The Empathy Engineer

Sid Chattopadhyay

Table of Contents

Serendipity

Abir stopped looking at the comments in his blog post on his phone and looked up. He could see the train taking the bend slowly, as if reluctant to come to the railway station. At six feet, he was more than a head above the teeming crowd of passengers waiting to embark on the train. The daily passengers were hanging out of the train, perching precariously on the edges of the doors. Pocketing his phone carefully, he submitted himself to the crowd surging ahead near the train line, ready to hop onto the moving train if possible. He had to leave the last one and let it go because there were simply too many people fighting to get in and out. In the chaos, he had almost lost his backpack.

He was returning from the city after meeting some prospective clients who wanted to hop on to his social awareness data platform. They were small-business folks, traveling to Kolkata from far-off places to sell their handmade goods to make a living. They mostly sat by the roadside and on the sidewalks, selling their dolls, bangles, earrings, and other pretty objects that gleamed in the scorching sun. Typical to his routine in these last two weeks, he had talked to them, taken pictures of their wares, asked for the prices, and interviewed them about their lives. He had asked them about their hours-long daily journey to get back home and about their daily struggle to survive. They had been politely interested, and some of the ones who had smartphones agreed to hop on to his platform and try it out.

Abir's mother had also coaxed him to meet Riya, with whom she had arranged a rendezvous in the city. Mother had come to know about Riya from a distant relative. Riya and Abir had lots in common, Mother had confided. Riya was a software engineer like him and went to an English-medium school, like him. Even their families had similar status. To top it all off, she was fair like a glowing swan, his mother had gushed.

Mother wanted Abir to go and speak to her and meet her since he was going to the city every day anyway. He was visiting Kolkata after four years, and Mother had tried to convince him that this was the right time to start seeing some prospective girls, get married, and settle down. She had wanted Riya and Abir to meet before the parents on both sides talked more formally about their marriage.

After all, he had turned thirty a few days back. Now that he was doing so well in Silicon Valley, all the way back in California, it was time to settle down and have a family to raise in the USA, she had counseled.

Abir and Riya had met at one of Kolkata's biggest shopping malls, the South City Mall. Abir was not sure why that spot was chosen, but a boy visiting from the United States presumably did not want to roam around in the hot Kolkata sun. So they had met there and had coffee in Cafe Coffee Day. Riya had lots to say. About her friends. About the city she loved. About why she had agreed to meet him at all. Did he believe in arranged marriages? What exactly did he do in the United States? Why was his Facebook friends' list hidden?

After spending the entire afternoon together, roaming around aimlessly in the air-conditioned shopping mall, they had taken an Uber to the railway station. She had come to see him off at the Howrah train station, the major train hub near Kolkata, to make sure he could board the train back home. The train would be extremely crowded at this time in the evening, she had warned him, but it was still better than Sealdah, the other major train hub. He would have to take the train to a suburb, and from there, he would have to cross the river in a steamer. After that, he would have to take a rickshaw to his home. It would be a good two-hour journey.

The train ambled its way into this final destination station, and Abir readied himself to hop onto it. As the train came to a halt, he stood aside briefly, letting a sea of people pour out first, and then let himself flow with the crowd of people shoving and pushing to get inside. At last, he managed to get inside, and after treading on a few feet, he finally found a place to stand.

Riya had wanted him to take a taxi to his home in the suburbs of Kolkata, knowing that the trains would be crowded like crazy. Abir, though, preferred to take the train. The green electric trains made him feel connected to the people of Kolkata, to their lives and their stories. Besides, he felt he was making a tiny contribution to the environment by not riding in a gas-powered car back home, taking the emission-free electric train instead.

Shortly, the train started moving, and from the open door where people were hanging outside, a gentle breeze blew into his face, cooling him off and drying off the perspiration. He closed his eyes to savor the delightful feeling he got every time he boarded these trains in the evening. Despite the crowd, he enjoyed the gentle swaying of the train, the cool breeze, the many interesting people and vendors, and the laid-back outskirts of Kolkata as they sped by. People around appeared unfazed, accustomed to the squashing crowd. These were daily passengers to whom the struggle to go to work and at the end of the day to come back from work in the overcrowded trains was a daily routine—not to be avoided and not to be complained about. As always, some people traveled together, meaning to enjoy every moment. No sooner had the train sped up than they stood in a close circle, took out a large towel, hung it between them by their rigged contraption, and were soon busy playing cards, using the cloth between them as a makeshift table. Some onlookers watched, passing advice to their nearest contender.

Occasionally, a mobile vendor would come by, carefully treading his way among the crowd, selling his fare. Some would have jars full of lozenges, some with jars of sweets, and some others with salted peanuts. Tired, with lines formed on their faces due to the daily struggle to sell their stuff in stifling heat amid dispassionate passengers, standing and threading their way through them, the hawkers, as the local term went, would move around patiently from one compartment to the other to make a daily living.

Abir bought a packet of salted peanuts from the nearest hawker. He felt bad whenever he saw them and would invariably purchase something from every hawker who came his way, hoping his little contribution would improve their sales. He would either eat them right away or store them in his backpack to take home for his cousin Rimjhim or give them away to beggars if he found any on the streets.

Rimjhim and her parents were amused at his exuberance to interact with everything and anything that the city had to offer, though they did understand that Abir wanted to soak in all these experiences as a tourist to these parts of the world. After all, he was not a local. Before migrating to the United States more than five years back, he had been all over India, moving around to various parts of the country along with his parents while growing up. His father had been a civil servant, an esteemed Indian Administrative Services officer of power and position, transferring from one part of the country to the other. His parents had finally settled in a suburb near the eastern city of Kolkata after his father retired, in a sprawling three-story bungalow.

Abir checked his watch. There was more than forty-five minutes left before his station came up. He decided to spend his time productively by editing his latest blog and possibly publish it before getting off the train. He took out his phone, opened the blogging app, and started writing.

Hello blog visitor,

In today's blog, I will discuss a fundamental idea: can empathy be practiced daily, at every instance of life, by following an algorithm? I have often wondered about it, and I believe you can. To the uninitiated, empathy means the ability to understand and share the feelings of another. I will first quote four great leaders who have practiced empathy in their profound ways. Then, I will propose the algorithm as an extension to their thoughts.

Gandhi said, "You must be the change you wish to see in the world." If you want a more empathetic world, you must start practicing empathy at every moment of your life.

Mother Teresa said, "Not all of us can do great things, but we can do small things with great love." Small things. Small acts of empathy. Do all these small acts with great love.

Mandela said, "Education is the most powerful weapon which you can use to change the world." These words can be extended to say that empathy is the most powerful weapon to change the well-being of people in this world.

Tagore said, "I slept and dreamt that life was joy. I awoke and saw that life was service. I acted and behold, service was joy." Service. We must make our lives of that of servitude to the more needy, the oppressed, to the underprivileged, to the ones who need it.

The algorithm for empathy that I am about to mention is primarily derived from the profound thoughts of these great people. But since I am an engineer, I will give you a data-driven solution. Data, which we gather from our own experiences about the conditions of human existence. Data from YouTube videos of moments in people's lives. Data from our Facebook feeds, WhatsApp messages, emails we receive from a friend, search results provided to you by Google. Data from real humans, real thoughts, real emotions, real-life states. Data, which slowly adds up to form a common opinion of the people you know and, with time, creates a core idea about how humanity thrives in a chaotic world.

I will propose a simple high-level algorithm to practice empathy in any situation:

First, remove the "I and me" from "myself," so that your immediate needs are less important than the needs of others around you.

Then, consider all the data that you have about the situation and the people involved.

Next, extrapolate or interpolate the data to make an inference about the people or situations involved, before jumping to conclusions.

Finally, take action with opinion and purpose created with empathy for the other in mind.

In my next blog, I will dwell on some real-life examples where I use this algorithm to try and be empathetic to people and situations. Am I perfect at it? Far from it. It is my experience and experiment with life, where empathy is the fundamental key that will enlighten me, make me connect to humankind, of which I am a tiny part of.

This is Abir, your friendly empathy engineer! Keep coming back for more! Signing off from Kolkata, India. August 2019.

* * *

Abir hit the publish button to publish the blog and checked his watch. He would arrive at his station in five minutes. The train had become relatively less crowded, albeit there still were no empty seats to sit. He started making his way toward the ajar door to prepare to get down from the train.

By the time he got down from the train at his destination station and took a rickshaw to reach the dock by the river, it was dusk. The sun had decided to call it a day and was reclining on the red horizon at the other side of the river, about to retire for the night. The ferry, which was to take him across the river, had aligned itself gracefully by the bamboo docking side. The silhouette of the boat made a strangely impressive figure against the setting sun—the reliable one, silently carrying hundreds of passengers across the river every day.

All sorts of folks had accumulated to cross the river: the weary daily passenger returning home from work, the unkempt local vendor carrying a bicycle with large bags on each side of the handle, and mingling easily with them, a group of young people who looked at ease among the local folks, yet seemed to talk urban lingo and were dressed accordingly.

Abir picked up his backpack and prepared to embark upon the wobbly boat. He proceeded to the side, from where one could touch the tranquil waters breaking gently against the sides. The ferry motor had not started chugging yet. The daily travel folks were having their usual discussions about the train timings, the traffic jams on the roads down in the city, and the massive crowd that fought to catch the evening train. The smell of burning kerosene drifted across the boat; the tea vendor had started preparing tea on the ferry dock. A small boy in shorts and bare torso moved in and out of the boat, giving little mud pitchers with tea to the folks asking for the tea. Abir listened to the gentle murmur and concoction of sounds around him, subconsciously accepting a pitcher of tea from the boy.

"How much?" he asked the boy, reaching for his purse.

"Saat taka" ("seven rupees"), came the reply.

Abir gave him a ten-rupee note and told him to keep the change. He looked around, wondering whether to have the tea inside the boat or have it outside and come back in later. Deciding on the latter, he got up and made his way back onto the bamboo dock.

Amid the light buzz of conversation, he could hear the water splashing against the boat, making it wobble gently. Distant sounds of bells from the temple floated across the water. A pool of small boys swam enthusiastically across the river, the splashing sound making an excellent accompaniment to the chanting from an old woman in the distance, who was draped in a wet sari, putting flowers from the puja in the river.

"Excuse me, sir, do you have a lighter?"

He turned around to find a bespectacled young man around his age standing with an unlit cigarette in his hand. Abir shook his head and pointed to the tea vendor's stove. Lighting his cigarette, the young man turned toward the boat and puffed away somberly.

Abir looked away in silence, lost in an array of thoughts. The sun was now half-hidden behind the coconut trees across the river. The orange shade of the sky near the horizon made a splendid reflection on the water, occasionally interrupted by the odd branch of a tree floating on the water, or marigold garlands in their faded glory, forsaken of their inherent right around the temple deity's neck.

Marveling at the scenic beauty of his surroundings, he took out his phone to take a picture. For this picture, he wanted himself in it and realized that a simple selfie would not work. He wanted to appear small in the image to symbolize his tiny stature in the splendor of nature, embracing his journey.

A selfie would do just the opposite, and give over-importance to his presence.

Looking around, he saw his smoking neighbor nearby and proceeded to ask him to take his picture against the setting sun. He walked off to a distance where he would appear small and insignificant against the surroundings, where his only presence among his people would be a faceless silhouette.

His smoking acquaintance seemed to understand his directions and proceeded to take several pictures from different angles.

"Local to these parts?" he asked, after returning the phone to Abir.

"Yes."

"From the USA?"

Abir nodded, surprised.

"I came to know from your phone—we don't have this model around here yet," said his smoking acquaintance, making rings of smoke and surveying Abir through his lenses, apparently enjoying his surprised expression.

"The USA is a decent place to be in. My elder sister lives there. She has two kids," continued his smoking acquaintance, glancing at Abir. Abir nodded politely, finished his tea, and threw the earthen pot carefully between the bamboo poles, which made the base of the dock into the water below it. He felt comfortable doing it, knowing that it would dissolve gracefully in the water and not pollute it. A person on a bicycle was hurrying toward the ferry, determined not to miss this one. He stood aside to let him pass, wondering whether the nice seat he had occupied by the side of the boat was gone by then.

"I have been to the States—went a couple of years back," continued his smoking neighbor. "My visit to my sister's place in the USA was nice, although I must say that I felt sorry for them."

"Sorry? Why?" asked Abir.

His cigarette buddy threw the stub into the water below with a fervor, took out another cigarette, and offered one to Abir, which he refused. Abir looked anxiously at the stub, which had disappeared along with other trash that littered the river. This one would not dissolve in the water and would pollute it, he thought to himself.

"See, I didn't mean to sound offensive or anything," continued his acquaintance, lighting up his second cigarette. "It's just that I feel you guys are very privileged to be there. Over time, folks staying there forget the reality that they have left behind in this country. They try to hang on to their culture, which is unfortunately already diluted. So this leaves them in a stateless limbo where they are neither Americans nor Indians."

Abir did not reply and looked away silently at the setting sun as his acquaintance puffed away, dropping the ash down through the bamboo dock down into the river. Some more people had accumulated and were taking up seats inside the ferry. The distant boat was approaching this side. Their boat would start its way across the river once the other one came near enough. The tea vendor had folded his mat to make way for the pool of people who would be getting off from the oncoming ferry.

"I guess you don't quite agree," continued his smoking buddy after a while, throwing the second cigarette down the bamboo dock in the water below. Abir looked down anxiously once more as the cigarette stub hit the water below and floated away. Was this magnificent sacred river a trash bin, to be polluted with anything that was not required on the shores? He looked up to remind his smoking acquaintance that the river was the last place to throw away cigarette stubs but decided against it. His empathy for the immediate natural surroundings would perhaps not be well received by this opinionated and unmindful young man.

"You have a point. Every place has its pros and cons," Abir said politely, looking at his watch.

"I am Aniruddha, by the way," said his smoking acquaintance.

Abir nodded, looking up at the river. The distant boat was very near now, and soon, their boat would start chugging, ready to make its journey across the river.

"I didn't get your name," asked Aniruddha.

"I am Abir."

Aniruddha nodded and proceeded to take a third cigarette out. He paused, midway, to abandon the idea and adjusted his glasses as if thinking of a new channel of conversation.

"I should get on board now," said Abir.

"Yes, yes—I will join you too, but need to say goodbye to somebody first. Don't know where she went off to," said Aniruddha, looking around. "There she is, still talking on the phone."

He waved his hands to a young woman around his age some way off, who waved back and started walking toward them. As she came nearer, she saw Abir with him and stopped short.

"This is Shyamoli," Aniruddha said, nodding at her. Abir looked on as Aniruddha walked off to Shyamoli's side to talk to her.

13

The sun had finally settled, and the lanterns in the mud houses by the river had been lit. The soft lights on the lamp posts by the dock had lit up too, casting eerie shadows across the water. Their ferry motor started chugging. The few passengers who had been idling outside on the docks started getting on board.

Aniruddha went off with Shyamoli to say goodbye while Abir stood there alone. He watched them as she talked to him softly, her voice not carrying over the sound of the motor on the boat. He watched as Aniruddha waved goodbye to her and came over to board the boat. Shyamoli's hair floated with the breeze by the river as she stood at a distance, watching them climb into the boat.

With all its crew and passengers on board, the boat glided gently into the water to start yet another trip across the river.

* * *

Abir sat in the coveted place which he had secured earlier. Amidst the drone of the motor, conversation died out. He stared absently into the distant shoreline of the river which they had just left. By then, the sky was a dark shade of red. The boat had crossed half the river. He could still see the distant docking site where the boat had taken off. Shyamoli was still standing looking at their boat, a far-off silhouette under the yellow lights of the dock.

"What do you do in the USA?" Aniruddha eventually asked him, looking up from the newspaper that he was reading. Then he held up his hand in a dramatic gesture.

"No, wait. Let me guess; you are a software engineer."

Abir nodded.

"Ah—the typical dollar lust," said Aniruddha, smirking and taking off his glasses and polishing the lenses with his *kurta*. Abir ignored him, bending down to see if he could touch the water rushing by the boat.

"You know, it's such a waste," continued Aniruddha, putting his glasses back on. "I mean, you are a bright person, yet you are wasting your time working for a foreign company, to earn a few dollars. They are benefitting from your smartness, but what are you doing for your country? The country expects some great things from you. It spent resources on you, with the expectation that you will do something in return. But you run away from it all! Don't you think you are selfish?"

Abir did not reply; instead, he clutched his backpack anxiously. Whenever the boat was in the middle of the vast river, he became anxious. What if the boat sank? With so many people on board, the sides of the boat was almost touching the water.

Eventually, though, they reached the other side safely. The boat turned toward the flow of the water, parallel to the other waiting ferry, and gently floated in, as the other waiting ferry started another trip across the water. Once the boat touched the dock, people began tumbling out. Abir and Aniruddha waited until the others had disembarked the boat. Then, heaving his backpack, Abir followed Aniruddha out into the dock.

"You know, I keep thinking about it—I think I have seen you somewhere before and have heard your name as well," said Aniruddha, as Abir looked around for a rickshaw to take him home.

Abir nodded absently as Aniruddha pulled out his phone.

"Wait, wait, I think I know. You are the person who gave the TED talk on empathy and mindfulness in San Francisco, right? I saw it on YouTube," he said, flicking through YouTube to come up with one of his many videos. Abir glanced at it. It was taken a few years back. It was his first TED talk on this topic and somehow had reached a sizable audience.

"Yes, that's me," he said quietly.

"You are quite the celebrity then!" exclaimed Aniruddha, peering at him intently, as if seeing him in a new light. "But I don't quite agree with some of your views. I had left some comments in your videos, but I guess you don't remember," he continued, putting his glasses back on as if to see him more properly. "My point is simple. It's easy to talk about empathy, mindfulness, and all that if you are comfortable in a rich country, but it's hard to do all that here, to follow those principles in reality. How does one even go for all this fancy mind training stuff you talked about when money and comfort are scarce and basic livelihood is hard to come by?"

Abir stopped looking for a rickshaw and turned to Aniruddha.

"You do have a point," Abir said politely. "But don't you think that empathy and mindfulness is a state of mind and should be, as such, independent of one's situation?"

Aniruddha folded his hands combatively as if preparing for a debate.

"It's interesting how you view this," he said eventually, sounding indignant. "First, follow the dollar dream, earn a lot of money, and once you are at a good place in life, start talking about empathy and mindfulness, mind over matter, mind training, and all that. How does it even help me get my life every day?"

Abir smiled at his indignance, unperturbed. He had heard this view countless number of times. He wished he could tell Aniruddha that this was the precise level of mind training that had automatically not make him react to Aniruddha's provocations. He was used to dealing with combative and opinionated people. His rounds with venture capitalists in the Silicon Valley, at various talks, and debates with his coworkers had made him get used to these varied views: some supportive, some argumentative, and some downright belligerent, like that of Aniruddha's. It did not bother him; instead, from years of training his mind to follow his empathy algorithm, he automatically wanted to find out the root reason why somebody would bring on these points with a negative passion of such intensity.

"Yes, your point is certainly valid to some extent," agreed Abir calmly. He went to a rickshaw puller and told him where he wanted to go. Aniruddha looked somewhat surprised at his unperturbed expressions, and a reluctant expression of respect came over his face. His demeanor became less truculent. He took out his cigarette packet and took out the third cigarette, lighting it up, as Abir watched on in silence.

"What?" Aniruddha asked, as he looked up, lighting his cigarette to realize that Abir was looking at him somewhat solemnly. "Are you going to judge me on how much I smoke? Going to pitch me about your empathy for nature talk on this now?" he asked, throwing his ashes on the road and looking around to toss the empty packet by the roadside. Abir held up his hand and took the empty cigarette packet from him, deciding to throw it when he found a suitable place or a dustbin to throw it into.

"No, I am not judging you, Aniruddha," he said, patting his arms kindly. "Anyways, I need to go now. Thank you for taking the lovely pictures by the setting sun. Goodbye."

He climbed up on the rickshaw and asked the driver to start pedaling. The street lamps were alight on this side too, perhaps brighter than the other side, casting their yellow light on everything around them. The small shops by the side of the road had lit their lanterns— some more fortunate ones lighting electric bulbs with electricity stolen from the closest electric pole. The *jhaal muri* (spicy puffed rice) vendor was busy selling the popular concoction in conical paper bags. The roots of a tall banyan tree made cozy sitting stools for urchins nibbling on freshly roasted corn. The air was filled with the sound of chirping of birds setting in the tree for a good night's sleep and the chatter of folks returning from the dock.

As the rickshaw started ambling up the road, it reached an elevation when Abir could look back at the other side of the ferry dock, far away, and he could just see a small dot of a person still standing on the other side of the dock under its yellow light. He presumed it was Shyamoli, looking to see if Aniruddha had reached safely.

* * *

The rickshaw puller, an old man in unkempt clothes, wearing glasses with lenses making his eyes look like bees, labored his way across the road. Abir felt anxious, and abashed, to be sitting comfortably while the old man drove him, pedaling away vigorously to negotiate bends and potholes on the road. Would the little bit of money that this old man made with his rickshaw enough to sustain his family? Why did he have to work anyways, and not be with his family, with his grandchildren?

After a little while, he asked the old man to stop, halfway to his destination. He got down from the rickshaw. Paying him the full fare, he started to walk the rest of the way along the road, as the surprised old man looked on.

When he eventually reached the railway station, the railway gate was closed as usual. Although the gates were down, and the distant train was blaring its horns, people were still crossing the railway lines. Most of them were on foot, some on bicycles, and some on scooters.

Instead of crossing to the other side, he walked up to one of the platforms. He sat on an empty bench, feeling slightly fatigued. He usually loved doing that. He would sit there and observe the people getting in and out of the train. Another great attraction for him was the band of singers and musicians, who sometimes performed at the station. Sometimes, there would be a single singer with a *dotara*, sitting on the platform, singing, and playing at the same time. He loved these folks and their unadulterated view toward music.

There was a pair of musicians singing *Shyama Sangeet*—devotional songs for goddess Kali. Abir closed his eyes in delight, swayed by the sheer melody and beauty of the interpretation. After they finished a song, he took out a bunch of rupee notes and dropped them into the box, smiling slightly at the look of gratitude given to him by the musicians. He watched them silently as they started another song, the music getting sometimes drowned by passing trains.

He felt his phone vibrating in his pocket. He picked it up after looking at the number—it was his mother.

"When are you coming home?"

"Almost there," he said shortly and disconnected the phone.

He decided to remain on the platform for some more time. The journey had fatigued him. The beautiful songs rejuvenated him, and he wished he could sit there the entire night, just to listen to them.

He noticed his phone ringing again. In the noise of the train station, he could barely hear the ringtone. He picked up the phone and looked at the number. It was an unknown number.

"Hello?"

There was silence at the other end for some time.

"Hello, who is this?" he repeated.

"This is Shyamoli."

Abir's heart froze, and his hands felt numb. Suddenly, the platform seemed to disappear from around him. Everything dimmed around him as if an invisible volume knob had turned off all the noise from the surrounding.

"How are you, Abir?"

His throat constricted him, and he could not utter anything.

"I am using a telephone booth to call your international USA number," she continued after a pause. "Looks like your USA number has not changed even after these four years."

A silence followed, where each second felt like years. Abir felt that he should be saying something, but could not bring himself to do so; his throat constricting him with wild emotions to hear her voice again after four years.

"I did not speak to you when I saw you with Aniruddha. I guess I was too stunned after seeing you after all these years, and I did not know whether you would like to talk to me," she continued.

"It was good to see you today, Shyamoli," he said finally, hoping he sounded casual. His mind whirled around, trying to find an opening to start a conversation, to ask her all the questions that were left unanswered in these last four years.

"I see your TED talks on YouTube. I have been following your blog posts for the past few years. It's so good to see you doing such great work with technology and humanity through your social data platform and your blogs," she said.

Abir felt his heart hammer wildly. Shyamoli following his blogs—what did it mean? He had not heard from her in these four long years. Unknown to him, his blogs were being read by somebody who was the key reason he had started them in the first place. What did she think of them? Why did she never try to connect with him even after following him in his blogs?

"Thank you. I feel deeply about my work," Abir said, trying to sound casual, in a supreme effort to not betray the turbulence he felt in his mind. To think that he would bump into her again, in these suburbs of Kolkata, of all places. To find her with another man. What was the coincidence? Why did it have to happen? Why did she have to call? Especially when he had been trying to forget how he felt after seeing her with Aniruddha.

"Don't you have anything to tell me anymore?" said Shyamoli after a long silence. "Back then, you had so much to tell me."

Abir felt he needed to tell her that even in these four years, there was not a single day when he had not thought of her. But how would she react to this? His voice constricted him, and he could not say anything. He pressed the phone to his ear, hoping that he would find the courage to feel normal and talk again.

There was an uncertain silence at the other end, and the phone got disconnected. Abir realized that she had cut off the conversation.

The station came back to life, as if in slow motion. Things whirred around him again: the people, the crowd, the trains, the vendors, and the musicians. He looked around, dazed, as if noticing the events, the people, and the platform crowd around him again after an eternity.

He stared at his phone, at the unknown number. Shyamoli was the reason he had not visited India for the last four years. What were the chances that he would bump into her again, after such a long time? That too, in the least expected of spots. Was there some unexplained cosmic connection that made their paths cross? What were the chances? There must be a reason for this.

He would have to figure it out. But not now. His mind was drained from all energy after his chanced meeting with Shyamoli.

He got up from the bench and walked out of the railway station, feeling fatigued, letting himself into the flow of the hundreds of people rushing out of the platform.

A first meet

Abir peered down from the flight window as it prepared to land at the San Francisco International Airport. It was 2013, a time when he had graduated with a degree in computer engineering and had worked for a couple of years before accepting an offer from Silicon Valley in California to join a software company of his dreams. At twenty-four, he had already achieved what his parents called a first-class ticket to fame and glory—a six-figure salary with excellent benefits at the heart of technical innovations and a mind full of hope and innovative ideas to change the world with technology.

He looked excitedly at the vast landscape which cradled the San Francisco Bay Area. This was home to Google, Facebook, Apple, Intel, Twitter, and many other revolutionary tech companies that created products that changed how humans interacted with the world, with each other. Busy highways and empty lands ambled past as the plane gradually lost height, preparing to descend into the distant runway.

At Kolkata, when his flight had finally left the Dumdum airport to start his journey, the air below had been hazy. The coconut trees stood proud but tired, dilapidated buildings stood wearily, but cheerfully aware of their place and ancestry. The busy streets below, with the crawling Kolkata traffic, had slowly become dimmer and more distant, as he left the only place he called home. Throughout the flight, he had listened to music on his MP3 player. It was given to him as a parting gift. He listened to music from both the countries, in languages that he knew, in the sounds he had grown up with.

His would-be roommate, Ayan, picked him up from the San Francisco International Airport, in his ancient and rather old car, a Toyota Corolla. Bespectacled, and sporting a solemn mustache, Ayan had the quintessential academician look which he wore with elegance. Abir had contacted Ayan through a common friend. It happened that Ayan, too, was looking for a roommate in his tiny two-bedroom apartment in Palo Alto near Stanford University, where he was a postdoctoral student in Chemistry. Abir had fitted the bill of a potential roommate perfectly.

Abir occupied one of the rooms that was given to him in the tiny apartment. It would be his temporary abode till he found a place of his own to stay if he chose to. His company had provided corporate apartments to him for the first month, but he had decided to become Ayan's roommate instead. It was especially comforting to come to a foreign country for the first time to find somebody who was from his homeland, spoke the same language, and probably had the same values. Besides, the corporate housing would not suit him because he did not know how to drive. He could take the Bart. He had looked up the nearest Bart stations, but having a roommate with a car certainly fared much better than left to oneself.

He spent the first few days drifting in and out of sleep at odd times, waking up late at night, feeling strangely hungry. Ayan understood this effect of jet lag and kept food for him in the fridge. He had pre-arranged a twin mattress for him and had his room cleaned and vacuumed. Abir had heard about the work expectations from a postdoctoral student at Stanford, and he felt grateful, and guilty at the same time, knowing that Ayan skipped his lab on a weekday to help him settle down.

Ayan had a female visitor on the second day, who identified herself as Srija. She stayed in Ayan's room till late at night. When she appeared the next evening again, Abir made them out to be a couple of sorts and not just mere friends. She happened to be a Bengali too and acquainted herself with him in no time. Srija was a student at Santa Clara University and had read comparative literature at Jadavpur University in Kolkata. She had met Ayan back in the days in Kolkata when he was at the Presidency College. Abir assumed that they had planned to come over to the USA together.

In the few days before he was to join his work officially, Abir made the best out of the time he was awake, spending time with Srija and Ayan, who had gone out of the way to make him feel at home. They invited him for all their meals, which they made themselves in their sparse little kitchen in the evenings. Abir helped them out by loading the dishwasher and giving them company. After dinner, Ayan and Srija would go into Ayan's room, and Abir would go back to his room to sit with his laptop, to try to get out of his loneliness and get accustomed to the deafening quietness of the place.

* * *

One Saturday evening, two weeks since he had settled down somewhat to a typical routine of sorts, Ayan asked him whether he wanted to go to a get-together at Srija's relatives' place. Abir was not sure whether these people expected him to appear with them and was hesitant, but Srija was particularly adamant that he went along with them. He reluctantly agreed to go with them, riding in Ayan's car in the backseat.

Srija's relatives lived in a sprawling two-story house overlooking the south San Jose mountains. A winding road led to the sloping driveway. Cars of several luxury models were lined around the roadside. Distant lights twinkled from the houses strewn around the mountains, as if lanterns in the sky, beckoning casual onlookers to look at them in wonder. The high building silhouetted against the darkening evening sky, dazzling in its splendor.

Abir followed Srija and Ayan inside the house, taking off his shoes and dropping them along with the piles of shoes left outside by guests who had already come. The house was teeming with people, all dressed in traditional Indian attire. Srija instantaneously made herself at home with the people, and he realized that she must be knowing these folks well. Ayan kept him company for a while as he nodded politely to a few kind folks who had come up to talk to them. A lady, whom he assumed was the host, sympathized with his jet lag and rushed off to fetch strong coffee for him. Her husband, in his early sixties, and with receding white hairline, looked at him through puffy eyes, with a glass of whiskey in his hand.

"Welcome! Enjoy yourself. Mingle with the crowd," he told Abir, his tone slightly slurry.

As the party progressed, Abir learned about the host, Arun uncle as Srija called him, who had a Ph.D. in computer engineering and had migrated to the Silicon Valley decades back, when the tech boom had not started. He had worked on semiconductors and circuit design and had minted his millions during the tech boom in the late nineties. Abir got acquainted with a few other people, most of whom seemed to be in their fifties and well-settled in their lives. They were mostly empty nesters, whose kids had graduated, or were in college, leaving behind their wealthy parents to enjoy their comfortable lives in Silicon Valley.

He carefully avoided the alcohol bar that Arun uncle kept in one of the rooms, which had become the focal point of people flocking around and for conversations. He did not drink and had to fend off several kindly folks who had come up to him with drinks and had asked him why he did not have drinks with him. Srija and Ayan had already made themselves comfortable with a bunch of folks, and he decided it was best to fend for himself.

After a while, he felt thirsty and decided to venture into the kitchen for a drink. He looked around to find a glass, and finding one, he tried to figure out the best place to get some water.

"You can take water from the fridge—here, let me help you."

He turned around to find a girl around his age standing with an empty glass in her hands. She had a kitchen towel hanging from her shoulder, and her hair was tied in a tight bun. She wore an apron, and it looked like she was heating up food in the oven, getting them ready before dinner began.

"Thank you," said Abir politely, as she filled up water and handed it to him.

"Would you like any other drink? Soda?" she asked as she continued putting the bowls of food inside the oven to heat them up. Abir shook his head politely, wondering whether he should be helping her with her work. As she struggled to lift a particularly heavy bowl, he decided she really needed some help.

"Here, let me help you with it," he said, putting down the glass into the sink and rushing to her side. She looked at him, startled, and smiled.

"No, it's alright. I can manage myself. Please do go ahead and enjoy the party," she said, finishing loading the food in the oven and turning it on. She continued doing other work in the kitchen, arranging the spoons and ladles, and Abir thought it was prudent at that stage to leave her to her work.

"Can I check out the backyard?" he asked, noticing a sliding door that led out to the back of the house.

"Yes, of course," she said, walking over to the sliding glass door and pulling it open. Abir thanked her and went outside, shutting the sliding glass door behind him.

It was a large backyard, with a section of small trees along the fence. A large lawn with immaculately cut grass made a green carpet. A row of flowers adorned the walls, which overlooked a small hill receding off into the black sky. It was a dark evening, and although it was a full moon, whiffs of floating clouds obscured it, making the soft diffused moonlight lighting up the distant looming trees eerily.

Abir sat down on one of the benches in the backyard, feeling slightly cold. The gentle breeze reminded him of the breeze by the river Ganges, which would reach as far as his home. In the evening, everybody would go up to the roof on the third floor, which was a favorite hangout for his family. His cousin Rimjhim, and his uncle and his wife would invariably drop by, as was a daily custom. It was morning this time in India—he wondered what his father would be doing at this time. If he was not traveling, then he would probably have come back from his morning walk, picked up the newspaper, and would have glanced over it while having his morning tea. Dadu, his grandfather, who woke up in the wee hours before anybody else did, would already be having his tea on the third-floor room where he stayed alone. His mother would be praying in the prayer room, with the sweet smell of incense drifting around the house.

As he thought about them, he felt listless and forlorn. Did he need to come all the way away from home, from his people, to come to this strange place, with its magnificent, distant beauty which he could not internalize? Silicon Valley had attracted him for its tremendous energy and the innovation that seemed to seed from this place, yet he could not distance himself from the fact that he was far away from his people.

"Missing home?"

Abir started back from his reverie and looked up. The girl from the kitchen was standing in front of him. Her hand wrapped around to shield herself from the chill. She had let her hair fall free now, and the gentle breeze made them fall around her face. The apron was gone, and so had the kitchen towel. Abir made way for her to sit down, and she sat down beside him on the bench.

"Sorry, I did not get your name," he said.

"I am Shyamoli. I know you, though—you are the new software engineer roommate of Ayan's. Srija told me about you."

"How do you know Srija?" he asked.

"We are acquainted through a distant relation," she said, looking up at the dark sky, shivering slightly due to the cold. Abir followed her gaze. The moon was transitioning between one cloud to the other. The halo on the clouds made a perfect circle, as if teasing the moon, daring it to come out. The gentle breeze made the leaves on the trees in the big backyard rustle softly, as if making a rhythm to an unheard song in the air.

"This is a strangely beautiful place," Abir said in wonder.

Shyamoli smiled, looking at the moon. The breeze seemed to lush down a little bit, as if to understand why two young people sat in the moonlit backyard silently. Abir sat in silence, savoring the moment, the atmosphere, the gentle breeze, which seemed to carry his thoughts. Shyamoli sat in silence too. The moon appeared from behind the stray whiff of cloud, as if it was a silent spectator, applauding and celebrating the moment.

"Is this your favorite place in this house, Shyamoli?" Abir asked after a long silence.

"Yes, especially this time of the evening," she said, picking up a piece of paper that was lying around in the lawn, putting it in the trash can, and coming back to join Abir on the bench. Abir could suddenly feel her closeness, her perfume. He felt a strange tinge of thrill go over him, and he wondered whether he was being inappropriate to sit so close to her, given that he hardly knew her at all.

"I am very new to Silicon Valley," he said, getting up from the bench and sitting down on the grass in front of her. "In reality, I had no idea the weather would be like this. This is a far cry from the hot and humid weather back in Kolkata."

"How do you like your new job here?" asked Shyamoli.

"Well, it's just a few weeks, but I think it's going to be exciting. I love computer engineering and coding, and of course, Silicon Valley is *the* place to be in, in this entire planet."

"How do you write code all day?" asked Shyamoli, smiling at him. "I am not a computer engineer, but from whatever I have heard, it sounds boring and dry."

"Well, it depends on the perspective," said Abir. "Programming is like creating little packets of life, you know. Computer programs spawn, live, and die, like life around us. Sometimes I feel they know it and have a secret life within themselves, oblivious to us, the creators. Perhaps akin to how we borne our lives, created by our creator if there were any."

"That's an interesting insight!" said Shyamoli.

"Yes, I feel there is a connection to the silicon world and our world. There is a will to survive in computer programs, in a certain way, and response to stimuli in some sense. But even if they were conscious, there would be no way of knowing that."

"What made you think like this?"

"Well, I studied artificial intelligence in college. I believe intelligence is inherently linked with consciousness. But the problem is, I think consciousness does not exist beyond itself and is hard to prove or disprove. For example, I have no way of knowing whether you or anybody else around me is conscious. I can only infer it from their response to stimuli, their expressiveness, through the language they use to describe situations and feelings, and the likes."

"That's a new thought," said Shyamoli. "I never thought of it like that. But do you think artificial intelligence will have real feelings?"

Abir looked at her thoughtfully.

"Maybe someday," he replied. "Perhaps they will have feelings like we humans do—like those of anger, fear, respect, empathy. Or perhaps they have other emotional measurements which do not necessarily map to ours. But then, even if they do, we will have no way of telling them, except by observing their reactions to situations."

The moonlight was falling on her big black eyes, which sparkled in radiance, fully turned on him, intrigued—eyes that smiled at him and questioned his. He automatically smiled at her, feeling shy, and felt her eyes smiling back at him, questioning his intense gaze on her. He suddenly felt a shiver run through him that had nothing to do with the cold outside, and he dropped his eyes, embarrassed. He had gotten up from the grass to talk about artificial intelligence, as was his nature whenever he got excited. Shyamoli was following his words, smiling at his exuberance and spirited descriptions.

He stopped his discourse abruptly, turned toward Shyamoli, and asked anxiously, "Am I boring you?"

"Not at all," laughed Shyamoli, her voice ringing across the walls of the garden, reflecting from the fence. "Incidentally, I can see that you are more of a computer scientist than a typical software engineer."

"Why do you say that?" asked Abir, surprised.

"None of the software engineers that I have met think of their work like the way you described it. It's a job for them. But you don't describe your work in the typical techie way."

"Is there a typical techie way of looking at things?" he asked, intrigued.

"Yes, there is. I am not a computer engineer, but something in your lingo is different."

"Possibly," admitted Abir.

"Srija said you were a topper in your engineering college."

"Yes. Is that a big deal?"

"It can be, to some people. How was your undergrad engineering experience?"

"It was fun. I grew a beard," said Abir solemnly, stroking his chin.

Shyamoli laughed out loud.

"Is that the only thing you remember about your engineering college days? Growing a beard?"

"I remember my friends and some good times, and some good teachers and professors," he said shortly.

"You sound reluctant to talk about it," she said, smiling at him.

"Yes, you are right," agreed Abir. "And that is because I do not have a high opinion about my undergrad experience."

"Why not?"

"Well, I perceived an academic hierarchy, where the better-ranked students looked down on the lower-ranked ones, and there was a certain sense of elitism. Also, most people were not well rounded and spent most of their undergraduate lives trying to outdo their peers in grades and other superficial objective measures of success."

"Oh," said Shyamoli.

"What is the *oh* about?"

"Well, I was expecting a different view from you, given that you seem so passionate about computer engineering."

"Yes, I do sound rather negative about my undergraduate experience, don't I?"

"You certainly painted a gloomy picture," she said, smiling.

"Well, it is somewhat gloomy, albeit it's really subjective. Don't get me wrong, Shyamoli. I made some great friends there. The atmosphere in my institute was great for engineering and intellectual pursuits. The campus was absolutely gorgeous, and for most of my stay, I enjoyed myself. Competition was fierce and often exhausting, but at the end of the day, it's all for the best, I guess."

"So, what is your real complain about?"

"My main complaint is about the selection process for undergraduate students, which seemed to favor people with high intelligence, than those with a well-rounded development or high emotional quotient. That's not necessarily the wrong way to select students, but I think it can improve."

"What would you change about the entrance tests?" she asked, sounding intrigued.

"I wish they had tests around measuring emotional quotient, creativity, and empathy, which makes a person truly useful to society at large. Unfortunately, most students selected to study engineering had a general notion that intelligence was everything. As a result, these institutes are creating generations of goal-driven individuals, whose values of success lie in scores and numbers throughout their lives—how much they earn, how quickly they get promotions, what is their position in their corporate career, how big their house is—objective and cold metrics of success."

Shyamoli nodded, wrapping herself up tighter in the cold breeze.

"Isn't it like that everywhere?" she said after a while. "Most folks here in the Silicon Valley do everything they can to put their kids through Ivy League schools if they can. It is as competitive, and perhaps bordering on ruthless, as it is back in India. I have heard of some parents who hire college counseling companies in middle schools to prep their kids for college or university of their dreams."

Abir nodded thoughtfully, chewing on a grass blade. He sat silently, savoring the slight chill, the breeze, the strange moonlight which seemed to illuminate everything around them mysteriously.

"Anyways, what about you?" he asked eventually after a long silence.

"What about me?" asked Shyamoli, smiling.

"What do you do here?"

"Does one need to know everything?" she asked, her tone lilting.

"Well, no, but let me make some guesses," he said.

"Go for it," she said.

"OK, for one, you are thinking of doing a Ph.D."

"That's a far shot! But then, you are actually right. How in the world did you guess that?"

"You said I talked like a computer scientist, rather than an engineer. Like you said, this is a lingo not typically used by nonacademic folks. In fact, there is something in your lingo which makes me believe you are academically inclined, with a mind to pursue academia further."

"That's a really long shot, but you took your guess correctly. Yes, I am thinking of doing a Ph.D. in cognitive psychology after I finish my masters."

"Which makes me easily deduce that you are a grad student on a visa, and you stay with Arun uncle and his wife, and they are your local guardians."

"Very true! Again a really bold guess, but it's absolutely correct. How did you know the last bit?"

"Data and hypothesis, that's it, Shyamoli," said Abir, enjoying her surprised expression. "I am a man of data and algorithms. You provided lots of data, and I took some educated guesses based on the probability of outcomes."

"OK, I can understand about the grad school part. But how about the fact that although I stay here, this is not my home, really?"

"Well, I just—umm—made an informed guess."

"What made you think I am not Arun uncle's daughter?"

"Well, it's all a guess based on data and reasoning, really, like I said."

"Well I certainly don't look like either of them" said Shyamoli. "Also, you were talking about data. So does your data add up to the fact that I have a dark skin color, and both Arun uncle and Pooja aunty are fair-skinned?"

"Oh," said Abir, startled. His deduction had indeed been based partially on Shyamoli's dark skin complexion, which was a stark contrast to her local guardians' fair skin color. Not that it mattered to him, but this had been an observation, a data point, used for his deductions, along with other data points.

He toyed with a blade of grass, evading her question.

"So you *did* make your guess based on my dark skin complexion?" asked Shyamoli after a pause.

"Look, I don't mean it like that," Abir stammered, feeling inappropriate all of a sudden. "I have a long formed habit of speculating based on reasoning and data."

"You deduced it like a scientist with empirical evidence, and that's perfectly fine," said Shyamoli. "I am not ashamed of my skin complexion. My complexion is dark, that's all. There is nothing awkward in deducing lineage from skin color, although it's not always accurate."

Shyamoli sat in silence, wrapping herself closer and rocking to keep herself warm. Abir looked at her anxiously. Did he inadvertently start a topic which was not comfortable to Shyamoli? Was she now annoyed at him?

"Do you know what my name *Shyamoli* means in Bengali?" she asked after a while.

"Yes. It has connotations around having a darker skin tone," said Abir, embarrassed. "I am sorry, Shyamoli. I truly am. I did not want this conversation to go this way. Just so you know, the only significance of your dark skin complexion is it being a data point, one among many factors that I had used to come to a logical conclusion when following an algorithm of sorts."

"I understand perfectly well that you meant no negative connotations," said Shyamoli. "No, really, it's fine. Don't look so uncomfortable! You were just thinking about it logically, like a person of logic and rationality, and I appreciate your honesty. To all my American friends in my grad school life, I am exotic because I am strongly colored. Well, maybe not for my Indian people, because it's not a favorable color."

"Yes, I have observed that being dark is not a favorable state in our society. What we all need is a colorless society," said Abir, feeling relieved and happy that Shyamoli had understood his point and was not offended.

"A colorless society! That's an interesting concept. What does it mean?" asked Shyamoli.

"I have pondered on this concept for quite some time," said Abir, warming up to her interest. "Just imagine a colorless society, a world of people where humans did not have any colors. I think a lot of societal prejudices would have disappeared, or at least lessened, no? No more comparing between brown versus white versus yellow versus black. There would be more empathy for each other. In fact, color is merely a metaphor for variation; you can extend it with any concept that varies across a spectrum: variation in language, variation in culture, or whatever. I think it puts a lot of *ism* in people's minds."

"I see. Colorless! What a lovely concept," said Shyamoli. "But I have to disagree on one thing though—I think color brings the variety in this world that is required. Otherwise, it's all mundane and same, no?"

"Yes, indeed," agreed Abir. "Color is required, literally, and as a metaphor. Opinion based on color is wrong, again in reality and in metaphor."

"I have heard of subtle color-based profiling here in America, too," said Shyamoli. "But I have never really faced it in Silicon Valley. This place is the closest to being a colorless society, now that I come to think of it."

"Yes, indeed. And why not?" observed Abir. "Silicon Valley is a melting point of intellectuals and goal-driven individuals, who think with their minds and are more open to variation. Yes, this place seems to follow the colorless principle very well, I think, although I have only been a few weeks here; I don't have any data set to compare with."

"Ah right, you would need a sizable data set to come to a conclusion," said Shyamoli, smiling. "But indeed, a colorless world would have been nice. You have given me serious food for thought."

"Good," said Abir happily. "In fact, it's almost a rainbow when it comes to skin colors in India, no? Stratas based on color are bound to happen. For example, meaning no irreverence, haven't you faced prejudice in India for your dark complexion?"

"Yes, I have," said Shyamoli, turning solemn, as if thinking of her experiences. Abir looked at her gently, waiting delicately to make sure that Shyamoli took this conversation in the right spirit, as a stimulating one, and not intended to highlight her dark skin complexion. He waited gently for her to clear this. Shyamoli seemed to read his mind, and she smiled at him reassuringly.

"It's inherent in humans to create strata," he continued, relieved that Shyamoli was taking the conversation in the right spirit. "It makes them comfortable to be ahead of the race, by some means or the other. Be it color of skin if that is an advantage! If not, then some other form of pointless superiority, say the name of the family, or social strata, or opulence. There will exist strata in this world as long as this is a metaphorical colors in all societal constructs. And this is the fundamental cause of lack of empathy in several situations. What we truly need is empathy and mindfulness imbibed into the way of thinking in everything."

"Yes, indeed, that's so true," agreed Shyamoli.

"Isn't it?" continued Abir. "Just opening one's inner eyes and considering empathy in everything solves a lot of issues. Wars. Racism. Prejudice. Crime. Power struggle within society, even in small groups of people. Everything can be resolved if empathy becomes a regular theme in one's outlook, in one's upbringing. It starts at the cradle and needs to be a way of life. In fact, empathy should be a mandatory subject in schools."

He paused from his discourse, looking at Shyamoli to judge if she was getting bored with these rather intense discussions. Indeed, it did not seem to be the case. Shyamoli sat rapt in attention, apparently enjoying his insights and views and the passionate way he delivered them. Abir felt buoyant and happy. Already he was savoring her company, glad to be present with an elegant and intelligent person like her. The breeze was back, blowing with enthusiasm, making Shyamoli's hair fall around her face, as she tried hopelessly to keep them off her face. Abir sat silently, enjoying the breeze, his thoughts on this moment.

They heard Pooja aunty calling out to everybody to have food, and he realized that it was dinnertime already. He ignored the summons and instead got up from the grass and sat beside Shyamoli again on the bench. He did not care about the food, nor Pooja aunty calling out. He felt he could spend the entire night in this backyard, talking with Shyamoli. However, he had to stop short as the sliding door opened, and Srija and Ayan came out of the house to call Abir. They paused a bit when they saw Shyamoli and Abir together.

"Shyamoli and I were enjoying this wonderful backyard," Abir said hastily as if trying to justify why he was sitting so near her.

"Shyamoli, should you not help aunty with the food?" said Srija curtly to Shyamoli. Shyamoli got up hurriedly and went inside. Srija turned to Abir, disapproval written all over her face.

"Ayan and I had been looking for you, Abir. If you planned to come here to chat with Shyamoli all alone, you could have called us too," she said coldly. Abir felt abashed, wondering what excuse to bring up for his rather long absence from the other folks at the party. Did he appear rude to disappear like this from the well-meaning people who had expected him to mingle with them, to turn himself in into their mundaneness?

"Let's all go in—I am hungry," piped in Ayan smoothly, pushing Srija toward the house, beckoning Abir to follow them. Srija cast an angry glance at Abir as she led the proceeding back into the house.

The party invitees were sitting wherever they could. Some were on the sofa, some on the decorated Persian carpets, and a few on the stairs. Abir was impressed with the spread of food. He had seen them being heated by Shyamoli firsthand but did not realize the extent to which Indianess was revived and prevalent. Goat *curry*. Chicken *tikka masala*. Big prawns floated on coconut curries, as did roasted and charred spicy eggplants, mashed to their elements. The steaming rice sat at the corner, ignored for the large part due to the large bowl of *biryani* that took center stage on the kitchen island. Containers covered with aluminum sheets promised mouth-watering desserts to follow.

Amidst all the festivities, he realized after some time that Shyamoli was missing. She was nowhere to be seen. Taking a rather heavy plate in his hand, laden with food that Pooja aunty had coaxed him to help himself with, he strolled around the living room, family room, back to the backyard, hoping to talk to her again, but she was nowhere to be seen. He knew that she stayed at this house; had she gone upstairs to her room then?

His search was interrupted by somebody singing a song from the family room. Turned out, it was Srija. She was joined by another male voice, somewhere around the corner of the sofa, immediately accompanied by a crude set of beats played with enthusiasm on a tabletop by a third individual. To Abir's amusement, the song ended with loud applause. Trust Srija to steal the limelight, even though she did not even sing tunefully, he thought to himself. Was there something about the orchestrated and carefully careless actions, and the timing of it all?

Or was it all to do with the fact that Srija seemed to be accepted readily by this crowd? If that was so, was Shyamoli too accepted by this crowd? Or perhaps, she wasn't?

Abir occupied an empty part of a sofa and sat, legs folded, head tilted back as if poised to disappear from the crowd. His mind was on Shyamoli. He wanted to be near her and talk to her, but she was nowhere to be seen. Why was nobody asking for her? Why was she not a part of these celebrations, even though she was as much a part of this gathering as Srija was, if not more?

As the night progressed, and everybody got done with desserts, Shyamoli still did not appear. He decided it was not worth staying in this party anymore. A general slumber had fallen on the assimilated guests. He went to the kitchen, dejected, to throw his plate away, and went back to Ayan to tell him that he was feeling sleepy.

That night, after they returned from the party, and he had called it a day, Abir could not sleep. Alone in his room, his mind was ringing with Shyamoli's smile, her soft voice, her hair falling around her face, her brilliant and dancing eyes in the moonlight. He wished he had stayed the entire night talking to her in Arun uncle's backyard.

Inclusion

Abir became busy with work gradually. He was not new to corporate software engineering culture, having worked for a few years at Bangalore back in India before coming over to the Silicon Valley. He did get a pleasant culture shock, though, when he started working in his new office. He soon found out, within a few weeks, that his international colleagues were interesting and kind folks. Also, most importantly, they were definitely more disciplined than he had ever been. They were early risers, came to work early, and went home at the right time to maintain their personal time and pursue their passions. They worked hard, worked out hard, gossiped less, and were eager to learn new technology to stay ahead in their careers. He liked the way they were politely interested in India and was charmed about how little they knew about the country. A few of them still seemed to think that marriages happened on elephants, and that most houses were made of mud and thaw, and that snake charmers adorned the streets at will. He was amused when Steve, the other occupant in his office cubicle, described his keenness in knowing Indian girls. He told him a story about his short affair with an Indian girl, about how she made spicy food, and that she had big beautiful eyes.

Steve's story made Abir think of Shyamoli, like the countless number of times in the past few weeks. He had thought of getting in touch with her, but he did not have her number. He sometimes thought of asking Srija for her number, but the incident at the backyard put him off. He did not foresee Srija being friendly with his request.

Also, he was not sure Shyamoli would appreciate a call just like that; would that seem too desperate? After all, he just had a conversation with her, only one time at that. He had been expressive, and she had been mostly receptive and listening. But now that the moment was gone, he wondered whether he had been too pedantic.

It made him anxious to think about the final impression that he had left with Shyamoli; perhaps she had found him too forward? He was surprised with himself. Usually, he was quiet around most people, preferring to listen than talk, but somehow he was free and opinionated around Shyamoli. Perhaps it was something gentle and receptive about her demeanor that had opened him up. But had he opened up too much, and not allowed her to speak?

Before he knew it, two months had passed. Ayan had taken him around to some places, driving him around the green and posh localities of Menlo Park, and around the Stanford campus. On the weekends, if Srija were not around, they would go out to random drives along Highway 280, enjoying the scenic view. Sometimes, they would go down south using 101 all the way to Morgan Hill, enjoying a detour through the Evergreen winding hilly roads. The Sikh Gurdwara in San Jose became their most favorite spot to visit. Cradled in the splendid Evergreen hills, the Gurdwara offered a spectacular view of San Jose and a large part of the Bay Area.

On these random drives, Abir finally got to see the woods, mountains, bays, and oceans that he had heard so much about, before coming to the Silicon Valley. His first long trip was to the majestic Yosemite National Park. Ayan, Srija, him, and two other lab mates of Ayan had packed up in his small car. The five of them made merry in the four-hour-long drive to Yosemite. He found the view near the Half Dome, the popular tourist spot inside the national park, spectacular and breathtaking. He could hear a waterfall faintly and could see it between a foray of trees. The hiking trail had people of all ages: small kids, young boys and girls, and old men and women going up or coming down the path.

In all these trips, Abir had hoped against hope that somehow Shyamoli would be included, but he gathered over time that Srija did not seem to be particularly friendly with Shyamoli. After their first visit to Arun uncle's place, Srija had not mentioned Shyamoli at all, as if she did not exist. This attitude irked Abir. There was no mention of Shyamoli in any of their conversations. He realized that there was a sort of understanding between Ayan and Srija to not mention her in their discussions, even inadvertently.

* * *

One day, when more than a month had gone by since he saw Shyamoli for the first time, Abir ventured to ask about her casually to Ayan. Srija was not around, and he felt this was a good occasion to talk about Shyamoli.

"Do you guys not include Shyamoli in your activities at all?" he asked casually while putting some potatoes in the microwave oven to cook. In these first two months, he had already learned a few things about cooking. This time, Ayan was preparing goat and potato *curry*, the classic Bengali dish usually popular as a lunch option on Sunday afternoons. It was a nontrivial process, but Ayan seemed to be well aware of all the spices and the methods to cook. Abir was his sous chef of sorts, trying to be useful by peeling the potatoes and washing the utensils.

"Why do you ask?" asked Ayan.

"Well, I mean, Shyamoli and Srija are somewhat related, right? So I was curious about this."

"I guess Shyamoli is a bit of an introvert and a loner," said Ayan.

"Really?" said Abir, surprised. "On the contrary, she appeared quite sociable when I chitchatted with her that day at Arun uncle's house."

"Hmm, maybe. I don't create these social circles—Srija does," said Ayan. He resumed cooking, adding bay leaves on a hot oil, ready to prepare the spicy sauce, and cook the meat thoroughly before pressure cooking it. "As a postgraduate academician, I have to focus on my academia. I really leave it all up to Srija to create our social circles, whatever there is. Srija does not seem too keen to include Shyamoli, but you are right there about Shyamoli, though. Personally, I find her to be really well behaved, genuinely nice, but a somewhat quiet and introverted person, like I said. Also, she seems too busy being an invisible caretaker for Arun uncle and his family. The potatoes are done; peel them, will you?"

Abir realized that Ayan was reluctant to talk about this and that this was largely due to Srija. He passed him the peeled potatoes, deciding not to pursue the topic. He thought to himself that if he wanted to befriend Shyamoli, he would have to skirt around Srija somehow.

* * *

Soon, it was October. It was the most anticipated time of the year because it was time for *Durga Puja*, the most looked forward celebration by Bengalis. Bengalis all over the world looked forward to Durga Puja. Durga Puja is a Hindu festival, notably celebrated every year by the Bengalis, which hails the victory of the ten-handed goddess of power, Durga, over *Asura*, the demon.

It was not so much about the religious aspect that made him look forward to this event; instead, it was the atmosphere, the sound of the religious cymbal, the ceremonial drums, the sound of the conch, the prayer recitals, the people, the attires, the food, and cultural programs.

He loved the *Mahalaya*, the story and song routine that was broadcasted at dawn seven days prior to the start of the Durga Puja; the hauntingly beautiful melodies, accompanied by the stunningly powerful recitals by the late great narrator Birendra Krishna Bhadra, describing how Durga, the goddess, was empowered with weapons by the other gods to defeat *Asura*. He loved the Durga Idol, the decorations, the lion on which she stood, the snarling and ferocious face of the *Asura*, and the spear which was finally used to defeat the *Asura*. He loved the smell of flowers mixed with incense and other ritual offerings. He loved Durga Puja and felt excited like a child every time that time of the year approached.

Abir and Ayan listened to the *Mahalaya* by streaming it from YouTube seven days before the start of the Durga Puja, as was the tradition back home in India. Back in earlier days, before there was Internet, people in Kolkata and Bengalis all around India used to wake up very early in the morning, seven days before Durga Puja started, to listen to the Mahalaya broadcasted over the All-India radio. With the advent of YouTube, that unique charm was somewhat diminished, because one could hear the *Mahalaya* all year round,

40

but at the same time, it also made it possible for them to follow the same culture thousands of miles away.

Listening to *Mahalaya* signaled the beginning of the most exciting festival in the year. This time, it was special because, for the first time, he was far from India. He was curious to see how this cultural phenomenon had permeated through the vast distance into this heartland of technology. He started counting the days for the Durga Puja to officially begin in the Silicon Valley.

* * *

Abir's visit to one of the more significant Durga Puja events in the Bay Area turned out to be an anticlimax. A plain white tent-like structure, with a mid-sized Durga idol, stood on the grounds of a college campus booked over the weekend to celebrate the festival. It was a far cry from the magnificent structures, the grand Durga idols, that he had seen back home in Kolkata. He felt slightly disappointed, but reasoned to himself that it was not expected that the busy Silicon Valley engineers would find time to create elaborate structures like those back home.

He did appreciate the shiny and traditional Indian dresses that everybody wore for the special occasion. The ladies wore *sarees*, and Abir could make out exquisite designs on the *sarees*. The men wore traditional *kurtas*. Ayan and Abir turned up to the Durga Puja in their magnificent traditional Indian dresses. Srija did not put on a traditional dress, much to Ayan's annoyance. Ayan threatened not to be around near her if she dressed this way when she could have worn the elegant Indian dress that he had presented last year, but Srija started something about women's rights and individualism. With a foreboding that this outing would be spoilt by their bickering, Abir felt it better to leave them alone, and excusing himself, he mingled into the crowd accumulated before the idol to have their batch of prayers.

As the prayers ended, the *dhaak*— sacred drums—started playing. Abir felt his pulse racing with anticipation, waiting for the classical beat to start and the people around to start dancing with it. He got up, unable to resist himself, and made his way through the crowd to where a couple of middle-aged men were playing the *dhaak*—not so well, he realized ruefully. He waited for some time to see if a more groovy beat would start, but it looked like they would not like to give up their once-a-year chance of glory by trying to play these drums and hoping people would start to dance, as was the ritual.

"Can I try?"

Another man, probably in his mid-thirties, had appeared. He sported long hair and looked like a musician. The one playing the *dhaak* nodded and handed the stick to him. Nobody had started to dance, and he could see the disappointment in his eyes, as with the other person who was hanging around with him. The long-haired musician fellow went and placed the *dhaak* carefully in front of his knees, even as Abir watched in fascination. He took the sticks in his hands and folded his hands to pray to Durga, sticks in his hand. Then he opened his eyes, swung the drum sticks, and hit the drum.

The sound that emanated as the sticks hit the drums seemed to send an electric shock around the surrounding. Position himself carefully, the long-haired musician person started playing classical *dhaak* groove that he was so used to listening to. Abir listened, fascinated, feeling joyful all of a sudden. He felt intoxicated with the essence of it all, his thoughts taken by the pure joy of listening to the intoxicating groove, the classical *dhaak* beat reverberating powerfully around.

And suddenly, as if out of nowhere, a throng of men and women gathered in front of the deity. Abir saw, to his joy, the slow twirl of these folks, their feet keeping up with the beat to the *dhaak* drums, their hands in the air, in one joyous unison, dancing to the rhythm, reverberating in front the Durga idol. He felt as if Durga's eyes were turned on them to bless them, even as the *dhaak* player played with a power that seamed through the men and women gathered together to dance. More people joined, in a wild, clamorous joy, their feet dancing along with the *dhaak* beats in front of the goddess Durga, the dance of power, the dance of joy, the dance of triumph. The conchs were blown in unison, their sounds reverberating with the loud voices, calling out in unison "Durga mai ki jai" ("Hail the mother, Durga").

Abir felt elated at the joyfulness in the air, the beautiful union of positive thoughts of utmost power weaving inside the minds of the men and women. His mind followed the groove, the happy feet of the people dancing, reveling in how culture united people.

And amidst the crowd, he suddenly saw Shyamoli, standing serenely as a bystander, watching the group of men and women dancing. His heart froze for a fraction of a second as he saw her, her long hair dropping down graciously over a traditional Indian sari, her face lit with happiness and excitement. In her eyes, he saw the same happiness that he felt on hearing the *dhaak* being played, on seeing the dancing women and men. He felt a jolt of joy go through his mind, his heart beating wildly all of a sudden. She was looking intently at the joyous crowd, even as several women came over to form a ring of circle to dance. Her large eyes lit up, like candles, as she clapped with the drums, savoring in the radiant energy around her.

As Abir watched, Srija came and stood beside Shyamoli, clapping along with her. As the dancing intensified, the women forming the ring of dancers called on other women nearby to join them. A few women near and around Shyamoli were asked to participate in their dance. They participated happily, the crowd around the dancing arena intensifying. They called out to Srija too to join them, and Srija joined the large circle that the women had formed to dance to the intoxicating dhaak groove

For some reason, the dancing group of women did not invite Shyamoli to join them.

* * *

The college campus where the Durga Puja was being celebrated hosted a dedicated performance hall. Abir looked at the list of events that was about to start in the afternoon. There would be a few plays and dances in the afternoon. In the evening, a professional singer from Bollywood would be performing.

43

Abir entered the auditorium, feeling listless. The sight of Shyamoli being left out by the group of women, and not asked to join in their dance, kept ringing in his mind. Shyamoli had disappeared from the crowd of onlookers after a while, and he felt dejected. He was really looking forward to having a conversation with her again, but now he did not know whether she was there on the campus at all.

He ambled around aimlessly inside the auditorium, without any purpose, thinking whether it was time to go back home. The hall did not have an audience yet. There was more than an hour left for the performances to start officially. The performers were lounging around in the empty seats, looking on at folks in the stage checking out the stage, the sound, and the lights. A group of little kids were on the stage, rehearsing their positions for the play they would perform.

Deciding to be useful in some way, he walked up by the side steps on to the stage side wings to see if anybody needed any help. Back in his college days, he had often hung around backstage to help out his friends when they performed during intra-college cultural competitions. He was never a part of those programs, but he used to love hanging around backstage. Something was thrilling about the preparation, being backstage, to be part of the teams, waiting in anticipation for the performance to start officially.

A few kids ambled past him to join the stage, preparing for one more last rehearsal for one of the songs before the audience came in. A cape slipped off from one of the kids, and somebody went past him hurriedly to the kid to help put on her card back in place.

He was thrilled to realize that it was Shyamoli.

He looked breathlessly, his heart beating fast, as she gracefully went past him. Her long hair touched the floor as she knelt down, tenderly holding the little girl and pinning in the cape back into her dress. She got up, and turning around, her eyes met Abir. There was a flicker of recognition, and she smiled.

"Hello," she said.

Abir nodded, feeling suddenly tongue-tied and embarrassed at being caught staring at her. He could not believe his luck that he had bumped into her again and that she actually recognized him. Shyamoli went on to another small boy who was wearing a crown, which seemed to be falling down because it was too big for him. His heart pounded against him, and he wondered how he could start a conversation with her. He noticed a stapler lying on the side wing. Grabbing it, he went over to her.

"Maybe you can cut the crown, fold it around to make it smaller, and restaple it back," he said. "It will make the crown fit his head."

"Oh, what a clever idea!" she exclaimed, appearing to be delighted. Abir took the crown in his hands and carefully cut the side. Then he rolled it further to make it smaller, holding it happily as Shyamoli stapled it back. He could feel her nearness to him, and it made his mind go all the way to the evening when she was with him in Arun uncle's backyard.

"Are you a volunteer too?" she asked, putting the crown back on the little boy's head, who looked happy to have a crown that fit.

"Well, I am now," he said.

Shyamoli smiled at him.

"Are you one of the directors of this kids' play?" he asked.

"No, no. I am merely a background helper and the costume person. One of my uncle's friends is the director of this play, and my aunt is the costume lead for this play. I helped her—they wanted somebody to prepare the costumes for the kids."

"You made all the costumes for these kids?" asked Abir, amazed.

"My aunt gave the overall direction for the costume designs. I merely made them."

"I see. So your aunt product managed this thing, and you engineered the dresses," said Abir.

"Ah, you corporate engineering folks—always putting things in this light," said Shyamoli smiling. "If you have to put it that way, yes, my aunt sort of decided on what kind of dresses the kids should wear at a high level. I created all their dresses."

"Impressive! That must have been a lot of work."

"Well, I had done a lot of sewing back home, and this was a nice project to have. It took some time, yes, but I enjoyed the process."

"The costumes look absolutely gorgeous," said Abir warmly. "And they are so intricate and detailed! I am sure this play will be a hit."

Shyamoli smiled happily. A few more kids had joined the stage, their parents hovering around anxiously, with the director giving advice, telling them where they should stand on stage, from which side they should enter. This would be the first item of the afternoon performances, right after a short introductory speech by the Chairman of the organization. The kids looked excited and somewhat scared.

Feeling that he would be more of a hindrance than a help at these final stages of the preparation for the play, Abir stood unobtrusively near the side wing, silently observing Shyamoli, as she rushed to another teenage girl who was trying to tie her hair. He looked in wonder and admiration at her as she helped the girl tie her hair, taking a pin from her own hair and using it. He looked at her big eyes shining with excitement, mingling with the kids and the youth with ease, moving around adjusting their dresses, listening to them—eyes that were as lighted and as innocent as those of the kids whom she was helping.

After a while, the audience lights went dark. The afternoon programs were about to start. From the side wing curtains, Abir could see the audience teeming in. Although he was not part of any of the programs, he felt his excitement rising. Was he associating with the kids play simply because Shyamoli, too, was a part of it? Soon, the stage went dark. The kids were crowded around on the wing, waiting for their turn to go on to the stage. He got up hurriedly and went by the side wing so that he was not blocking their entrance. Shyamoli stood amidst them, along with the play director, making last-minute adjustments to their dresses, whispering encouragements.

Soon the play started, and the kids went on to the stage for their performance. Abir went near Shyamoli and stood beside her. Together, they watched the play, enjoying the performances, the somewhat accented Bengali from the kids, and the background music. For him, it was one of the most beautiful moments that he had in a long time, to be able to be near her, not talking, but feeling her presence.

After the play was over, the kids came back to the side wing, happily chatting between themselves, reveling in the spirited and prolonged applause from the audience. Abir looked on happily as a few kids came and hugged Shyamoli, who was standing with bottles of water and passing on to the kids as they flopped around. Abir quickly went over and brought more bottles of water as Shyamoli passed them around, feeling happy that he was finally useful.

As the rolls were called out, the creators behind the play went on stage to receive their dues. For costumes, Pooja aunty was called out.

Somehow, Shyamoli was overlooked and not called on stage.

* * *

As the curtains closed finally to signal the end of the kid's program, Abir turned to Shyamoli, feeling puzzled.

"Hey, wait, why didn't they call you on stage?" he asked.

"Oh, Pooja aunty is the lead, so they called her," Shyamoli said calmly. "I merely created the dresses."

"Hang on—what do you mean you *merely* created the dresses?" said Abir frowning. "Without you, all this would not have been there. You are the ones who did the costumes, not your aunt!"

"Oh, it's OK, really. I don't mind," said Shyamoli, looking slightly troubled.

"But this is ridiculous! *You* are the one who actually made all the dresses, yet they did not mention you at all!" said Abir indignantly. "There is absolutely no doubt that a large part of the success of this play goes to the months of work that you did to create these beautiful costumes. Did you notice that when the anchor called out the costume lead, the audience gave the loudest applause? That applause was meant for *you*, Shyamoli! Why is your aunt taking it all on her? The least she could have done was to call you out personally!"

Shyamoli stared back at him, with a hint of a smile at his indignance.

"It's OK, really. I enjoy doing all this," Shyamoli said simply. "Making the dresses made me happy. Getting to be the lead and getting all the applause makes Pooja aunty happy. Everybody is happy, so it's all good."

Abir looked at her in wonder, marveling at the clarity of her explanation.

"You know, you are like those *Ten-X* engineers in Silicon Valley that all companies want," he said, helping her pack up her assorted items in the bag she was carrying. "You take on all the development work, creating these fabulous creations, which would have taken ten people to do."

"That's an interesting analogy," remarked Shyamoli, as she high-fived the last kid who had walked out of the stage.

"The only difference here, Shyamoli, is that the *Ten-X* engineer gets paid likewise," mused Abir. "But what is your payment here?"

Shyamoli looked at him serenely, smiling at his persistence to express his unhappiness over her work not being acknowledged.

"I guess my payment is the joy I get in creating these dresses," said Shyamoli after a while, zipping up her bag after fitting all her assorted items for the play. "My biggest payment is the happy smiles of the kids when they try on the dresses that I made."

Abir smiled at Shyamoli, admiring the profound simplicity of her thoughts.

The stage, which was empty with the curtains closed, was being prepared for the next event. Abir waited patiently beside Shyamoli, fingers crossed, hoping she would not go off somewhere else. He racked his brain to come up with a plan to stay on longer with her and decided to take the most obvious approach.

"Looks like there are going to be some more performances. Let's watch them from the audience?" Abir asked, hopefully.

"It's more fun to watch it from the side stage," she said. "Let's watch them from here?"

"Sounds like an excellent plan," he said, and quickly grabbed two chairs and put them down.

Shyamoli sat beside him.

Some other program had started—a Bengali play by adults this time. Abir did not try to understand the play much; he was too elated that he was sitting next to Shyamoli. Though not directly looking at her, he noticed her every move: the way she laughed at the jokes on stage and the way she handled her long hair that fell on her face occasionally. It thrilled him when she would suddenly lean toward him, her lips near his ear, and whisper something, about the actor on the stage whom she knew, or giggle about the makeup goof-up of another actor whose mustache seemed to be slipping off. Abir could hardly hear what she was saying when she did that. He was mesmerized by her presence, her essence, her perfume, and her smile. In a fantasy dreamland, he was already flying high, along with Shyamoli, where only they existed.

* * *

"I did not find you later that day. Did you not join the party at all after our chat in the backyard?" Abir asked, as he and Shyamoli strolled outside the auditorium.

The local cultural shows were over, and they were back in the open air. After dinner, a professional Bollywood singer would perform in the evening. Abir did not have a ticket for the evening show, and he did not care. All he wanted was to be with Shyamoli every moment of that day. The evening had descended upon the venue grounds. Children ran amok among the crowd, colorful in their dresses, their excited squeals and laughter adding ornamentation to the exotic atmosphere. The area near the idol had started getting crowded again—the evening prayers had started.

"Oh, that day—no, I had to go upstairs to call my mother. I had promised that I would call her," said Shyamoli.

"I see. I thought it was something to do with Srija; she seemed particularly sharp."

"Oh," said Shyamoli. "Why do you think so?"

"Well, I mean, Srija asked you to help Pooja aunty with preparing and serving the food. She too is related to them, I guess—she could have helped them too, no?"

"She was a guest. I would not expect her to help," said Shyamoli.

"Well, if she was a guest, then she had no right to ask you to help!" said Abir. "Whichever side you take, it points to the obvious that she was just rude and overbearing with you."

"Does it matter to you if she was rude to me?" asked Shyamoli softly, looking sideways to him as they walked back to the Pandal.

Abir wanted to say yes, it made him angry, and that he had been thinking of that evening every day. He decided not to express his thoughts. He thought it would look a bit incorrect to show that he had already started to care about her, after just two meetings with her. It would seem inappropriate, bordering on being desperate.

Abir tried to show his casual disinterest by merely shrugging and looking away, as he dodged a couple of kids who had run straight into him in their playfulness.

* * *

"Are you still seeking your colorless theory in everything you see?" asked Shyamoli as they sat on a grass lawn opposite the auditorium entrance.

"Yes, I dwell on it once in a while," said Abir. "In fact, while the other cultural programs today were going on, I was thinking to myself that cultural appreciation too is vastly colored."

"How so?"

"OK, so let's analyze the program where the chorus sang songs by *Rabindranath Tagore*. So again, going back to my colorless theory, had the world not being divided into *them* and *us*, by color, would you have imagined where Tagore would have stood? He is a combination of the best playwrights and the best music composers of all time. He composed more than two thousand songs, wrote numerous novels, and was the first non-European to receive a Nobel Prize in literature. He literally single handedly redefined a vast landscape of Bengali culture and definition. He was an absolute genius, and the personification of a person specially handcrafted by God to start a cultural and artistic revolution in India. I personally find him no different than an ethereal combination of Shakespeare and some other famous European music composer."

Shyamoli nodded in agreement.

"Yet just look around," continued Abir fervently. "Most people here in America don't know him, haven't heard his music, and seem to be vastly indifferent to what he was, or what he did, for literature and music which transcends beyond the Indian subcontinent. And then, look at the other direction of cultural and musical appreciation. We know all about the famous cultural artists and cultural patrons that Europe had to offer over the centuries. Shakespeare. Bach. Beethoven. Mozart. Why is this so unidirectional? If *we* know about the great European and American cultural influencers, then why not the other way around? Why don't *they* know about our cultural influencers?"

"You have a point," said Shyamoli thoughtfully. "We had heard of Shakespeare from our childhood. Our school syllabus had plays by Shakespeare. We read about Beethoven, but I am sure none of the kids in any European country, or here in America, ever heard of Rabindranath Tagore."

"Exactly," said Abir.

"Do you think this is something to do with colors?" she asked.

"Yes, it absolutely is!" said Abir. "In fact, it's not special to Europe, to America, or to any country or culture. It's just human nature to create strata by color."

"Yes, you told me that last time," she said.

"In fact, I saw a color-based profiling today too," said Abir after a while, weighing his words carefully.

"Where?" asked Shyamoli, intrigued.

"Well, I noticed that you were not included in the dancing group of women today morning," he said, looking at her gently to make sure she saw it just as a discussion.

Shyamoli looked startled.

"You were there?" she asked.

"Yes, Shyamoli, I was there," he said quietly. "I saw those so-called glamorous women dancing to the beautiful *dhaak* groove, reveling in their artificial glamour and glory, enjoying all the attention from the onlookers, smiling at the right moments to the camera folks to have their glamorous photos taken, to be uploaded to social media. I saw you standing by, and I saw those women call other women around you and ignore you automatically. I hate to say this, but they ignored you simply because of your dark skin color, Shyamoli. Perhaps they did not mean to be unkind to you, but they did it automatically, without thinking, because ignoring dark-skinned people is hardwired in their hearts and their minds, Shyamoli."

Shyamoli stared at him, lost in his fervor, her eyes suddenly brimming with tears, as Abir pulled some grass off the ground in anger.

* * *

The sun had set. Abir sat with Shyamoli on the grass, oblivious to the surroundings, to the time, to the occasion. He felt he was in heaven, in the presence of a sublimely graceful diva, whose sheer presence elevated his happiness to a supreme level.

"Let's eat something," he said in a while. "You worked hard today. You need a treat, and I am hungry too."

He went over to the stalls with Shyamoli to buy some typical Bengali food. Together, they savored *phuchka*—the famous Kolkata crunchy and spicy street food—and egg rolls.

"Do you miss Durga Puja at home?" Abir asked, munching happily on an egg roll.

"Oh, terribly," said Shyamoli. "You know, for me, Durga Puja has been all about family. I especially loved the extraordinary designs of the Puja pandals all over Kolkata, and my family used to wake up in the wee hours of the morning and used to roam around the city, pandal hopping."

"Yes, that's a popular thing to do," said Abir, smiling at her exuberance.

"Yes, isn't it?" she said brightly. "And what amazing pandals! Such beautiful structures—temples, castles. Such intricate designs, such magnificence."

"I guess the pandal here is a far cry from what you are used to seeing at home," he said.

"Well, yes," said Shyamoli. "Although it still brings people together, for me, though, what I miss most is my family."

Abir nodded gently. As he took out his wallet to pay for the food vendor, Shyamoli stopped him.

"Please, let me pay," she said, taking out her purse. "I wanted to thank you for helping me backstage."

As Abir watched her pay the vendors, he reasoned to himself that this could perhaps be an appropriate time to take her phone number, so that he could possibly ask her out some time, but as he thought about it, he hesitated. Would it seem inappropriate? Besides, he still did not have a mobile phone of his own—a fact that surprised anybody who knew about it. Where would he store her number? Scribble it on a piece of paper? That sounded weird and desperate.

He heard his name being called. Turning around reluctantly, he found Srija walking toward them, calling out to him. This was not a situation that he looked forward to, and in his joy at being with Shyamoli again, he had completely forgotten that he had come over with Ayan and Srija and that they would eventually look for him before going back home.

He sighed ruefully and prepared to call it a day. As with last time, Srija stopped short when she saw him with Shyamoli. Shyamoli and Srija exchanged pleasantries, and Srija complimented Shyamoli on her gorgeous Indian dress. Abir looked on in amusement, noting the forced appreciation in Srija's voice, even as her eyes looked angry and distressed to see Shyamoli looking so sublime. Ayan looked as placid as he always did, but his eyes were alert, as he looked at Abir and Shyamoli. Thankfully, it was all a formality, and soon they left, leaving behind Shyamoli, who wanted to wait for Arun uncle and Pooja aunty to show up before she went back home.

As he returned with Ayan and Srija that evening, Abir sat dreamily at the back of the car, wishing he had a phone and that he had Shyamoli's number with him, so that he could drown himself in her soft voice. He was leaving behind his people, the scent, sound, and scenes of Bengaliness, taking with him the same feeling of dizzy euphoria that he had felt the last time he had talked with Shyamoli. He closed his eyes in happy guilt as he thought of her long hair and her beautiful large eyes, soft and calm, and fantasized himself lying on the grass with his head on her lap, looking up at her as she patted his hair, entangled in a silent time warp which had no end.

An unbalanced equation

After Durga Puja, Abir settled down with the fast rhythm of life in Silicon Valley. The end of the year 2013 was approaching fast, and it was already mid-December. It was hard to believe that he had been in Silicon Valley for almost two quarters now; it felt just yesterday that Ayan had picked him up from the San Francisco airport. While initially, he had missed the comforts of being in India, he was now well accustomed to the mini India that dwelled within the heart of Silicon Valley. Thousands of Indians resided in California, a large percentage of them being in the Silicon Valley. Numerous Indian festivals happened all year along. There were Indian grocery stores all around the valley. It was easy to obtain Indian food through hundreds of restaurants around the Bay Area and through the host of catering services who could provide Indian food at home directly. In this multicultural melting pot, Indianness thrived joyfully in its essence.

He stayed connected with his parents, especially his mother, who would call him almost every alternate day and ask about his work and his time at Silicon Valley. His mother had been a college lecturer. She had held several faculty positions at various universities and colleges in different parts of India, as they moved around the country along with his father. She had taught mathematics at a senior level in college. Much of Abir's mathematics outlook, and his preparation for engineering college admissions tests, had been fueled by his mother. She had picked up computer programming of late, writing code in the Python programming language for fun, and would sometimes ask Abir coding questions which had mathematical foundations. She had recently retired from teaching, taking an early retirement, but continued to give private mathematics coaching lessons to college and high school students at home once in a while.

Abir discussed everything with his mother. About his work. About the beautiful weather in the Bay Area. About his colleagues. About Ayan and Srija.

But for some reason, he could not mention Shyamoli.

He did not know whether it was something that he should think about. He had met Shyamoli only twice. He did not quite know when he had started thinking about her. Every time he thought about her, he felt happy. Her big, beautiful eyes stayed in his fantasy, and often he found himself daydreaming about spending time with her.

Somehow, he felt his mother would not appreciate this side of his story, so he carefully avoided any mention of Shyamoli.

* * *

The fall colors were giving way to more dull shades in nature. There was a sharp chill in the December air. The first bout of shower had already occurred in the valley. Abir had settled into a pattern in his life, between work, home, and his tech passions. Ayan would come home late in the evenings in the weekdays, and more often than not, he would also disappear in his lab during the weekends too. Srija was less frequent to their place now, and Abir had a feeling Ayan was meeting her in other places, out of respect for Abir's privacy. Abir felt guilty about this and had on more than one occasion mentioned that Ayan was most welcome to have Srija over.

More often than not, Abir was alone at home. In those times, he felt lonely and thought of Shyamoli. He did not have a mobile phone yet, a fact which surprised almost anybody he met. Somehow he could live without a mobile device. He would make all his video calls home from his laptop. They had a landline phone, and it was sufficient for him to receive calls from home when he was around. He did not have Shyamoli's phone number either, albeit he reasoned that, after having met and talked with her only two times now, it would be a bit awkward to just call her. Would it be appropriate? Would she deny his approach for friendship, thinking he was too forward?

Abir revived the last time he was with Shyamoli. He thought of the conversation with her, in the inebriating October breeze, in the Durga Puja pandal. He had felt intoxicated by her sheer presence. He spent a lot of time rewinding the entire event in his mind several times and replaying it. He wished he could talk to her again, in the inebriate breeze, sitting on the grass.

Out of boredom, Abir finally opened an account on Facebook. He looked up Shyamoli immediately but realized to his disappointment that she was not on Facebook. His first Facebook friend was Srija, who added him herself. He got to add a few more folks and invariably received many more friend requests. As he expected, Ayan did not have a Facebook account, and he did not seem to care to have one.

Abir realized shortly that it was straightforward to use Facebook, or any social media for that matter, but after getting Srija's updates continuously in his news feeds, he realized, though, that she had mastered the art of promoting herself through Facebook. It fascinated him to see her post everything about her life on Facebook daily, especially pictures of where she went, in a carefully articulated manner, which revealed a lot besides the innocuous images. She would also share random thoughts from the web, which she thought appropriately described her apparent intellectual side.

Right after the Durga Puja in October, Srija had uploaded a dazzling picture of herself with Ayan on Facebook, which also included Abir, to his surprise. For some reason, it annoyed him. He considered it bordering on invasion of his privacy, because he did not recall being in that picture, and neither did he want to randomly appear in Srija's photos. To his chagrin, she tagged him in her photo almost immediately after adding him on Facebook, which irked him because he felt he was not looking good in the picture.

Soon, he found himself analyzing Internet content as a person with inclination for everything data would. He enjoyed the varied YouTube videos—of music, of love, of stories of people, and of random talents who would never be famous if YouTube was not there. He enjoyed the interesting Facebook posts, the unusual stories. Every person in his ever-growing friends' list, or those of extended friends' list, had some sort of a story and life event to share. He felt happy at the way people around the world took to Facebook with a gusto, sharing every part of their lives. He enjoyed the supportive comments made to posts about each other—the encouragements and the appreciations.

He started appreciating the core personalized feed ranking algorithms which caused these YouTube and Facebook feeds to show up for him. He had an inkling about the algorithms of connectivity used, but he did realize that the primary force behind these feeds were the data from people themselves. People. People, and their cultures, emitting data about themselves in a perpetual endeavor to showcase their lives as colorful journeys. These feeds were not relegated to the locality where the events happened. Posts and videos from the remotest parts of rural India were seen by well-off people from the United States. A random street singer from Honolulu was becoming an Internet sensation on YouTube, getting new gigs, money, and livelihood. There was a global sharing of life conditions, of cultures, and of the happy and sad tales of people and their lives.

He realized that Internet entities like YouTube, Google, and Facebook played a huge role in creating a base for people to develop empathy for each other. Every now and then, inspiring stories about people helping each other in crisis came up. Humans helping animals in floods. Brave firefighters and police officers risking their lives to save victims. Of donation drives for critically ill people. Of charity, of hopefulness, of small tales of love, of sympathy, of kindness, and of empathy.

Abir felt proud to be a computer engineer, to belong to a tribe of people whose work affected the way people engage with each other, at the way data and information got shared across cultures and regions, and at the way it was helping global consciousness slowly conform to one single identity of fundamental and core humanity. Slowly, but surely, these Internet phenomenons would create a consciously chosen, global, and fundamental gist of being human.

* * *

One Saturday afternoon, a few days before the Christmas vacations began, Shyamoli called on Abir's home landline phone. Ayan and Srija had gone out for a movie. He was alone at home, reading articles on data science and engineering.

"I am in your apartment complex. I had tried calling Srija on her cell phone, but she is not picking it up," said Shyamoli over the phone.

"How long will you take?" asked Abir, panicked, his heart racing in elation about this unexpected turn of events that would make him see her again. He looked around his house; it was a mess. He was wearing a set of boring pajamas and t-shirts, had not shaved in a week, and the last thing he wanted was Shyamoli to see him look like a ragamuffin.

"I am almost outside your door," she said. Abir put down the phone in alarm and hurriedly changed into something decent, running between rooms in a frenzy. There was a knock at the door, and when he opened the door, he was slightly breathless.

Shyamoli stood outside, with a paper bag in her hand. On realizing that he was alone in his home, she looked a bit embarrassed as he let her in. She put down the paper bag on the table.

"So this is your place," she said, looking around.

"Yeah—well—there is nothing to look at," said Abir, feeling breathless and suddenly shy at being in her presence.

"I think it's perfectly lovely. Also, you don't have an uncle and aunt to sponsor you and keep you in a villa on a tilla."

"True," smiled Abir happily. "Do you want to have tea? I was thinking of making myself some."

"You don't have to be a perfect host. Sit down—I can make tea for us," she said, walking toward their little kitchen. "By the way, I got some food that I cooked today morning. Some chicken *curry*, *prawn masala*, and *aloo poshto*."

"How wonderful," said Abir. "Did you come all the way to give us all this?"

"I had come to the Safeway near this place in Mountain View to buy some groceries for home. Arun uncle wanted to eat a special chicken *curry* which I make for him, so wanted to get the chicken from here. I told Srija that I would be coming along in the afternoon. I guess she will be here shortly."

"I am sure Srija will be delighted," he said.

"This food is for all of you, by the way—Srija, Ayan, and you too," she said.

"Great. By the way, let me make tea for us. That's the least I can do. Why don't you sit down and relax?" said Abir, hurriedly getting the tea leaves from the top counter. Shyamoli nodded and went out of the kitchen.

"I love the balcony," she called. She had walked outside to the balcony. At least it was not unkempt, Abir thought in relief. It was his favorite place. The branches of a tree brushed against the railings of the balcony lightly. Often, squirrels would come hopping onto the balcony. He was the most frequent visitor to this place of their little home. Once in a while, Ayan accompanied him, but when Srija was around, they rarely ever came to the balcony. In that sense, the balcony in a way belonged to Abir. The trees made a beautiful fence around the balcony, creating a canopy of sorts, where he could not be seen by passersby on the parking lot down below on the ground floor. At first, seeing Abir, the squirrels would flee, but gradually, they had become accustomed to him.

He took the teacups in a saucer to the balcony, with some biscuits on the dish, touching the cup. They had a small plastic beach table with two matching beach chairs on the balcony.

"Thank you, this is wonderful," said Shyamoli. "Did you know, there are two squirrels on this tree! They are not afraid of me at all."

Abir nodded as they sat in silence for some time, watching the squirrels. He felt elated to be sitting with her again and hoped fervently that she would not decide to leave, given that the others were not there. He did wonder, though, as to why she was there to meet Srija at all, given that he had the distinct impression that Srija was not favorable toward her. He decided not to think about that aspect at the moment. Her presence, and the beautiful weather to compliment it, made him forget everything else except her. Although it was just late afternoon, it was slightly cold, and the hot tea made yet another pleasant addition to their setting.

"The December breaks are coming soon. You will go and visit home, I guess," Abir said.

"Well, no, I have not thought of it," said Shyamoli. "How about you?"

"Uh—I don't know," Abir replied, thinking it over. It had not occurred to him to go home during the winter holidays. When he had come here several months back now, his first instinct had been to question his decision to come all the way. Now well into his work, his outlook had changed, and he realized, to his surprise, that he had not given a thought about going home at all during the coming winter breaks. He did not have a plan as such, except to perhaps go out to Los Angeles or some other place during the Christmas vacation.

"Oh, you software engineers—you don't have much vacation, do you?" Shyamoli asked playfully.

"Well, I can take a couple of weeks off, I guess. And then there are the Christmas vacations and New Year too," he said.

"Come on, then you should go," said Shyamoli. "I am sure your parents want to see you. I miss home so much—I haven't been home since I came here. But I have tons of work that needs to be done in the winter break. But I am sure you are more free than me, so you should go and surprise your parents. Besides, what will you do in the winter vacations anyways?"

Abir shrugged, sipping his tea solemnly, watching her. He wished he could tell her that all he wanted in the holidays was to see her every day, every moment. Till even that morning, it was all a fantasy, a happy thought that in some dreamland, he and Shyamoli would be together every day. But now that she had manifested herself in his presence, it was more of a reality than before. Would he get the courage to ask her out one of these days? Even the thought made him nervous. What if she rejected the idea? This was all nice at the moment, the serendipity delightful in its uncertainty, and it did not make sense to break this growing friendship with some overly romantic moves which could jeopardize all of this.

He noticed her large, eloquent eyes, highlighted with dark black eyeliner, her hair falling around her face, and her ebony tone reflecting the light from the setting sun. He noticed the way she laid her hands lightly on the table. The entire aura and her sublime graceful femininity bedazzled him, blurring everything around him, everything except her.

"I was thinking about social networks and their influence in our lives," he said eventually, trying a more reasonable course of conversation so that he appeared casual.

"You mean Facebook?"

"Yes," said Abir. "I opened an account some days back, and I really enjoy going through all the feeds now. I am almost an addict now. It provides a lot of interesting data about people."

"Ah right, you would like it, of course, given your passion for data," she said, smiling.

"How come you don't have an account on Facebook?" asked Abir.

Shyamoli looked at him curiously, and Abir suddenly felt embarrassed, realizing that he had given away the fact that he had searched for her on Facebook. He hurriedly took his empty cup and pretended to take a sip out of it.

"I never thought of opening an account," said Shyamoli, smiling slightly, ignoring his failed attempts to sip from an empty cup.

"Well, you should," said Abir, putting his cup down. "It's more than just gossip and life status. It is a good way to really understand the world of humans beyond pretty pictures of decked up ladies. It really opens one's eyes to the different cultures around the world. But the thing that strikes me most is the appalling conditions that some people stay in. It's one thing to be casually concerned about them, but a whole different thing to actually see videos of their lives and misery when they surface in the timeline feeds. I really think we take our living conditions for granted."

"You sound genuinely empathetic toward their plight," said Shyamoli, smiling at his fervor.

"Yes, I am Shyamoli. I have always grown around wealth; God had been kind to my family and me. Truth be told, it was all due to a lot of effort on my dad's part to work really hard, do the right thing, and take his career to a level that made my life very comfortable. Many people work hard and don't get their due. My dad did get his due, though. We, as a family, did get our due. For example, I have lived in bungalows for most parts of my life, all over India, due to my dad's status as an Indian administrative service officer."

"Wow, that must have been fun," mused Shyamoli.

"Well, I guess so. But at the same time, my dad insisted on looking at the world at a grassroots level. He used to take me to local tours sometimes, to these places where people were living in real poverty, merely getting by their lives. It made me upset, and I used to sort of dislike being so much far better off than them. These visits made an impact on me, I guess, and I have always wondered about this strange distribution of wealth. This skewed distribution of wealth makes an imbalance in the distribution of empathy too."

"I am aware of this, too," said Shyamoli after a pause. "You know, my father has similar views too and tells me that this is a theme that occurs in his classes sometimes."

"Oh, how interesting! By classes, did you mean college classes? Is he a teacher?"

"Yes, he is a college lecturer."

"That's cool. For how long has your father been teaching?"

"From as long as I can remember," she said.

"Where? In Kolkata?"

"Yes."

"Do you guys stay in the city in Kolkata?" he asked.

"Well yes, we stay in the city—in north Kolkata," she said, her eyes lighting up. "Ours is a joint family. My relatives from my father's side live in the same complex, on different floors of the house. It's a bustling household."

"That must be really fun," he said wistfully. "My life had been the exact opposite. Most of my life, I have stayed all over the country and have not really been near a bigger family. I was an only child, and both my parents worked, so I spend more time with the servants at my home than with them."

"Oh, that must have been a bit hard," said Shyamoli sympathetically.

"Oh well, each one to one's life, I guess," said Abir, somewhat morosely. "It's better now, though. Since my dad retired a few years back, we came back to Kolkata. Now there is a lot of family nearby. My cousins Rimjhim and Manik live nearby. But then, when my parents moved to Kolkata, I went to Bangalore! So in a way, it had all been the same for me—almost always away from an extended family."

"Well, everything has its pros and cons," said Shyamoli kindly, smiling at his morose expression. "Since we are in a joint family of sorts, privacy is pretty less. But, indeed, I had never felt lonely in my life."

Abir smiled at her. He felt happy in her presence, just like last time. The place, the context, and the surrounding had disappeared from him, and the only thing that mattered to him was her presence. It was getting slightly dark, days being much shorter in winter. The squirrels had disappeared, and a row of birds in a long, splendid formation flew over the sky.

"Well, you are continuing your joint family existence here too, to some extent, I guess," he said after a while.

"Well yes," said Shyamoli, "I am so grateful to have some kind of a family, a local guardian, to stay with, although I had not really met Arun uncle before. He is related to us very distantly, and I saw him the first time I came here. But he is very kind. He lets me stay in his house with low rent."

"You pay rent to your uncle?" Abir said, surprised.

"Well yes, of course," she said, looking surprised at his surprise. "And it's only fair, I think. I get to stay in my own room in their big air-conditioned home. Why should I stay for free?"

Abir nodded silently.

"I do feel abashed at times to hold on to their hospitality, especially Pooja aunty, because, after all, who am I really to her?" continued Shyamoli. "But I think I am a decent live-in guest and make myself useful by doing household chores for them, like cooking all their meals and stuff."

"You cook *all* their meals?" asked Abir, raising his eyebrows in surprise.

"Well—yes," said Shyamoli. "I make their breakfast before I leave for college. They both work, so lunch is all set for them. I make dinner for them when I get back from work."

Abir's thoughts went to the first time he had seen her, months back, heating up food and preparing the kitchen, all alone, while everybody else was having fun at the party. It all added up now.

"My uncle and Pooja aunty are so busy at work. I make sure they are comfortable. I cook all their meals, make their beds, tidy up their home, and clean all the kitchen utensils. If they had a daughter, I guess she would have done the same. It's the least I can do."

"I doubt it if any daughter would do that," he said quietly, weighing his words carefully. "I think it's very kind of you to help them out. In fact, I don't think anybody would take on the role that you have taken. But I am not sure you realize the service that you are providing to your uncle and aunt?"

"Oh, I don't see it like that at all. In fact, I enjoy doing all the household chores."

Abir remained silent, wondering why would somebody want to cook all the meals, and do all household chores, and on top of that, pay rent to stay. When did she get time to do her academic work— the main reason for being here in the first place? It seemed too un-selfish to him, and he felt a small tinge of resentment at the stupen-dous free service that her uncle and aunt were getting. To him, she was too simple to really understand that she was vastly over-paying for her accommodation, in terms of paying rent, as well as being an invisible caretaker for Arun uncle and Pooja aunty. That's what Ayan had meant, he recalled suddenly—that she was too busy being an invisible caretaker for her uncle and his wife. He realized that this was a person who would just be simple, grounded, and calm, like a person who does not question others' motivations but sticks to one's work.

His heart pounded for her with a sudden fervor that he could not understand. He had known her for only a short time, and this was their third meeting. Why did he care for her so much? He had never seen anybody whose eyes reflected such purity, eyes that saw only the good in others, a reflection of a soul that found it difficult to comprehend cunningness and complications in the society.

"Did you ever think of staying independently of your own?" he asked eventually, deciding to pursue this topic, despite realizing that Shyamoli was hesitant to talk about it. He felt he needed to get to the bottom of this strange arrangement, which seemed to have negative benefits.

"Yes, I wanted to," she said. "But Srija told me that her aunt was growing old, so was my uncle, so my staying at their place and helping them would be the unselfish thing to do."

"How is Srija related to you?" he asked after a while.

"She is related to my aunt."

"Oh, I see. So you and Srija are not really related by family?"

"No."

Abir suddenly realized the entire game behind this. It seemed to add up finally. The whole setup made him angry, and he could see some manipulation on Srija's part, which he did not like. The peculiar arrangement in which Shyamoli lived her life in the Bay Area did not make sense to him. This was not right in his eyes, but he did not want to say anything right then, lest she got offended. He racked his brain to change the topic.

"It must be fun to have a sibling. I am an only child," he said eventually, hiding his frustration and trying to sound calm.

"How does it feel to be an only child?" she asked, looking somewhat relieved to change the topic.

"That's an interesting question. I don't know, really. I mean, I do not have enough data to compare to. Being a single child has certain benefits, I guess. For one, my mother has all the time and attention for me. She calls me every other day, and we are close buddies, really. I tell her everything: what I do here, the kind of work I am doing. She is getting into computer science these days, more as a hobby than a necessity. We sometimes write code together."

"How nice," said Shyamoli, smiling.

"Yes, it has been like that most of the time. My father is a workaholic and still travels most of the time, doing government projects all over the country."

Shyamoli nodded, collecting her cup and Abir's empty cup, too, in preparation to keep it back in the kitchen sink.

"I have often wondered what it's like to have a sibling," Abir said.

"Well, I have always enjoyed having a sibling," said Shyamoli. "In my joint family, I had one cousin whom I grew up with, although she is now married and lives in a different place. My own little brother is the cutest human being in the world and is the closest person to me in my life. When he was younger, he used to spend all his day making mischief and trying to prank me. He has grown up now and is a sophomore in high school. So far, he seems to adore me."

"Who in the right mind wouldn't adore you?" said Abir without thinking.

Shyamoli blushed, and Abir realized the folly of his innocuous comment. He felt embarrassed, and she looked down at her hands in sudden confusion.

Her phone rang at that moment, changing the context, to his relief. It was Srija calling her.

"Ayan and Srija are done with the movie and are coming over," she said.

"I see," said Abir.

He got up from his chair and paced up and down in the room, thinking out the situation, while Shyamoli took the empty cups to the kitchen, meaning to wash them. He did not stop her. Instead, he looked on as she automatically washed the cups, her well-used-to hands rinsing the soap and neatly scrubbing the sides of the cups. She must have done this a thousand times, he thought angrily. How could somebody be so naive and simple?

He decided that it was time he started giving her some sense, to protect her from all this. He decided it was time for him to take a stance.

"Shyamoli, don't take it otherwise, but I really think you should leave before Srija sees me with you," he said, as she dried the cups to put them back neatly in the drawer above. Shyamoli looked at him, her big eyes wide with surprise. Abir nodded at her reassuring.

"I am not driving you out, Shyamoli, but I wouldn't like Srija to see me with you alone. She will say something rude to you again, like the last time she found you chatting with me alone, and I can't stand it."

Shyamoli stared at him apprehensively, looking troubled. Abir debated to himself whether he should voice his thoughts about what he thought of her situation. Perhaps his opinion about the true colors of his uncle would pull her away from him. After all, she knew him only from a few conversations, but come what may, it made him angry and frustrated at her situation, and he decided to speak out anyway.

"I don't like what's happening in your life, especially the way you are staying with your uncle, Shyamoli" he said. "You might think I am intruding in your life choices and that I am wrong about them because I hardly know them. But if you consider me as a friend, or even a well-wishing acquaintance, I think you should really reconsider an option to move out of your uncle's home and live independently."

She stared at him, apparently at a loss of words. Her eyes looked distressed, and it made Abir deeply unhappy.

"I really mean it, Shyamoli," he said quietly, despite his mind being in turmoil at her distressed expression. "I think your uncle and his wife are simply manipulating you into working like a live-in caregiver, who also happens to pay rent! This is absolutely absurd! If they need all-day care, ask them to hire a full-time stay at home caregiver, which, by the way, would probably cost them half their salary. You don't need to do this. You did not come all the way to the Silicon Valley to become somebody's free stay-at-home caregiver. You came here to pursue your intellectual passions, to pursue a life of academia. You don't have to let Srija manipulate you!"

Shyamoli put down the cups that she had been holding, and went over to get her purse, turned away from him. She zipped up her purse in silence, as Abir watched on.

"I can take care of myself, thank you," she said after a while, turning back him, her voice soft, but determined, "I am staying over with my uncle and aunt not just at Srija's counsel, but by my own sense of duty too. I think it's good to take care of older relatives. Besides, the work is not killing me, and I enjoy their company too."

"You are doing them a favor, which they are not returning," said Abir debatably. "When I first saw you, you were working alone in the kitchen, and everybody else was having fun, yet when I met Arun uncle and Pooja aunty, they looked perfectly fit and healthy! Then why were they not taking care of their own kitchen? Why you? That is not taking care of elderly relatives—that's just serving them for a pittance! The entire setup is wrong!"

"You mean your data does not add up here?" she asked, regaining her calm self.

"Exactly! It's an unbalanced data equation. The algorithm does not make sense. You are being exceptionally kind with negative benefits!"

"I think kindness is not for any benefit," said Shyamoli, smiling slightly at his indignant expression.

"Well, maybe, but there is a process to it," pursued Abir. "There's no use being cryptic here, Shyamoli. You are doing some work, and you are not getting paid for it. It's as simple as that. It's like working for a company here in Silicon Valley for free. Just like that. And it's not your company either, neither is it a startup which can give dividends some time in the future. It's just free service."

"I thought it's all about free service here in Silicon Valley?" said Shyamoli, picking up her bag. "Look at Google. Google Search is free. So is Gmail. And so is Google Maps. Yet look at the happiness that these services are giving to everybody—all for free. Not everything needs a payment, Abir."

"Oh, come on," said Abir, throwing up his hands in the air. "Surely you are not comparing your service to those provided by Google? That's not even a comparison, Shyamoli! Accepted—Google is a phenomenal institute by itself, and all the beautiful services that I get from Google are free. But that's a completely different thing, Shyamoli! They are, after all, a profitable company. For you, you have zero profits! In fact, it's all loss for you as far as I can see! It's a terrible deal with negative benefits!"

"Well, it's not a terrible deal like you make it out to be," Shyamoli said calmly. "I get to make food, which I love to do. I love to care for a family, and I get to do that too. Not everything can be explained with data, logic, and profitability, Abir. Is my uncle and his family getting a free service? Probably yes, as you point out. Does it affect me? No. In fact, I get to enjoy their company, their love, the people they receive. It's wonderful to have a sort of family of my own here. I miss being with my joint family back home. I get a little bit of that here. When I was in India, I did all the work at my home. I am doing the same thing here."

Abir remained silent, marveling, yet again, at her simple views of life. He smiled at her, and she smiled back.

"For me, happiness is all about belonging—to a family, to society, to a culture," Shyamoli said softly. "So what if I cook a few meals for free or clean the home once in a while? It's my home too because I live in it. I would have prepared meals for myself anyways—why not then make meals for the others in my home too? It makes me truly happy when they appreciate the food that I make, and it makes me happy that they are comfortable when they come back home after a tiring day. It makes me happy to see their smiles of happiness to be looked after."

"You are also tired when you come back home after a grueling day being a grad student," said Abir. "Who looks after you then, Shyamoli?"

"Somebody will come along when I need it," she said, smiling. "God will send the person when I truly need somebody to help me and look after me."

Abir looked deep into her eyes, thinking about the simplicity of her outlook on life, love, and equity. As he looked at her pristine eyes, he could understand her side of the world, about it being all about family, about being accepted in a family, about empathy for the elderly, about providing selfless service to people who needed them. He wondered at the profound purity of her thoughts and smiled at her automatically in genuine admiration.

"I think your uncle and aunt are really lucky to have you stay with them," he said fervently. Shyamoli looked embarrassed at his praise and looked down at her hands shyly.

"In fact, may I extend that to say that anybody who gets to know you is lucky?" he said softly, looking into her eyes. Then, without thinking about it, he held out his hand to hold hers. She did not take it away. She stared back at him, holding his hand, her eyes smiling, seeming to seek some meaning from him. He gazed at her, and everything seemed to dissolve around him except her beautiful and bright eyes staring back at him. She, too, seemed to be mesmerized by his gaze as she looked back. They stared at each other in silence for a while. Then she smiled back at him, bade him adieu softly, opened the door silently, and went out.

Homeless

Christmas, followed by New Year's eve, came and went, and soon, it was 2014, a brand new year. His last meeting with Shyamoli was always on Abir's mind, consciously and subconsciously. Her thoughts, and their conversations from the previous three times that he had met, kept on whirling in his mind, creating different experiences and versions of the topics they had discussed. Her words made him think about the idea of doing something selflessly, without expecting any relevant payment, just for the sake of loving doing it.

With the advent of a brand new year, Abir started jogging in the nearby park after coming home, as a sort of New Year's resolution to exercise daily and stay fit. The park was a few blocks away from his apartment complex. It was a beautiful park, lush green, with canopies of trees over the walking trail.

On his first day, he almost ran into a homeless old man sleeping under a tree. Abir had not noticed him at first in the dim light of dusk. During this first encounter, Abir thought he was merely an eccentric rustic old man napping under the tree. When he found him sleeping under the same tree the next evening, and the next one, he realized that this was the place where he slept. The evenings were cold, and the nights were colder. The old man kept under a torn old blanket, wearing a woolen cap to keep his head warm. During the first few days, Abir had been afraid of this sleeping, mysterious stranger, wondering if he was a criminal of some kind and if it was safe to jog in the dusk with so little light. After a while, he got used to seeing him under the tree. The park would be mostly empty in the evenings, and he would be one of the few people who stayed back, either to jog or walk their dogs. The homeless man would be sleeping at those times in the evening, and once in a while, if he was awake, he would just stare away at nothing.

Every time Abir saw the homeless man, he felt bad for his condition. One unusually cold evening, as he was making his rounds around the park during his evening jogging session, he noticed the homeless man shivering. He felt bad for him, as always, and after the first few rounds of the park, he stopped near him, panting slightly, feeling warm.

"Feeling too cold, mate?" he asked.

The old man looked surprised at being spoken to. He was probably not used to being addressed directly by the park visitors, especially not about his well-being.

"Nah, it will pass. I have God to protect me above, watching over me with his satellite," he said, pointing upward in a dramatic fashion, squinting his eyes. He became silent again, closed his eyes, and rocked himself to and fro.

"How long have you been here? Don't you have a home or shelter of some kind to go to?" asked Abir.

"Nopes, mate. I ain't got no home or shelter to go too. I am not well off like you, my friend."

Abir looked at him, wondering what he could do to help this man beat the cold. He decided that it was time for action and took off his jacket.

"Here, man, you take this jacket. Hope it will keep you warm," Abir said, handing over his jacket to him. The old man made a V sign with his two fingers.

"God bless you, sir, for your kindness," he said, putting it on hurriedly.

Abir was still feeling warm because he had been running for some time, but he knew he would feel pretty cold soon without the jacket. He started jogging again, this time toward his apartment, which was a few blocks away. He reached his home in ten minutes and tugged at the door thankfully, for it was getting cold.

It was locked.

He checked his pockets and realized that he had forgotten his keys back inside his home. He knocked for some time and suddenly remembered that Ayan had mentioned something about going to Srija's place in the evening. Usually, Ayan would be around at that time, and Abir would just go out to run. He always took his keys along with him, but as luck would have it, he did not have his keys with him that day.

Abir realized that he was now genuinely stranded outside his apartment, on a cold night, without his jacket, for an unknown amount of time.

He waited for some time, and as it started getting colder, he started panicking a bit. The last thing he wanted was to get hypothermia. He did not have a mobile phone, and for the first time, he realized that it was time that he had a mobile phone with him. He knocked on a few doors of the adjacent apartments and realized that nobody was around. It was a Friday evening, and presumably, people were out partying.

Slowly, it started getting deeper into the night. After sitting for almost an hour outside, hugging himself to keep the cold out, he decided that he would have to take some emergency actions. He realized that he would need to jog around again if he were to avoid acute hypothermia. He ran up and down the stairs and then went out to the parking lot to run around, and soon enough, he was feeling warm enough to manage.

While running around, he saw lights and heard voices from one of the ground floor apartments, and he decided to ask for help. The condo had some kind of a party going on. He knocked at the door, and a middle-aged woman opened the door. She looked at him suspiciously.

"Sorry to disturb you. I stay in this apartment complex. I got locked out by my roommate, and it's freezing outside. Is it OK if I make myself warm inside?" Abir asked politely.

"Do you have an ID with you?"

"Sorry, no. I know I should be carrying one, but I got out to jog in the park nearby and left everything at home."

"There is an apartment caretaker who should have the master key to most of the apartments. Why don't you go and ask her for the keys?"

"Do you know where she lives in this apartment?" Abir asked, his teeth chattering from the cold. The woman told him the location and closed the door.

Abir started jogging again to keep himself warm, running around the apartment. He found the apartment and was relieved when somebody answered.

He explained his predicament and eventually got to enter his apartment.

Abir went into his room and went straight inside his quilt to make himself warm. As he snuggled comfortably inside his quilt, he thought about the homeless man. How did he fare nights after nights of miserable cold, when he found it hard to withstand even a few hours of cold at night? He felt deeply troubled about the strange ways of life. Did his jacket really help the homeless old man?

He thought about his experience for that evening as he lay down on his bed. He was denied entry into an apartment to warm himself, despite it being so cold outside. He had all the signs of a well-cared-of, affluent, and social young man, yet even then, he was denied entry. The apartment homeowner did not display any signs of empathy for him.

Then what chances did an unkempt old man have, who obviously looked impoverished and homeless, to get help from the so-called genteel part of society?

Nil, he realized.

Thinking about the old homeless man and his sad condition, he fell asleep.

* * *

Abir had vivid and wild dreams that night. He felt he was flying high in the clouds, without wings. The world was far below, enticing him to stop by and have a look, but every time he tried to gaze down at the beautiful contour flying by below, a black cloud would come by, hide his vision, and drench him. He wanted to get down to see the beautiful Earth, but he just could not fly down, as if a strong wind was blowing him away, further and further away. And on that lush green Earth, far below, he could see Shyamoli calling out to him, her large and beautiful eyes brimming with tears, her voiceless screams asking him to come down, to protect her, as he desperately tried to get back to her, but instead got further and further away.

He woke up with a start and realized that it was all a dream. It was well past morning. His body and head was burning from heat, in an apparent high fever. He could not lift his head as he laid down on his mattress. He drifted off to sleep once more and continued dreaming a similar dream, in a different context, distressing him.

After a while, he opened his eyes again to find Ayan by his side.

He smiled feebly at him, realizing that he had people around him to take care of him, unlike the homeless man.

* * *

Abir was down with a high fever the entire weekend. He had temperatures many times before, but nothing had felt like this. He felt unusually drained out this time, unable to raise his head, unable to eat, and generally feeling down. Ayan took care of him, sharing his meals with him, heating them up for him, leaving behind bottles of water by his side. He skipped his weekend labs to stay with Abir, working on his computer on the small table near their kitchen, mindful of any need that Abir might have.

Lying on his bed, Abir kept thinking about the homeless man. He had been out in the cold for just a couple of hours and had caught a fever. How did that old man even stay there, night after night of bitter cold, sleeping out there in the open? His thoughts went back to the thousands of homeless beggars he had seen on the streets of India: men, women, and children. He had got sick just being out for a couple of hours in somewhat harsh conditions. How did those people fare in their lives, living in harsh conditions every single day of their lives?

As he looked around himself, noticing his air-conditioned and comfortable room, signs of opulence everywhere, a kind-hearted roommate taking care of him, he realized that there was something inherently strange about the world and its ways. It need not be so dramatically different for individuals.

If everybody was human, then why were conditions that they lived in so dramatically and drastically different? In the animal kingdom, things weren't as radically different. All animals stayed in the same condition out in the wild.

He realized that most human sufferings were created by humans, not nature.

* * *

Pooja aunty threw a party for Srija's birthday in February, and Abir was invited by them. It was supposed to be a surprise party, and Pooja aunty was calling some of the folks who knew Srija.

He felt elated at the hope that he could be seeing Shyamoli, but at the same time, felt resentful that Shyamoli continued to stay there, helping out her aunt in her somewhat peculiar lifestyle. He understood her reasons, but that did not change the fact that his opinion about her local guardians was getting rather low. It also made him anxious at the prospect of seeing her—he was not sure if she would favor him after the last episode, mainly because he had been cynical about her being with her uncle and his family.

Did she think of him as a hard, pragmatic, data-driven computer engineer, a stark contrast to her gentle, grassroots level views of life? If that was true, she certainly must be having a low opinion about him, he thought morosely. Did he speak too much that day, advising her on matters which he, perhaps, understood little of?

True, he had held her hand the last time he was with her, and she had not taken it away. He had held her hands for only a short while, but to him, it had felt like an eternity. He had drowned in her gentle, beautiful, big eyes—eyes that reflected nothing but simplicity and a will to be of servitude to others. Eyes that told many untold words, words which danced around, unspoken, as if a lush spring of the most fragrant essence. And this was what made him more anxious. He would rather not see Shyamoli's beautiful eyes ever again, than see those eyes look at him with disdain.

All these thoughts gnawed in his heart, and he felt anxious and worried at the prospect of falling from the eyes of the most wonderful woman he had ever met in his life.

* * *

Ayan and Abir went to Arun uncle's place at the allocated time, apparently to prepare to surprise Srija, who would be coming over later. Privately, Abir was sure that Srija knew everything about it and would just pretend as if she knew nothing about the surprise event.

They reached earlier than anticipated, and he looked around hopefully for a glimpse of Shyamoli. Not finding her around, he decided to go to the kitchen, knowing that she would be there. His heart skipped a beat when he found her in the kitchen, looking exactly how he had seen her the first time months back, her hair tied uptight in a bun, wearing an apron, sweat coming out of her forehead while putting heavy containers of food in the oven. She looked busy, and happy, as if the prospect of giving a surprise party, and being involved deeply in the process, was particularly enjoyable to her.

Abir felt a pang of guilt when he saw her face, her eyes alighted doing something she loved. He had almost talked her out of it, and he realized that he had probably been a bit too nosy and opinionated about her life without really fully understanding the underlying dynamics of her thought process. Would she be happy to see him? Or would she try to avoid him and not speak to him at all, lest the reference from their past conversation came up again?

He felt anguished at these thoughts and decided that it would be best to avoid her. He decided to leave, and at the same time, Shyamoli looked up to find him staring at her. She seemed embarrassed for a moment, and her hands stopped midair, stopping the work she was doing. Abir stared back at her, suddenly forgetting his intent, forgetting everything, except the fact that he was with her once more. They stared at each other for a while. Then he silently went beside her and took the heavy bowl of food that she was preparing to heat and put it in the heating oven.

"Thanks for helping out," said Shyamoli shyly.

"No problem," said Abir. "I understand that you enjoy doing all this, so I want to have a share of your joy."

"Did you get the share?"

"Yes," said Abir simply. "Besides, I get to be by you once more. What can I ask more?"

Shyamoli looked embarrassed, and she hurriedly started arranging other items in the kitchen, as Abir looked on.

"I heard you got a high fever and were in bed for days?" asked Shyamoli after a pause, in an apparent attempt to change the topic.

"Yes, I got locked out of my apartment without warm clothes on a rather cold night."

"Oh, how terrible!" she exclaimed. "Ayan told my uncle about that incident. Apparently, you were without your jacket. Why would you venture out in the cold without a jacket on?"

"Well, I had a jacket on when I went out. But I gave it away."

"You gave away your jacket?" asked Shyamoli surprised, stopping her activity to look at him, her eyes questioning.

"Well, yes—it's an interesting story, but let's skip it. What's for dinner today?"

"You are avoiding the story, Abir," said Shyamoli smiling. "You just gave your jacket randomly to somebody and caught a cold?"

"Does that bother you?" he asked, looking at her eyes. She looked embarrassed at the way he stared at her, but did not take her eyes off him. He looked deep into her eyes, and suddenly, everything dimmed from around him, and the only thing that existed were her intoxicating, big, and beautiful eyes swimming in front of him.

"Will you continue staring at me, or are you going to answer me?" asked Shyamoli after a prolonged silence.

"Ah, OK, right," Abir said, his ears growing hot and red all of a sudden. He forced himself to break his eye contact with her. He paused for a while, trying to remember what he was trying to talk about.

"Right, so if you want to know, I gave my jacket away to a homeless man," he said eventually, recollecting his train of thoughts with an effort. "I had seen him every day, and that particular night was really cold. He was shivering, and I gave him my jacket. But as luck would have it, I did not have my keys, and Ayan had gone to Srija's place. So I was left out in the cold for more than two hours."

"My goodness me!" exclaimed Shyamoli. "That might have been really rough!"

"Yeah, well, it all passed, but I did catch a fever. Ayan put me back in shape in a couple of days, bless him. But it had me thinking about the homeless man. I mean, there is so much disparity in human living conditions. Here it's less. In India, or for that matter, in most developing countries, it is drastic."

Shyamoli nodded in agreement, resuming her work.

"In fact, after this episode, it got me thinking about privilege, about empathy, and about the strange distribution of wealth, which is probably the direct cause of most unhappiness in the world. I was thinking about the theory that humans are the key reason for human suffering."

"You do have a point," observed Shyamoli.

"Yes, I am convinced about my theory," said Abir. "For example, look at animals. Have you seen animals of the same species, living in the same geographical region, live drastically different lifestyles? It's unheard of. Yet look at humans. Skyrises and slums coexist in the same geographical region—especially in third world countries. Wealth distribution is very unequal in general between humans. For example, wealth distribution is absurdly skewed in the San Francisco Bay Area. Software engineers earn significantly more than other folks."

"Yes you are probably right," said Shyamoli. "Maybe that's why the average house prices are also so skewed in the Bay Area? Perhaps that is causing homelessness?"

"Exactly!" said Abir, warming up to the discussion. "Skewed income results in skewed increase in home prices. Median household income for a California couple last year was around fifty thousand dollars per annum—I think around that range. But look at median home prices and the cost of living in a decent neighborhood! Simply not comparable!"

"Do you think the homeless man you encountered was a direct result of this skew in income?"

"Possibly," said Abir. "In general, what I mean to say is, humans are the main cause of human sufferings."

"It's an interesting theory," agreed Shyamoli.

"I have seen some poverty in India because my dad used to take me to some of his surveys to connect to the poor folks at a grassroots level," continued Abir, helping her set the spoons in a container. "I did not fully understand their plight, sitting in my dad's government car, well-fed and comfortable. But when I was stranded outside for two hours with no warm clothes that day, I truly understood the meaning of despair—well, to a small degree, but it was a firsthand experience."

"Indeed," said Shyamoli, looking at him, her eyes concerned. "How are you feeling now? Are you better?"

"Do I look any worse than before?" asked Abir anxiously.

"No, you look great, as always," said Shyamoli, turning away from him shyly. "But I do agree with you about underprivileged folks. Like you, I, too, have seen a lot of destitute, homelessness, underprivileged, orphans, battered women back in India. The disparity is stunning. But then, it's changing, and many of them get help. Some efforts are organized, like through NGOs. And some others come unexpectedly from kindhearted people, like what you did."

Shyamoli stopped and smiled at him, apparently in admiration for his kind deed.

Abir felt his heart skip a beat.

"After my experience that day, I have been seriously thinking about getting involved with some NGOs. I want to work for the underprivileged. Especially homeless folks, to start off with," he said.

"That is a great thought," said Shyamoli, turning to look at him, her eyes blazing with passion. "You really should. If you want some quick initial information about the options to help out, you can research some NGOs in Kolkata. I will give you their names."

"That would be great," said Abir warmly. "But I am curious—how do you even know about these NGOs?"

"Oh, it's all due to my father," said Shyamoli. "He keeps himself super busy with social activities to enrich the betterment of the underprivileged folks back in Kolkata. I used to help him out when I was in Kolkata."

"How interesting. How exactly does your dad do this?"

"He teaches underprivileged kids for free when he has time after school," she said, her eyes lighting up. "He teaches two nights during the weekdays and afternoons on the weekends. He works with three different NGOs. Right now, he is helping lead a school for orphans and underprivileged kids. He teaches there and is also the joint secretary responsible for obtaining funding for the school."

"How amazing is that!" exclaimed Abir in genuine admiration. "Your dad is quite a remarkable man! I would love to meet him."

"My father has a general reason for doing this," said Shyamoli. "He thinks the distribution of well-being should be the key focus. Material wealth will follow automatically. That's why he focuses on the well-being of the people he helps—their mental well-being, physical well-being, psychological well-being."

"That's an excellent point of view," said Abir. "Well-being is indeed more important than material wealth. In general, people need to be aware of other people's plights. What's worse is that most people, even at this modern age and time with information overload, oversee these issues. The fundamental way to get rid of hardship and inequality is through developing a sense of kindness and empathy as a social norm, as a culture. Only when people are empathetic toward the other's plight can they come up with means to help them out. Once this becomes a social standard, distribution of well-being automatically equates out proportionately."

"Well, you displayed true kindness that day when you gave your jacket away," said Shyamoli, smiling again, as if that single act of Abir was ringing in her head recursively, making her happy every time she thought about it. "That was an act of true empathy, and I am delighted you did it for the poor man. We need more people like you in Kolkata, where the need is really high."

"Are you trying to recruit me in your dad's activities?" asked Abir. "If you are, I am more than willing to help out. Servitude is one reason, and there are other reasons too."

"What other reasons are there to help out my father?" she asked.

"Well, another great reason is that I get to spend more time with his brilliant and beautiful daughter, whom I cannot seem to keep my eyes off today," he said, looking at her eyes unwaveringly.

Shyamoli blushed scarlet red and hurriedly concentrated on setting up spoons for no reason into the spoon container, which was already set up. Abir went by her side and helped her, and she let him help her. She paused her activity every once in a while as his hands brushed her hands occasionally. She seemed flushed and embarrassed but pleased at the same time.

"I sometimes wonder how technology can be used to abate this massive mis-distribution of wealth and well-being," Abir wondered aloud as he helped her out as if nothing had happened. He felt he needed to be more pragmatic in his conversations with her so that he would not appear to be hitting too hard on her.

"You are a man of data," said Shyamoli, changing her stance with apparent relief and taking on a more casual tone. "You can probably put data to good use here. Think about it."

"I am already," said Abir.

"You are?" asked Shyamoli in wonder.

"Yes. For one, I think all NGOs need data. Solid, eye-opening data. I can help them by creating a free search engine from open-source technology which is tailored for hunting out social injustices, statistics on poverty, distribution of resources, and all that."

"A search engine?" asked Shyamoli, startled. "Like Google?"

"Yes, a specialized search engine which will only search for web pages dedicated to data and human service for the underprivileged."

"That is an absolutely marvelous idea," exclaimed Shyamoli, stopping all her activities and looking at him, her expression exalted. "I am really eager to see this search engine. Have you started building it? But wait, I guess you will need some time and perhaps more resources to get this done."

"Oh, don't worry, this is Silicon Valley! People are jostling over each other, trying to outdo each other with one innovative idea over the other. Writing a custom search engine is not a big deal. I already have some ideas for a prototype."

"Wow, I am really impressed," Shyamoli said breathlessly. "I cannot wait to tell this to my father. I am sure he will be excited."

"Yes, yes, of course, all in good time, but let's not hurry," cautioned Abir. "I would like to take a rather conservative approach and first see if it is of any use at all. It all looks good on paper, but I have to make sure this cannot be easily done by the Google search engine itself with some smart queries. But this is not the only idea I have. I have a few more ideas for a general social upliftment and empathy platform, albeit they are not well-formed yet. I will have to brainstorm on them a bit."

"I can help you with data sources," said Shyamoli brightly. "At least, I can connect you with NGOs back in Kolkata, from where you can get lots of information that you might need to get started."

"What kind of information?" asked Abir intrigued.

"Well, you can get real examples of human kindness when it comes to empathy for the underprivileged," she said, her eyes shining. "All sorts of people come over to help. The organizations work with all levels of people, across the vast horizon of West Bengal and beyond in India. You can call them from here—they will be happy to talk to you and provide information to you."

"Good good," said Abir happily. He smiled at her exuberance, struck by her enthusiasm. She stared back at him as if she was seeing him in a new light. They stared at each other for a while. As always, the world around him disappeared as he looked at her eyes melting against him, shining with a curious yearning expression.

"Let's see how the party is progressing," said Abir, suddenly feeling embarrassed at the way she looked at him. She nodded as if in a trance and followed him.

* * *

Abir enjoyed the party immensely. Not that he was a particular fan of Srija, given that he still believed that she was partly to blame for being the reason that Shyamoli ended up serving her uncle and aunt for altruistic reasons. But at that moment, he did not care. He was deliriously happy to be near Shyamoli.

He observed her every move, the way she mixed gracefully with the crowd, quietly and elegantly. He also saw things from a different angle after Shyamoli threw light on the arrangement she had at home. He realized that she had perhaps chosen a lifestyle that was in line with her lifestyle back home in India. He could see the affection in her uncle and realized that he treated her like his own daughter, and that made her really happy.

Abir's eyes followed Shyamoli the entire evening, lost in her elegance and grace, admiring her every move, every word. He got lost in the sparkle in her eyes, the effervescence of her smile. He took multiple helpings of the delicious food she made. He was delighted when Arun uncle announced proudly that his beloved niece had made all the arrangements. He clapped the hardest and longest as everybody applauded her.

It amused him to see Srija displaying a mixed bag of emotions—those of outright jealousy that Shyamoli was getting accolades for her thoughtfulness, her food and for the beautiful decorations, and mixed with that, a genuine admiration and gratefulness for the effort she had taken to make her birthday an extra-special one. It delighted him when Ayan went to Shyamoli and thanked her personally, and he half laughed at Srija's jealous looks as she saw Ayan talking animatedly with her. Knowing Ayan as well as he did, Abir knew that Ayan's thanks were heartfelt and sincere with gratitude for making his girlfriend's birthday an extraordinarily special one.

Several times into these kinds of social settings, Abir had discerned the silent game that Srija had been playing, conniving frivolous and petty occasions to try and prove her superiority over Shyamoli. He also realized the silent battle that Shyamoli was having to thwart off Srija's ill-wishing endeavors.

Abir was sure that this occasion, too, was designed by Srija to make Shyamoli work for her. It delighted him the way Shyamoli turned the tables on Srija, by taking away all the accolades and good will.

He realized that somewhere within Shyamoli's calm and gentle demeanor, there lay a fierce spirit that only women of the highest quality had. A spirit that made her utterly sublime and graceful, yet at the same time, extraordinarily strong and determined. A spirit that automatically exuded infinite kindness, yet, at the same time, radiated a strange power which could shake the Earth when required.

Abir smiled to himself, thinking of Shyamoli, feeling extraordinarily proud of the most wonderful woman he had ever seen in his life, as he sat in Ayan's car's backseat when they went back home that night.

* * *

Dear Shyamoli, this is Abir. I just got a mobile phone for myself finally after so many months—can you believe it! You are the first person I am calling from a mobile phone in America and also the first person I am leaving a voicemail to. Give me a call back to this number if you feel like it. Or text me. I can't wait to hear your voice.

Abir made his first phone call after buying his phone and left his first voice message. He had finally bought a smartphone, and the first person he called was Shyamoli. He obtained her number from Ayan, who gave it to him after making him promise not to tell Srija that it was he who gave away Shyamoli's phone number. It irked Abir to see this level of secrecy and effort to make Shyamoli stay away from him, or perhaps the other way around, but he was too happy to get her number to think about it for long.

Abir bought an Android phone. He had researched several phones with Ayan and Srija's inputs. The iPhone seemed right, especially when it came to sheer exterior quality, finish, and camera quality, but he realized that he was more of an Android person because of the openness of the platform. Ever since his conversation with Shyamoli, he had been thinking of building some kind of an app for social awareness of empathy. He did not have any definitive idea but had a general idea of what it should do or achieve. He realized Android's openness would help him create app prototypes somewhat more quickly than on an iPhone.

After he left the voicemail to Shyamoli, he waited anxiously for the entire day, hoping and praying that Shyamoli would not find his call too intrusive.

After dinner, he got a text back from Shyamoli.

Dearest Abir, welcome to the world of instant mobile communications. Are you coming over with Ayan and Srija tomorrow to celebrate Holi at our place? I can't wait to see you. Yours Shyamoli.

* * *

Dearest Abir. Yours Shyamoli.

These words made his world go around in a strange fantasy place, where nothing mattered and everything was like a dream. He clutched his phone, looking away dreamily into space even as Ayan talked to him about his new research directions over dinner. He helped Ayan clean up their tiny dining table in a dreamy trance, stashing the dishes in the dishwasher in a misty haze, as Ayan continued to describe his work at the lab. Ayan and he watched TV, and in every character in the TV show they were watching, he could see Shyamoli's face. As Ayan went on to his room to sleep, he clutched his new phone, looking at the text, feeling a sense of giddy joy that he had never felt in his life.

Dearest Abir. I can't wait to see you. Yours Shyamoli.

Abir read and reread the text multiple times. He did not reply back immediately but instead laid down on his bed, staring at the ceiling, looking at the clock, as it slowly ticked away. It was near midnight, and he thought it would be unwise to call her or text her. Perhaps she was asleep. He would meet her the next day to celebrate Holi at Arun uncle's place.

Tomorrow. Just tomorrow, he would go to Shyamoli's place once more, to celebrate Holi, the Hindu festival of colors, the celebration of love. He would be there to play Holi with her soon.

Dearest Abir. I can't wait to see you. Yours Shyamoli.

Rainbow in the sky

Abir never quite knew how it all happened. Or whether it was on Earth or in Heaven. Or whether it was anywhere in his consciousness or in some strangely ethereal place where there were only songbirds, and beautiful music, and wildly beautiful fragrance. He never quite knew how, or if at all, he had felt anything before. Or if the intensity of his joy was matched in the real world.

It all started happening in the small room at the corner of the second floor in Arun uncle's house, where Shyamoli took him to show him the view from her bedroom. In that room, Earth and Heaven came together to make the world around him an oblivion, when Shyamoli suddenly closed the door and turned to him, looking at him, her eyes lit up like two bright candles.

The world around him stopped when she took those few steps toward him, which seemed to take an eternity.

Everything around him blurred into oblivion as she put her arms around his neck, tilted his head softly toward her's, and kissed him on his lips.

And suddenly, all the feelings in the world exploded within him. Suddenly, as if by magic, everything around him disappeared—the only sense that existed was Shyamoli's hot lips on his, her hands tightly around his neck. His mind played tricks with him, making lights and colors splash across his mind in an intoxicating concoction, as she pushed him on the bed and laid down beside him, her arms around his head, her lips melting against his. His body refused to cooperate, and his hands laid limp on his side, as Shyamoli embraced him and played with her lips on his, saying his name softly again and again.

He did not quite remember how he had finally gone home. They had kissed for what felt like the entire afternoon, and thankfully, nobody had come inside the room. Everybody was downstairs, enjoying Holi, the festival of colors, the festival of love. Everybody downstairs was smeared in colors—colors of all shades and forms and hues, even as bubbles of all colors seemed to emanate in the room where Abir and Shyamoli locked their lips together.

Abir could have continued for eternity, not wanting to let her go, but common sense had prevailed both of them, and Shyamoli, her face dazzling and radiant, hardly meeting his eyes, had left the room abruptly when they heard somebody calling out for her. He was left in the room, his head swimming with the intensity and reality of it all. It sunk into him that like him, she had thought about him all this while, from the time they had first met.

He did not remember how long he was there, in that room, sitting on the bed, as if not knowing where he was. He did not remember how he finally went downstairs, unnoticed in the bustle of people who had accumulated at large to play Holi. He responded mechanically to a bunch of people who jumped on him to smear his face with colors. He just remembered how he had spent the rest of the evening, and how the party had gone late into the night, and how his eyes had followed Shyamoli all the time, when she went about in her usual business, helping out her uncle's wife to distribute the food, her face radiant and flushed, colors all over her face. In his eyes, nobody existed in the world but her—her beautiful face, her suddenly shy eyes which would not look at him directly, but was always aware that his eyes were on her all the time.

* * *

Abir called Shyamoli from his workplace the next morning, immediately after reaching work, and she picked up his call instantly, as if she were waiting for it the entire night. Suddenly they were both tongue-tied and shy, not knowing what to say, how to say, but the delicious silence singing volumes than all the ballads in the world would not have. That evening, Shyamoli drove over to Abir's office after her classes, and in his frenzy of seeing her again, he could hardly stay waiting in the office, wanting to see her immediately. When she finally called him, breathless and ecstatic, telling him that she was parked in the parking lot of his office, he ran down the office building, into the parking lot where she was waiting. He jumped into the passenger seat, his heartbeat doubling at the prospect of seeing her. He stopped and looked at her beautiful, big, shy eyes, her face flushed and radiant.

She drove a little bit to a secluded place and stopped the car, waiting shyly for him to say something, and this time, he bent over to her side, and she let him pick up her face by her chin. He kissed her lips with an intensity that he did not believe he had in him. It was her turn to melt away in his kiss, her lips parting as he pressed his lips against hers, her hands around his neck once more, neither wanting to let the other go.

In a dream-like daze, they drove to an empty park away from prying eyes of the curious, away from relatives and roommates waiting at home. The evening shades of the sky played magic on the surrounding. Shyamoli sat on a bench, and Abir laid down with his head on her lap, looking up at her face. He gazed at the starry skies above and felt that he could stay there for an eternity.

* * *

After that day, Abir and Shyamoli met daily in his office on weekday evenings and in parks and other natural areas on weekends. They went to places which were far from either of their homes, lest anybody else saw them together. During the weekdays, after spending the entire evening together, Abir would reach home pretty late after dinner. After a few occasions, Ayan had come to accept this, and he had dinner alone when Srija was not around. If he did suspect anything from his roommate's sudden deviation from routine, he did not show it and did not pursue him on this topic.

Often, when Shyamoli came over to Abir's office, she would bring food with her for them to eat together—Indian food which she made herself at home. She and Abir would sit in her car's back seat, and more often than not, Shyamoli would feed him while he lay on her lap.

Together they spent moments of ethereal, blissful time. Moments which he wished would go on for eternity, when the first few bouts of shyness was coming down, when Shyamoli's presence, essence, eyes, voice, and countenance was in his wakefulness and in his sleep.

Abir and Shyamoli's relationship did not seem to be apparent to the people around them. Perhaps it was the way they met in his office, or maybe it was because Abir never went to her place alone, and she too never asked him to come over.

Abir understood her desire to be secretive, and he contended being with her in the various odd places that they met. Parks. Shopping malls.

After all, a secret so beautiful needed to be safe at all costs.

* * *

Arun uncle hosted a birthday party for Shyamoli in May. Srija and Ayan were invited. It would be a small affair with only a few folk.

To Abir's chagrin, he was not invited.

He complained about it to Shyamoli when she came over to his office the next evening.

"So they did not invite you?" she asked him, laughing at his woebegone expression, twirling his hair with her finger, as he laid down with his head on her lap in the back seat of her car, in the deserted park near his office.

Abir shook his head angrily.

"They don't associate you with me, maybe that's why" said Shyamoli soothingly.

"But they called me to Srija's birthday."

"Well, you are Ayan's roommate, so it makes sense," reasoned Shyamoli. "They have no idea about you and me, about our relationship. It's *my* birthday. Why should you, Ayan's roommate, be invited? Only Srija is invited, and Ayan automatically comes in with her."

"But still, why ignore me completely?" Abir asked moodily.

"They are not ignoring you, Abir. Arun uncle and Pooja aunty probably don't have a reason to call you to celebrate *my* birthday.

They don't know about us. Besides, it's just a few people—a small family affair kind of thing."

"So I am not part of your family?" he asked her angrily.

"Yes, of course, you are, to me. But not to them," Shyamoli reasoned.

"Could I not attend that party somehow?" he asked.

"Well, I am not going to invite you, or ask them to invite you, if that's what you are trying to get at," she said firmly.

* * *

When the day of the birthday party arrived, Abir felt left out and resentful, especially after Srija made a splash about it.

"Sorry, we have to go without you, Abir. Especially knowing that you get along with this Shyamoli quite well," she said, looking at him shrewdly and smirking. Abir wondered whether Srija had guessed something about them, but he did not care. He did not reply, staring hard at his laptop screen instead, looking at nothing.

After Ayan and Srija left for the party, Abir walked to the nearest Bart station and rode to his office. He could not bear to stay at home alone when the others were having fun at Shyamoli's birthday.

Abir spent the entire evening in the empty office, working on a complex piece of C++ code for three hours continuously. It was not critical to get it finished, but he thought it would be best to keep his mind busy.

As it got deeper into the night, Shyamoli texted him, every hour after ten, but he refused to text her back. At midnight, Shyamoli called him three times in a row, and he finally relented and picked up the phone.

"Why aren't you picking up the phone?" she asked, sounding concerned.

"Happy birthday," Abir said dully. "I have a gift for you."

"Why are you talking so formally? Why aren't you coming down to meet me?"

Abir walked downstairs from his office room and went to her car parked outside in the empty parking lot. Shyamoli opened the passenger side door for him, but he ignored that and sat at the back seat, her gift in his hand.

"Don't want to sit beside me?" she asked.

"No."

"Don't want to talk to me?"

"Can you drop me home?"

"No, I won't," said Shyamoli, as she started the car and started driving out of the parking lot. Abir sat silently at the back seat as Shyamoli drove through the empty roads, zooming along the highways.

"Hungry?" she said after a while.

"Yes," he said. He had not eaten anything after lunch. It was almost twelve hours since he had any food. The fact that everybody was having a good time, enjoying themselves, including Shyamoli, whereas he was spending time at his work for no reason, that too on the weekend, was ringing in his mind. He felt especially resentful that Shyamoli had not made a big deal of this and let it pass as if it did not matter to her that he was not a part of her birthday celebrations.

Shyamoli drove along, and soon, they were in an almost empty parking lot at the Stanford shopping mall.

"Let's eat inside the car. Then I will drop you back to your place," she said, coming out of the driver seat and opening the trunk. She took out a plastic bag with boxes of food, opened the rear door, and sat beside him.

"I can't eat all that," said Abir, looking at the spread.

"It's not all for you."

"Oh," said Abir, suddenly feeling guilty, realizing that she had been starving the entire evening because of him. He looked on, feeling abashed, as she arranged all the food in the back seat of the car, complete with plastic spoons and a large piece of cake in a paper bowl wrapped in metal foil. She looked tired, like somebody who had not eaten anything at all the entire day.

"I am sorry," he said, patting her cheek gently. "You should not have starved yourself. Why did you starve yourself?"

"How could I eat when I knew you would not be eating any-thing?" she said, unwrapping the cake. She pulled Abir down and made him lie down with his head on her lap, took a piece of cake, let him take a bite, and took a bite out of it to break her fast.

* * *

"I never proposed to you formally," Abir said. "Now it seems too late! I should get down on my knees one day and make the for-mal proposal."

They were sitting in the Santa Cruz beach. It was July, and the weather had started becoming hot enough for people to start flock-ing to the beaches. Abir had driven Shyamoli's car. He was still on a learner's license and took this opportunity to drive someplace at a long distance to practice. Saving a few rough moments when he slowed down the traffic on the left lane on the hilly road and was consequently honked down to the right lane, Shyamoli thought he did pretty well.

"Indeed, now that I come to think of it, you never proposed to me formally," Shyamoli said, pouting her lips in pretense sadness.

"I am a terrible boyfriend, no?" Abir asked anxiously.

Shyamoli turned to him and looked at him solemnly.

"I don't like the word boyfriend," she said.

"You don't?"

"No, it's too western and cheeky. You are my soulmate."

* * *

"I think I know why you never proposed to me," said Shyamo-li, adjusting her sunglasses. They had been at the beach the entire afternoon. By then, it was evening, but the sun still glared at them, making it hot. At the same time, a slightly chilly wind blew from the ocean, creating an exotic mix of shades of temperature.

"You do?"

"I think you did not propose to me because I am an easy-going person," she said.

"Oh, well, I don't know," he said, smiling.

"Did you know that Ayan proposed to Srija twice before she agreed to be with him?"

"Oh, her!" said Abir dismissively.

"You don't like Srija?"

"Not in the least," said Abir, dusting sand off his legs. "She annoys the hell out of me, and I don't like the way she behaves with you."

"Yet she is at your place all the time with your roommate, and it seems she enjoys your company too."

"I don't know how Ayan puts up with her really," said Abir, lying down on the sand. "She bosses him around all the time, and she is always conniving something or the other. I find her a big fraud."

"That's not a nice thing to say!" said Shyamoli.

"Maybe," said Abir, covering his eyes from the glare of the sun. "Not that I have a habit of discussing people, because I think it's not a correct occupation of one's time. But Srija has all those quintessential traits which interest me as an interesting subject of observation. I like to analyze the data I have about people like her."

"Ah, right, you would, of course, want to look at everything from a data angle," said Shyamoli, smiling.

"Well, yes, Srija provides lots of interesting data through her demeanor and activities. Data, which helps one develop a deep understanding of human psychology and the prejudices practiced by society at large."

"What data would that be?"

"OK, so the most interesting thing about her is that she has limited intellect and class, but has to somehow portray herself as a supremely intelligent and classic being!"

Shyamoli did not reply and looked at him silently, intrigued.

"As such, I can give you all sorts of anecdotal evidence that made me come to this conclusion," continued Abir. "For example, I have noticed that she thinks nothing of copying anecdotes and proverbs from the Internet and passing them off as her own. I detest these pseudo-intellectuals who do nothing for anybody, but have learned the art and trick of hoodwinking people into believing their copied thoughts as their own."

"You are being rather unkind on her," said Shyamoli, laughing at his indignant expression. "I think she has her flaws, but all humans have flaws."

"I know you like to see good in everything," said Abir frowning. "But don't forget that she is rude to you whenever she wants to. Also she cooks up these evil little plans to show her superiority over you once in a while. I detest her for this attitude."

"Oh, I ignore that," said Shyamoli. "Srija comes from a family of well-known people; her parents are very well off and respected back home in Kolkata. She has been brought up on certain ideals of superiority, I guess, based on their social position."

"Does social position dictate superiority?" asked Abir. "I have a strong suspicion that Srija's views of the world are colored by the kaleidoscope she carries with her, and that kaleidoscope has probably been passed on to her from her family. But the most disturbing part of all this is the fact that she gets to control my relationship with you in a weirdly subtle way. Why are we hiding our relationship from everybody, especially from her? I don't like the way that even after ages of being together, we are hiding our relationship. We are adults, for heaven's sake. Nobody can tell us what to do or how to conduct our lives. This is abnormal and not healthy."

"Yes, I do realize that I am not too keen to have Srija see you and me together," said Shyamoli. "But it's more than just her. I wish I could explain it to you."

"You don't have to explain, Shyamoli," said Abir. "I understand it perfectly well. You are tightly intertwined with Arun uncle and Pooja aunty, and hence to your extended social circle here in the USA, and as well as back in India. You don't want rumors to go around, because it's not seen positively back in India, although I personally think it's all hogwash. But tell me something; if that is the key reason that you are keeping your relationship silent from your uncle and aunt, then why are Srija and Ayan out in the open as a couple, live together for most of their time?"

"They are different. Srija and Ayan knew each other from India. Also, Srija is not a dependent or staying with anybody; she works here, is independent, and is free to do what she likes."

"Shyamoli, you are independent too! You, too, are free to do whatever you like! This is America. This is the place which gives people the freedom to choose their own lives, with minimal interference from the world, from society. That is one of the main reasons why I love this country; it gives people space and freedom to live and express themselves. What are we afraid of in this country?"

Shyamoli did not reply and instead looked at the distant waves silently.

"Shyamoli, don't take it otherwise, but I really think you should learn to speak up when Srija is rude to you," he said gently, carefully hiding the frustration in his voice lest she felt hurt. "And she is rude to you almost all the times I have seen her."

"It's not easy for me to speak up," Shyamoli said, after a pause, looking slightly troubled.

"It's not easy for you because the Indian society back home had crushed your confidence, just because you are dark-skinned," Abir said. "And they have done the exact opposite with Srija, who got all the goodwill from that same society, just because she has a skin color which is favorable to the Indian society at large!"

Shyamoli looked at the distant silently.

"Tell me something, Shyamoli," continued Abir. "How many times have Pooja aunty's friends asked for you? I have seen you serve food to these people, making them comfortable, being inclusive, being kind, being the gorgeous person that you are, which makes you so special to me. But do they include you in return?"

"Well," said Shyamoli, sounding uncertain. "They are nice to me, Abir. I mean, all these folks have been kind to me."

"Of course they are kind," said Abir. "Bay Area Bengalis are kind in general. But what I mean is, do they really try to include you in their society? Do they try to get your phone number, to call you to their places, to really, *really* befriend you? Do they embrace you in their lives, ask you about your parents, about your family back home? No! Every time I have been to these gatherings, it's been about Srija and not you. They take an *active* interest to know her."

"Well, I haven't thought about it this way," said Shyamoli. "Besides, all this does not matter to me, really."

"Well, maybe it does not matter to you, and I am sorry to put it so bluntly Shyamoli, but your dark complexion has sealed your place in society—especially our society! Over time, you have been subtly conditioned to expect less, want less, to try to be useful, to serve."

Shyamoli stared at him silently.

"Try as you may Shyamoli, our society will never, *ever*, get rid of prejudice based on skin color," he continued, getting up and pacing up and down. "They just cannot get rid of the imperial mindset that has been hardwired in their brains. Like I said the first time I met you, what we need is a colorless appreciation of people. But no! That just won't happen in our society. You don't get to see it because you have been *conditioned* to expect less over time, like I said. It's a systematic, subtle way of subjugation that society has been imposing on the darker-skinned folks. It's hardwired into the essence of being human, manifesting itself in a polite veneer in all aspects of life, in all conversations, in all societal relationships. On the surface, it's all good. They are friendly with you, you say. Of course, they will be friendly! Why not? You are a wonderful person, a great cook, with a sense of servitude and humility written all over you. Anybody would be friendly with you—not just them! But tell me, if you were to go to one of these typical social gatherings, would an unknown person, who knew nothing about you, come over and befriend you, just like that? Probably not! But if Srija went to the same place, chances are that a random person, despite knowing nothing about her, would ask about her, try to include her in their conversations, invite her to one of their social gatherings. All this happens because society ranks people by the color of their skin. It's as simple as that."

"You really seem to be angry with the society over this," said Shyamoli, smiling at him.

"I am, Shyamoli! The fundamentals of empathy and inclusiveness goes for a toss simply because of the color of skin! It's a deep-rooted pathetic prejudice that our society just cannot get over. Color, just color. They will make huge judgments, and weigh their perception simply based on the color of skin! They will admire your skills—your cooking, your wonderful manners, your calmness, your sense of responsibility, and whatnot! But you have to *work* for it, show them that you are so good, and then perhaps they will accept you a little bit. They will notice you only when you have special talents and attributes which far outweigh their preference for color."

"Why do you care so much whether I get accepted as is, or whether I have to work hard for it?" she asked, smiling at his indignant tone. "I would rather work hard to get recognition, rather than get it for free. It's not as bad as you make it out to be, Abir."

"You mean you think my observations are incorrect?" asked Abir.

"No, what you are saying has a tinge of truth in it," said Shyamoli quietly. She looked afar at the ocean, and Abir followed her gaze. "People don't include me and overlook me sometimes. Like when I was watching all the women dance during the Durga Puja last year—they overlooked me and asked Srija and the other women around me to join them. I too sometimes wonder, had I not been able to do all the things that I can do, would anybody have ever wanted to befriend me, want to know about me at all? Perhaps not. If they had overlooked all my attributes, and only looked at me—the vanilla me without any attributes—would they still include me? Probably not. But does it matter to me? No. I would rather work for my position and pride than to get it for free for reasons other than for what I am."

Abir looked into her calm and beautiful eyes, and, like every time, he felt mesmerized by their clarity. Yet again, he was touched by the simplicity of her outlook on life.

Shyamoli turned and smiled at him.

"I only care to be accepted by you and your family," she said simply and put her head on his shoulder.

The moment she rested her head on his shoulder, Abir forgot all his anger. He put an arm around her and stared away at the ocean, marveling, like every time, the profound innocence and simplicity of her explanations.

He also felt worried.

He and Shyamoli had been together for several months now. They had met for hours everyday, and to him, it felt as if they had been together for years. He had not given a thought about acceptance from family. For him, it had always been about him, about her, about them.

Shyamoli's comments on acceptance made him realize that to move forward with her into a more formal relationship, they would need family approval from both sides.

He had no doubt that her family would be warm and would be welcoming him. Something about her graceful demeanor and behavior reflected her family energy, and Abir already felt relaxed about the prospect of seeing them formally sometime soon.

The thing that he worried about most was his family.

He had not mentioned Shyamoli to his parents at all, keeping it a secret. He felt guilty about it once in a while because he knew Shyamoli had told her parents about him almost immediately after they started going out together. True, she had kept their relationship a secret with her extended society, but had made it open quickly with her parents.

From his side, somehow, he could not bring up the conversation about Shyamoli with his parents, especially his mother. His mother and him talked very often on the phone, and it was all intellectual from her side: about his progress in his career, the projects he was doing, and about his plans for the future. It was all to do with rise in his life, about power, about fame, and about wealth. In the hunger for success in her son, his mother would probably never be able to fathom the other side of his life; Shyamoli, whose calm presence and connection at a grassroots level to humanity, had changed his views and directions in life forever.

For the first time in his life, he felt that he had deviated a lot from his family's views about the world. They were already miles apart in their thoughts, and somehow, introducing a simple and root-ed person like Shyamoli to them seemed like a tough job.

* * *

It was September. The fall colors ran wild around in the San Francisco Bay Area, marking the valley in hues of orange, gold, and red. The canopy of trees had turned into garlands of colors, inviting

100

cars and people to ride through them. In a few weeks, another Durga Puja would come.

Abir finally obtained a California driver's license. To celebrate the occasion, he bought his first car—a blue Mercedes Benz coupe. He went with Shyamoli to the Mercedes Benz dealer on Stevens Creek Boulevard in San Jose and let her choose the external color and the internal hue. That weekend, he took her to San Francisco, to drive through the Golden Gate Bridge against the setting sun, opening the roof so that she could extend her hands up in the air to feel the rushing wind as they drove. They ate out near the Pier 39 at Bubba Gump Shrimp. By night time, they made their way back to the Bay Area, ambling slowly down with the traffic.

As he drove back with her, she looked more thoughtful than usual.

"Everything OK?" Abir asked Shyamoli, gently prodding her on her cheeks.

She turned and smiled at him.

"You bought your first car, and that, too, a really expensive one. You have come a long way," she said.

"Not my car. Our car, Shyamoli, our car," he reminded her happily.

"Are your parents happy that you got such a fancy car?" she asked.

"Well, yes, they are! I told them right after buying it. They are absolutely delighted."

"Did you tell them I helped you select the color?" she asked.

Abir suddenly felt guilty. She looked at him in the eyes and seemed to read his mind and understand that he had not even mentioned her to his parents.

She turned away from him and looked outside at the traffic rushing by, as Abir looked on in silence at the road, feeling anxious and guilty all of a sudden.

* * *

101

Abir waited, somewhat nervously, in front of the laptop as the Skype video call connected. Shyamoli had bought a laptop for her dad by sending money home, and this was the first video conference call on Skype. She had asked Abir to be with her in the frame. Apparently, her father too expected to see him in the video call.

As the Skype call connected, he waved brightly to the man on the screen, preening from his large thick-rimmed glasses. Shyamoli's father looked nervous about seeing him and seemed to struggle with the controls on the laptop, trying to make the speaker volume louder. Shyamoli instructed him, speaking loudly, till he could figure out how to increase the speaker volume.

"Shyamoli talks a lot about you, sir," said Abir. "I am especially interested in your work with the NGOs."

Shyamoli's father nodded, smiling widely.

"Yes, yes, so I hear. Shyamoli told me about the computer software that you have been working on. I have told some of my colleagues about you. You are a very kind young man."

"It's a little thing really," said Abir, feeling embarrassed at his praise. He had been working on the Search Engine in his spare time. It was not as satisfactory, and he realized that mere algorithms would not help him connect with the underprivileged part of the society, primarily because they were invisible at large to the Internet world. He had started thinking about other angles to help fit technology with empathy, and so far, ideas were vague.

"No, no, it's the thought that matters," said Shyamoli's father. "It starts with the thought to be of service to others. It is the motivation that is the most important thing, and I am very happy to see you try."

"Thank you, sir, this means a lot to me," said Abir.

"Kindness is the greatest gift of life," continued Shyamoli's father. "You have been kind to my family, my daughter, and I thank you from the bottom of my heart for taking good care of her in a foreign land. Of course, her uncle is there, but you have stood by her all this time, and I am really thankful to you. She, too, is grateful for your company, and I pray to God that you are always together. As a family, I am grateful to God that Shyamoli has got such a wonderful friend in you."

Abir nodded, struck by the extreme simplicity with which Shyamoli's dad welcomed him to their family. To him, it felt as if he had known him for ages.

He remained silent for a while as Shyamoli continued talking to her father. He excused himself in a while and got up to have a drink of water, feeling that he would end up betraying the emotion and gratefulness that he felt if he spoke another word.

Returning to his seat, he sat opposite Shyamoli, away from the laptop screen and camera. Shyamoli looked at him and smiled, her eyes moist. Abir smiled back at her, his eyes bright with gratitude at the warm welcome that her family gave to him.

Gone too soon

The new year of 2015 was approaching fast. Another Durga Puja came and went by in October. The fall colors had started disappearing, like every year around this time, and a sharp, but pleasant, cold nip was getting introduced in the air. The sun called it a day earlier than ever, letting a lot of starry skies to be enjoyed.

Abir had become good friends with Shyamoli's father. Since their introduction, Abir had chatted with him almost every week when Shyamoli called him. He started calling him Biren sir, as he was called by his students back in Kolkata. They would discuss various details of operations that the NGOs did. He heard ground reality tales of compassion by random people who went out of their way to help the underprivileged. He marveled at the simple way Shyamoli's father went about life. He appreciated his insights, wisdom, and compassion, and realized that he was another role model, along with his own father. He summed him up as the quintessential example of simple living and high thinking.

Ever since Shyamoli bought him a laptop, Biren sir had learned to operate it as best as he could. He put it to good use, using Google to search for resources, doing Skype video calls with people all over the country, creating posters and pamphlets, and using Google spreadsheets to keep account of his activities.

He seemed particularly amazed at the real effect that technology had on being a steering platform for everything good that was happening around.

"Technology has changed the face of the Earth," he said one day, as he chatted with them on a weekend evening. Abir and Shyamoli were in Central Park in Santa Clara that evening, after visiting the library there. Abir wanted to look up books on charitable work across the world at the Santa Clara library. Central Park was just behind the library. A magnificent park, the thing that attracted them the most in that location were the ducks. Hundreds of ducks lived nearby, using the pond and fountain that was at the heart of the park. Abir and Shyamoli often spent several hours on the weekends just ambling around in the park. It was far from his apartment in Palo Alto and equally far from east San Jose where Shyamoli stayed. It was a comparatively safe haven of sorts, where they would not be spied on. They would sit for hours, watching the ducks and their families waddle past them, jumping into the pond, and coming back to the land, refreshed.

"Yes sir, I completely agree," said Abir, taking over the head-phones from Shyamoli to chat with Biren sir. "In fact, my dad also says the same thing. He told me just the other day that Google Maps saved him. He was looking for an obscure house in old Delhi where his car could not go. He used Google maps to walk through the narrow old Delhi gullies and ended up at the correct address, which otherwise would be really hard."

"Yes, indeed," said Biren sir. "In fact, the most extraordinarily kind thing that these companies in Silicon Valley have done is to make all this free. Do you know, even the economically lowest stra-ta folks here in Kolkata have started using mobile phones now? And look at the wonderful things they can get, all for free, just because of the great work done by Silicon Valley companies like Google. Now they can search for anything from their mobile phones and get real information. About jobs, about opportunities, and all that. They now have the world's information in their hands, so it's harder to cheat them of their rights."

"Indeed," agreed Abir. "It's extraordinary how you and my dad think alike! He, too, keeps telling me that the lack of data and infor-mation are the key reasons why the less privileged people get cheat-ed of their rights. Now with information in their hands, they are more equipped to face the natural prejudice in our society against the economically weaker people."

"What a great thinker your father is, Abir," said Biren sir. "How is he doing? You told me last week that he had traveled to Delhi. Is he back yet?"

"No, not yet," said Abir ruefully. "I keep telling him not to travel so much, but he is always meeting somebody or the other, or involved in some Government-consulting project. He does all this for free, mostly to keep himself intellectually engaged and active."

"What a great man your father is," said Biren sir reverentially. "I would like to meet him once."

"Yes, indeed, sir," said Abir warmly. "In fact, I told my dad about you too. He is very impressed with the work you are doing. He said teachers like you with a heart on social welfare are the true backbone of our country."

Biren sir's eyes suddenly seem to become moist. He took out his spectacles and wiped his eyes. Abir smiled at him kindly, realizing that Biren sir felt emotional, and if he said anything, he would betray it. Abir had faced a very similar feeling of gratitude when he had talked to Biren sir for the first time, and he knew this feeling.

He waved to him kindly, and they disconnected.

* * *

"Dad, I was talking to Biren sir about technology," said Abir. His father was chatting with him on Skype from the guest house he was putting up in New Delhi. "And he too thinks that technology has changed the face of Earth significantly. You do remember Biren sir, don't you?"

"Ah, right, your friend's dad," said Father. "How is the gentleman doing? I was quite impressed with your description of his work. It's especially heartening, and somewhat inspiring, to see somebody going all the way to help underprivileged folks with the best asset that one can have—time and a will to serve."

"Yes," said Abir. "He goes out of the way to help people who are impoverished and underprivileged. I think he is a remarkable man."

"Absolutely," said Father warmly. "In fact, I am glad, son, that you are trying to help him out with your resources. Let me know if you need me to lend out a helping hand to him, especially with some financing."

"Yes, dad, I am trying to help him out in my ways," said Abir. "He won't hear of taking personal financial help from me for his social upliftment activities, so I am trying to build some useful tools using technology."

"Excellent!" said Father. "By the way, you were talking about the search engine you were building to help him out. How is that coming along?"

"Not that good, dad," said Abir ruefully. "You can do all those things by doing smart custom queries on Google. Google has the entire Internet scanned. One can create smart queries to bring on the results. Custom search engines probably won't be that useful."

"Hmm, OK," said Father. "Never mind. Keep trying, son. Anyways, I need to go to sleep now. I am feeling a bit tired. I have to wake up very early tomorrow morning for a meeting."

"Dad, take it relaxed," said Abir. "Do you really need to do all these travels, now that you have retired? Why do you need to do these projects anymore? When will you ever really retire?"

"How can I ever retire son, when my country needs me?" Father said. "There is always something to do, and as long as I have energy in me, I will continue serving my country."

Abir's heart filled up with pride as he disconnected his phone.

* * *

His search engine having failed to some extent, Abir decided to pursue other directions of using engineering resources to aid in spreading the message of empathy. He had a vague sense of direction about increasing visibility and sales of the impoverished small traders who sold small goods. He wanted firsthand information on the kind of marketing model that the sellers in Kolkata used to sell their small fares. He decided to talk to Shyamoli's father about it.

"Biren sir, how do the small traders in Kolkata get to live by selling their stuff?" Abir asked Shyamoli's father over Skype.

"Do you mean the small roadside traders who sell flowers, toys, jewels, clothes, and the likes on the roads?"

"Yes," said Abir.

"Ah, you mean the Kolkata Hawkers. Yes, they get their stuff from in and around Kolkata. I think they have a Hawkers union of sorts, which unites the hawkers and helps them distribute their fare and places of operations."

"I have seen that they often sell their stuff on the pavement on the roads. Do the people have problems with them occupying the legal footpaths by the roads?" asked Abir.

"Yes, there have been movements over several decades, some in recent history, to remove the hawkers from the pavements so that pedestrians can use those pavements instead of getting on the road to avoid them. There have been people supporting either side of the story. Some are against the hawkers, and some are with them. After all, the big question is, where will they go?"

"Yes, one needs empathy at a social level for these people," observed Abir.

"Yes, empathy is required in all actions against illegal sales," said Biren sir, "But it has to flow equally in both directions. The common man needs empathy to understand the plight of these small traders; they have no place to go, and they need to get by their lives by selling their wares. But at the same time, the common man pays taxes to enjoy the basic amenities provided by the Government, things like enjoying a comfortable walk on the pavements. If these traders occupy the pavements, what happens to the people who want to use the pavements?"

"Is this still an issue these days?" asked Abir.

"No, it's much more improved. Small traders have their designated places to sell their things. People enjoy the pavement of the roads in general. A middle solution of sorts has been reached, and the economy is doing OK for these small traders. It's not that bad in reality. You can see designated areas for these small traders in places like Chowringhee, Chandni Chowk, and the likes."

"I see that the Government has found a solution of sorts then," said Abir.

"Yes, Abir," said Biren sir.

"I was wondering how to use engineering and technology to help these people out," said Abir.

"Abir, what is the exact definition of engineering?" Biren sir asked.

"Well," said Abir, "Engineering is the branch of science and technology concerned with the design, building, and use of engines, machines, and structures."

"So when you call yourself a computer engineer, what exactly do you do?"

"Well, sir, I design and build software systems, mainly built around the aspect of data, machine learning, and artificial intelligence."

"So essentially you build things, I think?" persisted Biren sir. "Like the search engine you told me about?"

"Well, yes, sir," said Abir.

"So, I guess if you are thinking along the lines of compassion and empathy, then from what you describe, I think you can also engineer, or at least influence, abstract human qualities," said Biren sir.

"What kind of qualities, sir?" asked Abir, intrigued. "You mean things like emotions, sympathy, and all that?"

"Yes, Abir," said Biren sir.

"That is a great food for thought, sir," said Abir, feeling excited all of a sudden. He was now slowly seeing a direction that would combine his passion for engineering and servitude.

* * *

Christmas vacations were in a few weeks. Bay Area was getting ready for another hiatus from their busy Silicon Valley life. Abir had already spent one and a half years in the Bay Area. He had already obtained a promotion at work and was a tech lead and manager. It was a remarkable rise by any standards, albeit he did not feel surprised. He was used to obtaining success fast and efficiently. His technical acumen was hailed in his company. The company stocks rose, its fortunes rose, and so did Abir's.

His parents wanted him to visit home. They had not seen him in this one and a half years and were eager to see him. He decided to go home to Kolkata for a few weeks. He wanted Shyamoli to come too. It was a bit late for tickets, which would mean the tickets would be expensive, but given his latest promotion, he felt it was well deserved. Also, going home together with Shyamoli seemed like a great idea to him.

He told Shyamoli about his plans to visit home in a short notice.

"Sorry, Abir, I can't go home right now," said Shyamoli tentatively.

"Why not?" he asked, surprised. "It's been a long time since your family saw you."

Shyamoli turned away from him, and Abir knew that she was hiding her tears.

"Hey, look at me," he said, putting his arms around her. "What is stopping you from visiting them?"

"I have too much work left to complete my thesis," she said.

"Is that the reason?" he asked. "Why didn't you tell me? I can postpone my visit and go home later with you. It would be fun to take a long flight together."

"Why should we go together?" said Shyamoli.

"Well," said Abir, taken aback. "What a thing to say, Shyamoli! You and I—we do everything together. Might as well go home together to visit, no?"

"Well, yes," she said. "But sometimes I wonder if we are there yet to do that."

Abir looked at her, feeling puzzled by her subtle hints, which he could not somehow decipher.

"You are not getting what I mean, are you?" she said, looking at him with a curious expression that he found foreign to her. He turned away from her, feeling puzzled, and Shyamoli caught his hands to make him turn and face her. He turned around and looked into her eyes. As always, everything disappeared away from the surrounding, and he felt as if he was floating into oblivion. Her eyes looked at his, as if seeking answers to questions he did not quite understand or comprehend.

"I am feeling confused, Shyamoli," he said in a while, feeling anxious. "I cannot read you right now."

"Abir, how long will we continue being in this state?" said Shyamoli, laying her head on his shoulder. "Where is our relationship heading? You said we should go and visit home together—like a couple—yet your parents don't even know about me! When will they ever know about me, about us, Abir?"

"Shyamoli, do they really need to know now?" he asked flippantly. "We are adults. We can continue our life here without letting them know."

Shyamoli looked deeply unhappy all of a sudden, and he looked away, feeling flustered. He realized he had to finally face his greatest fear—that of telling his parents about Shyamoli. He was less worried about his father because he knew he would be open to anything. It was his mother that he worried about the most.

* * *

"Dad, I wanted you to meet Shyamoli," said Abir. They were taking on Skype on a weekend morning. His father was still in Delhi. This was his last tour for the year. It was night in India. His father had connected from his hotel room. It looked like he had already packed and was ready to head back home to Kolkata.

"Hello Shyamoli!" said Father, his deep baritone voice almost shaking the laptop speakers.

"Dad, Biren sir is her father," said Abir, nodding at Shyamoli.

"Ah, right," said Father. "Your father is doing great work with social upliftment, Shyamoli. Please convey my regards to him."

Shyamoli nodded. She looked tongue-tied and shy in front of Abir's father, even though he was on the laptop screen.

"Do you work there with Abir?" asked Father.

"No, I am a grad student of Psychology," said Shyamoli shyly.

"Ah, Psychology! Good. What do you plan to do after masters?"

"I plan to do a Ph.D. in cognitive psychology."

"Excellent!" boomed Father in enthusiasm. "One should continue formal education for as long as they can. I had wanted Abir to pursue a Ph.D. in computer science and engineering. But he stopped studying after completing his bachelor's degree in engineering. He wanted to get into the tech world and all its gory details!"

Shyamoli turned to look at Abir and smiled at him, who shrugged his shoulders.

"My best wishes to you, Shyamoli!" said Father. "The world needs bright students like you. Also, convey my best wishes to your father. Your father is doing great work with a human touch. So will you eventually."

Shyamoli looked down at her hands shyly as Abir smiled happily. His father had to sleep early to catch the flight back to Kolkata. Abir waved to him, and he disconnected.

* * *

"Hello, dad, did you call?" asked Abir. It was Sunday night and merely nine. Abir was planning to go to sleep early so that he could wake up early the next morning and go for a jog.

"Hey Abir, yes, I just landed at the Kolkata airport."

"Was it a good flight?" asked Abir, wondering why his father was calling him at all. His father flew all across the country often, and it was not a routine to call him during the flights. Realizing that this call had a different purpose, he got up from his bed and went to the balcony with his phone.

"I wanted to chat with you about something," said Father briskly.

"Yes, go on," said Abir, piqued.

"Listen, so I guess Shyamoli is more than just your friend, is she not?" Father asked, coming straight to the point, in his usual style.

"What a thing to say, dad!" said Abir. He and his father rarely ever discussed these kinds of topics with him, and he suddenly felt awkward.

"Are you denying or accepting it?" continued Father.

"Yes, she is my special friend, dad," said Abir.

"Are you serious about her?" asked Father.

"Yes, dad, I am!" said Abir.

"Well, that's good, I guess," said Father. Abir did not reply, waiting for him to talk more about it.

"Listen, son," said Father after a pause. "Did you talk to your mother about Shyamoli?"

"No, dad, I have not spoken to mom about her yet," said Abir, feeling anxious all of a sudden.

There was a pause at the other end.

"Well, you know your mother," said Father. "You should talk to her about this. She still sees you as a baby, and I think she is not— well, how to put it—she is not ready for this side of your life."

"Why not, dad?" asked Abir, starting to feel dejected.

"Well," said Father, sounding awkward. "Listen, I will tell you my side. After I talked to Shyamoli yesterday, from my brief interactions, she seemed really nice—grounded, soft-spoken, and obviously brilliant. And I do really think highly of her father. I am sure they are a perfectly lovely family. I think you are a mature adult, and I am nobody to interfere in your life. But son, you do realize that this is not a good time for all this? You have your career to look at, your future. Now don't jump up to judge me. I am the last person to lay judgment on these things. But do keep that in mind."

"You are saying all this keeping mom in mind, right?" said Abir, finding it hard to conceal his disappointment.

"Yes, I am," said Father. "You know I am a straightforward man, Abir, and I like to talk straight. Yes, son, you should let your mother know about Shyamoli. You know, I have no issues. But do give your mother time to let this sink in. I am sure she will be receptive eventually."

"Eventually?" asked Abir, feeling unhappy.

"Listen, son," said Father after a pause. "I know what you are thinking. You are thinking, this is the twenty-first century, and you are a young independent man. So why do you need to get permission in the first place, right?"

"No, dad, I am not thinking about that at all," said Abir.

"Well, OK, if you say so," said Father. "But anyway, let me finish what I was saying. You should realize that it is one thing to be carefree, have a girlfriend, have a good time, and all that. But it's one whole other thing to make a system and a society work. Let me repeat—I have high regard for your Biren sir, for his family, and I think his daughter is a fine young lady. But whatever decision you take, make sure that there is some semblance of connection between the two families that you are going to unite. I am personally fine with you going ahead with your current state. I am nobody to interfere in two young adults making a decision like I said. But keep this in mind."

"Dad, I am not quite getting you," said Abir, feeling dejected. "Why don't you just say that you talked to mom about Shyamoli, and *she* made you say all this?"

"Err," said Father, sounding embarrassed. "I did talk to your mother right after you made me chat with Shyamoli. I made a good case for her and told her you might be serious about her."

"And what did she say?" asked Abir, starting to feel anxious again.

"She asked me all about her," said Father, suddenly sounding awkward. "I told her about our brief conversation."

"Why doesn't mom talk to me directly, dad?" said Abir, feeling bitter. "Why this roundabout way through you? Why such an evasive attitude?"

"Well—umm—don't say that," said Father. "Listen, Abir, your mother has the best intentions for you in her mind, you know that, right? She just wants you to—you know—how to say it—just concentrate on the right things. You know, the right metrics, as you would have put in as a data person. Just think about all that, that's what she had to say."

Abir's heart sank. He held onto the phone, suddenly feeling low and dejected.

"Don't feel dejected, son" said Father, as if reading the state of his mind. "It's all fine, I think. Just make sure that you and your mother are on the same page. I know Shyamoli means a lot to you. But keep in mind that you, your career, your life, and your aspirations mean even more to your mother. I think you should respect her wishes and make your intentions with Shyamoli clear straight away so that there are no surprises or animosity."

Abir stared at the dark trees by the balcony. It was a moonless night. The winter chill had set in, the cold setting deep into his skin.

And along with it, a chill set in his heart. He suddenly understood what this was all about.

"Dad, let's be frank here," said Abir quietly. "Did mom ask you about Shyamoli's skin tone? Did you tell her that she is dark-skinned?"

Father remained silent. Abir waited for him to confirm it. When his father remained silent and did not say anything, his suspicion was confirmed.

He stared bitterly at nothing from his balcony. It was exactly as he had anticipated: that his mother would have a deep-rooted prejudice against dark-skinned women. A prejudice which formed a negative idea about Shyamoli in her mind, even before she saw her, met her, or talked to her. A prejudice against dark-skinned women so strong that it surpassed anything and everything else.

"I will call you guys later, dad," Abir said, feeling utterly dejected. He disconnected his phone abruptly.

* * *

"Abir, why haven't you been picking up my phone?" asked his mother sharply when he picked up her phone. Mother had been calling him for two days, but Abir did not pick up her phone. Every time he saw her call, he felt anxious and dejected.

"Well, I have been busy with work," said Abir evasively.

"Well, that's good," said Mother warmly, "I am so proud of you, Abir! You just got your promotion. I am sure you are working very hard and planning for your next promotion, your career, your dreams of opening your own company, and all that."

"Yes, mom, I am," said Abir shortly.

"That's what I told your father too," continued Mother. "I told him that you had no time for idle distractions. You are a man of purpose, of intellect. You are made to do great things, be a leader in Silicon Valley, to make an impact. You are born to lead, to make a big name for yourself. I told him that you did not have time for emotional nonsense, romance, and all those distractions. There is an

115

age and time for everything. At your age, you are, I am sure, concentrating on what matters."

"I am not quite following you, mom," said Abir, feeling irked at the roundabout way Mother was trying to come to a conversation about Shyamoli.

"Oh, just a mother's advice, Abir," said Mother evasively. "Anyways, you are a man with a vision and direction of life. You have always reached for excellence. That is why I am so proud of you. I told Ruku mashi about your promotion, about the Mercedes Benz you bought as a first car. She is so proud! I told her that you are putting all your concentration on the next promotion and, then, to buy a home in Silicon Valley in a few years."

Abir remained silent. He realized that his mother had mentioned everything there was to say about Shyamoli. She had subtly dissuaded him in all possible manners, but without actually even talking about it. Despite his annoyance at the strange twists in the context and intent, he could not help smiling at his mother's tactics.

"Tell dear Ruku mashi that I will bring her a large box of chocolates for my promotion this time. Not that she needs any more chocolates to get fatter," Abir said sarcastically, putting his phone down.

* * *

"Are you sure your luggage won't be too heavy?" asked Shyamoli. They had come to the Target supermarket in Palo Alto to buy chocolates, electronic gadgets, and other gifts for Abir's family. It was mid-December. Abir was to leave for a three-week visit to Kolkata on the thirty-first of December.

"Don't worry" said Abir. "The main items in my bags will be gifts anyways. I am hardly taking any clothes with me."

"Well, you should take your red t-shirt," said Shyamoli. "Also, the formal black shirt. And your red pants. You look good in those."

"You seem keen to make me dress well," teased Abir.

"Oh, you never know," said Shyamoli solemnly. "Maybe your mother would want you to go and meet some girls."

116

"What do you mean by that?" asked Abir, raising his eyebrows. Shyamoli did not reply and walked silently beside him, pushing the trolley. Abir looked at her, wondering what was going through her mind. He had not discussed his conversation with his mother with her at all. He did not see any reason why his mother's acceptance or rejection of Shyamoli's presence in his life mattered to him.

It was his life, his choice, his love.

What worried him, though, was the general notion that the two parties were starting to have about each other. He could clearly perceive a subtle animosity from Shyamoli, even though he had never told her about his conversations with his mother.

"You did not answer me, Shyamoli. What's going on?"

"Well, I have a feeling that your parents are not very happy about me, are they?" she asked.

"Well," said Abir, feeling awkward all of a sudden. "Really, all these things are last on my mind now. I mean, you and I are together, in this beautiful place, buying gifts together for our families. This is all that matters to me right now."

"Oh, so they *did* have a conversation about me with you?" she asked, frowning.

"Look, can we drop this topic?" said Abir wearily. He was not in a mood to become a negotiator between two parties who already seemed to be making opinions without even meeting each other. "The most important thing is, how do I even live without you for three weeks? It looks like a tough job."

"Oh, you and your diplomacy," said Shyamoli angrily, pushing the trolley hard and walking ahead away from him in a huff, as Abir looked after her anxiously.

* * *

"Biren sir, I heard you fell unconscious during class! Are you alright?"

Abir was talking with Shyamoli's father over Skype, along with Shyamoli. It was late afternoon in India and late night in California. After their visit to Target in the morning, Shyamoli had driven back home in a huff, and Abir spent the entire day alone, feeling resentful that Shyamoli did not appreciate his efforts to come to a conversation with his over-expecting and prejudiced mother.

Shyamoli had learned that evening that her father had fainted during work. He had to be carried off to the staff room by his students. She had made frantic calls at home and had remained tensed and upset as the night progressed. Her father had finally regained consciousness and was back at home. She had been trying to get in touch with him, and she could finally see him over Skype, connected by her brother. Abir had made a video call from his home, and Shyamoli had connected to the call from hers.

Shyamoli's father did not reply but smiled feebly. Shyamoli clutched her hands hard, not talking, and Abir could see on the screen that her fingernails had made marks on her wrists.

"What happened, sir—was it something to do with low pressure?"

"I am not sure. This had happened to me once a few months back, but I had regained consciousness quickly. Not sure what this was. I still have pain in my upper stomach. It is indigestion and bloating, I think."

"Did you do a doctor check-up?" said Shyamoli, sounding scared. "When is Dr. Reddy coming to see you? I have told you umpteen number of times not to overwork! You will not teach during the weeknights for your NGO school from now on! It's an order!"

Shyamoli's father smiled, happy to be scolded by his daughter.

"I agree with Shyamoli, Biren sir," said Abir gravely. "Exerting yourself is not a good idea. We do not know the real cause of your fainting like this. This is the second time. I really think you should get an opinion from a doctor. I also think you should take complete rest from all your NGO activities."

Shyamoli's father smiled at Abir's concerned voice.

"God will protect me, my son and my daughter. Yes, Shyamoli, Dr. Reddy will visit me tomorrow—he is too busy in his chamber today. Abir, I can take physical rest, but what will happen to those hundreds of my poor children who are waiting to learn, to be fed in my little school? They need meals. They need education. If I take a rest, who will take care of them? Provide funding for their existence?"

"Yes, I understand all that, sir," said Abir, "But surely you can take a break from all this and simply delegate the work to others?"

"My best worker was my dear Shyamoli when she was here in Kolkata. No, I will have to oversee all this myself, or otherwise, our funding will dry, and the school will eventually close. All my dreams will perish. I have to look at my priority."

"Sir, with humble regards, your priority is your health," insisted Abir. "You should concentrate on getting well and do a check-up to determine the root cause of your fainting. I am visiting India in a few weeks. I will go and meet you in person and try to understand your work. I will try to rope in my contacts from my dad too. Then Shyamoli and I can start taking responsibility from here in the USA once I am back here. These things are not too hard, given the connectivity with Skype and phone. I am sure we can manage somehow. But your immediate priority should be to take a break from all this now."

"You are so kind, Abir," said Shyamoli's father, his eyes suddenly brimming with tears. "Shyamoli's mother and I are thankful that Shyamoli has you in her life. How wonderful your family must be to raise such a kind and compassionate young man like you."

"Father, you should rest now," said Shyamoli softly. "Please, for my sake, stay away from your social work for a week to start with. You can resume when we get a green signal from Dr. Reddy."

"I will, Shyamoli," said her father, closing his eyes with exhaustion. "I feel blessed right now thinking that God has been kind to me to give me a wonderful daughter and, with you, another kind young man. Once I retire from all this, together, you two will march on with your ideals of empathy and social welfare. You will shine in the light, showing compassion and empathy to people all over. All the world needs is love. Just love."

Shyamoli and Abir looked at him as he closed his eyes to sleep, looking peaceful, and Abir suddenly felt his eyes tear up at the great thoughts and hopes that this exemplar man had for him, for her, for them.

* * *

The next evening, Shyamoli got a call from Kolkata. Biren sir had died peacefully at night in his sleep, his heart attack undetected.

Thunderstorm

It was the New Year of 2015. As the country celebrated the New Year, the narrow gully that led to Shyamoli's house felt unusually quiet. Abir asked the taxi driver to stop at the entrance of the gully because the taxi could not go any further inside the narrow lanes. He entered the house to find a brick-floored corridor surrounded by walls, with a three-story home peering down at him. He recalled that Shyamoli's was a joint family, and the different floors were occupied by her relatives.

There was a somber atmosphere in the house. An old man was sitting on a rocking chair by the staircase to the upper floors. Assuming that it was Shyamoli's grandfather, Abir stooped down and touched his feet in reverence.

"Bless you," mumbled the old man, peering at him through thick lenses.

Abir smiled soberly at him and walked into the hallway to go up the stairs. Shyamoli had mentioned once that her family stayed on the third floor. He went up the stairs, his excitement palpable. It was fourteen days since Biren sir's demise, and the *shraddha* ceremony was being held in his memory. Shyamoli had flown over from San Francisco to Kolkata two weeks back after learning about her father's death. Abir had just landed in Kolkata the night before.

As he climbed up the stairs, he found a throng of people sitting on the stairs on the way up, dressed in somber white, talking in low voices. He made his way slowly through the swarm of people and went near the entrance to a spacious apartment crowded with people. He looked inside. A large portrait of Biren sir was on a small carpet on the floor. It was adorned with garlands. The sweet perfume of incense filled the room. Several elderly women were sitting in front of Biren sir's portrait, wearing white sarees, peering at his picture silently.

Abir's eyes swept the room for Shyamoli. As he looked at a corner, she emerged from inside. He observed her talk in whispers to her mother, whom he now noticed, sitting along with the elderly women. As he watched her, he felt slightly out of place. He waited by the door patiently, waiting for her to notice him. When she eventually looked up, her eyes fell on him, and she stopped what she was doing, her eyes suddenly welling with tears. Instinctively, Abir felt like rushing to her and hold her in his arms, and as she stared back at him, he felt that she too wanted the same. Despite the sorrow in the atmosphere, she smiled at him, and in an instant, he forgot the surroundings and context, for he knew immediately that she was smiling for the first time in these two weeks, and this smile was reserved for him.

* * *

"Did you have trouble finding your way here?" asked Shyamoli, holding Abir's hands. "I should have sent somebody over to receive you. The gullies leading to our home are so narrow and confusing."

They had come to the terrace, where there were preparations to feed people with food that Biren sir loved. Cooks, bare torsoed and clad in *lungis*, were preparing food in huge pots. A small white pandal covered the large utensils where they kept the food. Rows of chairs and tables were set up on the terrace.

"I just had to ask where Biren sir's house was, and people immediately pointed me to your place," he said gently, caressing her cheeks.

"Your parents must be delighted to see you," said Shyamoli after a pause.

"Yes," said Abir. He sat beside Shyamoli silently on the terrace of their apartment, looking serenely at the dusk sky.

"Arun uncle sent a small gift for your mother," he said after a while. "I got it along with me here."

Shyamoli nodded silently. She seemed unusually quiet, and Abir naturally took it to be due to her father's sudden demise.

"Did you buy your return tickets to San Francisco?" he asked gently after a while. "If you want, I can buy it for you—you have so much going on in your life."

Shyamoli looked at the distant houses silently.

"I have something to tell you," she said after a while, a bit uncertainty, looking at him. Abir looked into her eyes, and in her eyes, he saw an expression foreign to him. For some reason, the expression suddenly gave him a strange sense of foreboding. He had never seen that expression in her eyes, as if tentative, hesitant. He suddenly felt oddly troubled.

"What is it?" he asked, almost in a whisper, his heart hammering.

"Abir, I am not coming back to the USA anymore."

* * *

Abir did not remember the last time when he had felt such a shock in his life. He stood on the edge of the terrace by the wall surrounding it, facing away from Shyamoli, looking bitterly at the adjacent colorless houses which blocked the view to the older parts of Kolkata. The sound of buses, autos, and the omnipresent noise from the streets made a continuous, dull background to his thoughts. He realized that he was suddenly getting angry and checked himself before he spoke up.

"You made such a big decision and did not even think of consulting with me?" he asked, forcing himself to speak calmly to respect the occasion, despite his mind being in a furious turmoil.

Shyamoli looked down at her hands, looking unhappy.

"I cannot leave this place anymore," she said softly after a pause. "My father was the only one working in the family. With him gone, suddenly, it's all very different. I can't leave my mother or my little brother, who is still in high school. They need me. I need them. We need each other at this time."

She stopped and looked at him anxiously. Abir nodded to convey that he understood this perfectly well.

"The head from father's college got in touch with me," she continued tentatively after a while. "He is working on getting me a teaching position at his college, here in Kolkata. I am thinking of taking up the offer if it goes through."

Abir stood there silently, digesting all this information. He felt his world crumbling, his natural assurance to life, future, and happiness, suddenly in jeopardy.

"So many things happened, and you did not plan on telling me at all about all this till now?" he said, feeling utterly bewildered. He sat on the ground in front of Shyamoli, feeling dejected.

"I would have let you know," said Shyamoli softly. "I was not in a state to call you earlier. I meant to talk to you immediately after the *shraddha* ceremony."

"Shyamoli, I think you can maintain your family from the USA," said Abir, forcing himself to be calm and reason logically. "You have already applied for a Ph.D. in the USA. Once you join a Ph.D. program with a scholarship, you will get paid even better, and you can easily support your family by sending money to your mother for maintenance."

Shyamoli remained silent, looking down at her hands.

"Besides, what am I here for? You can support your family from your stipend back in the USA, and I will support you, or I can support all of us. Why come away from Silicon Valley completely?"

Shyamoli looked afar, her expression hard to decipher. He looked at her, his mind working fast. He could not allow this to happen at any cost. Shyamoli moving over here to Kolkata virtually meant a massive blow to their life and their relationship. He had to think of something fast, something desperate, just to be with the woman he loved.

"It's more than just monetary support," she said quietly after a long silence. "My family needs mental support. My brother is too young to take care of my mother. My mother does not work. I cannot just leave them here and go back to the USA. They need me. I need them. We need to stay together as a family as a unit. Abir, you need to understand my problems."

"I understand all this, Shyamoli," said Abir. "But what happens to us?"

Shyamoli did not reply.

"What happens to us, Shyamoli? Tell me, what happens to us?" he repeated, getting angry. He could not fathom how she could say all this so calmly. Did she not envision what would happen to them if she stayed back in Kolkata and he went back to the USA? He looked at her, and for the first time, he felt as if he could not recognize her. Was this the same Shyamoli who once could not live for a single day without talking to him for at least five hours every day? Was this the same Shyamoli who could not let a single day pass without seeing him at least once? Yet here she was, making drastic decisions in her life without thinking of them or having a concrete plan for them. How could she take all these decisions without letting him know?

"Please, let me take care of you and your family," Abir said fervently. "You have to come back to the USA with me. I will have your mother and brother come over too so that she can live with us."

Shyamoli said nothing, biting her lips.

"Abir, can the other way around happen? Can you come over here to Kolkata?" she asked tentatively.

As Abir looked at her, he suddenly saw through her predicament. She was the one who was at a vulnerable point in her life. It was much harder for her to make decisions, given the situation. She had huge responsibilities. Knowing her as well as he did, she would never leave behind her responsibilities behind to pursue her dreams. For her, family was, and always had been, the most critical entity.

He realized that he would have to leave his position in the USA and would have to simply come back to Kolkata and work here instead. That would not be too hard. He realized that this was the best and simplest solution to their problem. He had a couple of contacts in the few software companies that Kolkata had to offer. He was sure he could move here, and it all looked rosy.

He felt relieved. Despite the solemnity of the situation, he smiled at Shyamoli, and she smiled back at him as if reading his mind.

"Yes, Shyamoli, that could happen. I will move back to Kolkata for you. But give me some time. It will take a few months, but I will be back here."

Her eyes lit up like candles, and he felt a surge of happiness at the sudden decision. She sat quietly, hugging her knees due to the slight January Kolkata cold as if thinking out something.

"What about your parents?" she said eventually. "Will they accept this drastic change in your life?"

"Oh, I am sure they will be delighted to have me come over to Kolkata and near them," said Abir happily. "In fact, my dad had wanted me to look up opportunities in Kolkata before taking up the job in Silicon Valley. Of course, in terms of career, this is not a good move because Kolkata has limited opportunities in software. But that's fine for now. It should all work out well eventually."

"Well, what I mean is," said Shyamoli quietly. "Will your parents accept the fact that *I* am the main reason you are moving back here, despite it not being a good career move for you?"

Abir understood her point, and suddenly he felt less elated.

"Do I need to tell them about us?" he asked after a while. "Maybe I can just move over here first, and then we will go from there?"

"Abir, why are you hiding me from your mother?" asked Shyamoli, looking deeply unhappy. "You keep evading it, even after all this time! I don't want to be that secret woman in your life, Abir, whom you cannot even introduce to your family! You know that for me, acceptance and family is everything. I don't want to live a lie anymore, Abir. If you move here, you should tell your parents that you are moving here due to me, due to us."

Abir looked at her somberly, deciding that the time had come to face his biggest fear.

* * *

Abir walked anxiously beside his mother as they entered the narrow gully which led to Shyamoli's house. They had come to the city for shopping. He had bought some new *kurtas* to wear during Durga Puja back in Silicon valley. He had bought two magnificent *sarees* for his mother and new dresses for Rimjhim and Manik. On the way back, Abir had insisted that they pay respect to Biren sir's memory by visiting his place. He had also briefly told Mother that he wanted her to meet Shyamoli. His father was not in town, and Abir had only his mother to bring along. Mother had not said anything to support or oppose his plans for the day, but he did notice that she was brooding and seemed sharper than usual.

"Why is this gully so narrow?" asked Mother irritably. "Can't even ask our driver to bring the car all the way here."

"North Calcutta roads are narrow, mom," said Abir. "You should know that better than me."

"Have you been to this Biren sir's place before?" she asked sharply.

Abir nodded as they entered the complex.

As they made their way up the stairs, he felt stressed. He had an inkling that Mother was not looking forward to meeting Shyamoli at all. It perplexed him, albeit the reason for him had already been laid out by his father in an offhand way.

They found Shyamoli's mother waiting for them near the staircase landing, looking anxious. Abir had told them that they would be coming along to pay respect to Biren sir's last rites. He smiled at her and touched her feet in reverence. Then they entered their apartment.

* * *

Abir stared at the ceiling fan turning morosely in his bedroom. It was evening, and he and his mother had just come back to their home after visiting Shyamoli's. He closed his eyes wearily, thinking of the afternoon, feeling dejected.

He had gone to Shyamoli's place, hoping it would be an innocuous first meetup between the two most important women in his life.

But what followed was a nightmare.

Shyamoli's mother had been flustered as she welcomed them to their apartment. Abir had folded his hands in front of Biren sir's picture, which was the prominent one on the wall, adorned with garlands, with the sweet fragrance of incense filling the room. Shyamoli had worn a traditional Indian saree, and to Abir's eyes, she looked different and, somehow, more mature and homely than how he remembered seeing her even a few weeks back in the USA. Abir had suddenly felt shy before her. He wanted to see her through his mother's eyes, to see her wonderment, and waited for the entire time for that moment when Mother would smile at Shyamoli and try to befriend her.

Nothing like what he hoped for really happened. His mother was stiff from the moment they set foot at their home. Throughout the short visit, the conversation was mostly one-sided, with Shyamoli's mother trying to engage them in conversation, asking about their journey to this side of Kolkata, fussing over their food. Shyamoli's younger brother appeared once and peered over his horn-rimmed spectacles solemnly at them, and before Abir could engage in a conversation with him, he disappeared back into his room.

Shyamoli was shy in the beginning. After some time, though, her expression changed to that of quiet puzzlement, as Abir's mother continued to show complete disinterest in her. His mother did not talk to Shyamoli at all, as if she did not exist in the room.

Finally, by the time they got up to leave, nothing had been asked about Shyamoli, or her family, or Biren sir.

Her presence was not acknowledged by his mother, as if she was completely absent from the room.

His mother refused to eat any of the food prepared by Shyamoli and did not drink water either.

There was a heavy awkwardness in the air as he and his mother rose to leave.

As they went down the stairs, Mother asked him loudly enough for Shyamoli and her family to hear: what did he see in a dark-skinned girl like her?

* * *

Dark. That summed up his mother's opinion of Shyamoli. How ironic it sounded, especially given that the colorless theory that he stated everywhere was created precisely to oppose this prejudice.

Dark. A simple word that consumed all beautiful adjectives that could have described Shyamoli and her essence.

Dark. A single word that defeated all the purpose and ground to dust Shyamoli's elegance, intelligence, brilliance, responsibility, calmness, and sheer internal and external beauty.

Dark. That was the only thing Mother saw in Shyamoli. Not her smile and not her bright eyes when she looked at him, and them. Not her look of anxiety to somehow be a part of them. Not at the carefully prepared sweet delicacies that she had made, especially for them.

Dark. A word which made a sweeping generalization, a word which overlooked and outweighed every aspect of Shyamoli's essence. One powerful, crushing word that broke all other hundreds of positive virtues into pieces.

Dark.

* * *

As he stared at the ceiling above, Abir realized that he had made a grave blunder in introducing Shyamoli to his mother. His father had subtly warned him about this. He realized that it was not required, at this present day and age, to get parent's approval. He could have just moved over to Kolkata and continued a relationship with her. True, Shyamoli had always been particular about being accepted by his family, but that could have waited. He could have kept it all a secret.

But then again, would Shyamoli have liked it—to be that secret woman in his life who could not be introduced to his family of prejudiced individuals?

He closed his eyes, his mind unrest, suddenly foreseeing a tsunami of negative energy that was about to enter his life.

* * *

For the next few days, Abir tried to call Shyamoli, but she did not respond. He sent her text messages, which she did not return either. Meanwhile, his mother was not on speaking terms with him either. She seemed deeply disappointed that he had chosen such a woman as his life partner, that too, without any prior consultation or warning.

His mother's anger toward him did not worry him.

What worried him most was Shyamoli's silence. This was extremely uncharacteristic of her, and it made him worried sick.

Abir spent the next few days contemplating his next steps to get back to speak to Shyamoli and talk about their future. She had not responded to any of his phone calls, texts, or emails. He had to go back to the USA in a few days. It was a strange crossroads in his life. Even his father was not around to counsel him. He did not want to phone him on these personal issues.

He decided that it was best to go and meet her in person straight away.

* * *

Abir rang the bell at Shyamoli's house, his heart hammering. He had made the arduous journey all the way by taking a train and then a taxi to her place. He had purposefully not asking his driver to drive him there in their family car. It had taken him a full two hours to reach her home. Unused to traveling in crowded train compartments, he was exhausted and unkempt.

Shyamoli opened the door and let him in silently. He touched Shyamoli's mother's feet, presented her sweets, presented a bouquet of flowers to Shyamoli, and presented the book he had meant to give to her younger brother. He left his shoes reverently outside the home. As always, the sight of her filled him with happiness. He forgot, for a moment, that she had not been talking to him for the last several days.

"Can we go out for a walk so that we can talk?" he asked her hopefully.

"You can say what you want to say here."

Abir stared at her, realizing that things were not going as planned. As her mother quickly got up to go inside, he said, "Why are you shutting yourself off from me? What did I do?"

Shyamoli did not answer immediately. Instead, she went to the kitchen and brought out cold orange juice for him and handed him the glass, sitting down across him. Abir did not like her formality but decided to accept the glass with an equal formality. They sat silently as Abir sipped the juice quietly, looking at her.

"Abir, I think your mother made it very clear what exactly she thinks of me," Shyamoli said abruptly. Abir looked at her in surprise. Somewhere along the time that he had known Shyamoli, he had never seen this side of her. Her soft tone was gone, and there was an authority and sharpness in her voice, which he found odd and foreign.

"Shyamoli, it's your life and mine," he said gently. "My mother's opinions do not matter."

"Well, you will never understand things from a woman's point of view, will you?" Shyamoli said sharply. "For you engineering people, it's all about getting through something as if it were some kind of a project! Life is not a project! Your mother's disdain toward me was as apparent as anything when she came over with you that day. You are thinking of this as a one off relationship between a man and a woman. It's not. At least, not in the society that I live in. When we talk about a formal couple, we talk about the families, about being accepted by each other's family. This is not just about two individuals."

Abir stared at her, his mind feeling fuzzy. Her voice, her tone, and her views were all foreign to him. He realized that he had seen her in his light, in a surrounding and ambiance back in the USA, which was conducive for thoughtful discussions, informed decisions, and mutual admiration. He also realized that he was now talking to the head of a family, a family which was at a low point, and with Biren sir's death, the old Shyamoli that he had known had also gone. This was a new person, whose views of life were hard and meant to protect herself and her family at any cost.

He sighed, and for the first time since he had met Shyamoli back in Arun uncle's place, he felt at a loss of words and in confidence. He looked helpless at her as if suddenly scared to confront her. He felt bewildered that it was his mother who had all these views, yet he was the one to get all the flak.

"Look, I am going to fly back to the States in a few days," he said eventually, stammering a little. "You and I can think about all this later when things are better. I am sorry you had to go through this. I truly am. But to be honest, don't you think you weigh too much on just my mother's opinions? After all, it's us who need to be together. What happens to us?"

Shyamoli got up, picking his empty glass, and went back to the kitchen with it. Abir got up and went to the kitchen to be near her.

"You still did not answer me, Shyamoli," he said patiently. "What happens to us?"

Shyamoli did not reply as she neatly washed his glass and put it back into the counter. Then she turned around and went to the balcony. Abir followed her.

"Abir, union happens between families, at least here in India. It's just not two individuals coming together. Your mother rejected me. She rejected our union. Can you even imagine the drama and prejudice that is to unfold if we are together, every day? There is absolutely no question of us uniting over her disapproval. I have enough stress on my plate now to even think about getting into a family and live bitterly, unaccepted, and insulted at every step of my life."

"You asked to meet her, remember?" said Abir quietly.

"Yes, I asked to meet her, because I had a foreboding about all this. And I now clearly see why," she said, her tone hard.

Abir turned away from her to hide the uncanny sinking feeling in his stomach, looking at the colorless houses facing the balcony.

"Shyamoli, this is the twenty-first century," he said after a while, collecting his thoughts. "You and I don't need my parents' approval to have a life together. Why are we even having this conversation?"

A light breeze made her hair flow across her face, like the way he loved. He raised his hands to move the hair from across her face, but she stopped his hands.

"Stop trying to deviate me unnecessarily to ignore my views," she said, her voice icy cold.

"Shyamoli, I am not ignoring your views," said Abir. "I apologize for my mother's attitude, but those are her actions, her attitude, not mine. What was I supposed to say? You know my point of view on this matter very well. What can I do if my mother does not think like me? What could I have done that other day?"

"The least you could have done was to defend me," she said, tears trickling down her eyes.

"Defend you? How?" asked Abir, troubled to see her tears.

"When you and your mother came the other day, and she behaved as if my mere existence in the room was painful to her, you should have made the situation and vibe correct. When your mother dared to insult me further by refusing to eat anything that I had painstakingly made for you and her, you should have had the balls to stand up to me. She knew very well that we are at a low point in our lives, yet she overlooked all that with utter disdain and indifference. And finally, when your mother said those obnoxious racist words about my skin color, you should have made a bloody scene. But you did nothing! Absolutely nothing! You have high ideals, great theories around an empathetic world, fancy empathy engineering projects, big lectures on colorless societies, and whatnot, but all of them failed when you had to actually defend me in reality! Then suddenly, your eloquence disappeared!"

Abir stared back at her, looking at her expression of loathing and hatred. His mind was slowly becoming unclear. Was it all a dream? Was all his love for her gone down in vain at a crucial time? Where everything about him stood in ridicule, to be detested by the very person to whom he had given his heart away forever?

"Don't look at me with those watery eyes as if you don't understand anything!" continued Shyamoli, her usual calm voice getting shrill with anger. "I suddenly see through you now. You are the kind of men who lurk around to trap women by their practiced charm, but when it comes to reality, you can just think of yourself and how to have something that you want. You wanted me for some reason, so you will do anything to get me, trying to blend together systems that don't work. Your mother has been raised in a society that values the color of skin more than anything else. She detests and looks down on people with dark skin. It's as simple as that. And you are too childish and pathetic to even understand that."

Abir looked back at her, his feet trembling, hardly able to stand up and face her.

"Here's an advice to you. Don't be so spineless!" continued Shyamoli, her expression scornful. "If you are too much of a mama's boy, then go and live her dreams! You spineless men will never understand the issues that dark Indian women face throughout their lives! You haven't seen life as it is for people like us, who try to be excellent in everything, yet get put down simply because we are dark-skinned! I have simple views of life, and all I want is respect— and that seems to be the last thing that I can get from your family! Don't come around and try to force unions that only benefit you. Your mother clearly detests my kind. And I detest her kind too! You think everything will be fine, but it never will be. You have great theories around a colorless world. It's a bit rich, given that your family is a prime example of why you need a colorless society in the first place!"

"You are fighting with me to get over her insults?" Abir asked, his voice trembling with distress.

"No, I am not fighting with you or just for myself," Shyamoli said, her big eyes lit up like angry dots of fire. "I am fighting for justice. What your mother did was to wage war against me and my type. She waged war against the dark-skinned women in Indian society who struggle to get accepted, to get respect. And I am going to fight that war, because it's a *dharma* war—a war of ideologies, not just my personal war. I cannot let your family insult me and my type. And you are not any different from them. It's all a mask, and in reality, you are just likely to be like them. You are a part of a family who thinks it's OK to come over and accept my hospitality, yet insult me with utter disdain to assert their superiority simply because

I am dark-skinned! It's a fundamental human rights violation! I refuse to associate myself with this family! And I refuse to entertain you further, who does not have the courage, or fortitude, or balls, to stand up for what's right and what's wrong!"

Abir stared at her speechless, his mind numb, not knowing what to say. He felt stupefied, and not knowing what to do or how to react, he put out his hand again to touch her hair, like the countless times he had done before. Shyamoli pushed away his hands rudely with a finality foreign to him.

"I am not your toy, Abir, and don't you dare touch something you don't own" she breathed, her face flushed with anger and an unknown expression that Abir had never seen before. "It's always the same, no? Women will be objectified—always! Be it *Draupadi*, to be given away by *Yudhishthir* as if she were an object, or *Sita*, asked to prove herself, again and again. Always an object! Always compared and judged! Always told things on their face, as if what they feel does not matter! And to aid it all, there are these pathetic men across history who will bow down like cowards and won't have the balls to stand up and defend their women! Like you!"

He gazed at her eyes—eyes that stayed in his thoughts all the time. Eyes that had become an integral part of her essence, like a fragrant mist engulfing his soul. Eyes that floated subconsciously in his dreams and his wakefulness.

Eyes that now looked at him with an expression he had never seen—an expression of hatred and deep, bitter disappointment.

Shyamoli looked distant, foreign, as if they had never known each other. There was a steely resolve in her eyes.

"Abir, I think you should forget me," she said, her tone stinging him with its clarity. "Let me get on with my new life, my new responsibilities, here in Kolkata, and you can get on with yours in the USA. You have been diplomatically avoiding a meetup between your mother and me. Thank you for bringing your mother to our story finally! She reflects the society and the world you belong to. It opened my eyes to what I was getting into! Not anymore! Please let me be, and please leave. You and I can never unite. And please don't insult yourself further by trying to get in touch with me again.

Instead, devote your time to be a *real* man, to make a *real* impact on this world. Learn to defend the oppressed, to truly practice empathy instead of making fancy intellectual theories, and not be an utterly pathetic and spineless coward."

Shyamoli looked at him for one last time, her face drawn together in disgust, tears of anger and rage falling from her eyes.

Abir raised his hands slowly toward her face, one last time, to wipe away her tears.

"Don't you dare even touch me, you coward. If you do, I will scream," said Shyamoli shrilly, shaking all over. Then she ran away inside her bedroom.

Abir stared after her for one last time, as she ran inside, as if even his sight disgusted her. He went to the door of her apartment and trudged out in a trance, not looking back, his head bowed, feeling heavy, too heavy to keep up. He started climbing down the stairs with trembling legs. There were no words of endearment or good-bye from her. No sweet goodbyes that were always reserved for him.

Shyamoli closed the door of her apartment with finality, as Abir climbed down the stairways slowly, his body shaking uncontrollably. He stepped out of her house into the narrow gully and went away.

Move On

The cool night breeze, blowing on Abir's face as the rickshaw ambled its way away from the railway station, helped him think more clearly. Listening to Shyamoli's voice on the phone after four years was a dizzying experience. The entire day had been topsy turvy. First meeting with Riya. Then his chanced encounter with Shyamoli and her acerbic friend Aniruddha. Abir believed that events happened due to a reason. What would be the reason for this series of events, all happening within a short period?

The rickshaw driver expertly avoided people on the road, swinging around the random crowd walking in the middle of the road and occasionally blowing the rubber horn when it was hard to turn around. The sound of this horn made up for the sound of this town, as did the white tube lights in the shops.

Abir alighted from the rickshaw in front of their three-story bungalow-style home. An iron gate marked the entrance to the house, followed by a collapsible wrought iron gate. Bhutto, the manservant who stayed at their home from morning till night, opened the gates for him, taking his backpack and bringing him lemonade, which he seemed to have prepared for him anticipating his arrival. Abir finished the lemonade in a gulp, went to his room on the second floor, and laid down on his bed, shoes on, staring at the ceiling fan which had started gaining speed. The house lizard behind the tube light peeked its head as if to make sure it was him and not some other intruder.

Mother entered the room.

"What's the matter? Did you meet Riya?"

"Yes."

"So what happened? Why are you lying down on your bed? Are you ill?"

"No. Just a bit tired."

Mother hovered around a bit, arranging his room. Abir knew that she wanted to ask him about his rendezvous with Riya in Kolkata. He kept silent, watching the fan blades turn perpetually. Sensing his reluctance to engage in any conversation, she went out of his room and left him alone. He remained lying on the bed, staring at the ceiling fan blades spinning. He felt emotionally exhausted, and the last thing he wanted was to talk to anybody.

He heard the doorbell ring downstairs and heard his father come in. He could listen to him talking to her, probably asking about him. "What did he say? Uncommunicative and distant as usual?" he heard Father say, deep disappointment in his baritone voice. He heard Mother mutter something undescriptive. Abir stayed put in his bed, eyes closed. Through the open window, he could listen to the occasional quack-quack of the rickshaw horns as they sped through the streets down. The calendar made a monotonous rustling noise as it rubbed against the wall due to the gentle breeze from the ceiling fan.

Before he knew it, he fell asleep.

* * *

Abir woke up to the sound of barking dogs and sat up, startled. What time was it? It was tranquil outside. The house was silent, except for the steady ticktock of the clock on the wall. He was sleeping with the same clothes he had worn the day before. The mosquito net surrounded him, confining him, as if he was living in a small room on top of his bed, with the nylon mesh walls all around him. Bhutto must have put that on while he was sleeping.

He got up and parted the curtains of the window of his room— it faced east, and he could see the faint hint of orange in the eastern sky. He glanced at the clock. It was five in the morning. He tiptoed past his parents' room and took the staircase to the roof, taking his laptop along with him.

The refreshing air outside, not yet burdened by the bikes, auto-rickshaws, cars, or people, made him more awake than he was some time back. The slightly orange sky made the aura for the sun to peep up from the horizon soon, against the silhouette of the tall coconut trees, standing proudly against the light shade. The birds had started their clamor, and occasionally, an enormous flock of cranes would fly across the sky.

He stood on the edge wall of the roof, with a light breeze blowing on his face, breeze from the river Ganges, not so far away. In the deafening quietness he was so unaccustomed to in these areas, he could even hear the faint hoot of a train from the railway station a few miles away; it would not be heard otherwise. The first rays of the sun erupted, suddenly, from behind the distant houses, blinding for an instant, and he turned his eyes away.

He logged in into his blog and stared at it, wondering how to describe his feelings at the moment. He then started writing a new blog.

Dear Blog Reader,

Thank you again for dropping by my blog. Yesterday, I had promised that I would share anecdotes from my own life about how I practice empathy and mindfulness. Certain events happened, and I am happy to say that I am in a position to share with you some examples of how I am practicing mindfulness and empathy. I am far from perfect, but I wanted to share my perspective with you nevertheless.

I met with three strangers in my life yesterday. Well, two were strangers. The third one was one of my best friends, my soul mate, who had turned a stranger. Each person had their own intention of interaction with me.

The first one was interested in my outer material self, as it appeared to the world, to the society. This person had formed an opinion about me based on my somewhat redundant and unnoticeable communications. The second one interacted with me by placing me in a category and assuming that I represented that category. He was not a particular fan of this category and ended up having all his interactions with me based on that single assumption. The third one saw me after a long time, and had deemed me unworthy a while back, and was merely curious to see how I fared in this world.

In all these interactions, I was the one questioned, scrutinized, and made answerable. In each of these interactions, my side of the story was not sought after, not analyzed. It was not what they had to offer to me. It was what I had to offer to them. Questions were for me to defend and for them to throw.

In all these interactions, I, in myself, remained immaterial. It is a perfect situation because that is what I have been practicing for the last four years; to become irrelevant, take the "me" out of "myself" and make myself invisible so that I can pass smoothly among the many layers of human emotions, without creating undue perturbance.

The first one was going to make a big decision in her life and had every right to scrutiny me, my life, my past. She had all the questions to ask, and I had some fortitude to respond appropriately to respect her desire to really know me more before deeming me worthy of friendship. I looked at the small amount of data I had about her, and when I took the "me" away from "myself," I could see clearly with my mind and could understand and respect her motive clearly.

The second one had probably faced bitterness facing the Indian system, which had rendered him unavailable to the resources that are prevalent in more affluent countries. At least, that was the data that I inferred from the few words spoken with him. I put the "me" out of "myself," ignored the fact that he was trying to insult me at every step, and instead, decided to look at the bigger picture from his point of view. He was resentful of my apparent good fortune to avail those resources, and hence, he had every right to be acerbic. He questioned my humble efforts to spread the message of empathy, and I think he had some excellent points.

The third one had rejected me on her own accord as I was unworthy of her, yet she expected me to be communicative when she called me. But again, I got back to my training, analyzed the situation methodically, and looked at all the data that I had. I realized that I had very little data about this third situation. But nevertheless, I could mitigate my unhappiness by merely looking at it again from her point of view, perhaps without much data. Perhaps there was a message that I had failed to read those years back.

To my readers, today I would like to close with one import-
ant note about human behavior that I have observed. To understand
it, go back to your high school physics, and try to recall the deep
connection between frequency and energy. Every human has a fre-
quency, and when two humans interact, their frequencies interact.
Their energies cut each other. The final amplitude might increase
during constructive interference and decrease during destructive in-
terference. Extrapolate it to multiple humans, interacting, by will or
forced to, and suddenly, you have a cataclysm of energies.

Do not despair when this energy seems harmful to you. Instead,
look at the data available to you and take yourself to a plane where
you can see the full perspective. If you can do that, you can over-
come anything.

And if you do not have any data, just move on calmly, peace-
fully.

On a closing note, be what it may, always remember that any
interaction that has some emotion attached to it is a real human
interaction. Be happy that you feel it, whether it is negative or pos-
itive. That means you are alive and emotionally sound, and as long
as you are alive, practice empathy, in the way I have engineered it
for you. One day, your practice will rebound back to you and will
give you relief when you need it.

This is Abir, your friendly empathy engineer! Keep coming back
for more! Signing off for now from Kolkata, India. August 2019.

* * *

Abir stopped writing the blog and hit publish. In the last few
years, he had steadily acquired a bunch of hardline followers, who
seemed to adhere to his thoughts, read his blogs religiously, made
comments, shared his posts, and often sent him questions. At times,
the issues would be personal, with details of their lives that he
wished they would not share. They would ask him questions, about
situations, about his thoughts on how to deal with them, how to
be mindful and empathetic. He had often responded. Sometimes,

he had desisted from responding directly because the questions had been too personal.

Besides the blog, he had started his mindfulness and empathy data platform a year back as a formal project. It had been somewhat inspired by his own thoughts in his blogs. Initially, the platform had been a personal quest to rope in facts about local artisans, local cultures, from places around the world. He had started curating all this information from the Internet, intending to research on how empathy and mindfulness for people had a correlation with people's connection with the underprivileged and the downtrodden.

He was visiting Kolkata after four years, to a place that had changed dramatically. His suburb town had grown out of proportion, and there was significant traffic in front of his home. All around, he could see growth. More multistoried apartment complexes. More cars. Better dressed people. It seemed the economy had opened, and despite the increase in pollution and crowd, it made him happy to see that people seemed happy and excited about their future.

His parents had visited him a couple of times in Silicon Valley in these last four years. They had observed, with pride, his rapid progress up the corporate engineering ladder, as he became an engineering director in his company. He had bought a home in Sunnyvale, at the heart of Silicon Valley, at his mother's wishes. When his parents visited, he took them around to visit typical touristy places in the USA: Los Angeles, New York, and Florida. He got his parents to meet Ayan and Srija, who had finally married and had started living in their own apartment.

In all these activities, no mention of Shyamoli was ever made, as if it was a wrong detour in the path of their little family of three people, bound together to measure life's success in their own metrics.

His parents, though, seemed to ignore the quiet change that had come over in their son's demeanor. Their once opinionated and cheerful son had become silent, introspective, and stoic.

Back home in the USA after that fateful visit four years back, he had disappeared from all social circles, avoiding people. His only constant connection to the Bengali social bandwagon had been Ayan and Srija. Not that he had a choice. Not having Shyamoli around anymore, his single link to normalcy was his association with them. In his frenzy to forget Shyamoli, he had spent long hours at his office, often working late at night. He did not see a point in returning home, which meant nothing to him anymore, knowing that Shyamoli would never be with him anymore. He had shunned himself off from people, from the society, and taken to blogging and creating his data platform.

His visit to Kolkata this time was to connect with local NGOs, local artisans, marketers, and other folks. He had decided to start small, with a place he knew. He had visited the city regularly during this visit, visiting different organizations to see if they would like to hop on to his platform. He also asked the local artisans and small traders to join his free platform and provide information on the goods they sold. It would be straightforward for them to hop on to his platform from mobile phones, which had suddenly become omnipresent with even the lowest strata of society. He wanted to emphasize, in particular, the handcrafts created by these impoverished folks. His platform was a location-aware data platform, which provided information about the goods that these small traders had to sell, pointing the shopper to the closest small trader based on the location of the shopper's mobile device which used this data platform service. He hoped that his free data platform would enable people to connect directly to these underprivileged folks and the goods that they had to sell, which would then create a sense of connection at a grassroots level to their lives and their crafts.

It had all been all growth for Abir in these last four years. To anybody observing him, he was a typical successful young techie in the Silicon Valley, rising the corporate ladder with ease and demonstrating all the prized characteristic desired in Silicon Valley: hard work, intelligence, a sense of purpose, and being adept with the right technologies that the valley cared about at the moment—artificial intelligence, machine learning, cloud, and big data.

At this stage, when he had just turned thirty, his mother had suddenly changed gears, as if waiting for him to reach this stage. She had been talking about him getting married for some time now.

Abir had put off her advice with a quiet indifference. Every time she talked about marriage, he envisioned her taking rounds of families of potential would-be brides for her magnificent son, keeping an eye out for the right girl to be with her high-flying, high-achieving son, whom she had molded with her own hands.

It was a routine he detested in every manifestation.

He had agreed to meet Riya just to satiate his ever nagging mother. In reality, he wished he could tell Mother that he could never live with another woman, or love another woman, because his heart had bled away too much four years back.

* * *

Abir stared at the road below from the terrace. It was dawn. Several people had started their day. A few cars and motorcycles had started using the road.

He heard the door of the room on the roof open. Dadu, his grandfather, emerged from the room. Thin and lanky, he was clad in his omnipresent *dhoti*, the traditional Indian dress worn by men, mostly at home these days, his slim bare torso holding the *poitey*, the sacred thread Hindu Brahmins wear, dangling onto him.

Dadu was nearing eighty but was surprisingly agile for his age. Every day, he would get up at the wee hours in the morning and go for a walk. Abir never knew precisely where he went. On his way back, Dadu would bring the morning newspaper with him and would sit in his room and read it till Bhutto brought his morning tea. It was a routine he had heard about, from the time his parents had moved back to this Kolkata suburb. His grandmother had passed away long before his folks had come back to Kolkata. Dadu stayed alone in this single room on the third floor of the building.

Abir's interactions with Dadu had been limited to visits during summer holidays when he was at school, or when sometimes Dadu would come over to their place. During his college days, he had seldom been to Kolkata and did not see much of Dadu. What amazed him most about Dadu was his impeccable English; it was splendid, with a British accent sometimes typical to English-educated folks from the pre-independence days. During his school days, Abir would pen down letters, in blue inland cards, and Dadu would reply, in his sprawling handwriting, which would invariably start with "My dear young man." Abir would sometimes send him pictures of him with his friends, and Dadu would, in turn, send him pictures of Kolkata, cut out from newspapers.

He waved to Dadu as he came near him. Dadu sat down on the mat with him and looked at the distant sky.

"Do you want to stay in the USA forever, or do you want to come back home here?" asked Dadu suddenly. Abir looked at him, startled. It was unusual for Dadu to say anything, that too, a direct question like this.

"I don't know, Dadu."

"I remember you made that tiny robot of yours when you were in school. You and your friend—what's his name—I forget—you tried to make a computer out of matchboxes and magnets. Do you do all that in your job?"

Abir shook his head, marveling at the simplistic nature of the question. Dadu peered at him silently. The dawn had started breaking into the morning. The road below had begun to attract its regular travelers: people on bicycles and occasional rickshaws. Dadu would have left for his morning walk, but he would not go today; after all, his grandson was here with him on the rooftop.

"I read your writings on the computer sometimes," said Dadu.

"You do?" asked Abir, surprised, marveling that Dadu could operate a computer.

"Yes. Your father reads them out to me from the computer sometimes. I also look at your speeches on the computer."

Abir looked on silently at Dadu in wonder. He had never realized that Dadu would follow his work so carefully. He realized ruefully that he had hardly spent any time with Dadu on this visit to India.

"What do you think of my work, Dadu?" he asked.

"I see a lot of pain in all your writings and talks, Abir," he said simply. Abir looked at him, startled, as Dadu peered back at him through his spectacles. He suddenly felt his eyes tinge with tears, and he turned his head away. After a while, he turned back again to face him.

"Why do you say so?" he asked.

"I have seen a lot in this world, and any change in a person happens due to a reason," said Dadu. He peered at Abir solemnly, and he looked back at him, unwavering. "You have suddenly grown up, Abir. All grown up. Serious. Unromantic. Uncommunicative. Working too hard. Mechanical. Almost like some kind of a robot that you used to build."

Abir did not reply, staring silently at the horizon at nothing.

"You have become very hard on yourself, Abir," continued Dadu, his old wrinkled eyes suddenly looking worried. "You go about your work like a military person. It's good to be stoic. A man needs to be balanced and stoic. But not so much. But it is all happening for a reason, I think. What is the reason?"

"Do you think everything happens for a reason, Dadu?" Abir asked.

"Yes, everything happens for a reason," said Dadu simply. "You had great views on everything. You were vivacious, inspiring, and talkative. You are now all wound up. You have become almost silent, as if you want to disappear from the world, to make your existence invisible. Your only communications are through your talks on the computer that I see. But even those are bordering on being too serious, too deep, too spiritual. Why is it so? What is the reason?"

Abir smiled at his prodding ways. It was uncharacteristic of Dadu, and he must have a strong reason for pursuing him for an answer. He remained silent, looking away at the orange sky.

"What is your latest article about?" asked Dadu, changing the subject.

"It's about meeting some people for apparently no reason," said Abir.

"All the people you meet in your life have a purpose and reason for you. It's up to you to seek the purpose."

Abir nodded, looking at him silently. What was the reason that he bumped into Shyamoli again? What could be God's intention there? She detested him and had thrown him away as being unworthy and immature. True, he had not forgotten her, and there was not a single day when he had not once thought about her, but that was because he still had strong feelings for her, which his weak mind could not get rid of. But all this was past. She was already with Aniruddha. Were they married or still only a romantic couple? He did not know and did not want to know. Why did he have to get in touch with her again? What was the reason?

"You talk about empathy and mindfulness. Why is that different from meditation?" asked Dadu, breaking his reverie.

"There is a relationship, certainly," said Abir, coming back to the present. "The only difference that I see is that meditation helps one know oneself and connect to oneself. In my mindfulness and empathy notes, you will notice that I talk about connecting with people around, with nature, with empathy and understanding."

Dadu peered into him silently as he fidgeted with the little loose strings which stuck out from the mat that they were sitting on.

"Stay mindful, Abir, or you will lose yourself one day," Dadu said, getting up to go for his morning walk.

* * *

There was a sound of somebody walking up the stairs, and Abir looked up to see Manik, his cousin, coming through the door leading up from the stairs. Manik and his dad lived in a small house across the pond adjoining their home. Manik's mother had passed away when he was just a toddler. His dad owned a tiny stationery shop down the street. Manik had gone to school for some time, but academia did not come to him quickly. Having failed grade ninth two times in a row, he had given up and had instead concentrated on learning how to repair electrical gadgets. With time, he had done a reasonable business for himself, repairing TVs, fridges, microwave ovens, and CD players in his tiny electronics repair shop on the other side of the railway station. Abir always marveled at how a person who failed ninth grade twice and gave up school, given up for being a poor student of everything, could learn the intricacies of electronic circuits so well that he could repair sophisticated electrical gadgets.

Manik was the odd jobs person in the household. Whenever anybody from his house or that of his uncles' had some odd jobs, Manik would be summoned. He would get the fish from the pond, break and peel fresh coconuts, get medicine if somebody had a fever, fix fridges, TVs, and fused bulbs.

Always smiling and happy, no occasion was complete where Manik was not there. If one of his cousins' birthdays came, the birthday was not finished until Manik had a piece of the cake, or had not sung happy birthday with gusto, or had not prepared a little dance routine to entertain the guests.

Whenever Abir had visited Kolkata in his earlier days during summer vacations, Manik would be his best friend. Slightly younger than Abir, Manik was the gateway to everything fascinating about the Kolkata suburbs that folks living in other parts of India sometimes do not have access to. He and Manik would disappear in the suburb streets, then free of traffic, with no solid roads to take the brunt of developing households and apartment complexes all over. They would run after ducks waddling across the ponds. They would fish in the pond with a makeshift fishing rod made with bamboo sticks. They would build tiny electrical circuits from odd assortments of batteries, shouting out with delight and congratulate each other at seeing little bulbs light up magically when the wires connected. Tired and dirty after tramping around starting from early morning to noon, they would sit together to eat at their house.

Manik was listening to FM radio through a pair of Bose headphones, the tiny radio tucked away in his pocket. Abir had bought the Bose headphones and the radio for Manik from the USA this time. Since then, these had been Manik's constant companion, and he bore them around proudly. Manik had always dreamt of owning a set of Bose headphones to listen to music always while working, or not working, or at home.

"What's new, brother," asked Manik, hopping on beside him. "Why up so early? You are usually a late sleeper—I have never seen you up so early."

Abir nodded silently at him.

"What are you doing with your computer?" asked Manik.

"I was writing a new blog," said Abir.

"What is it about?"

"About meeting people for no reason. I was talking about it to Dadu too."

"Whom did you meet?"

"Oh, an old friend who has abandoned me."

"You mean that Shyamoli girl?" Manik asked.

Abir looked at him, startled.

"How did you know, mate?" he asked, surprised.

"I just guessed. You told me about Shyamoli some years back, remember? You also showed me a photo of her."

"Yeah, I might have," said Abir, "But how did you know that I might have bumped into her?"

Manik fidgeted with the headphones for a while, and Abir had an inkling he wanted to hide some information.

"What is it, Manik? Tell me."

"I have seen her a few times the opposite side of the river," said Manik evasively. "So I guess chances are high you might have bumped into her."

"With another man, right?" asked Abir quietly.

Manik nodded and looked away, avoiding his eyes.

"Tell me, Manik, do you think she is married to this guy?" Abir asked, feeling strangely empty. "Or do they look like lovers? Is she is in love with him? Is he in love with her?"

"Don't know, man, don't know," said Manik, looking at Abir unhappily. Abir looked away, and Manik put his hands on his shoulders.

"You alright, brother?" Manik asked gently.

Abir turned to him, his eyes tearing up.

"No, you are apparently not," said Manik ruefully. He ruffled Abir's hair and got up.

"Forget all this and move on," he said. "Yes, you really need to move on, brother. Your mother told me that you had gone to the city to meet a girl. If you think she is decent, get married and move on. I know you are not the marrying type, but you will pine yourself away for this Shyamoli girl. Forget her man, and get married, have a family, and just move on. Otherwise it's going to be hard for you. Anyways, talk to you later. I have got to fix the light bulb in the guest bedroom of your house."

* * *

Abir stayed back on the terrace, looking at the distant horizon, which had the sun now peeping up. The milkman rang his bicycle bell down near the gate. Abir could see him down in front of his home. He came in a bicycle, with two big drums of milk attached to the two sides of the cycle. He had known this fellow for ages. Hari kaka. His mustache had grown whitish, and there were wrinkles in his face, lines of wisdom developed out of time. Hari kaka found him watching from the roof and waved to him, and Abir waved back.

There were running feet up the stairs and soon he was joined by Rimjhim, his cousin. Rimjhim lived a few houses away and was his uncle's daughter.

"Tell me tell me what happened yesterday," she chirped, jumping down beside Abir.

"Nothing."

"What do you mean nothing happened!" said Rimjhim indignantly. "Did you meet Riya didi at all, or did you run away?"

"Why would I run away?" asked Abir, lying down on the mat, "I met her."

"And?"

"And what?" asked Abir.

"What do you mean *and what*! Did you like her?"

"She is brilliant and amazing," said Abir quietly.

"Are you going to marry her or not?" Rimjhim asked impatiently.

"Maybe the question should be the other way around, Rimjhim," he said, smiling at her calmly. "As in, will she find me fit to be married to her?"

"Oh, shut up," said Rimjhim, pulling his nose playfully. "Any woman who gets to be my brother's life partner is lucky."

Abir did not reply, turning around from the sudden ray of sun peeking from behind the coconut tree, blinding him for an instance.

He wished he could tell Rimjhim that she was so wrong, because no woman wanted to have a spineless coward for a life partner.

* * *

Over the next few days, Abir's indifferent reply about Riya did not please his mother. He did not say no. He did not say yes, either. Mother said nothing to Abir, but he heard her mutter darkly behind the kitchen counter to Rimjhim's mother.

Abir avoided his mother carefully. He spent most of his time alone in his room, writing and editing his blogs and preparing material for another TED talk around the corner. His only interactions with his family was during meal times.

Seeing him in a brooding mood, Manik proposed that they should go around to the Ganga ghats in the evening, like old times, and eat salted peanuts and lemon tea. Abir went with him, and they sat silently, his sights on the opposite side of the river as if seeking Shyamoli's silhouette, which he remembered vividly from their chanced meeting a few days back.

"Why, it's my empathy engineer friend."

Abir turned around reluctantly to find Aniruddha sitting on a bench in the stall. Abir nodded as Aniruddha came and sat on a bench opposite them.

"I read your latest blog. You seem to mention me."

Abir shrugged, looking away, taking a sip from his pitcher.

"I am sorry I appeared to be angry" continued Aniruddha, ignoring Abir's reluctance to engage in a conversation with him. "I did not realize it, but saw your note and realized that I might have been a bit rough."

"That's OK," said Abir politely, looking around for a trash bin to throw his pitcher away.

"Is he your friend?" asked Aniruddha, looking at Manik with distaste, who had stopped listening to his headphones and had come near them, his hands folded.

"He's my brother," said Abir coldly.

"Oh, I see," said Aniruddha, turning around and asking for another pitcher of tea and lighting a cigarette. It was going to be evening soon, and like every evening, the birds had started their vociferous journey back to their nests.

"You know, we never got to talk that evening, but Shyamoli was also in the USA some years back—remember that young woman I introduced you to? I told her about you—that you stay in Silicon Valley and all that. It looks like both of you were in California around the same time."

Abir did not reply. Instead, he got up from the bench to pay for the tea for Manik and him.

"Do you know her personally?"

Abir turned around swiftly to see Aniruddha standing behind him, casually taking out his purse to pay the tea stall owner, but his eyes intently on him.

"I do," said Abir quietly.

Aniruddha paid the tea stall owner silently. Manik came and stood beside Abir, his eyes on Aniruddha.

"How well do you know each other?" asked Aniruddha, turning around and folding his arms.

"How does it matter to you?" asked Abir.

"It does matter," said Aniruddha, now very close to Abir, with a hint of a glare in his eyes, his stance menacing. Manik instinctively came between Aniruddha and Abir, and the air was suddenly belligerent.

Abir felt anger build up inside, and his mind training quickly made him realize that he needed to neutralize the situation by simply avoiding it. Turning to Manik, he beckoned him to follow him as he went out of the tea stall. He could feel Aniruddha staring after him, his expression indecipherable, as he and Manik walked toward the rickshaw stand.

"The third stranger that you mentioned in your blog—that was Shyamoli, wasn't it?" Aniruddha called after him, following him. Abir did not respond and continued walking.

"Did you happen to talk to Shyamoli that day after our boat ride?" asked Aniruddha, catching up with them by running a bit, panting slightly with the effort. Abir stopped and turned to him.

"Yes, Aniruddha. Why are you asking?"

"Shyamoli is very happy with her life. It's best you don't come again near her—*ever*—and interfere with her happiness," said Aniruddha, glaring at him.

Abir raked his mind to find an appropriate answer to this rather extraordinary claim. How did *he* interfere with her happiness at all? Shouldn't it be the other way around? She was the one who parted ways, not him. She was the one who called her that day after the ferry ride, not him.

It all seemed wrong. The data was misleading. The inference was wrong.

"For your information, *she* was the one who called me, not the other way around," Abir said, quivering with distress all of a sudden. "And anyway, why am I even talking to you about my personal life? You and Shyamoli are together now, so be happy! Why do you care now? Goodbye."

Aniruddha looked at him, his expression indecipherable. Abir boarded a rickshaw and asked Manik to hop on along with him.

"Brother, do you want me to go and break this bastard's nose?" asked Manik, his hands clenched, looking back and glaring at Aniruddha, as the rickshaw started ambling its way over the bumpy roads, away from the ghats. Aniruddha stood there at a distance, looking after them, his silhouette standing out in the distance against the setting sun.

Abir stared darkly at the road ahead as the rickshaw made its way slowly on the bumpy road. Why did he have to bump into Shyamoli, of all people? With her call that day, everything had changed. Like the first time that he had seen her, back in the USA, years back, when she was staying with her uncle. Everything changed when he had first seen her then, and like that, everything changed when she left him. Over the last four years, he had come to terms that they were not to be together again, and then this entire episode occurred, which was turning out to be more than just a chance encounter.

When he returned home that evening, he made up his mind.

There needed to be a closure to all this. For good. He could not linger in his past and let his life fade away in uncertainty. Shyamoli had moved on, and there was no point lingering on to the inevitable. He needed to move on too.

The only regret he had was that there was no formal closure to the end of their relationship. A deep regret that perhaps she would always think of him as that spineless coward who could not defend her when she needed it the most.

He had to live with it for the rest of his life.

That evening, over dinner, Abir told his parents that he was ready to go ahead and marry Riya if she had not rejected him already, and that too, as soon as possible.

A formal meet

Abir sat at the rear seat of his family car, lost in thoughts. He was on his way to Riya's home, to meet her at her parents' resident, along with his parents, as a formal initiation to their would-be reunion. His boss at work had allowed him to extend his stay by two weeks.

There was general rejoicing in the air, and his mother finally seemed to be elated. She and Father chatted happily about the last time they came to the city together, their little family of three.

When Abir had told them his decision over dinner, they had been initially stunned, but soon after, there had been frantic phone calls between Riya's parents and between Abir's mother. Abir got the impression that they had been talking all the while as if they knew he would make up his mind in their favor and that it was just taking a bit of time.

His mother had summoned Rimjhim and her family to tell them the news. Rimjhim had already started making plans for the dresses she wanted to wear for the wedding. The dresses had to be very different, of course. There would be one set of matching dresses for the engagement ceremony. Then there would be another matching set for the wedding ceremony at Riya's place. Then, of course, there was the reception done by Abir's parents.

Rimjhim's parents had lots of opinions about how the marriage reception invitation card should look like, what food should be catered on the day of the reception, and other details. Rimjhim had proposed that Abir should ride a horse, like how the north Indian grooms went to the bride's place. And that was not new to Kolkata either, she said breathlessly. Why, only that other day, her friend's sister's BFF's would-be husband had come on a horse. That, too, a white one.

Riya's home was a large pink house in Jodhpur Park, one of the most upscale and posh locations of Kolkata. A formidable wrought iron gate, with pillars marking the number and name of the owner of the house, marked the entrance. A "beware of dogs" sign hung prominently on the gate. Abir and his parents waited outside the gate after ringing the bell a couple of times, as the angry sounds of a barking dog came from the house. Eventually, a man-servant came to fetch them and asked them to sit in a large room with splendid decor and sheen and wait on Riya's parents to appear.

Riya's parents appeared after some time and made a great fuss of Abir and his parents. They asked him all about the USA, about Silicon Valley, about the stock prices of his company. Riya's father talked about their various trips around the planet and how Riya grew up in front of their eyes, from a little girl to a young woman with personality and attitude. When Abir's mother finally asked where she was anyways, her father said she was out for a tennis match with her friends and would return shortly.

Riya eventually appeared when her parents had started coaxing Abir and his parents to start lunch. Clad in shorts and t-shirt tennis dress, she jumped onto the many sofas in the drawing room, waving hello to Abir's parents. His mother was elated on seeing her and started asking her how her tennis match went, where she went to play, and how long she has been playing.

After lunch, Riya's father suggested that Riya and Abir go around exploring their bungalow and the terrace while the elders caught up. Riya took Abir to the garden on the roof on the third floor, showing her room on the way, adorned with plush toys and pink decor throughout. The terrace overlooked other homes nearby, each competing with the other in their size and opulence. The neighborhood trees and the canopy on the adjacent roads made a pleasing contrast to the brick and mortar homes.

"When are you leaving for the States?" asked Riya.

"In two weeks."

"Did you find your way through the crowded train that day?" she asked, sitting on a canopied chair and table set on the terrace and beckoning him to have a seat. "I hate those trains. Always crowded. And the vendors are such a nuisance!"

Abir remained silent, wondering whether to mention to her that it was precisely due to the vendors and their delightful assortments of snacks that made him savor the train journeys. He decided not to say it, in reverence to her views.

"Have you been to these local trains recently?" he ventured to ask instead.

"Only once. It was a nightmare! Those sweaty, low-class people sitting next to me made me want to throw up. And the vendors are the worse. Even my driver does not like to take these local trains."

Abir was not sure how to react to this. Was it an insult to him that he preferred these trains? Was Riya displaying extreme arrogance? Or had Riya been unlucky to board a local train on a particularly rough day with sweltering heat and overcrowded compartments? His trained mind selected the last option: that she just might have had a bad day on the train. He decided not to pursue this topic and hunted around in his mind for another subject to converse on.

"Do you have a lot of friends in the USA?" asked Riya, putting on her Prada sunglasses.

"Yes, there are a few. One of my best friends there was a room-mate when I was staying in an apartment complex. He married last year, and I have moved on since."

"You told me last time we met that you bought a house in the heart of Silicon Valley. Where is it?" asked Riya.

"It's in Sunnyvale," said Abir.

"How big is it?" she persisted. "How many stories?"

"It's a twelve-hundred square foot single-story house with a small backyard."

"That's small! Do you know, my dad's house here is around five thousand square feet?"

Abir did not have an answer to that. He reasoned that since she was used to staying in a mansion, a twelve hundred square foot home would indeed be a small one. Real estate was expensive in the San Francisco Bay Area. His house had cost him close to a million dollars—an astonishing price for a very modest home. He could have told Riya that, but his practiced mind made him overlook the tone and color of her statement.

"I had a few questions for you," said Riya. She got up abruptly and gestured him to do so too. "Come, let's go to my room. It's too hot here."

Abir followed her downstairs through the winding stairs, wondering what questions she had. A little while back, he had only glimpsed at her room. This time, he could take note of the plushness of the large room, its decor, the many panels, and pictures, soft toys littered carelessly on her bed. The theme was dramatically pink: pink walls, darker shades of pink curtains, even the door having a pink tinge. He sat on a pink chair in her pink room, as she sat on the bed, her feet crossed, hugging a pink heart-shaped pillow.

"OK, here's my question. Do you have a girlfriend?" she asked abruptly. "OK, that's not a nice question, I guess. Did you have a girlfriend ever?"

"Yes," he said quietly.

"Oh, I see," said Riya, "Does she live in the USA?"

Abir shook his head.

"Do you still think about her?"

Did he think about her? Abir mulled this question over. He and Shyamoli had met every day when they had been together, talking on the phone for hours. She had engulfed his thoughts, his mind, his existence. Even though she was not with him anymore, her essence reverberated with him often, even four years after she had rejected him. In these four years, he had never looked at a woman ever since, fearing that he would be rejected anyway. True, she had found a closure and had moved on, but, in his mind, he still had not seen a closure, a legitimate finality to officially end it all. Riya's question was a legitimate one, he reasoned to himself, and of course, she had every right to ask him this question. It dismayed him to think that just when he was coming to terms that Shyamoli was not in his life anymore, he had bumped into her. After that instance, her memories were fresh in his mind.

He looked into Riya's questioning eyes and realized that at this stage when he was setting his life with another woman, he had to give his full concentration on her. He had to train his mind even harder to forget Shyamoli and concentrate on the present and the immediate future.

He shook his head in denial, perhaps a bit too vigorously, but it seemed to satisfy Riya for the moment. At least, she did not pursue the topic, but sat in silence, as if pondering the next interview questions that she had prepared for him. She surveyed him, twirling a key ring as if deciding what other angles to pursue. Abir felt a bit anxious but decided to stay put.

"What typical bad habits do you have?" she said eventually after a long pause, putting down the key ring and sitting cross-legged on the bed. "Let's see now. Do you smoke?"

Abir shook his head again, his thought instinctively going to Aniruddha and how the entire saga of getting to see Shyamoli started off with him, asking for a cigarette lighter from him. It was only a few days back, yet it seemed as if it was ages since the entire episode of seeing him with Shyamoli happened. Maybe he rehearsed and reanalyzed the scene so many times that it had etched into his mind like an old but powerful memory.

"Well, I smoke," Riya said casually. She got up and closed the door more firmly. Abir felt uncomfortable to be inside with her, alone, with the door all closed. Wondering what her motive was, or what she wanted to ask in such confidentiality, he waited anxiously, waiting for further interrogation, sitting on the edge of the chair.

"Look, I don't know why mom and dad are trying to make this match, but frankly, I am not your typical wife material, if you know what I mean," she said, bringing out a packet of cigarettes, and lighting one up, surveying him from within the smoke.

Abir did not reply, but looked on, waiting to hear more.

"You look like a quintessential boring vanilla typical Bengali mama's boy. You don't look like a person who likes adventures, or has any demands, or any views or opinions for that matter. So, if you are looking for a good little wifey, I am not the one."

Abir remained silent, feeling even more anxious than before.

"I am a frank person, and I appreciate frankness too. So very frankly, you look even older than you are, and a bit too serious, as if you have the world's burden on you!"

Abir half smiled at her, thinking in his mind that her observations were indeed entirely accurate. That's what Dadu, Manik, Rimjhim, and others said about him these days.

"And are you always so uncommunicative and boring?" she asked, irritation in her voice.

Abir smiled at her candidness but remained silent.

"Does my smoking bother you?" she asked again after a pause as if wanting to engage him in a conversation. Abir shook his head, suppressing a cough, as he always did in the presence of cigarette smoke. She continued surveying him as if thinking of further revelations.

"OK, one more thing. I have had lots of men friends in my life. I had a few romantic involvements too. I don't have one now so that you know. After marriage, I will continue to have men friends and will go out with them once in a while."

Abir nodded politely to convey that this was perfectly fine with him.

"I am a travel freak," continued Riya, blowing rings of smoke. "I might go off on my own, or with some guys, to travel around in the USA. You can join me if you are free, of course. Do you have any issues with that?"

Abir shook his head, and Riya continued her terms.

"I am working right now, and after we are married, I expect to continue working. I hope to get a job in Silicon Valley."

"Riya, your first priority should be your career," said Abir quietly.

"Excuse me?" asked Riya, as if surprised that Abir had a comment or an opinion finally.

Abir looked at her silently. He wondered why she was getting married at all, that too, to a boring vanilla man like him, in her own words. She had her career, had lots of men friends as she mentioned, and looked happy and content staying in Kolkata. Why did she want to marry him anyway and move to the States? That too, with somebody whom she did not know at all, when obviously she had many other options? It did not seem to make sense to him.

"I like to travel around the world too. Once in a while, I would like to go on world tours as a couple," continued Riya, throwing cigarette ash into a makeshift ashtray out of a Coke can. "My mom and dad have gone to most major places in the world: Paris, London, Rome, Sydney and all, and I have always accompanied them. I would expect to continue going to these places during our anniversaries, birthdays, and other occasions."

"Certainly," Abir said politely. "Whenever and wherever you wish."

Riya finished her cigarette, drowned it in the bathroom flush, and sprayed some perfume in her room. Beckoning to Abir that his interview was over, she went out of the room and downstairs to meet the rest of the family, with Abir tagging along behind her.

* * *

"What a lovely girl" gushed Abir's mother as they made their way back in the evening to the suburbs. "Such a significant and influential family. Such a large home. And she is fair like milk—looks like Goddess Saraswati."

Father nodded in agreement. "She did not change from her shorts," he added, as an afterthought.

"Yes, I noticed that too," said Mother, frowning. "But she came from a tennis match. I would not expect her to change into a formal Indian dress immediately after that. How lovely she looked in her shorts. Like a royal, glowing white swan."

Abir looked absently out of the car door, hardly listening to them. It was dusk. The posh and canopied streets were behind them now. Somewhere along the road, in the northern and older part of Kolkata, he would pass by where Shyamoli's house was.

As they turned a road, a sharp pang went through him. He remembered that this was the turn that led to Shyamoli's home. He looked at the narrow gully that would lead him to her place. When he had gone to visit her last time, four years back, she had waited demurely for his family, adorning her beautiful saree, her face flushed with the excitement of seeing him again. His eyes blurred with the pain of it. He could hardly suppress his yearning to just stop the car and run down the narrow gully, to go to her home, and ask her for the last time why she cut him to pieces that day.

He closed his eyes, determined to wipe that memory from his mind and not to think of the incredible cruelty dealt to him by Shyamoli. He had to move on, fast, before life engulfed him and took him to a place of no return.

"Can we get the engagement ceremony done as soon as possible?" he said quietly from the back seat, ignoring his mother cast a happy glance at his father. "I need to get back to work."

* * *

Abir went to the city again two days later to meet with another potential client who would possibly hop on his platform. Mother insisted that he called on Riya on the way back and have dinner with her parents in their home, and obedient to her wishes as always, he called Riya to meet up.

After finishing the meeting with his client, Abir waited patiently in the hot afternoon sun at the Shyambazar five heads point, looking out for Riya to show up. He had told her that he could find his way to their place himself, but Riya's mother had wanted Riya to pick him up, and he had conceded to her wishes respectfully.

Riya appeared in some time in her white BMW, driving herself, and opened the door for him to the passenger side. Abir hopped in beside her.

"Let's go somewhere before going home. Where do you want to go?" Riya asked.

"Anywhere you want," he said politely.

"You don't ever have a choice or opinion, do you?" she said, frowning, pushing the accelerator pedal hard to make her car surge forward. "You know, I am meeting you all because mom wanted me to pick you up and take you over to our place for dinner. I was swimming in my club swimming pool. Because of you, I didn't even have the time to properly dry my hair!"

"I am sorry," said Abir, concerned. "Really, I could have come over myself to your place in the evening."

"No, it's OK. You don't have to be so damned polite and agreeable all the time," Riya said irritably. "Anyways, let's go to the nearest shopping mall and have coffee in the food court. It's too hot outside, and it's hours before it's time for dinner."

Abir looked at the sweetshops and street food vendors as they ambled along the busy Kolkata roads. He always tried street food whenever he was in the city and was especially partial to *phuchka* and egg rolls. He wished they had tried some street food but was sure Riya would be alarmed at the thought of eating from these roadside food stalls. He did not judge her for this. It was her upbringing, her choice, and indeed, there was a tinge of unhealthiness to these stalls. Of course, for him, it was different, but for this moment, what he thought of did not matter.

As he looked at the busy road ahead, with Riya driving impatiently, navigating the unpredictable Kolkata traffic, he felt that he was doing a poor service to this woman, to whom he would be engaged in a few days, by being mundane, uninteresting, and bordering on being unattractive in every possible way. He did not want to be like this, but somehow, in the last four years, he had found it difficult to talk to anybody. She was being candid, honest, and upfront all the time, and was prepared to be with him for life, and certainly did not deserve his weak vanilla presence.

As they stopped at a traffic signal, a small thin street urchin ambled up to them with a bunch of roses to sell. Abir reacted automatically, as he always did when he saw these child vendors. He noticed the sweat gleaming on the little boy's forehead. Should he be not playing with his friends, instead of selling fares to make a living for his family? As always, he felt a sharp pang of pity when he saw the little boy, and instinctively, he rolled open the car window glass. He beckoned the boy to come near their car and bought some roses from him. As always, he tipped the small urchin significantly more than the price of the roses, smiling automatically at his delighted toothless grin.

"Why did you overpay him so much?" demanded Riya, as Abir rolled up the car window glass.

"I always tip off street vendors. You asked me about my bad habits. Here is one," said Abir, smiling at her indignance. The roses still had thorns on the stems. He gingerly plucked them off with his nails, and turning to Riya, he gave them to her, feeling somewhat uncertain, while she waited for the light to go green.

He felt slightly anxious giving her the flowers; would she accept it? Or would she just discard it as a mundane behavior from a plain vanilla boring man?

"Oh, thank you," Riya said, looking at him in surprise. She put the flowers carefully on her lap and continued driving.

* * *

Riya was rather quiet in the shopping mall coffee shop. As he paid for her coffee, she turned to him and asked: "I read your blogs last night."

Abir nodded at her, his eyebrows raised quizzically, and asked: "And?"

"You seemed to mention me indirectly," she continued. "Looks like I was asking too many questions about you that day."

"Oh, not at all!" he said, then added, after a pause, "Are you OK with the blog? If not, I can remove or edit the blog if you want."

"No, I think it's fine. Seriously, you don't have to be so agreeable all the time," Riya said, almost snapping at him. They sat on a booth, facing each other. Abir sipped his cold coffee, waiting for her to say something.

"I read your other blogs too," she said after a pause. "But did not understand some of it. You talked about empathy for nature; how does one even show empathy for an inanimate, non-living thing, like a river, for instance?"

"By not polluting it, not throwing trash in it, by protecting it," said Abir quietly, his mind going to a few days back, at how Aniruddha had thrown all his cigarette stubs casually into the river without

164

a care in the world. How many countless such stubs he might have thrown over these years, he wondered.

Riya looked at him, uncharacteristically quiet, as if waiting for him to say more.

"Every entity that we interact with needs our empathy and kindness, whether it's a living entity, or an inanimate part of nature," he continued. "It's a simple concept to sustain the cycle of life. If I pollute the river, the water creatures suffer, and so do other parts of nature which are associated with the river. The entire ecosystem becomes imbalanced, which leads to abnormal climate change and other phenomena over time. One small act of empathy for nature, by one person, can go a long way to create and spread the message to preserve this world and its cycle of life."

"Hmm, I see," said Riya thoughtfully. She kept silent for some time, stirring the coffee, looking down at the cup. Abir surveyed her calmly, wondering what she was thinking of.

"You also mentioned two more people in your latest blog, whom you apparently met on the same day," she said eventually, weighing her words carefully. "How did their reference come in?"

"Yes, I met this young man on my way back home after meeting you. He seemed particularly sharp with me. If this had happened a few years back, I would have felt upset or angry at his provocations, but now I always question the deeper issue, rather than the symptoms."

"What symptoms?" asked Riya, interested.

"His getting angry at me was a symptom of something deeper," said Abir. "I try to be mindful in these situations and follow the empathy algorithm that I mentioned in my blog. For this particular person, I tried to put myself in his shoes, trying to understand why one would behave like that even with a stranger. I think I might know the issue, so I let it pass. Does it make sense?"

"You suddenly sound very communicative!" said Riya. "I can now see that you just need to get turned on in a particular way!"

Abir smiled at her candidness, and Riya smiled back at him, looking at him in his eyes. Her hazelnut eyes cringed when she smiled. He realized that she was surprisingly attractive in her own ways, something which he had never noticed hitherto. His thoughts had always been on Shyamoli, on her eyes, her hair, her face, her lips, the way she talked, her graceful body movement—everything about her. He had not looked at any other woman's physical attractiveness ever since those four years back when she had rejected him. Instead, he had automatically concentrated on their persona and intelligence during any interactions that he had. It was a convenient and well-appreciated behavior and outlook, especially for his female acquaintances. His polite disinterest in a woman's natural look, but noting their intelligence and persona, had created quite a flutter among the women he had interacted within these past years.

With Riya too, it was no different. He had taken an impassive, respectful, and pragmatic approach to this entire episode. Nevertheless, he did realize that she was indeed attractive. He looked straight into her eyes, and she smiled back, suddenly looking confused.

"What are you looking at?" she asked, her tone playful, as she put her sunglasses on her head and played with her hair to tuck them behind her ears.

"I never noticed that you had hazelnut-colored eyes," Abir said simply. "You have beautiful eyes, Riya. If I were a painter, I would focus on your eyes first to start painting you."

Riya seemed pleased to hear this and embarrassed at the same time. She dropped her eyes and stirred her drink vigorously, pretending to concentrate on it, as Abir continued surveying her. He felt she had something more to say about the blog, and he had an inkling what that would be but waited for Riya to start it.

"About the third person," said Riya eventually. "Can I hazard a guess that it was your ex-girlfriend?"

Abir sighed and concentrated on his drink, thinking of how to respond to this. His inkling was indeed right—that she would eventually get on to this topic. It certainly seemed to make sense that Riya would prod on it. He remembered his first meeting with Shyamoli, when they had played an involuntary guessing game, trying to learn about each other through deductions. That was six years ago, but it seemed like yesterday. His interactions with Riya reminded him of that night in Arun uncle's backyard when he had met Shyamoli for the first time.

"Yes," said Abir eventually.

Riya seemed prepared to ask more questions, but for some reason, decided not too. Abir did not want to discuss this either. It was one thing to write an obscure blog for his fans, which focused more on the mind training and thinking pattern, but quite another thing to discuss the actual people, especially when talking about his ex with his current woman friend.

"So this girl lets you go despite all your empathy and mindfulness?" asked Riya after a long silence.

Abir did not reply.

"What's her name?" she continued.

"Shyamoli."

"Shyamoli means dark-skinned, right?" asked Riya.

Abir cringed at this, as he had done on a few occasions when somebody else had pointed it out, but decided to ignore her views.

They finished their drinks in silence and were about to leave when he felt a tap on his shoulder.

He turned around to find Aniruddha standing behind him, a slightly sheepish smile on his face.

* * *

"Hello, here is my empathy engineer friend again."

Abir stiffened. What was the probability that they met again, away from the suburbs, at this odd hour, in this very shopping mall? It looked almost as if they were following each other around. There had to be some strange unseen connection to all this, a contrived plan by the almighty to prolong his misery by making him bump into people who reminded him that Shyamoli was not in his life anymore. Or was Aniruddha following him, knowing his whereabouts by some mysterious cosmic connections?

Aniruddha seemed to read his mind too.

"This is three times in a row in a few days that we are meeting. It seems like this is destined, don't you think?" said Aniruddha.

Abir kept his seat and looked on coldly at Aniruddha.

"I wanted to apologize about the other day," continued Aniruddha, standing over Abir, still holding the sheepish grin, ignoring Riya. Abir looked up to him and nodded unsmiling, hoping he would just leave.

"What apology?" asked Riya. "Abir, is this a friend of yours?"

Abir did not reply. Aniruddha took off his glasses and polished them with his kurta, as if pondering whether to re-start their conversation. Abir shuffled uncomfortably, wondering if he would make an excuse and get out of this situation. This was the last place where he wanted to start a conversation with this acerbic young man. Things seemed to be going fine with Riya, and Abir was coming slowly to terms that he would move on with her. He did not see any reason why Aniruddha should continue to interfere and interact with him.

"Can I talk to you in private?" Aniruddha asked Abir, putting on his glasses and looking at him solemnly.

Riya flared up at once.

"What's so private? What do you want to share that cannot be shared in front of me? Why don't you just tell him here?" she said rudely.

"Sorry, it needs to be private," said Aniruddha dryly, walking toward the cafe door and beckoning Abir to follow. Abir rose and got up reluctantly to follow him outside the cafe, as Riya looked after them, mystified.

* * *

"Look, I wanted to apologize about the other day," began Aniruddha.

"Yes, you told me that already," said Abir, wondering what all this was about.

"I told Shyamoli about our little altercation that day, and she is really angry with me. She says she won't talk to me unless and until I apologized to you for saying that you need to get out of her life."

"Oh," said Abir, stunned, his heart hammering suddenly.

"Shyamoli gave me your USA phone number to call you up, and I had meant to, but I saw you enter this shopping mall with your—what is it now—your fiancée? Girlfriend? Whatever! I saw you enter this mall with this female, and I thought I might as well take this opportunity to talk to you directly instead of calling you."

Abir nodded, his mind in a curious turmoil on hearing that Shyamoli had known about their little altercation. What did she think of him? Did he do anything wrong once again?

"Anyways, I hope you don't have any hard feelings," continued Aniruddha. "I realize that I don't really know your background with Shyamoli. But I think I should also tell you that, after she saw you that day, she seems particularly unhappy and dejected. She mentioned briefly that she knew you, and somehow I put two and two together and figured out that you were the reason for her anxiety. I was rude to you precisely for that reason. Anyways, have a good day."

Aniruddha turned to leave, and as he started walking away, Abir called out, "Does Shyamoli continue to work with the NGOs that Biren sir used to work with?"

Aniruddha looked surprised.

"You knew Biren sir?" he asked curiously. "How did you even know him? You stay in the USA, right? How well did you know Biren sir?"

Abir pondered over this question silently. He wished he could tell Aniruddha about the hours of discussions that Biren sir had had with him four years back, with Shyamoli on his side. The thought made him smile.

"I used to know Biren sir very well, Aniruddha," Abir said quietly. "In fact, if you must know, I had talked to him over video chat even the night before he died."

Aniruddha took his time to digest this information, taking off his glasses, polishing them, and putting them on in his trademark style.

"You didn't answer my question, Aniruddha," continued Abir. "Does Shyamoli still work in those NGOs?"

"Well, maybe she does," said Aniruddha evasively. "And even if she does, or does not, why should I tell you her whereabouts? So that you can now go and stalk her? I told you before, she is happy. Very happy doing her work, leading a normal life. Don't you go around following her and make her miserable again, increase her anxiety."

"I am not following her, Aniruddha," said Abir patiently. "It was a chance encounter with you and her at the river dock. As it is with you and me today, as you admit. Why would I follow her around? Why would I make her unhappy?"

"Well, she seems very withdrawn and anxious these few days since she had that telephone conversation with you," said Aniruddha frowning. "Did you tell her anything nasty on the phone?"

"No, we just said hello on the phone," said Abir, suddenly feeling low. Why was Shyamoli feeling anxious? Did he inadvertently send across a negative vibe in his inability to talk to her over the phone? What wrong did he do again? She had rejected him years back. Why did she call again? What did she expect of him?

"Well, anyway," continued Aniruddha. "Can I tell her that I met you and that you accepted my apology?"

"Yes," said Abir, feeling dejected. "But you still did not answer me about whether she works in that NGO."

"Like I said, I don't want her to see you and become anxious again," said Aniruddha.

"I am not sure why keep on harping this, Aniruddha," said Abir wearily. "I can understand you are protective over her because you guys are a couple. But you should also hear the other side of the stories. Did you read my blog at all?"

"What the heck do you mean we are a couple?" said Aniruddha angrily. "Shyamoli and I are merely friends! You see Shyamoli with another man, and you assume automatically that she has moved on romantically? You talk about data all the time—this time, you got the data all wrong!"

Abir stared at him at a complete loss of words.

"And yes, you are right. I am protective about Shyamoli," continued Aniruddha. "I have been Biren sir's student, and from that angle, it's my best interest to be protective about Biren sir's daughter. But not everything relationship need to be romantic! And speaking of Shyamoli, from what I can make out, you should not be seen around near her at any time. Your very presence seems to make her upset and distressed, and I cannot stand it."

Abir's trained mind automatically filtered out all the negativity and accusation in Aniruddha's words and concentrated only on the information. The fact that Aniruddha and Shyamoli were friends, and not really a couple, should not have mattered to him, yet he felt slightly troubled to find that this piece of information gave him enormous relief.

"Look," continued Abir patiently, "I admit I did not have data about you, but that is beyond the point here. Also, I apologize for thinking that you and Shyamoli are romantically involved. And I understand your protectiveness about her, but you, on the other hand, should have all the data too. If you must know, she decided to part ways with me, not the other way around. Now you are telling me she is getting distressed after seeing me. What does this even mean? Don't you think the lines of accusations are one-sided? Seriously, I really think you should read my blogs in more detail, Aniruddha! You are making assumptions based on half-baked data. You said Shyamoli is feeling anxious after seeing me that day. Does it automatically mean that I am the one to be questioned, to be blamed?"

"Well, at least you should worry about the fact that she is feeling anxious after meeting you!" said Aniruddha sarcastically.

"Well, I do worry!" said Abir. He felt annoyed all of a sudden, and despite his years of training, he felt he could not bring himself to pursue his angle of empathy. "I really need to talk to her to take this burden off each other, to make it all clear, but you won't tell me her whereabouts! And you know very well that I cannot simply barge into her house full of people just like that!"

He paused and passed his hands over his forehead. These days, it always hurt him when he felt especially agitated. His practiced mind wanted to calm him, but somehow, for once, he could not let an algorithm of mind activities take over his feelings. Aniruddha looked at him solemnly, as if thinking out an appropriate angle to pursue to resolve this dispute.

"I think she is looking for closure," said Aniruddha quietly, deviating from his usual aggressive countenance. "If you ever cared for her, you should make it an amicable closure for her so that she does not feel dejected at your presence or at the thought of you. Maybe that's why she called you that day. But I think you did not give her a chance to make that closure. I think she feels wronged."

Abir suddenly felt himself growing angry, and despite his years of training, he could not control the rage that built up in his mind slowly. He felt it was incredibly unfair that, like always, he was the one to be scrutinized, to be questioned.

"Aniruddha, tell your precious Shyamoli to stop and think, for once," Abir said after a pause, his voice starting to tremble with distress. "Tell her to get the idea of being wronged out of her head. If you get a chance, remind her of Arun uncle's home, the night in the backyard, when I had seen nothing in the world like her eyes. Remind her, Aniruddha, of all the hopeless words of love and endearment that I reserved for her. Remind her, Aniruddha, of the nights when we held hands under the sky, where nothing existed except the feeling of her, me, and us. Tell her that she may have found me unworthy, but I can vouchsafe that if there was anybody who felt for her, who truly understood her, who would have held her hands and protect her, like hands on the softest petals of flowers, it was, and always will be, me. Also, tell her, Aniruddha, as much as she might hate me, she needs to understand herself better than she tried to understand my type because I did nothing wrong. Absolutely nothing! The only wrong that I did was thinking with my heart and fall hopelessly in love, which is the worst decision one can make in one's life. Aniruddha, tell your precious Shyamoli to get over her ego, her sense of being wronged. Tell her, nobody did any wrong to her. Tell her to get a life, move on, get married, have kids, and get on with her life, and let me go. Tell her to release me from her image, so that I can move on in peace, and so can she. And Aniruddha, please do remind your Shyamoli that she is a person of intellect and remind her that data is important. Tell her to look at the damned data, past and present, extrapolate correctly, verify facts, and then come to a damned conclusion logically. If she knew me at all, she would have stopped to think twice before getting distressed in my presence."

Abir felt his face go hot and red with rage. Aniruddha stayed put in his spot, and for once, he looked shocked at Abir's intensity. Abir stood tall over him, his six feet seemed to loom over powerfully, and Aniruddha shrank back instinctively, looking suddenly scared.

Abir stared back at him, his trained mind gradually forcing him to let go of his rage and utter dejection at the brutality of the opinions. Slowly, he breathed more relaxed and forced his mind to calm down.

After all, Aniruddha was merely reacting to what he believed was right.

Nobody looked at the data.

Nobody verified the data.

They believed it blindly, for whatever reasons, and made conclusions. Aniruddha was not to blame.

Abir realized that his algorithms on empathy were still limited to his own practices. It would take a lot of time for people to truly understand the meaning of looking at data, look at both sides, and come to a conclusion.

In a little while, he could make his mind regain the calm that he had trained himself to feel in all adverse situations. He patted Aniruddha kindly on his shoulders.

"You are a good friend to Shyamoli, Aniruddha. Stick by her side. Let no harm come to her. Also, tell her not to worry. I think it's all fine between us. She can get along with her life happily," he said. Then he turned around to leave Aniruddha there, to go back to the coffee shop, back to the woman with whom he was to spend the rest of his life.

As he was about to enter the coffee shop, he felt a hand on his shoulder. He turned around, feeling tired and fatigued. It was Aniruddha, his expression oddly exalted with reverence for Abir, whom he seemed to see in a new light.

"I have a question for you," Aniruddha said. Abir nodded, unable to speak. All the intensity had suddenly drained him of his energy, and he felt he needed a rest.

"Am I to hazard a guess that the woman you are with is your fiancée?" asked Aniruddha.

Abir shook his head.

"OK, a soon to be fiancée?" persisted Aniruddha. Abir nodded.

"I wanted to give you the answer to your question before I leave. Yes, Shyamoli still works at that NGO. She will be there today in an hour. Here is the address. It's not too far from here. And here is her phone number" he said, handing him a torn piece of paper, casting a contemptuous glance at Riya, who was busy putting on thick dark red lipstick voluminously on her lips, looking at herself in a small pocket mirror and making pouty faces to see her lips more clearly. "I have no reservations over you going over to meet her. After all, you were good friends once, and you have every right to seek a formal closure to all this so that there are no bad feelings anymore. Go and meet her today and get it all cleared. It will be beneficial for both of you in the long run and help you guys move on amicably."

Abir stared at the piece of parchment on which Aniruddha had hurriedly written an address and a phone number. He stood for some time, staring at the address, then went inside, feeling fatigued, as Aniruddha turned and left.

Yes, he had to meet Shyamoli one last time to seek out a formal, amicable closure. Also, most importantly, he needed to make sure that she was happy and that there was no more bitterness between them.

Closure

Abir stood in front of an iron gate, his heart beating fast. A grassless lawn and a yellow two-story old building stood beyond the gate. He paused for a bit before entering the gate. He was not entirely new to this place. Four years back, he had made video conference calls with Shyamoli's father, who also used to come here to teach on the weekends. He had a mental vision of how the complex would look like, given the descriptions by Biren sir. It looked exactly as he had imagined in his mind, given Biren sir's descriptions.

Riya had dropped him off at the gate, driving over straight from the shopping mall, promising to pick him up in two hours after getting a facial. As he waved her goodbye, he felt oddly relaxed, at the prospect that he could finally have a conversation with Shyamoli, to find a closure to the relationship that had haunted him for the last four years. He hoped that he could perhaps end on a friendlier note. But most importantly, he hoped that Shyamoli was doing fine.

Abir closed his eyes and calmed his mind, drawing from the years of mind training, which had let him be relaxed in different situations. Then he entered the building and took the dark stairs to go upstairs, remembering that Shyamoli's father had mentioned a room with an open window on the second floor; he was sure Shyamoli would be there. He landed on the second floor and heard gentle murmurings of young children talking in a room.

He slowly made his way to the room and looked inside.

Shyamoli was sitting on the floor on a mat, her hair tied in a plastic head cover, wearing a white lab coat. A hoard of unkempt children sat around her, looking eagerly at a small glass beaker that she was holding in her hands. The room was bare of any necessities, and everybody was sitting on the floor.

Even as he watched, the beaker's content changed colors, and the children around clapped enthusiastically, jostling with each other to see the magic of the simple chemical reaction. Abir's face automatically broke into a smile, reflecting that of Shyamoli, who had now joined the kids in their delight, laughing at the childlike and unadulterated joy at seeing something as innocuous as a simple chemical reaction showing changing colors.

As he looked at her, his trained mind automatically subtracted himself from the surrounding, and he felt that he would be intrusive if he appeared at this time to interfere with the happy energy in the room. Surely Shyamoli would not like to see him there, he reasoned to himself, feeling a sudden pang of despair. He realized that he had already found the answer that he had come seeking to these doors. Her laughter, and the light in her eyes, said it all. Shyamoli was happy. Truly happy. She was where she had always wanted to be—in servitude to others who needed it. Perhaps that is what Aniruddha had meant. He had no place beside her anymore. He would only add to her anxiety.

He turned to leave, and at the same time, Shyamoli looked up, and their eyes met. As always, an electric shock seemed to emanate from the surrounding, spreading a shiver through him, and he stayed rooted there as if transfixed. His practiced mind told him to remain calm, to not let his emotions run over his reasons, but for once, he could not control himself. He felt a shiver go through him as years of tender thoughts came floating as strings, to engulf him and his mind. She looked back at him, her hands frozen with the beaker in her hands, her eyes locked with his.

Abir went inside the room silently. The other kids took no notice of him, thinking he was one more volunteer. Shyamoli stared at him in a trance, as Abir stared back at her. After a while, the reality of the surroundings and the kids brought them back to the present. The moment he set eyes on her, all his plans to remain calm, to let his mind take over his heart, became difficult to implement. His senses got dissolved into oblivion by the present, Shyamoli's presence and essence engulfing his mind.

* * *

176

Abir became a silent assistant to Shyamoli as she went through her science demonstration class. There was no escaping now. He was in a strange stupor that he had not felt for years. Not a single word was spoken between them, presumably because it was not the time to say anything. Shyamoli passed on small test tubes to groups of kids, and Abir tagged along with her, automatically making himself invisible as he effortlessly and silently helped her pass on the test tubes, helping her set up the fun little experiment for the kids to perform. As she knelt down to help a group of kids with the science experiment, and as the afternoon sun shone on her face, he dreamed of being with her alone in the universe, for the last time in his life, where he could spend the entire day just watching her face, her big beautiful eyes, seeing the world through her eyes, eyes reflecting the pure unadulterated joys of the happy kids around her.

* * *

"Did you come all the way just to be my assistant?" asked Shyamoli while packing up the science experiment chemicals and other materials into a cardboard box. The experiment was over. Another volunteer had arrived to take the raucous kids to the next event. As the kids lined up to follow the next volunteer downstairs, a few of them came over to hug her, and she returned their hugs. Abir's thoughts automatically traveled six years back, during Durga Puja at Silicon Valley, where Shyamoli was on the side of the stage to help out the kids with their dresses for a stage play. Some kids had come over that day too, just like today, to acknowledge her selfless service.

Abir stood at a distance, unobtrusively, forcing himself to be calm and nonreactive, where, in reality, he felt that this was the end of time, the final days when it would be all over with Shyamoli.

He looked at her, noting her happiness in interacting with the ones who really needed all the kindness, and despite his natural subconscious joy on seeing her, he felt a strange sense of betrayal.

He felt a sudden rush of bitterness, a feeling that he had held back for years: pain at his betrayal by Shyamoli, by his parents, betrayed by the little world which he had clung on too ardently. He had put his heart open, and with that, taken away the protection that one would need in case it bled. It did bleed, and Shyamoli was the reason for it, whether it was her fault, or his, or the circumstance.

He looked on to her happiness and realized that she had indeed moved on, and was truly happy. He realized that everyone he had interacted with was happy. Shyamoli was happy. So were his parents. And Rimjhim. And her parents. And Manik. And Dadu. And Ayan and Srija.

Everybody was happy, except him.

His happiness on seeing her ebbed away from him, like a lush spring which suddenly loses its water during a harsh dreary summer. As Shyamoli turned to wave the final kid out of the room, he closed his eyes to calm himself and, with a supreme effort, collected himself for the moment as Shyamoli turned to him to face him.

* * *

"I had come by to see some clients for my social platform. I recalled Biren sir mention this place, so came along to check it out," Abir lied, hoping to sound convincing and casual enough. Shyamoli looked at him silently, her eyes questioning. He looked around the room, and for the first time, saw a picture of Biren sir on the wall. He had almost overlooked this frame, in his internal turmoil at seeing Shyamoli again. He walked over to the frame, peering at the picture.

"I am glad you are doing such a great work by following Biren sir's dreams," he said, hoping he would not revive old memories or make her sentimental. He was relieved to find her not flinch or react to this statement but merely look on.

"How is your brother doing?" he continued.

"He is studying engineering in Bishnupur."

"Ah, good for him," he said. "Bishnupur is far from this city, so he must be staying in a hostel there I guess?"

Shyamoli nodded silently.

"How is your mother doing?" he continued after a pause.

"She is no more," she said quietly.

"Oh," he said, shocked. "I am sorry. I did not know."

Shyamoli shook her head to convey that it was alright.

"When did this happen?" Abir asked anxiously.

"A year after my father left us," she said. She did not seem dejected at her loss anymore. Her voice sounded toneless as if she had moved past these emotional turmoils—as if the thoughts did not trouble her anymore. Abir felt somewhat relieved that she was past her losses. He sighed and looked down at his hands, feeling dejected.

"I am sorry you went through such a hard time, with your loss," he said, avoiding her eyes. Shyamoli did not reply, and Abir realized that he needed to change the topic to avoid bringing the context back to her past, which would surely make her unhappy.

"The kids really seem to love you," he said in an attempt to change the topic. "Your little experiment was really successful, I think! In general, kids seem to like you."

"Thank you," she said. She stood uncertainly, as if thinking of a continuation of their conversation. "You did not tell me why you came over. Do you need material for your blog?" she asked after a pause.

Abir felt his feeling of dejection overcoming his thoughts once more. Shyamoli's question seemed correct, but there was something about the tone and context that made a sharp pain go through him. He realized, again, that he had made a mistake to come over. Shyamoli had gone over him and moved on—moved on mentally, moved on spiritually, moved on in every possible way.

He realized that he needed a graceful exit plan so that no hard feelings lingered over. At the same time, he felt he had to clear a few questions with Shyamoli.

"Why do you think I came over, Shyamoli?" he asked after a pause, despite realizing that this question was not an answer to her question. She did not reply. Instead, she turned around and started collecting the assorted objects strewn around on the floor to throw them away in the trash can. She turned away from him as if she had suddenly forgotten that he was there. Abir looked on at her silently as she cleared the floor and started packing her bag, still looking away from him.

"I should leave now," he said eventually, feeling his head getting dizzy with the suppressed emotions at Shyamoli's apparent nonchalant. The intense feeling of betrayal and being wronged rose within him again, even as his practiced and trained mind tried to sedate these feelings by methodically trying to subtract himself from his emotions. Did it really matter if Shyamoli appeared nonchalant or not? He methodically subtracted himself from the situation and automatically felt empathetic toward her situation, about her loss of her parents, about her loneliness in this world.

As he turned to leave, Shyamoli turned to look back at him.

"You look tired," she called out. "I should at least be a good host to you. Come, let me buy you some cold drinks before you leave."

* * *

Abir sat on a chair in the cafe a few blocks away from the NGO, as Shyamoli went to the counter and ordered cold drinks. Despite feeling low and dejected, he felt surprisingly relaxed. He sat in silence, looking at his phone as she went to the counter and ordered cold drinks to stave off the scorching late afternoon heat outside. She, too, looked relaxed, as if merely meeting an acquaintance after a long time, with a duty to make him feel comfortable and at ease. He could smell her perfume, which had not changed in these four years. His mind went back to the first day that he had come to know her at her uncle's place. He noticed the t-shirt that she was wearing. This was the t-shirt that she had worn that day. He smiled to himself at the clarity of this memory.

"What are you smiling at?" asked Shyamoli, coming back to the table to wait for the drinks to come.

"You wore this t-shirt the first time you and I met at your uncle's house," he said, surprised to find his own voice so casual despite the emotional low that he felt.

"Yes, indeed," she said. "In fact, you are also wearing the same t-shirt which you had worn that first day. It's a strange coincidence."

Abir looked down at his t-shirt in wonder. Yes, indeed it was the same t-shirt.

"It's my favorite t-shirt, I guess," he said.

"Well, you can say this is my favorite t-shirt, too," she said.

"I see that your perfume has not changed either," he said.

"You remember my perfume?" she asked, sounding surprised.

Abir pondered about this question. It did not make sense to him. Remember her perfume? What did it even mean? He remembered her perfume, all the dresses she wore, how long her hair was, the ornaments she wore, the shades of lipsticks that he had encouraged her to wear. He remembered the colors of the dresses that he had advised her to wear. He remembered the smell of her books. He remembered the color and number of her car, the number of times he had gone around filling air in her car tires, her favorite ice-cream place.

Yes, he remembered everything about her, and her question made no sense to him.

* * *

Abir had his drink in silence, looking down and concentrating, not looking up. Shyamoli sat on the opposite side of the table, sipping her drink.

"How is your work coming along?" she asked eventually to break the silence.

"Oh, it's OK," he said softly, looking up briefly. He resumed sipping his cold drink. They sat for some time, neither of them talking. After a while, he finished his cold drinks and sat looking at his empty bottle. They sat in silence for a while.

"Thanks for the drink," he said eventually. Shyamoli did not reply and looked on to him in silence.

"How is Silicon Valley treating you?" she said eventually, her tone casual. "Are you married yet? Do you have kids?"

Abir wondered what the question meant.

181

Married? Kids?

Somehow these words hit him hard.

He realized once again that Shyamoli had moved on, emotionally and physically, moved on so far from him that she had forgotten him completely. If she remembered what he was like, even for once, she would have thought twice before asking these questions.

Once again, he realized that he should not have listened to Aniruddha and come all the way. He had come all the way to make it all amicable, to bring a logical closure to this so that he could move on, but Shyamoli's distant formality made it difficult for him.

Abir shook his head. He suddenly felt oddly empty despite feeling as low as he had felt in several years.

"I should really leave now, I guess," he muttered. He got up from his chair and made his way to the cafe exit.

"Why did you really come all the way, Abir?" Shyamoli asked, standing up as he tried to open the door to make his way out.

"I came to see you to find closure," he said simply, stopping on the way out and turning to look at her.

"A closure?" asked Shyamoli, her large eyes looking at him, her expression indecipherable. Abir looked at her silently. He was not in a position to discuss or negotiate anything. What did closure mean anyways? He realized that Shyamoli had made the closure four years back. It was him who was seeking closure. Shyamoli's last irresponsible question on his marital status sealed the deal.

He decided that if this was the final ending to a strange saga in his life, he had to do it properly. He came back and sat in front of her, his mind calm, his intentions resolute. Shyamoli sat down again. He felt his head throb with an unknown dark feeling that seemed to surge within him, like a drop of liquid slowly being heated.

"I bumped into Aniruddha in the shopping mall when I went there with my would-be fiancée," he said quietly. "He said he wanted to apologize to me for being rude. He also said that you were feeling dejected after meeting me. So I came over to make things amicable, and to ask you why you got dejected after seeing me."

Shyamoli stared at him silently.

"I am sorry if I inadvertently said or did anything to you," he continued. "I know you called me that day, and I should have talked to you naturally. I could not because I guess I still have some bitterness left in me. It's my problem. You can blame me if you want, but please do not get dejected because of me."

Shyamoli remained silent.

"I came here to get an amicable closure," he continued. "And also to tell you that you should get the idea of getting wronged out of your head."

Shyamoli looked away. Abir looked at her silently, realizing that she somehow still blamed him for what happened.

He decided it was time that he made things straight.

"You said you have been reading my blogs on empathy engineering and mindfulness for a while now, Shyamoli," he said quietly. "Are you sure you have read them properly?"

"Yes, I have," she said.

"Perhaps you did not catch one part of it," he continued calmly. "When I talk about practicing empathy every day, every moment in one's life, in every interaction, I talk about *everybody*. Empathy does not manifest itself as a flow of sympathy from the more privileged to the less privileged. That is akin to charity, not empathy. I do not talk about charity in my talks. Instead, I talk about empathy. I talk about looking at the entire picture, look at all the aspects, look at all the data, putting yourself in the shoes of the other, and then making an informed decision. This is not about victims and the victimized. It is about the right flow of understanding between people."

Shyamoli looked back, her eyes suddenly looking uncertain.

"By asking me so casually whether I am married or not, or if I have kids, you assumed a position where you are the victim, and everyone else is a culprit, moving on with their lives, leaving you behind," he continued calmly. "In all my talks, I talk about looking at data. But you do not seem to understand it. You threw away and disrespected the monuments of data that you had about me, about how I work and behave, about how you had seen me: data from my public profiles, from your memories of me, of us. You disrespected all that, and forgot to put yourself in my shoes, forgot to be empathetic to somebody who had laid open his heart to you, only to be bled in vain. You, of all people, should have known that I would not, could not, marry anybody—ever—till I found a reason to move on, found a closure."

He looked away at the discolored wall, his mind registering odd off-context things like the humming noise of the AC, as if seeking a connection to the physical world which was, to him, slowly getting devoid of any association with Shyamoli.

"When Aniruddha asked me to get out of your life that day, it helped me come to a decision, and find a closure of sorts," he continued. "I have decided to move on, get married. But I still wanted a formal closure from what we had between us all those years back. Your last statement, asking me casually if I am married, or if I have kids, has helped me come to a complete closure—finally. But I look at you today, and I realize that what I seek from this closure is perhaps futile. When I look at your complete and utter lack of empathy for me, or my life, or my well-being, I realize that I might have made a mistake in seeking closure from all this."

Shyamoli sat on the edge of her chair, looking flushed and troubled.

"In your zeal to play the victim, you made my family the villain," he continued, forcing himself to be calm, despite feeling his rage mounting every second. "My parents, especially my mother, had simply reflected a natural response based on her previous encounters with certain people. Perhaps she was wrong. But Shyamoli, you copied her sentiments and pasted it on my countenance and existence. You took her words as if they were my words, when both of us knew that I, of all people, am the most empathetic person who understands prejudice due to color more than most people. You did not give me even a moment to explain, to consider, to discuss. You did not seek data from me, seek explanations. You put yourself above it all."

He paused for a bit, his head hurting at the intensity of his suppressed emotions. Shyamoli looked on, her expression troubled.

"You are not always the victim, Shyamoli," he continued after a while. "Every person has a story, and the only way to understand that story is to practice empathy, and look at it with different contexts. Real, true empathy, when one let's go of one's ego, one's existence, and truly tries to understand the other person, look at all the data, and come to a good conclusion."

Abir clutched his head as the pain increased. Shyamoli looked deeply troubled, and her hands instinctively went toward Abir's head to comfort him. Abir waved her aside, in a mounting fury that he could not control despite his practiced mind trying all the algorithms subconsciously, which had almost always worked for him. His mind training had always worked, but somehow, this time, he could not control his mounting rage.

"Because of your ego, which consumed everything that we had, my parents almost lost their son emotionally," he continued, his voice starting to shake in distress. "All these four years, I have made my mother a villain. I did not come home for four years, and she struggled to connect with me even when she came over to California to meet me. I know she cried inside every time, crying out to me to connect to her, to come back to her. I was distant with my father, who did nothing wrong, and has always been supportive of me. All this while, I almost destroyed my parents by being aloof, by being distant. All this time, I believed that they were the reason for our separation. But I was wrong. Completely wrong. And to add to that, I was a pathetic and undeserving son. I broke the most precious relationship in my life—with my parents, who gave everything to make me happy, whose entire lives revolve around me. I made them my enemy—them, whose eyes light up when they see my smile, and whose sole purpose in life is to see me happy. I went away from them, just because foolishly, I made them the villains, and you the victim."

Shyamoli looked at him, her eyes welling with tears.

"I am not blaming you, Shyamoli," he said, feeling distressed to see her look unhappy. His trained mind overtook his emotions, as always, and he forced himself to become calm. "You did what you had to do, and I did what I had to. You separated from me because you felt that my family would never accept you, and perhaps you are right. I did not tell you all this to make you regret. You did nothing wrong then. But you still harbor a strong negative feeling for me, and that is where I think you are wrong. I was weak Shyamoli, that's all. I do not have any negative feelings toward you. It was your battle for justice, and I respect it that you sacrificed me for it, but still, it hurt. It hurt badly, and I lead an absolutely miserable, meaningless life for four years. You cut me to pieces, Shyamoli, and I have already lost four years of my life trying to regain my sense and purpose."

Abir rested his head on his hands, trembling with distress. He felt his phone ringing. It was Riya calling to tell him that she was near the NGO to pick him up. He picked up the phone with shaking hands and asked her briefly to wait for him outside the cafe. Putting down the phone, he smiled serenely at Shyamoli, as she looked back at him, her big eyes locked on his.

"I feel terrible telling you all this Shyamoli, especially because you are leading such a hard life," he said, as he got up from his chair. "You lost both your parents, your brother stays far from you, and I feel terrible right now talking to you in this tone, where all you need is comfort and companionship. And I feel terrible, because Shyamoli, you are, and were, so strong, and I was nothing but a spineless coward. But I do wish to make you understand that you should stop getting distressed due to me. It's all good between us. It should remain amicable between us. Please don't harbor negative feelings about me, about us. Anyways, I wish you all the luck in your life. I wanted to let you know that we are good. Please don't be upset over me, or what happened four years back. You are doing great work. You should continue this great work. You should not make yourself unhappy over a cowardly person like me."

His head felt heavy, as it had done four years back when Shyamoli had asked him to leave. At the same time, he felt relieved, as if a heavy load had lifted from him. He had come to a closure. And he could clearly see that Shyamoli had moved on and come to a closure as well. It took four years, but finally, it had ended formally.

He trudged to the door of the cafe and walked out, without looking back at Shyamoli, to meet Riya waiting outside.

* * *

Abir was mostly silent at Riya's home at the dinner table, even as Riya's mother made a fuss of him and tried to make him take second helpings of everything. She had prepared a sumptuous meal for him. It consisted of everything that he loved. *Potoler dorma*. Goat *curry*. Prawns. Kolkata's famous *mishti doi* and *baked Rosogolla*. Riya's father had joined the table to share dinner with him, and so had Riya. Riya's mother did not join the table; instead, she hovered around Abir to make sure he had all the right food on his plate. It made him feel anxious to be treated like royalty. He wished Riya's mother would sit down to have a meal with them and that he could simply help himself with the food, instead of her serving him.

Abir responded politely and meaningfully to all the conversations, his trained mind automatically trying to subtract himself and his immediate feelings from the surroundings so that he could concentrate on the needs of the others around him. He smiled at Riya's father's jokes, praised her mother's cooking, and respectfully listened to occasional comments from Riya, who seemed unusually buoyant that day.

"Where did you guys go today?" asked Riya's father jovially.

"I took Abir to the shopping mall," Riya said, glancing at him as if hoping to engage him in a conversation. Even in his dull and low state, he could make out that Riya had taken special attention to her makeup, perhaps more than usual. She looked beautiful, as he had observed in the shopping mall.

"Ah, you young folks!" said Riya's father, helping himself to some sweets. "When I was younger, I used to take your mother to movies and theatres. Then we used to roam around in the city, eating roadside food. None of your fancy shopping malls!"

"Well yes, dad, but nowadays it's impossible to roam around in the city," said Riya, folding her legs and sitting comfortably on the dining chair, as the maidservant piled food on her plate. She shook her head irritably, and the maidservant retreated silently.

"Why is it hard?" asked her father.

"It's so damned hot!" she said, screwing up her face. "And so many low-class poor people on the street. You cannot walk around in peace before some beggar comes up and shoves his dirty hands at you, asking for alms."

"Kolkata has always had its share of the poor, my dear," said her father. "This is a third world country, after all. When you move to the USA, you will see less of this."

"Dad, Abir thinks empathy can solve most of the problems in third world countries," said Riya, glancing at him, apparent pride in her eyes. "Did you read his blogs? I will forward them to you. Also, he has a lot of talks that he makes all over the USA and sometimes in other countries too. They are called TED talks. They are all on YouTube and have hundreds of thousands of views. Abir is a star in his own right!"

Abir smiled politely at Riya's father, who looked at him as if he had found a pot of gold. He felt embarrassed and decided to change the topic.

"Riya and I met this bright little boy selling roses on the streets," Abir said quietly. Riya looked at him as if surprised that he had a comment, but seemed glad that he was participating in the conversation.

"Dad, do you know, Abir bought flowers from him for me and overpaid him for no reason!" she chirped, giggling. "You should have seen the grin on that little rascal's face!"

Riya's father did not reply, but looked at Riya and at Abir, beaming, apparently happy that they were already interacting like a couple.

Abir kept quiet for the rest of the meal. After the meal, he decided to leave immediately. It would take more than an hour for him to go back home. He looked around for his backpack. It was missing.

"What are you looking for?" asked Riya as she walked with him to the door.

"My backpack," he said, trying to think where he saw it last.

"Well, you did have your backpack with you in the shopping mall today afternoon," said Riya.

"So did I," said Abir, "Do you think I lost it in the shopping mall?"

"No, I distinctly remember you went to that NGO or whatever taking your backpack with you. I think you must have left it there."

Yes, he thought to himself, he had indeed left his backpack in the room where Shyamoli was teaching. He remembered that he had taken it off to help her with the Chemistry experiments. After that, he did not remember carrying it.

Abir felt a chill go through his heart. He had to get the backpack back, and that would mean interacting with Shyamoli again. Shyamoli, who was bent on being casual and disinterested in him. He felt a cold sense of trepidation at the thought of asking her.

"Why don't you call the NGO and ask them to save it for you?" said Riya, "I can collect it for you tomorrow, and you can collect it when we meet next."

Abir did not reply, thinking that he would rather not collect the backpack again ever.

* * *

Abir stared at the tattered piece of parchment that Aniruddha had given him. It was dawn. He had woken up early, somehow being unable to sleep after coming back home from Riya's place the previous evening, and had come to the terrace at his home. He had worried about his backpack the entire night. He would have to get it back because it contained a diary full of essential phone numbers. But that meant calling up Shyamoli to ask if she had it with her. He could not bear to talk to her again, to hear her voice again. The closure from her side had been apparent. He had found the reason for his closure, and he did not want to restart communications.

The piece of parchment contained Shyamoli's phone number, given by Aniruddha the last day at the shopping mall. He looked at the numbers, trying to find her face in them, and realized that he could still see her everywhere, whether he wanted to or not. He clutched at the parchment and forced himself to be calm. This was the last piece of connection with Shyamoli that he had. He could either tear it up and throw it away, or make the last excruciating call to talk to her to get back the backpack.

As he looked at the parchment, he made up his mind. He would let the backpack get lost forever. Perhaps Shyamoli would throw it away anyways. But he did not want to meet Shyamoli again. He tore the parchment into tiny pieces and threw them over the terrace walls, tears rolling down his eyes as he saw the symbolic end of his connection with Shyamoli, the remnants of parchment floating away into the wind.

* * *

Hello Abir, this is Shyamoli. You left your backpack here at the NGO. What shall I do with it?

Abir stared at the text from the unknown number. He had torn away the piece of parchment containing Shyamoli's phone number just an hour back, and was sipping morning tea which Bhutto had made for him, feeling oddly relaxed. Somehow that had been a symbolic end to their romantic relationship. Her text did not incite the excitement that he had feared would be evoked.

"Throw it away," he texted back calmly.

"I can't do that. Please tell me a good way to return it to you," texted back Shyamoli after a while.

"Please throw it away," he texted back her again.

"Can I please call you?" she texted back.

Abir looked at the text, thinking about it. Despite it being from Shyamoli, he felt curiously calm. He stared at the text for some time and decided not to answer. He was done with that side of the relationship. It did not make sense to linger unnecessarily.

He long pressed the number from where the text had come from, and clicked "block" on the name, and put aside the phone.

He had blocked Shyamoli's phone, which was another symbolic way of cutting the ties forever.

Shyamoli was officially erased from his life, as he was making plans to move ahead with Riya to a new beginning.

The Ex factor

Dearest Abir,

I have been trying to call you for two days, but I think you have blocked my phone number. I have been mustering enough courage for these two days, and I am finally writing this email to you to this Gmail account, hoping you still have it and read it once in a while. Or even if you have, I am not sure you will want to read my emails anymore. I can understand why you would want to avoid me forever, and if you feel you need to, delete this email.

I saw the pain in your eyes when I last saw you two days back, and I am really lost for words to the terrible wound that I have inflicted upon you. I feel I have struck and pierced the heart of somebody as beautiful and innocent like you, who left it open, unprotected, for a black and hateful serpent like me.

You had come for a closure, and I realize that a simple and profoundly pure soul like you will never understand anything beyond your timeless and eternal love. A love so passionate that you believed it would be strong enough to withstand forces wanting to break it all apart.

I wanted to share my reasons with you, every day, for these last four miserable years, but did not find the moral courage to tell you, worthless that I am, or write to you, or to communicate to you, as to why I had to let go of the most precious possession in my life. You.

Let go. Just two words with such a powerful meaning. Let go.

I let you go because, Abir, true happiness comes from the union of your collective thoughts and relationships with people. With me, you would have never found true happiness, because, had I come to your life, you would have cut off ties with the other people in your life, people whose love is truly precious to you, as I was precious to you too.

You once told me a concept around equations not matching. With me in your life, your equation would not match. Never. It would always be an unbalanced equation. Your family would never accept me. I would never be happy with them and would have forever worked toward their support. You would never be happy—ever. All through your life, you would have struggled to balance this equation, which is not supposed to ever get balanced at all.

By rejecting our union, I supported and represented the nameless and voiceless women who are not favored due to prejudice in society. As I told you those four years back, I stood up for "dharma," for the injustice meted out to people who do not fit a particular social picture. I stood up for what I thought is incredible injustice on these women, often meted out by women themselves.

I know I don't deserve forgiveness for the cruelty that I dealt you, just to fight my battle. You asked for a closure. My email will probably make you seek closure once again. I hate myself for continuing the misery in your life.

But rest assured, I think you are in good hands.

I saw the woman who picked you up in her car from outside the cafe. You said you were with your would-be fiancée in the shopping mall, and I presume she is the lucky one. She looks classy and absolutely beautiful. I looked on, feeling happy for you, when you smiled at her and sat beside her, and I looked at the admiring way she looked at you. You and her look absolutely heavenly together, and fit the image that the society has when making matches. She will automatically fit into your society, and I think with her, you will find true happiness that you deserve.

I am sure she will never take your heart in her hands, wring it and cut it into pieces, like I had done.

In our culture, demonesses have always being portrayed as black. My face, too, is black, like that of the classical demon in our mythologies. And I have behaved with you like one. I truly stand for a demoness and have acted like one, by cutting your heart to pieces and letting it bleed and die.

The beautiful woman who came to rescue you that day from me is your Goddess, and she is the one who will let you finally come to a closure and make you free from a horrible demoness like me. She will stitch your heart back, nurture it, and make you healthy again.

I wish you all the luck in your life with her. She is lucky to get a beautiful person like you as her life partner. I think you will find your closure and be able to move on with her.

As a parting gift, although unworthy of it, I would like to keep your backpack with me as a last remembrance of what you have done for me, for my father, for us.

-Shyamoli

* * *

Hi Shyamoli,

I wanted to reply to you yesterday, but was caught up with some work. Anyways, coming quickly to the point, I will not dwell too hard on your use of terms and connotations in your email, but I do have a request.

Never, and let me repeat, never again belittle yourself in front of anybody. Ever again.

You called yourself a demoness, and made a veiled reference of dark women and demonesses in our culture. I am deeply disappointed in you! You, of all people, should deviate from these racist connotations!

Comparing yourself with a serpent? A demoness? What kind of a bizarre middle age language is this??

This is not the Shyamoli I know. These four years have changed you, made you look down on yourself. It makes me really sad, because that's not how I have looked at you.

Is it because of us, because of what happened to us? Why, Shyamoli, why? Why are you taking all the blame on yourself? No relationship is more significant than what you mean to yourself, where you stand in your own reference point. You berate yourself with extremely negative connotations, and I am deeply saddened by your stance.

You have the profound strength to stand up for all the wrongs done by a prejudiced society: a society especially biased against people who don't fit a particular social image. I salute you for your strength, which meant breaking something as precious as what we had between us. You stood up to the true ideals of women empow-

193

erment, the power to take a strong decision, and not get bogged down by chauvinism encouraged and propagated by society as a subtle method of subjugation. I truly admire you for taking a stance against racist views in the society, and in my mind, you have done the most honorable thing that could be done.

Also, back then, in me, you would have found a weak and immature person who could not look at the bigger picture. You must not demean yourself in front of somebody like me, who was so weak as to allow a beautiful flower, like you, to wilt away due to insult and profound humiliation, but did not have the galls to stand up to the forces that caused it to fade away.

I do admire you—everything about you. I think we are moving ahead with our own lives, with our personal goals, and individually, we are making progress, going toward the same goal of servitude for humanity.

But in all this, I do have one complaint of sorts.

I wish you had included me in your quest for social justice before rejecting me outright as a worthy partner four years back. It would have stopped a lot of heartache on either side. I would have happily partnered with you in your journey, not as a romantic partner, but perhaps as a partner in a quest for social equality and empathy, which seems to be our common goal.

With your email, you made your explanations clear, and I thank you for that. As mature adults, we should now let the past go. I sincerely apologize for being dramatic and sentimental that day over the text messages and consequently blocking you. I have now unblocked you on my phone. You should feel free to give me a call, or WhatsApp me, whenever you need my assistance. I will be happy to help you with any of your NGO activities.

Feel free to keep the backpack, but I think I have a few documents and an old diary inside it, where I keep phone numbers from my clients (I am still strangely not tech-savvy over these little things like keeping phone numbers and prefer to scribble my imprints). If you find that old diary, I would like to have it back sometime.

And finally, let me repeat again. Never again, never in your lifetime, should you belittle yourself in front of anybody. Ever. You are an extraordinarily strong woman, with brilliance, calmness, nobility, and elegance to match. You have the supreme power to stand up to "dharma," as you rightly said, to what is right and wrong. I am merely a shadow of what you are. Remember that, always, and never ever belittle yourself in front of me, or anybody for that matter.

Best regards,

Abir

* * *

Dearest Abir,

I cannot express the joy that your email brings me, knowing that you did read my email and even found time to reply. Deep down, I knew that you would respond because of your nobility in spirit.

I am sorry for using those words and belittling myself. But it is OK to belittle oneself in front of somebody as pure as you. I guess I will be less explicit about this now, but I do feel terrible for what I did with you.

But at the same time, I stand my ground. I could not have accepted a union where I am not received by the bigger society that you are a part of.

I am delighted that you have seen my point, and I have seen your side too. We have reached a closure of sorts, I think, as you would have put it.

And yes, you are right. Even if our worlds do not match, we should leave all this behind and partner up for the common cause of social upliftment. I will be absolutely honored to have you as a partner in these efforts and to get back our beautiful friendship.

I did find your diary and found a lot of phone numbers scribbled on the pages. Yes, I must admit that this is being surprisingly not tech-savvy, especially for a super tech person like you! I scanned all the pages and created a Google Drive folder for you and uploaded the numbers in a spreadsheet. I think going forward, you can use that shared cloud document directly from your phone to update the numbers.

I feel silly telling all these instructions to a tech guru like you! You can call it the habits of a teacher.

Yours Shyamoli.

* * *

Hi Shyamoli,

Thank God for your retransformation. Your last email reads more like the Shyamoli I know! And thank you for accepting me as a partner in your social efforts. I will be happy to provide my technical support by building websites etc. for your organization. Thank you for scanning all the phone numbers and arranging them so neatly in the spreadsheet. This reflects your usual kind self, which I have always admired.

Also, see, we have already started collaborating remotely. Hail cloud tech.

-Abir

P.S. I presume you scanned all the pages of the diary and kept the diary with yourself. What will you do with an old diary? Throw it away! It's got four years of dirt through all the places it has been through.

* * *

Dearest Abir,

I cannot throw away the diary because it contains your hand-writing. You are my friend, and I cannot throw anything away which belongs to a friend.

How did the engagement ceremony go? It was today, I guess?

Yours always,

Shyamoli

* * *

Hi Shyamoli,

The engagement ceremony has been delayed because Riya's father suddenly got sick and had to be hospitalized at Bellevue Hos-

pital in Kolkata. I am not sure what it is yet, but they might keep him for watch for a couple of days.

I will go to the hospital in Kolkata to visit him tomorrow morning.

-Abir

* * *

Dearest Abir,

I am sad to hear this news. May the almighty give him strength to bear the pain. I can understand the stress that Riya is going through at these times. I will pray for her and her family.

Yours,

Shyamoli.

* * *

Shyamoli: Dearest Abir, thanks for acknowledging my WhatsApp invite. Nice profile picture! Is Riya's father doing OK?

Abir: Yes, it looks like it's nothing too serious, but he needs some rest. I will visit the city to see him tomorrow. Can I drop by to collect my backpack then?

Shyamoli: Yes, you can come by to the same place to collect your stuff from the backpack. Like I said, I refuse to return the backpack back to you, but you can collect all that you need from there :)

Abir: It's not my backpack. You bought it for me five years back, remember?

Shyamoli: Of course, I remember. That's why I want it back now :)

Abir: Haha, OK, thou shalt have it!

Shyamoli: Bring Riya over too.

Abir: Oh, really?! Are you sure??

Shyamoli: Why not? I think it's unfair on her if she does not know about us, given that you are collaborating with me, now and presumably in the near future. And I would love to get to know her more. After all, you and I are friends, and your wife should be my friend too.

Abir: Ummm. Don't you think it's a bit awkward, Shyamoli? Why does she need to know about us working as friends, as partners in a common interest? We are merely collaborating and are good friends. I have other friends too. She does not need to know all of them right now. Then why you?

Shyamoli: I think it's more awkward to keep all this a secret, given our history. You and I are good friends. You are getting married to a woman who is going to be the most important person in your life. You should be open about us, you and me. Otherwise, it's unfair to her.

Abir: What if she sees you as an ex and not as a partner for social work? Will she feel comfortable around you? Frankly, the entire idea sounds a bit preposterous. She might just stop allowing me to contact you again.

Shyamoli: Then you have to respect her decision and throw me out of your life. Remember, she will be your better half. I am merely your friend. You are ideal in everything I have observed about you, my friend. So ideally, given our history, you should at least let her know that you will be working with me.

Abir: You are the one being idealistic again, Shyamoli! Not me :)

Shyamoli: I like your description of me—idealistic :). Yes, now that I come to think of it, that's what I am! Somewhat too idealistic, perhaps?

Abir: Yes, that's what you are, Miss Shyamoli! You are really a bit oddly idealistic. Nothing wrong in that, though.

Shyamoli: You called me Miss Shyamoli again after ages. Oh, it makes me so happy! I am so happy that you and I can talk normally now.

Abir: Yes, absolutely. Tell me, what can I do for your NGO?

Shyamoli: I am working with a home for impoverished women, and they need some tech help to set up a website, or other tech stuff like setting up a payment option for foreign funding. I could use your help.

Abir: Of course, I will help you set up the website! Give me a few weeks. Will talk to you later about it. Send me a rough design on what you think it should look like. I am getting called for dinner now...

Shyamoli: Where are you right now? On the terrace? Or in your room?

Abir: On the terrace. It's always my favorite place.

Shyamoli: Is that big coconut tree still by your terrace?

Abir: Hmm—yes, it's still there. Why do you ask? Also, I am a bit surprised—I don't recall you coming over to my house ever, so how do you even know about coconut trees by my terrace?

Shyamoli: You gave me your address once, remember? I simply checked out your home on Google Earth and saw the lovely tall coconut trees by your terrace.

Abir: How interesting!

Shyamoli: Yes, isn't it? We are connected despite being far away. By bits and bytes of technology and engineering, as you would have perhaps said. We will get even further away after you marry Riya. But the world is so connected due to these amazing tech revolutions like instant messaging, and I hope we remain in touch forever. Technology and Engineering is so beautiful.

Abir: Indeed it is—and you know, I feel so proud to be an engineer every day, because I think I have made that little contribution to this planet which makes lives better for so many people by helping them connect to each other despite being Geographically apart. I love being a computer engineer, to be able to contribute to all these great technologies.

Shyamoli: Indeed—and you are more than just a computer engineer. Oh wait, I used to call you a computer scientist, remember?

Abir: Yes, I do remember that, Shyamoli. Wow, those were the days.

Shyamoli: Indeed. And it makes me so happy to see you come all the way to now also call yourself an empathy engineer. It makes me so proud. I have read and re-read your blogs so many times and have often watched your YouTube videos in repeat mode. You are exceptional, Abir.

Abir: I am blushing right now, Shyamoli.

Shyamoli: :) :) :)

Abir: Anyway, I will get back to you shortly, Shyamoli, and we can get a basic website setup. Goodnight.

Shyamoli: Goodnight, Abir. Remember what I said about Riya. You should at least mention me and the fact that you and I will be working together in the future.

Abir: I will. It worries me a bit, but if that's what you want, I will tell her about you.

Shyamoli: You should do that immediately. Also, one more thing.

Abir: What?

Shyamoli: Delete this WhatsApp conversation. Otherwise, it will hurt Riya if she comes across this conversation between us later when you are married to her.

Abir: Oh! That's an interesting perspective. Yes, I will delete this conversation.

Shyamoli: Thank you. Goodnight Abir.

* * *

Abir told Riya about Shyamoli when he made his way with her to her home, after seeing her father at the Bellevue hospital. He told her briefly that he had met her in the NGO center.

"Is that where you left your backpack the last time you went to this NGO?" Riya asked.

"Yes," he said shortly.

"Is she married, this Shyamoli?" asked Riya after a silence, as they stopped the car at a light.

"No, she's not," he said.

Riya remained silent as she drove on. Abir felt that this was enough of an introduction to Shyamoli. He changed the topic as they ambled along the Kolkata traffic.

* * *

"I want to go and meet Shyamoli," said Riya casually after lunch. All throughout lunch, she had been quiet and brooding. Abir looked at her quizzically.

"Why?" he asked.

"You don't want me to meet your friend?" asked Riya, her eyebrows raised.

"Oh no, I don't mean like that," said Abir hastily. "I mean, there is no reason to see her right now. I deliver the project online and will work with a team of software volunteers from Silicon Valley. Her connection with me is mostly over the common social work we are doing. I won't be seeing her anyways after we are in the USA, so you and I don't really need to go and meet Shyamoli."

"You don't want me to meet her because she is your ex, right?" she asked, looking at him sharply. Abir did not answer and tried to be busy with a magazine lying around in her room.

"Well, you know what, I want to meet her at least once before you leave for the USA," said Riya, getting up to get ready. "Tell her to meet us in that cafe where I picked you up last time. I will drive us there."

* * *

Abir waited nervously at the cafe near Shyamoli's NGO—the same one where they had met a few days back. Riya had driven him there. He did not feel comfortable about all this and wished he had not listened to Shyamoli, or Riya. He was not sure why Shyamoli wanted to know Riya in person at all. Also, he could not understand why Riya was keen on meeting Shyamoli either. It was an odd gameplay which was getting hard for him to understand.

At the appointed time, Shyamoli appeared at the cafe, and Abir missed a heartbeat at her sight. He looked at her with a mixed feeling of awe and discomfort, as she came, her natural grace looking even more sublime. He noticed her eyes, dark and striking with dark black eyeliner that he had not seen her put on with such intensity. He saw her careful makeup, which seemed to highlight her face brightly, something he had never seen her put on before. Her dress was oddly formal and gorgeous, hugging on to her, lining the curves in her body, a far cry from the oversized casuals she wore the last time he saw her. He noticed her heels clicking on the floor and marveled at it, wondering when he had last seen her look so fashionable and attractive.

The icy coldness exuded by both women, even as they warmly greeted each other outwardly, did not go unnoticed by Abir. He sat beside Riya, and Shyamoli sat opposite them, wearing a warm and friendly expression. He looked at her, wondering what it was that was different beyond her apparent effort to look extra attractive. He soon realized, with a jolt, that Shyamoli had colored her hair, with streaks of brown shining among her ebony black hair. This was definitely new and, as he thought, very un-Shyamolish.

Abir had planned to be casual and jovial in this meeting, but soon found himself retreating to a silent zone, as he looked at the two women, feeling puzzled. The demeanor of both women was foreign to him. Shyamoli seemed too warm, too bright, too dressy. Riya, who was always dressy anyways and was generally outspoken, bordering on being arrogant in her demeanor, suddenly looked alert, trying to be pleasant, smiling at Shyamoli, apparently eager to know her.

During the entire get together, Abir kept quiet, smiling occasionally if one of them glanced at him to see whether he was following their conversation. He felt puzzled at the way Shyamoli kept putting her hands through her hair, a habit he had never noticed in her. He noted her dangling earrings, her dark rose-colored lipsticks, the lining around the front of her dress which seemed to slip ever so often. The more he looked at her, the more puzzled he got. This was a different Shyamoli, a Shyamoli he had never hitherto seen.

Shyamoli had to leave for another science class, and Abir could not help but feel relieved that she was not near Riya. He waved to her, not going near the door to see her off, even as Riya went to the door to see her off, hugging her warmly before she departed, a strange behavior that he had hitherto never observed.

* * *

After meeting Shyamoli, Riya drove Abir back to her home, where he was supposed to have dinner before leaving for the day.

This was the last dinner they were having together, before the engagement, which was due in two days. Abir would fly back to California after that, to come back formally to marry in a month or so.

Throughout the car ride back to her home, Riya seemed oddly jovial, as she talked about random things with Abir. This was a new experience for him, to see her jovial without her usual air of annoyance at Kolkata traffic.

As Abir made his way inside Riya's home and flopped down on a sofa in the drawing-room, her mother fussed over him and handing him a glass of lemonade immediately on arrival, predicting that they would be tired. Riya disappeared from the drawing-room. He sat down, listening absently to her mother, as she went on about Kolkata congestion, pollution, about how Riya had been driving ever since she was legally permitted to operate, and that she had made some more of his favorite dishes for dinner after consulting his mother.

After a while, when Riya did not appear at all, her mother beckoned Abir to follow her to Riya's room, and knocking at her door, she asked Abir to join her there, as she went back downstairs to set up an evening snack for them.

Abir entered the room to find Riya lying down with her head down on the bed. He sat down on the chair beside her and cleared his throat to make his presence known.

Riya turned around and got up. He sat down silently, looking at her quizzically.

"Are you tired?" he asked gently.

"No, just resting after all the driving," she said, smiling brightly at him. "I have never been to that side of Kolkata—it's quite far from here."

Abir nodded.

"Shyamoli seemed quite nice," continued Riya. She sat down on her chair, hugging her heart-shaped pillow, looking at the ceiling fan, which was turning morosely, somewhat redundant because the entire house was air-conditioned anyways. Abir waited patiently by her side, wondering what she wanted to say.

"Have you been in touch with her all these years?" she asked eventually. Abir shook his head. Riya stared at him and then went to her bed. She sat there, hugging another pillow, as she stared at the wall opposite her.

Suddenly she covered her face and burst into tears.

Abir got up, shocked at this sudden transformation, and came and sat beside her bed, distressed. He wondered if he had inadvertently done something wrong and waited anxiously for her to say something.

"Are you sure she is your ex?" she asked after a while, wiping her eyes and smiling at him oddly through her moist eyes. She got up and went in front of the mirror, looking at herself and at Abir's reflection in the mirror. She ran her fingers over her hair, and made it fall on her forehead, on her face, and turned around to look at Abir.

"You are not saying anything. Is Shyamoli really your ex?" she asked.

Abir nodded silently.

"Then why was she behaving like that?" she asked.

Abir looked at her, startled.

"Behaving like what?" he asked.

"Of course you don't understand," Riya said, waving her hands at him and sitting on the chair.

"What don't I understand, Riya?" he asked, genuinely puzzled.

"You never told me that Shyamoli is so utterly beautiful!" said Riya. "You made me think she is some dark, ugly maid who merely wants to hang on to you desperately by doing this stupid collaborative social-upliftment project or whatever you are onto."

"I never said anything about Shyamoli's appearance, Riya," Abir said quietly.

"Exactly!" said Riya. "You failed to conveniently tell me that she is so absolutely drop dead gorgeous! You made me believe that she is just dark. That's what her name meant anyways. But she is so hot and beautiful and is obviously beyond just being dark!"

Abir got more confused by this sudden change in angle. He did not recall having her ask him anything about Shyamoli. It was she who stopped asking about her after knowing that her name had connotations around having a dark complexion.

Besides, what had dark to do with beauty? Did being dark automatically disqualify a woman from being called beautiful?

He looked at Riya, feeling bewildered, as she turned to look at the mirror again. Abir saw her face slowly getting contorted with anger. He waited apprehensively for more outbursts from her.

"You are an idiot and a simpleton, aren't you?" she said, looking at him angrily. "You don't see anything, do you?"

"Riya, I am really confused now," Abir said quietly.

"I can't believe you can't see the obvious," Riya said, her expression furious. "Didn't you even notice what she was doing all the time? She could not keep her eyes off you! She dressed as if she came to date *you*, not to meet your would-be fiancée! Each and every aspect of her figure-hugging short dress was to flaunt her sexuality to you! Every line in her damned body screamed to be taken by you! Are you so blind as to not even notice how she drools over you? Friend—best friend—partner in business—my foot! She is head over heels in love with you, and you are too much of a pathetic mama's boy and an idiot to really read her vibes! What are you? Some kind of a blind sheep?"

She shook her head in disbelief and agitation at Abir's bewildered expression.

"If she wants you so much, then why did she let you go in the first place? Why does she have to now come to take something which is not hers to have any more? Why is she so damned confused in her life? That greedy bitch!"

Abir looked on in silence, as Riya sat down on her bed again, hugging her pink heart-shaped pillow.

"What shall I do now?" she said and screwed up her face to cry again, rocking to and fro. Abir instinctively wanted to comfort her. He hated himself at the moment for creating this distress in her, even though he was not sure whether he did anything wrong. Riya stopped rocking back and forth and looked at him.

"You made this plan to humiliate me, didn't you?" she said, tears flowing down her cheeks.

Abir shook his head.

"Riya, this is all a misunderstanding," he said gently. "Shyamoli and I are friends. Just friends. Besides, you were the one who wanted to meet her, remember? Where is all this coming from?"

"Where is all this coming from?" she said, suddenly standing up and looking around, looking wild. Abir looked at her in alarm. She picked up a heavy magazine and threw it at him with all her might. It hit his head, and he felt a sharp pain go through his forehead.

"This was all your plot to get rid of me, right?" she yelled, shaking in a fury. Abir looked in alarm at her expression, his head hurting him due to the blow from the magazine. She glared at him and suddenly picked up another magazine and threw it at him with all her might. He covered his face and ducked instinctively as the magazine hit the wall with a dull thud and fell down. He stood up stricken as she threw herself on a chair, sobbing.

"You cad, you two-faced liar! You took me there deliberately to have me see her and make me feel inferior," she said sobbing. Abir felt sad for her sorrow, realizing that her needs were more than his sense of bewilderment. It was her who wanted to meet Shyamoli, not the other way around. He decided not to remind this to her again. Instead, he went and knelt down in front of her, putting his hands on her hands to console her.

She threw his hand away fiercely and pushed him away with a force that made him fall on the floor.

He picked himself up tiredly and stood up, making up his mind that it was time to leave. Why did he always face these situations with women? Each and every time, when he never did anything wrong.

As he turned to leave, Riya ran and stood in front of him, guarding the door, not letting him out.

"Do you realize who I am?" she screamed, shaking in uncontrolled rage, as he backed into the room in alarm. "I was the most sought after girl in my School, in my College. I have had men drool over me all my life. Men belonging to families who can keep me in castles like a queen and not in your pathetic twelve hundred square foot hole in California. I grew up like a princess. A princess, do you hear? A princess worth thousands more than that black-skinned Shyamoli! You should just go back to her and let that beautiful black demoness engulf you with her greedy serpent tongue!"

"Calm down, Riya," Abir said quietly, his practiced mind over-looking all the insults hurled by her, making him see only the reason for this, justifying her behavior.

"Calm down?" she said, shaking in mad rage. She looked around to throw something else at Abir, and seeing the porcelain vase on her table, she picked it up, and as an alarmed Abir looked on, she threw it at him with all her might. He ducked in time, and the vase hit the wall, smashing into pieces.

A broken piece of porcelain bounced off the wall and hit his temple. His forehead burnt suddenly, and touching it, he found blood slowly oozing out.

Abir's eyes teared up at the profound unfairness of it all. He went into the bathroom to wash the cut. A thick streak of cut had appeared on his forehead. It was oozing blood slowly. He dabbed some wet paper on it and cleaned the wound with soap and water. He waited for some time for the blood to stop flowing.

He came out of the bathroom after a while, feeling dejected and distressed, the wound on his forehead burning. Riya was sitting on a chair, hugging a pillow, a resolute expression in her eyes.

"I don't want this engagement to happen," she said, her teeth clenched. "Get out of my room right now. Get lost!"

Abir looked at her silently as she looked away from him. He felt deeply unhappy. He closed his eyes for a while to let his empathy algorithms take over.

But somehow, the data did not add up. His empathy algorithm could not be used, for once, because the data was all jumbled up, corrupt, and unusable.

He realized that sometimes, when empathy was distinctly missing from the other side, one had to let go and move on.

"Well, neither do I," he said after a pause, feeling dejected, but determined. "Riya, you have physically abused me with utter disdain, and I cannot accept that. This is not the fabric that I expect to lay down our married life on. I am sorry it came about this way, but I consider this engagement null and void too. Goodbye."

Then he turned and opened the door and left her room.

BFF

"Did I get you in trouble with your fiancée?" asked Shyamoli shyly.

It was evening, and Shyamoli had finished teaching her final class at the NGO for that day. Abir had returned to the building where he knew Shyamoli would be teaching. He had left Riya's house without letting her mother know. It was uncharacteristic of him, but his usual calm self could not tolerate physical abuse. He shuddered to think what would have happened if the vase that Riya had thrown at him in her rage had hit him. He would probably have been seriously wounded and hospitalized.

"How did you even know that?" asked Abir, feeling slightly exasperated despite the stress that he was under after the episode. "I didn't even tell you anything about it!"

"Yes, you certainly did not say anything," Shyamoli said. "But your expression tells me you guys had a fight. Sadly I had a hunch it would happen."

"Really?" asked Abir. "Why did you have this hunch?"

"Riya had come to check me out, and I think she did not like me at all," she said calmly. "I am sure she was pretty mad about me being your best friend."

"Well, if you had figured it all out, then why did you ask me to tell her about you in the first place?" asked Abir, feeling annoyed. "And besides, you also wanted to check her out, no?" he added sharply, looking at her as if he was seeing a new side of her he had hitherto never observed.

Shyamoli looked embarrassed and hurriedly went over to the desk to continue her work.

"And did you have to make yourself look so stunningly beautiful today, of all days, Shyamoli?" he continued, half angry and half-amused. "You are beautiful anyways, Shyamoli. So why this extra effort today? What's with the extra dark eyeliner, mascara, blushers, dangling earrings, dark lipstick and all that? I bet you never put all that on ever in your life!"

Shyamoli did not reply, but continued to work, turned away from him.

"And what's with those absurdly high heels?" Abir continued. "When did you ever start wearing these ridiculously high heels, Shyamoli? Why did you have to deviate from your usual style so drastically just to give competition to Riya? That was not cool! It's obvious that you are not used to these two miles long high heels! For your information, you looked like a wobbly hedgehog on a skating rink."

Shyamoli giggled despite the seriousness in his voice. Abir frowned at her angrily, and she quickly straightened her face.

"OK, cool down," she said, her big eyes looking at him with pretense timidity. "Can I get Riya's number? Let me call up your pretty little fiancée and clear things up with her and tell her not to worry about me. I won't give her any more competition. Let me commiserate with her so that her majesty can fly back to the Earth from her heavenly abode."

Abir looked at her exasperated, then smiled despite himself at her sarcastic tone. He had never seen this side of Shyamoli, and somehow it delighted him despite feeling low at the entire episode.

"She was not my fiancée yet," he said wearily. "And anyway, it's all over now."

"Oh," said Shyamoli, looking at him with an expression he could not understand. "Please don't tell me you guys broke up!"

Abir nodded and sat down on the floor gloomily.

"I am really sorry to hear that, Abir," said Shyamoli in a small voice.

Abir sat on the floor for a while, staring at nothing.

"Are you feeling OK?" asked Shyamoli tenderly after a while.

"Yeah, well, I am feeling a bit shaky," said Abir unhappily. "I guess she sort of flipped out after seeing you."

"Are you trying to tell me that it's all my fault?" asked Shyamoli frowning.

"She seemed to imply that," he said. "And she was so angry about it all, and I was really stressed out. I wanted to mitigate the situation, but could not take it anymore when she threw a vase at me."

"She threw a vase at you?" asked Shyamoli incredulously. She came over to him. "What is that fresh cut on your temple? Is this something to with the vase she threw?"

Abir felt reluctant to get into the details of how or why this happened. For him, his empathy at that moment lay toward Riya, and the fact that she had seriously tried to harm him physically did not occur to him naturally.

"Umm sort of," he said evasively, thinking about the scenario and feeling a bit low. "I guess I deserved it."

"Nobody deserves to be physically abused in any circumstances. Men or women," said Shyamoli, her face turning red with anger. Abir stared at her in surprise—he had never seen Shyamoli so angry.

"When did she threw this vase at you? After she broke up with you or before?" continued Shyamoli, looking furious.

"Let it go, how does it matter?" he said. Shyamoli did not reply, and he could discern her anger rising.

"This is a strange reaction," she said, as if breathing fire.

"Hmm, yes," said Abir uneasily. "She saw you looking so—well—hot and beautiful—and she flipped out. She thinks we still have chemistry."

"Whatever the reason be, does that mean she gets to physically abuse you? Does she have no sense of decency?" asked Shyamoli, her voice shaking in anger.

"Let it go," said Abir wearily. "I wanted to ask you something else. Are we just friends, Shyamoli? I find it hard to believe that we are just best friends."

"I don't know," said Shyamoli, turning away from him. She packed her bag in silence. The next batch of kids had gone, and she was packing up for good for the day. Abir instinctively helped her, feeling as if this was the place where he belonged, and that being with Shyamoli was a natural continuation to his life.

* * *

"So what is your plan now?" asked Shyamoli after she was done with her evening class.

"I plan to be with you," he said simply.

"To be with me today?" she asked quietly.

"No, to be with you forever. I am done with all this. I want to be with you always every day."

Shyamoli stopped her activities and stared at him. He stared back deep into her eyes as if looking for a solution to his situation. Shyamoli dropped her eyes shyly at the intensity of her gaze.

"Why do you want to be with somebody who will not marry you?" she asked demurely, not looking at him.

"So be it. Marriage is not a solution to this. We will live our lives independently, but I need to be around with you every day, Shyamoli. Every day."

"You mean like a best friend forever—a BFF?"

"Yes, as a BFF, for lacking a better term! And if you say no even to this, I will get out of your life forever this time."

"No!" said Shyamoli sharply and instinctively grabbed his hands, as if the very thought scared her.

* * *

"What do you plan to do now, my dear BFF?" asked Shyamoli liltingly. They had reached her place. It was a tiny apartment, where she put up during the weekdays to be near her work. The apartment was kept neatly, with the pictures of Shyamoli's parents in frames, garlands around them as a respect for the deceased. The prominent artifact on display was a large study table, with rows of books, and a solitary table lamp.

"I really don't know," said Abir, jumping down on a couch. "Do you stay alone in this apartment?"

"No, I have a roommate, but she is away for a few days."

"I see," said Abir, feeling relaxed. He took off his shoes and stretched his legs.

"I think you should call your home and tell them honestly about what happened with you and this Riya creature," said Shyamoli.

"I noticed you called Riya a creature," said Abir, amused.

"Only a strange creature can physically abuse another person like this," said Shyamoli going to the kitchen to get water for Abir, sounding angry again. "It's just because of these pathetic and idiotic empowered and privileged women that the real feminist movement gets into a backfoot sometimes! These creatures never faced any women's issues in their super privileged lives, yet they take all the advantages of being a woman!"

Abir got up and followed her in the kitchen. It had the look of a well taken care of part of the house. Everything was neatly arranged, and he knew they would be.

"You sound genuinely angry, Shyamoli," he said, smiling at her intensity.

"Yes, I am," said Shyamoli shortly. "She physically abused you, as simple as that. She threw a vase at you, for heaven's sake! What if it hit you on the head? You could have had a serious concussion! This is completely unacceptable."

"Well, to be honest, her throwing things at me is last on my mind right now," said Abir. "Rather, I am concerned about what she must be going through right now. After all, she seemed to be getting quite fond of me in these few days."

"You don't have to practice your empathy algorithm all the time, Abir," said Shyamoli crossly, handing him a glass of water and walking out of the kitchen in a huff.

* * *

"It's getting late," said Shyamoli, looking outside. It was night, and they had finished a simple meal at her place. "You should go home. You should talk to your parents about Riya. I know she canceled the engagement and all that, but still, it's not fair on her parents, nor on your parents, if you keep all this a mystery."

Abir sat on the sofa, looking gloomily outside.

"I want to stay over the night with you," he said after a while. "I just don't want to go home. You know my mom. She will make a bloody scene and stress me out. I am already too stressed out."

"That would not be appropriate at all, Abir," said Shyamoli softly. "Besides, what will your mother think? That I kidnapped her son from Riya's place and kept him at my place overnight?"

"Yes, when she learns that you and I are together in this apartment, that too, without any adult supervision, she will probably flip out," he said. "It would certainly be against her values. And of course, against your strong Indian values too. But Shyamoli, I cannot help but think that you stick to Indian values and traditions a bit too much."

"That's the way I have been raised by my father—to value traditions," said Shyamoli quietly. "You and I are not together as a couple. Staying over together in this house, where you could have gone back home, is not appropriate. That's what our values tell us. Abir, I really think you should call your mother and go home."

"Looks like my mom has successfully intimidated us," he said, frowning. "You know, you are not obliged to respect her, because she had not respected you back then."

"Don't say that!" said Shyamoli, looking troubled. "She has a certain way of thinking which does not match ours, that's all."

She went and walked over to the balcony, and Abir followed her. They stood silently, surveying the murmur of a small market the spawned behind the apartment, which was still active at night.

"It will be childish to believe that we parted ways solely because of your mother's distaste toward women with dark skin," said Shyamoli, turning to look at him. "We are both adults. This is beyond just her views. She is a representative of a part of society which assumes superiority over people like me. I am against that mindset. Remember what I said four years back? About it being a war of *dharma*, of human rights."

"You said that in your emotional email to me, too," said Abir quietly.

"Oh," said Shyamoli, looking at him anxiously. "Are you still disappointed at me over that email? I meant every word I said, Abir. I treated you so wrong. At times, I still feel that I have played with your kindness and simplicity, just to fight my little battle with a prejudiced world."

Abir looked at her silently. Shyamoli stared back at him, and her expressions became curiously soft.

"Somehow, we women are really hard on you, no?" she said softly. "Me. Riya. Your mother. We really do hurt and reject you a lot, do we not?"

"You certainly do," he said, almost in a whisper, his throat constricting him suddenly with surging emotions. "But I was hurt the most four years back, when you broke my heart, and cut it to bleed, and made me want to kill myself and end it all."

Shyamoli covered her mouth as if to stifle a cry. She put her arms around him, pulling his head to her shoulder.

And for some reason, Abir could finally cry and shed the tears that he had held for years; tears that he had vowed never to shed for the relationship which made his heart bleed.

Bleed with the frustration of getting rejected every time from women when he meant nothing but good.

Rejected for doing nothing wrong, but always being in the wrong situation, at the wrong place, at the wrong time.

Shyamoli sat down with a thump on the floor of the balcony, her arms tightly holding him as he sobbed uncontrollably. Her tears flowed freely, along with his, as she desperately moved her fingers over his hair, hugging him tightly, as he wept openly. Slowly he stopped, and Shyamoli continued to hold him tight as if she never wanted to let him go.

* * *

The market behind the balcony was still alive with people moving around, despite it being midnight. The yellow lights hung from the poles were alighted, bright, and blazing. Moths hovered around the yellow lights as if magically attracted to them, circling round and round.

Abir and Shyamoli sat on the balcony. He had laid down with his head on her lap for the last two hours, and she had let him lie down in that position, stroking his head, wiping away his tears with her hands. He stayed put there, his feeling of hurt and being wronged

215

finally washed away with his tears, and his mind felt tranquil, with a supreme sense of peace.

Shyamoli looked at the market, lost in thoughts, and Abir simply looked at her, noting her face as the lights from the market fell on her. Her big eyes looked at a distance, and Abir knew that she was thinking of the day four years back. Back then, Shyamoli had been critical and sharp about his mother, his family, and vowed to never unite with his family. Yet now, she seemed to be less critical.

"You were furious over my mother's prejudiced attitude, Shyamoli," he said eventually. "You rejected me. You rejected all of us. But now you are defending her. I don't quite understand."

"I have learned to forgive and forget," she said simply. "Also, your blogs and talks helped me, Abir."

"Yes, that makes you find peace within yourself, Shyamoli," he said gently. "But it still remains the fact that it has done nothing for my mother, who is still as prejudiced as ever. My blogs and talks seem to have no effect on her."

"Yes, perhaps," she said calmly. "But I look at it differently now. Her prejudice comes from the over-importance of skin color that society has supported for ages. Now when I am slightly older and have seen the world a little bit more, I realize that the prejudice remains and will always remain. It's not just her and is not unique to her. This has been happening over time, to a lot of women besides me. And not just with women, men too. I have learned to feel less bitter about this, accept it, and move on."

They sat down on the balcony for some time, the gentle breeze blowing her hair, making it fall around her face, something which he always loved.

He gently moved the hair from her face and, in the process, accidentally brushed his hands against her lips.

"I really think I should not allow you to stay with me tonight," said Shyamoli severely.

"Why?" asked Abir, stretching his hands lazily. "You think I will come out of your friend zone and suddenly crave for you as the night falls?"

"Well, I did not mean that," she said, looking embarrassed.

"With you looking so beautiful, which rational man would have confidence with oneself when around you?"

"Shame on you!" she said, laughing. "It's not even twenty-four hours since you broke up with Riya, and now you are making passes at me? Flirting with your friend? So inappropriate at this time!"

"Well, you also came dressed to kill and give a competition to Riya when you came over to meet us, no?" he said, raising his eyebrows. "Was that not bordering on inappropriateness?"

"Well, this Riya creature certainly took great pains to do a character study of me!" said Shyamoli indignantly. "I bet she put all these thoughts into your head, no? She really flipped out when she got some competition for once! Bless her, but what an absolute idiot she is."

Abir did not reply. Instead, he looked her in her eyes, and she smiled at him.

"Well, I must say I am happy to see you like your old self," she said, "and not like the morose character that I saw some weeks back at the river when I was strolling with Aniruddha."

"Ah, well, I have gathered a fistful of experience about women, all in a single day, and I salute you guys for making things impossible to be deciphered by us dim-witted men," he said, half sarcastically.

Shyamoli laughed out loud.

"No, seriously. You lot are pathetic, and you know that!" he said, frowning. "First, you ditch me. Then you come over to see my fiancée, all dressed to kill, flirt with me, and as a result, she flips out and ditches me! You won't marry me, and you won't let anybody else marry me either! What do you want me to do—stay all my life in this stateless limbo?"

"Oh, can we change topics?" she said, turning away from him. "I have gone over this already."

"Well, OK. You made my would-be fiancée ditch me. So now I am your responsibility," he said. "I am going to hang on to you, whether you and I can get to stay together officially or not. You are a donkey, and I am your burden."

Shyamoli laughed out loud.

"Abir, I really think you should go back to your home. Your mother will worry, and again I will be the culprit."

"No, I won't. If you don't let me stay with you, I will sleep outside your door," Abir said.

Shyamoli's eyes suddenly lit up, as if holding back tears at his doggedness to be around her. Abir put his hands on her face gently and brushed away the hair from her face.

"It's tough belonging to a family like yours, isn't it?" said Shyamoli after a silence, half sarcastically. "So much control over a grown-up man! And such high expectations! They want a lot of things from you, and you concede and give them all they want. Mister hi-fi, overachiever, earns in hundreds of thousands of dollars, perfect role model of a son, super obedient, six-foot-tall, handsome, glamorous and famous. Every parent's dream, no? So naturally, they think you will get them the perfect glamorous daughter-in-law to represent their family. I think you failed them at that juncture. That's why so much drama!"

"Yes, I think you have summed it up perfectly," he said gloomily. "But such insane family expectations also helped me seek out the other side of the energy; empathy for the common person who truly needs it. Now that I am four years older—and wiser, I hope—I try to practice this in every situation."

Shyamoli nodded silently.

"And—I hope to pass it on to our children," said Abir.

"Oh—did you mean *our* children?" asked Shyamoli, blushing a bright shade of red.

"Yes," said Abir, looking into her eyes, solemnly.

"Shame on you!" she said, laughing, her face flushed with embarrassment. "You are thinking of making me your children's mother, even knowing that we can never marry? It may be OK in Western cultures, but a strict no-no in Indian cultures. What kind of a girl do you think I am? I will not even let you touch me anywhere unless and until we get married, and you are allowed to touch me properly! And since that cannot happen, technically, I can never be the mother of your children."

"Marriage is just an artificial social construct to balance the world of humans," said Abir. "I will abduct you from this society so that they stop having their diabolic influence on you. Then I will marry you because there will be no society around to care whether we got together or not. And then, finally, the natural will follow, as a man and woman together are programmed to do. I see my yet unborn children in your eyes, and I will be damned if I don't have them with you eventually—friend, BFF, partner in business or what-not—even if I have to wait a hundred years."

Shyamoli covered her face with her palms in embarrassment.

"Don't worry, it's all hypothetical and wistful" he said, pulling her hands away from her face. "I am a decent, typical mama's boy, remember? I will never touch you like that without your complete approval. And since you may never approve it ever, this is all a wist-ful fantasy, Shyamoli. But I will stay with you tonight, in this apart-ment, and Miss Shyamoli, you can't kick me out. You can sleep in your bedroom, and I will sleep on the sofa in the outer room."

He pulled her nose playfully and got up to stretch, as Shyamoli continued sitting down on the balcony floor, her face flushed and radiant.

* * *

Abir felt his phone vibrating in his pocket. He and Shyamoli were sitting on the couch—or rather, she was sitting on the couch, and Abir was lying down on her lap, like old times, his thoughts completely on the surrounding and around her, just looking at her face inverted, as he had seen them in his mind a thousand times.

He saw it was his mother calling. He picked it up reluctantly.

"Abir, I heard from Riya's mother that you disappeared sud-denly from their place! It's almost midnight now! What is going on? Where are you?"

"I am at a friend's place, mom," he said.

"What kind of childishness is this, Abir? Riya's mother tells me that Riya is very upset. When will you stop being childish and grow up? You are a thirty-year-old responsible grown-up man now! What's the meaning of this strange irresponsible behavior?"

"Riya and I are not getting engaged, mom," he said quietly.

"What! When did this happen? Are you out of your mind?"

"I am going to stay over at my friend's house tonight, mom. I will talk to you tomorrow."

"Your friend's house? When did you ever have friends in the city? Be more clear, Abir. Who are you with?"

Abir took a deep breath and looked at Shyamoli, who was looking back at him, her large eyes suddenly apprehensive, holding an expression that he had seen four years back when he had talked to her for the last time. His heart suddenly started beating fast. He was in a similar situation as he was four years back. His mettle and strength to hold his ground was being tested again. Try as he may, somehow he could not muster enough courage to bring up controversial topics with his mother, but this time, he had to pucker up and make it clear. He closed his eyes for a second and decided that this was the time he made it clear.

"I am with Shyamoli," he said quietly.

There was a silence at the other end. Abir waited for Mother to say something, but she said nothing. He had seen these symptoms before. She was too shocked to speak. He knew she would not talk to him and disconnect the phone. He was not wrong as he heard the phone get disconnected.

* * *

Abir woke up to find sunlight falling on his eyes from the window. He had fallen asleep on the sofa, true to his promise, and Shyamoli had gone to her bedroom inside. He looked around for Shyamoli, wondering why he was feeling anxious and unhappy despite being with her, and remembered that he had told his mother about him being with Shyamoli again.

Shyamoli had left a small note by his side. It was a Monday, and she had woken up early to go to work at her summer college session. She wrote in her note that she had made breakfast for him.

His coffee was in a small mug beside the stove covered by a plate. There was also a new toothbrush for him.

He looked at the clock and was surprised to find that it was already noon. He really had overslept significantly, he thought to himself as he had his breakfast after freshening up. He explored the books on the shelves to while away his time, although back in his mind, he felt he had a responsibility to call his parents, but knowing his mother, he knew she would not pick up his call. He decided that this was a time to enjoy and rejuvenate and not to worry about these details.

He knew Shyamoli would be back late in the afternoon. It would be good to make some lunch for her, he thought with sudden inspiration. He put on his shoes, locked the door, and went down the stairs. He went around the apartment complex and entered the market, which he had been observing from her balcony. Fishmongers and vegetable sellers in small shops with makeshift cloth ceilings balancing on bamboo poles made up for the shops. The shopkeepers sat on mats, shooing away flies as they busily weighed out portions of their items to the customers.

Abir looked around happily. These were his people, and these were the exact kind of people for whom he had made his social upliftment data platform for.

He took out his phone and started asking questions to some of the sellers who seemed to be selling handmade goods such as dolls, ornaments, and toys. He asked them if they wanted to be a part of his platform. Initially, they were politely intrigued, but soon, some of them got interested when they learned that it was all free and that all they had to do was to go to his App and enter some information regularly so that people knew what they were selling.

After chatting with the vendors, he decided to shop for ingredients to cook fish curry. He bought a fish, had its scales peeled off, and had it cut into pieces. He wanted to surprise Shyamoli with a fish dish, which he knew was her favorite. Ayan had taught him the recipe some time back, and he had tried it out many times, each time surprising himself with the taste he could produce.

Back home in Shyamoli's apartment, he started cooking, surprising himself with his own dexterity as he fried the fishes, and in parallel, prepared the sauce with mixes of cumin, tomatoes, turmeric, and ginger. He cooked rice in parallel, lightly frying them before boiling them and adding some bay leaves and cardamom to bring out the flavor that he knew Shyamoli liked.

By the time he was almost done, it was late afternoon. When he was putting the finishing touches to the fish *curry* with chopped cilantro leaves, the door opened, and Shyamoli came in, her face flushed with excitement at the prospect of seeing him. Abir instinctively went over to her, put his hands around her shoulder, and hugged her, and she let herself melt into his embrace.

"I have made some fish and rice for you," he said happily, taking the bowls of food and plates and setting them on the table. Shyamoli looked at them, and hurriedly went in, washed her hands and face, and came back to sit on the chair.

"OK, Mr. Chef, you can serve me," she said, her eyes shy.

"Certainly," said Abir, filled with happiness. He first put the rice carefully on her plate, making a mold. Then he made a hole at the center of the rice mold and carefully put the curry in there. Then he took two pieces of fish and put them gingerly on the side. Making a dashing bow, he asked her to start eating.

Shyamoli started eating with her hands, her eyes closing in delight as she savored the first bite.

"This is quite good. You have the makings of a great chef. But I feel bad eating alone."

"OK, I will come and join you," he said.

Shyamoli and Abir sat on the table, eating their meal silently, each aware of the other's presence. The afternoon sunlight fell on the mirror on a hanging bejeweled decorations on the wall, refracting the light and creating fragments of rainbows all around the place. To Abir, this was pure heaven where even the lights were fitting in to accompany him in the surreal feeling that he was having to be sitting down with Shyamoli for a meal, like old times.

* * *

Abir felt his phone ringing. It was evening. He was sitting on the table, editing a new blog on Shyamoli's computer, while Shyamoli sat beside him, reading a book.

He saw it was mother. He picked it up reluctantly.

"Are you done with the childish marooning? You should go to Riya's place and apologize at once!"

Abir chose not to reply or respond to her.

"And does this Shyamoli have no shame at all? What kind of a greedy person is she? Do you know what you are doing is so obviously inappropriate and shameful? I haven't told your father anything about it—I just said you were with some friends. Just imagine what shame this will be if, by chance, people get to know about you staying over at this Shyamoli's place instead of at Riya's. Doesn't Shyamoli's mother have any sense?"

"Mom, Shyamoli's mother is no more," he said quietly, moving over to the balcony so that Shyamoli could not hear his conversation. "She passed away some time back. Shyamoli and I stayed alone in her rented apartment where she stays these days."

There was a stunned silence for a few seconds.

"You mean you were alone with her the entire night? Just the two of you in that apartment?" Mother asked, almost in a whisper.

"Yes, mom, I stayed here," Abir said calmly. "I slept here overnight. I also made food for her when she went to work in the afternoon. She is reading a book right now. Do you want to talk to her?"

There was another stunned silence, as Mother digested all this information.

"You scandalous, worthless man," she said slowly after a prolonged silence, every syllable shaking with disgust. "What profound shame you have brought to our family. You dare to say all this with such confidence, you ungrateful brat! Did I raise you up to be so low minded? Do you even realize what a shameful thing it is to stay over with a spinster, and that too, alone? Do you have no shame, no sense of culture at all? When did you become so characterless?"

Abir's heart sank instinctive at the attack on his character, but he remained silent. It was her opinion, her words. He did not feel obligated to respond or make himself accountable.

"Just look at that dark female," whispered Mother, venom spewing in every word. "This witch is playing with your mind, and you are giving up Riya, the princess, and falling for a lowly, worthless female who is fit to be her maidservant?"

Abir remained silent, digesting her words.

"How did you figure out these strata, mom?" he said after a while, his tone courteous, but his mind slowly burning hot with suppressed rage. "What is it that gives you the right to call one person fit to be somebody else's maid, mom? Is it skin color? Is Krishna not dark-skinned? Is goddess Kali not dark? Did you ever really try to understand who Shyamoli is, what her worth is? Did you ever, mom? Or did you look at her dark complexion and came to a conclusion that she is automatically fit for subjugation?"

"Oh, so she has taught you moral values to suit the situation now," said Mother, her voice shaking with hatred. "When you realize that marriages happen between equals, you will realize what I am talking about. There are thousands of glamorous girls out there who would die to live with you, marry you, and have a family with you. This Shyamoli is conning you because it's a win-win for her, and it's a cunning strategy on her part."

"That's just your opinion, mom," said Abir quietly.

"Are you going to get away from that place, Abir?" asked Mother sternly.

"Not right now," he said quietly.

There was a silence at the other end. Abir waited, hopefully, hoping against hope that he would hear some form of encouragement from his mother.

"I refuse to talk to you anymore until and unless you come to your senses," said Mother after a pause. "And—I am deeply disappointed in you, Abir. Shame on you!"

The phone went silent, and he realized that Mother had disconnected the phone.

* * *

224

Abir stood on the balcony, looking at the market morosely. He heard Shyamoli open the door to the balcony, and turning around, he found her looking at him, looking distressed.

"Your mother must be really angry with you," she said in a small voice.

"Yep, she is," said Abir casually, going back inside and flopping down on the sofa.

"Oh," said Shyamoli. Her eyes teared up suddenly. Abir got up and went beside her.

"Hey, hey, don't cry," he said anxiously, as Shyamoli covered her face with her hands. "Come on, look at me. It's all OK."

"No, nothing is OK," said Shyamoli, sobbing. "I am yet again the cause for your unhappiness."

"No, you are not," he said firmly, patting her head. "My mom is like that—has always been like that! I have learned to ignore her views and crazy expectations over these years. And she has so many of them! Every year, she asks me about promotions. About my raise in salary. About the stock prices of my company. And every time I don't do something according to her expectations, she shows her disappointment."

"But she hates me so much," said Shyamoli, continuing to sob. "I am sure she must have blamed me for everything. I just get a lot of hatred for doing nothing. I asked you to go back to her, did I not?"

"Of course you did," said Abir, wiping the tears from her eyes. "It was my choice not to go back home. As it is now my choice to not go back home even now."

"Don't be so casual," she said, her eyes welling up with tears again. "Whatever you do, I am just your friend, and she is your mother. She has a hundred times more right over you than me. You should go back immediately and apologize to her. And go back and tell her it was all my fault."

Abir laughed out loud. Shyamoli stared at him apprehensively, as if not quite sure how to react.

"My dear Miss Shyamoli," he said, pulling her nose playfully, "You are one sentimental, over-idealistic character, are you not? Why should *you* take the blame on yourself, when it's not your fault at all! In fact, far from it, you gave me shelter and company when I needed it the most. Now, just relax! Let me make some tea for you."

* * *

"What happened?" asked Abir. They had been sitting on the sofa, just in each other's presence, not thinking about the future, or even what would happen at the end of the day, when Shyamoli's phone had rung. She chatted briefly and suddenly rushed off to change into outdoor clothes.

"I just got a call from the women's shelter where I volunteer. It looks like one of the women whom I had counseled is back at the shelter. Her drunk husband beat her black and blue today. She escaped and is now in the shelter. She really needs my counseling now. I will quickly go there by bus."

"I will come with you," said Abir, quickly putting on his shoes. "And let's take an Uber."

"What will you do in a women's shelter? Take rest, I will be back quickly."

"No, it's already night time. I will come with you and stay outside the building. I can't let you go alone at this hour," he said. "Besides, I am going to be your partner in all your social efforts, so might as well start that with this episode!"

Shyamoli smiled at him gratefully as they locked the door to go out.

* * *

Abir waited outside the gate of the shelter. Dim lights lit up the front of the building. Some other women volunteers were already there to console the abused woman, who was crying inconsolably. Her face was bruised with all the beating. Shyamoli had instinctively taken her bag with her, which contained first aid, some food, and water, although the shelter had them. It was getting dark, and in a few hours, it would become midnight. He had a quick chat with Shyamoli over text, and she said it would still take some time to console this woman, who had tried to commit suicide, but at the last moment, decided to run off and come over here. She would not want it to be a police case because she was afraid.

Abir waited outside, hanging around near a broken garage near the building. A few stray dogs ambled around, looking at him with their yellow eyes, hoping he had food. He searched his pockets to find some biscuits. He gave them to the dogs, watching as they nabbed up the biscuits hungrily, looking at him beseechingly, as if asking for more. He wished he had more food with him to give to these dogs. The shops were closed. This somewhat dingy side of Kolkata was not alive with people.

Suddenly, he heard a row coming over from the shelter. Instinctively, he ran over. A group of three men had accumulated by the door, and one of them, drunk, was shouting slurs and banging on the door.

Abir felt his heart freeze with fear. Shyamoli was inside. These men meant no good. He knew that the drunk one must be the husband of the battered woman, coming over here to take her back. He called Shyamoli urgently on the phone.

"Shyamoli, there are a bunch of goons banging on the door," he said breathlessly on the phone.

"Yes, I know," she said, sounding scared. "We are at the back of the house, hiding inside a room. I called the police, but I have no idea if, or when, they will arrive. I have also called Aniruddha, who will be arriving with some boys. Abir, stay away from this. Oh, I am so scared I brought you here. Please go back home to my place. Right now."

"What? Are you out of your mind? Shyamoli, you are in danger too! I have to do something right now!"

Suddenly, he heard the sound of wood splattering ominously. He looked on in alarm as one of the men almost broke the door. He started running toward the entrance, terrified, as the men started battering the door with more energy. He could hear women screaming from inside, even as the door splattered dangerously, about to break.

With a roar of fury, he rushed at the three men and pushed away the one banging the door to break it. One of the other men caught him by his collars and punched him on his face. Abir lashed back at him, hitting him square on his jaws, even as blood splattered from his nose. As this man fell, he felt another one hold him on his neck, trying to strangle him. He lashed around, and the second man fell off. By then, he was beside himself with rage and utter fear of what might happen to Shyamoli and the women if he could not stop these criminals.

Suddenly the door opened, and Shyamoli stood on the door, with a stick in her hand, along with the woman whose drunk husband had come to fetch her. She started raining blows on the goons, trying to fend them off, trying to escape. One of the men lashed out at her, and she fell down backward, unbalanced.

"Run, Shyamoli, run," Abir shouted, beside himself with fury, mad with anger that the goon dared to hit her. Shyamoli took hold of the other woman and ran toward the entrance gate onto the deserted road outside, screaming at Abir to leave them and run away with her, but he was beside himself with rage and continued to fight with the goons.

"Abir, stop it and run," screamed Shyamoli from the gate, holding on to the other woman, who was weeping profusely in terror. Abir fought it out, ignoring the screams from Shyamoli. The vision of Shyamoli falling down occurred to him recurrently, and it made him boil with anger. He lashed out to the three men, who had surrounded him, his fury overtaking his practical mind that he was not used to all this, ignoring the blood gushing out of his nose and mouth.

As he turned around to thwart off another goon trying to fist-fight with him, he saw the drunk man lift a heavy stick which was lying around and aim at him.

Before he could move away, the stick landed on his head, and he felt a sickening pain go through his head.

Everything became blurred around him suddenly, and a sharp din started in his head. A sudden high pitched sound in his head made all the noise around him drown out, as he fumbled and swayed, clutching his head, trying to keep steady.

And in the blurriness of it all, a vision rose in front of him. He saw Shyamoli rushing at him to thwart off the goons, as if in slow motion, her large eyes suddenly looking terrible in its fury. And at the same time, the door of the shelter opened fully, and a hoard of women poured out, sticks and utensils in their hands. He watched in awe, his head spinning with intense pain, his eyes blurry, as Shyamoli raised the stick in her hand, and the other women surround her, and suddenly, to him, they all combined to form the ten-handed Goddess Durga—the supreme Goddess of power. He smiled, bemused, kneeling down slowly, blood gushing down his face, unable to stand any more, as Shyamoli rained blows on the men with her stick, her face livid with terrible rage, the women around her rallying, the ten hands of Durga about to destroy the evil that dared to descend on them.

The goons stopped fighting and scampered out of the gate, even as he could see the soundless scream of fury from Shyamoli, the tidal wave of power from the combination of the women who stood tall like Goddess Durga, their eyes blazing with the power of twenty Suns. He could suddenly hear the sound of *dhaak*, of the powerful conchs in his head, as Shyamoli and the women stood their ground, their combined fury shaking the Earth beneath him, and his mind celebrated the descent of Durga from the heavens.

Abir folded his hands in front of them, in a posture of prayer, as if seeking blessings from the Goddess Durga who had manifested herself in Shyamoli—a radiant Goddess, the most heavenly one he had ever seen, with flaming eyes that scorched everything around in sheer blazing power and fury, the most powerful Durga idol that he had ever seen in his life.

Then he fell at Shyamoli's feet, unconscious, blood dripping all over the ground, gushing out from the deep open wound on his head.

Dawn of dusk

Abir felt he was flying inside a kaleidoscope of nothingness. Colors of all shades came rushing in, in an intoxicating concoction of effects he had hitherto never seen. The voices accompanying those colors were distant and, at the same time, near. They were soft and blurry and felt like threads of sounds strung together in a seamless ocean of ideas and concepts, all mangled together. In this dark, confusing world, why was not Shyamoli by his side? Why was he not lying on her lap, as he had done a thousand moons, for eternity, forever, with her hand on his head like a caressing angel, like the Goddess Durga, assuring him that he would be fine? Why was she not singing to him, her soft voice falling like pearls on the grass, like twigs on tranquil waters, making beautiful waves that he could immerse himself into? Why was Riya not hitting him, again and again, to punish him for his sins? Why was Mother not chiding him, again and again, bitter disappointment in her voice for failing to live up to her expectations? He could not open his eyes, to see these people, to understand why he could not communicate with them, and ask them, for the last time, why they had all rejected him, found him unworthy of them.

After drifting in and out of consciousness for two days, Abir finally woke up, opening his eyes feebly to find himself flanked by his parents and relatives. There were urgent murmurings as he opened his eyes, and an unknown male voice asked him if he could comprehend him, and if he could say his name. He realized that he could not move without feeling a blinding pain on his forehead. He closed his eyes and murmured his name. A few more questions followed, to which he could reply, painfully and slowly.

"No major problem with his memory," said the voice. "He is conscious now. Give him space, everybody. Please leave the room."

There was some bustling as everybody, except mother, left. He opened his eyes feebly to see her face, white, devoid of all emotions except fear.

"Let him take rest. I will give him his injection shot tomorrow," said the voice, which he realized must be a doctor. He looked around feebly to realize that he was home. How did he get here?

"Hello, mom," he whispered as she took his hand. Her hand felt cold, as if devoid of all energy.

"You should rest now," she said, fumbling around his bed, straightening the bedsheet. As she got up to turn the lights off, Abir whispered feebly, "Did anybody else come to see me?"

His mother stopped short and turned around. She hesitated slightly and then said, "Shyamoli is here to see you."

Abir felt a joyful shiver go through his body. Shyamoli. His Shyamoli. Mother said she was here. If she was here, where was she? He tried to ask her, but she had already turned off the lights and gone. He closed his eyes, slowly drifting off to sleep again, his mind picturing Shyamoli's big eyes as if they were looking at him, consoling him, caressing him.

* * *

Abir opened his eyes. It was evening. He could make out somebody sitting by his bedside. The light was dim, ambient from outside. The door was slightly ajar. There was absolute silence except for the breathing of the person next to him. He did not understand who it was, but instinctively spoke out feebly "Shyamoli?"

He felt a soft hand enfold his and felt the same shiver go through his body as he had felt every time Shyamoli had held his hand. A soft wet drop fell on his hands, and he opened his eyes to see tears drop down from her eyes, like pearls glittering under radiating lights. He savored the wetness of the tears on his hand, closing his eyes, feeling as if he was floating in the air, feeling absolutely safe, with nothing to worry about in life, as if nobody could touch him, nobody could disturb him ever. He closed his eyes, his head hurting him even in that small moment, and went to sleep again, smiling.

231

"Shyamoli?" asked Abir softly as he opened his eyes. It was morning, and he could see her sitting beside her. She smiled at Abir, and to him, she let in the sunlight through her eyes, her smile illuminating the room. He looked at her anxiously. Dark lines etched her eyes, and she looked like a person who had not slept for several nights.

Abir's mother entered the room to sit beside him, and Shyamoli rose up quickly, looking anxious.

"Thank you for visiting us again, Shyamoli," said Mother coldly, not looking at her. "Abir is awake, and you can leave now."

Shyamoli stared at her, her eyes anxious, and glancing at Abir, she left the room hurriedly. Abir looked at her as she left the room, feeling dejected. Mother looked away as she left, after which she sat beside him and patted his arms gently, coaxing him to go to sleep again.

* * *

"My first instinct was to not let her in my house. All this happened because of her. Look what happened to my Abir when he was with her. This Shyamoli brings nothing but misery to him, whether by purpose or by accident."

Abir could hear his mother talking to his aunt and Ruku mashi outside the door. She was speaking in a low voice, but he could still hear her. He laid down still, still feeling groggy from all the sedative medicines, feeling utterly dejected at her tone.

"Why did this girl come to see him at all?" asked Ruku mashi, her tone looking for a scandal.

"Well, she was the one who took Abir to the hospital in the city and gave us a call. But I did not want my baby to recuperate in the hospital, so I had him brought home after the first few days. But she came over to see him at our home too! My immediate reaction was to slap her hard because this happened when he was with her."

"You slapped her?" asked his aunt, sounding shocked.

"No, I wanted to, but I did not."

"What was Abir doing with this dark-skinned girl anyways?" asked Ruku mashi suspiciously. "Who is she? I have never seen her ever."

"Oh, she is just some random friend of his," said Mother casually.

"But you told me he had gone to meet Riya?" prodded Ruku mashi. "Where did this girl come in the picture? And how did Abir get injured at all? This is all a mystery to me."

"I will tell you everything later," said Mother. "Don't bother me now."

"Tell me, Boudi, what happened after Shyamoli came to see him here?" asked his aunt.

"I just asked her to get lost immediately," said Mother, her voice hard. "But she started weeping profusely, saying that she would go away from his life forever, but only after making sure he was alright. She said she would personally nurse him back to health. She said she was willing to sleep outside our door but could not bear to be away from him."

"So sweet!" said his aunt.

"Sweet?" said Mother angrily. "Just acting, if you ask me! These young kids know how to fake all this! But I could not kick her away because Abir's father insisted that she should be allowed to stick around to be near Abir. She has since been around to look after Abir."

"You let an unmarried girl stay in your house like this?" asked Ruku mashi, sounding shocked. "And also, look after Abir?"

"Oh, she does not stay here! No, no, absolutely not! Abir's father wanted her to stay in the guest room, but I put my foot down. No way!"

"But I see her early in the morning and in the evening too," said his aunt. "Does she live nearby in these suburbs?"

"Oh, she stays all the way in the city in north Kolkata," said Mother. "She comes early in the morning by train. Then she leaves to get back to work and comes right after work and stays back till the last train back at night."

"That's a lot of travel! Must be really hard on her," said his aunt, her voice sounding sympathetic.

"Well yes, indeed it is a bit hard, but she promised to put Abir back to shape, and she has to stick at it. I can never forget that she is the one responsible for Abir's serious injury. I shudder to think what would have happened if he had been wounded even more."

"Well, she seems to take care of him very well in these last few days," insisted his aunt.

"Well, she better do it," said Mother sternly. "I can't wait to see her off and never return to see my face again. But to be fair, she is indeed very dedicated to my Abir to make him feel better. But she made a grave blunder by allowing him to stay at her house. On top of that, she was solely responsible for what happened to him! Let her atone for her sins!"

"Abir stayed at this girl's house?" asked Ruku mashi, sounding scandalized.

"I will tell you everything later," snapped Mother. "Just learn to be patient! And not a word about it to anybody, or you will get it from me, Ruku!"

"I think you should listen to her side of the story too," said his aunt softly. "You know, I bumped into her downstairs yesterday, and she smiled at me, and her smile had an innocence which I liked."

Mother made an impatient dismissive sound.

"One smile caught your attention?" asked Ruku mashi, giggling.

"I think she is really pretty too," continued his aunt calmly, ignoring Ruku mashi.

"She is just dark-skinned!" said Ruku mashi scornfully.

"So what?" interjected his aunt. "I have never seen a girl so beautiful! Such nice features, big eyes, such nice hair! She is truly gorgeous."

"Oh shut up," said Mother dismissively.

"No, really!" continued his aunt. "You know, my Rimjhim is already smitten by her. She says Shyamoli didi helped her with her homework yesterday. I think my Rimjhim has a girl crush on her and told me she wants to grow up and be like Shyamoli didi."

"Stop praising her unnecessarily and get to the point! What are you getting at?" asked Mother irritably.

"I am saying, given that our Abir likes her so much, what is stopping you from getting them married? No, don't just shake your head—try and listen to what I am saying. Our Abir is so handsome, and whatever you say, I think Shyamoli is really pretty—dark complexion or not. You will have beautiful grandchildren because both of them are so good looking. They will make a great pair together."

"What nonsense!" exclaimed Mother angrily. "Where is the question of marriage coming from? Are you out of your mind?"

"It's just a thought."

"Nonsense!" spatted Mother angrily. "Don't talk about things you don't understand! I have no idea why you are talking about marriage, of all things!"

"Well, you have been nagging Abir about marriage for some now," said his aunt, sounding hurt at been rebuked. "I am just making a suggestion, which seems like a good solution."

"You seem to conveniently forget Riya!" said Mother angrily. "Riya has it all—the looks, the attitude, the opulence in her upbringing, the style, the arrogance! Plus, she is glamorous. Do you know, she plays tennis, lives in a bungalow in one of the most opulent places in Kolkata, and drives an expensive foreign car? Also, she is milk white! She is the one who will look right beside my Abir."

"You think this Riya will make Abir happy?" persisted his aunt.

"Yes, she will! I will make her come back to his life and make him happy. Mark my words. I don't know what transpired between her and Abir, but I will put it all right."

"But it is Shyamoli who is looking after Abir even as we speak, and not Riya" persisted his aunt.

Mother made a dismissive sound.

"Riya is not a nurse! Anyways, she will fit just fine with Abir. But first, I need to get rid of this Shyamoli. And don't you dare stick up for her like you are doing!"

"No, no, I am just stating some points," said his aunt, sounding scared. "And don't worry, Boudi—Abir will do the right thing and will bring the right woman to this home as his life partner. Right now, though, he is just too busy trying to make everybody around him happy, bless him. He is a real sweetheart."

"That he is," said Mother, supreme pride in her voice. "I am so proud of my Abir. You are right—he is an absolute sweetheart. I must have done something great in my past life to be blessed with a son like him. Look at his achievements at such a young age! I see his videos on YouTube, look at all the work he has been doing, read his articles on the internet. So intelligent! So passionate about what he does! So compassionate to others! Too compassionate at times, I think. He is my God. And only a Goddess of the highest degree, the best of women, can be a match with my Abir."

"You already have a Goddess walking your doors these days. You just can't see it," said his aunt in a small but meaningful voice, even as Mother made an impatient noise in disdain and got up to leave.

* * *

"Hello Abir, you gave us all quite a scare."

It was Ayan on the line. Abir smiled to himself—he always savored Ayan's calls.

"I am feeling better now, Ayan. How did you know?"

"Shyamoli called us and told us."

Abir was startled. In his drowsiness and confusion over the last few days, he had never asked himself; where was Shyamoli now? He had been so over the moon at her presence that he did not think it necessary to even think about it.

"Looks like she had been to your place all this while to look after you. Good girl."

"Yes, she has been here," said Abir, feeling a sense of elation that he had not felt in the last four years. Ayan put down the phone, and Abir went back to sleep happily.

* * *

It was late afternoon. Abir had just woken up from his slumber and could now sit up in an upright position, albeit his head still felt heavy. The sedating medicine was still in his body, and he was feeling unusually tranquil and sleepy.

The purdah on his bedroom door parted, and to his chagrin, Riya entered the room. Mother ushered her in silently and went off, casting a meaningful glance at her before leaving.

"How are you feeling, Abir?" Riya asked.

Abir smiled uncomfortably, wondering if she had overcome her mad rage at him. He looked at her nervously, hoping she would not start a conversation about Shyamoli with him again. Would there be no end to this?

"Your mother called me and asked me to come over to meet you," she said tentatively after a pause.

Abir stared at her, suddenly feeling annoyed. Trust Mother to continue her cunning ways to get what she wanted! He grimaced to himself, deciding that it was time he was firm. He waved her to the chair in the room.

"You should not have troubled with this long journey. Hope you did not lose your way?" he asked.

Riya shook her head and, after some deliberation, said, "I am sorry about the other day, Abir. I probably overreacted."

Abir shook his head and said, "No, you are not to blame. You merely got angry, and you were somewhat justified. I deserved it."

Riya looked away as if making up her mind on how to approach him. She got up from the chair and went to the mirror, looking at it as if contemplating what she wanted to say. She came near him, standing over him and looking at him.

"I guess we can forget what I said that day—about you and me not marrying," she said, twirling her hair. Abir looked on warily, not sure how he should respond. He felt vulnerable at this point. He could not take another dose of excitement or drama right now. Riya went over to the mirror once more, her high heels clicking on the floor of his bedroom. He wondered if his mother had noticed it— usually, everybody took off their shoes when they came in. Riya was already special, thought Abir to himself, feeling annoyed.

As Riya swung around from the mirror once more, he realized that he had never seen her wear Indian dress before. Her hair fell slightly over her face, and he realized that she had a hairstyling since the last time he saw her. There was something about the get-up that reminded him of Shyamoli, he thought with a start. What was it?

Was Riya copying Shyamoli?

Riya went over and closed the door. Then she ambled toward Abir, and he looked up at her apprehensively, suddenly feeling uncomfortable at the way she looked at him. Why did she close the door? She came near him, surveying him over her dense artificial eyelashes, fiddling with her earrings nervously, as if not used to dressing in this traditional way.

"What is it that this Shyamoli have that I don't have?" she said, coming near him. He could feel her closeness, the heat of her body, her strong perfume. He inched away nervously.

"Is she more beautiful than me?" she asked, moving closer to him, her hands touching his shoulders as he sat on the bed, her hair falling on his face. Abir turned his head to look away from her. Riya stood there for a while, looking down at him with an expression he could not fathom. He waited nervously, wishing she had not locked the door.

"You did not answer me, Abir. Don't turn away from me. Tell me, is Shyamoli more beautiful than me?" she whispered, sitting on the bed beside him. She put her finger on his chin and turned his face toward her. Her fingers went to his face, his lips, his hair. Abir felt hot and bothered and wished he had the strength to jump out of bed.

Riya put her arms around his neck and pulled his face toward hers, her eyes on him with a strange expression he could not understand.

Before he could push her off, she put her hands around his neck, tilted his face with her hands and pressed her lips on his.

He closed his eyes and felt nothing as she stayed in that position, her lips pressing deep into his, her tongue seeking his tongue. He tried to push her away gently, as she kissed his lips fiercely, not letting him go. The harder he tried to move away, the more fiercely she held on to him, burning his lips with hers, making them hurt.

"You can have me, Abir," she whispered, holding him tighter, her lips and tongue almost stifling him. He opened his eyes and turned away forcefully, breaking her lip-lock. Wiping her lipstick from his lips with the back of his hands, he unentangled himself and gently pushed her hands away from his neck.

Riya let him go and stood up with a jolt, her eyes blazing, as if she could not believe that he dared to reject her moves to be intimate with him. Out of instinct, Abir closed his eyes, fearing another physical assault from her, another outburst, more drama, more accusations. When nothing happened for a while, he opened his eyes again.

"So you do think this Shyamoli is more attractive than me?" she asked.

Abir looked at her quietly, not replying.

"Your silence says it all," she said.

She smiled to herself and sat down on the chair, contemplating Abir, as if looking for a new angle.

"So let me see," she said after a long pause. "You get rejected by all these women. First, this Shyamoli rejects you. Your mother rejects you. I reject you. Then this Shyamoli, seeing you after all these years, decides she wants to have you, by hook or by crook. She wants to be your partner in her stupid social upliftment things and whatnot. Pathetic! Where was she all these years when you were pining away for her? If she cared so much for you, she should not have treated you like this initially, right? She treated you like this for years, and you welcome her back. You have no shame, or self-pride! You just happily let her play her terms and let her back into your life as it suits her. In all this drama, where are you, Abir? Did she ever think of you, or what you went through?"

Abir listened to her silently, feeling slightly unnerved, realizing that Riya would be playing mind games with him for some time now, and he had to bear with her.

"This Shyamoli knows that you and I are going to be engaged and suddenly decides that she wants you," Riya continued. "What's up with her? First, she dumps you. Then she tries to steal you from me. And you obviously find her more attractive than me. What magic does she have?"

Abir looked back at her calmly, not replying.

"You are now suddenly attractive to her!" continued Riya, her face slowly getting contorted in anger, an expression Abir was familiar with. "You are attractive to most women anyways, the perfect marriage-material Richie-rich boy, no? Any random woman would want to marry you, marry to this family, married to this wealth. But no, you want this dark-skinned Shyamoli! What special attraction has that cunning black sorceress have? How does this dark-skinned woman even stand a chance against me, my class, my glamour?"

Abir looked back at her quietly, wondering how much of the mind game would go on and how long he would have to endure this torment.

"You are a pathetic bunch—you, your darky Shyamoli, your mother, this house. All of you," said Riya, her face becoming red with suppressed anger. Abir felt fatigued and wished somebody would come in to rescue him from her. Riya looked at him as if thinking over all that had happened, making up her mind to begin a new discourse. She got up to walk about in the room, ruffling her hair, looking at the mirror.

"Look at your mother. I mean, just look at her," she continued, turning to him, "You are a mama's boy, you don't see in her what any girl can see. Your mother is a cunning bully who conveniently leeches you for all the star status you give her and, at the same time, cleverly casts her disappointment at you as she pleases, to blackmail you emotionally and keep you in her control. I bet she rejected this Shyamoli in the first place because she is dark-skinned, but yet got your attention, which she could not tolerate. Serves this Shyamoli right, but that does not take away the fact that your mother is a typically chauvinistic, racist and manipulative bitch who feels superior just because she looks glamorous, and has an over-performing race-horse like you for a son."

"Don't talk like that about my mother," said Abir, feeling annoyed. Riya shook her hands at him impatiently, waving away his interjection.

"I don't understand how you are gentle with her, granting her all her wishes. You are gentle with all these people. You never seem to have a say or exhibit any retaliatory actions. They slap you when they like, then cry on your shoulder when they like! In all this game-play, nobody asked you how you felt about all this! You are the biggest pushover I have ever seen! Your emotions and feelings of being betrayed and hurt does not matter to any of these people!"

She got up and stood in front of the mirror in his room, looking at Abir in the reflection. Then she came back and took her seat on the chair with an air of purpose, looking at him. He stared back at her apprehensively.

Eventually, her expressions softened.

"Tell me something, Abir," she asked gently. "What is it that goes on in your mind when you deal with all these people, their utterly unfair treatment to you, and yet love them back? What gives you this utter peace and tranquility of mind?"

Abir looked at her and realized sadly that it was getting hard for Riya to get over him.

"What is it, Abir?" she continued. "What gives you this inner peace of mind to forgive others, to be calm, to be kind and empathetic despite the amount of cuts you receive through these people? Why do you have such a big heart?"

Abir stared serenely back at her, as she stared back at him, her eyes locked on his.

"You said it was your fault when I hit you that day, but you and I both know that it was all mine," she continued. "I had no right to hit you or abuse you in any way. I physically assaulted you. Yet even now, you are calm and unperturbed! What is this magic formula that you have to negotiate all this so calmly?"

Abir smiled at her.

"I want to soak in the negativity around me so that others can remain positive," he said quietly. "I have trained my mind to practice empathy at every step of my life. I have engineered my mind to be invisible, take *me* out of *myself*, so that I can try and put myself in the other person's shoes. For everything that you described, for every reaction from these people that you described, they have a deep-down internal reason for it. I get to see it only when I take *myself* out of it and look at it from a distance to truly try and understand their motives. Usually, I can do it after some effort. It's a mental training of sorts—an algorithm to practice empathy at every step. In fact, even right now, I am doing that, Riya."

He smiled at Riya, and she smiled back at him. He closed his eyes, his mind at peace, forgiving and overlooking everything that Riya had been trying to do or say. All this scrutiny had made him tired, and his bandaged head hurt again, but he felt good expressing his feelings to a neutral person as a first-hand experience, a far cry from the various TED talks he had given to generally receptive audiences.

"At the end of the day, it's love," he continued, his eyes closed. "Just love. Love for harmony. Love for life. I love to love, I guess."

He opened his eyes, feeling tired, and looked at her serenely. She looked back at him in wonder, her eyes bright, as if seeing everything in a new light.

Abir looked back at her, feeling sad because he knew that this was what Riya would like to get. Love. Powerful, all-encompassing love that he knew he could give and had it in him. He looked at her kindly, his practiced mind seeing only the positive sides of her presence: her beauty, her intelligence, her sensuality as she sat elegantly on the chair in her elegant dress.

He saw in her eyes yearning for him, and it made him sad for her. Although he respected and celebrated each person that had come to his life, he had a place in his heart and mind for only one woman. His Shyamoli.

"You deserve true love, Riya. You are destined to receive true love. You should move on," he said eventually, turning his head away to not see the tears in her eyes.

Riya looked on at him, almost beseechingly, her tears trickling down freely. Abir closed his eyes so that he did not have to look at her pain. He realized that in a few days, he had endeared himself to Riya. Was it her fault that made her react with such violence, made her abuse him physically, and break the marriage intentions? Abir's trained mind refuted this, and he put the blame on himself and the circumstances.

He opened his eyes as he felt a hand on his arms, soft and gentle. Riya bent down and put her arms around him, her tears wetting his face and neck. He did not turn away, letting her embrace him for one last time. He smiled gently at her and waved at her as she turned around abruptly and left the room.

* * *

"Shyamoli, you can keep the tray outside. I will take it in when Abir wakes up."

Abir heard his mother's voice outside the door, which was ajar. It was evening, and he had just woken up after a slumber and presumed that Mother thought he was still sleeping from all the sedatives. The news made him supremely happy, because it meant that Shyamoli was around in the house. He heard the soft click of glasses as the tray was put down and heard quiet steps moving away and down the stairs.

"Wait Shyamoli, I want to have a word with you," said Mother. He heard Shyamoli stop walking down the stairs and heard her come back near the outside sofa.

"Thank you for doing all this for Abir. After these weeks, Abir is finally feeling better. You are doing all this like a nurse, and I did not ask for a nurse. But you are making yourself useful, so I thank you for that, despite everything."

"Oh, this is the least I can do," said Shyamoli softly. Then, after a pause, she asked: "Why despite everything, Ma?"

"What do you mean?" he heard Mother ask sharply. "You caused all this. You know that, right?"

"I did not cause all this," said Shyamoli calmly. "Your son got involved in a scuffle that he is not used to and got hit by an inebriate goon."

"He went there at your provocation. You kept him at your house and asked him to join you," said Mother, her voice sounding angry.

"No, I did not ask him to stay at my place. He did it by his own accord."

"And why would he do that? Right on the day when he was supposed to be with Riya? What did you do?"

243

"Why don't you ask Riya what really happened? She was here in the morning. You could have asked her since you called her yourself."

"Don't be impertinent, Shyamoli! This is all a mystery to me, and I cannot ask Abir because he is so sick, and I don't want to trouble him."

"Riya threw him out of her house."

"She threw him out?"

"Yes. Riya threw him out of her house, and Abir came over to my place for comfort because he was upset."

"I see," said Mother, still sounding unconvinced. There was a silence.

"May I go now?" asked Shyamoli politely.

"No, wait. I have one more comment for you," said Mother coldly. "I see you trying to get in touch with my Abir again, trying to be intimate with him again, trying to win back his heart. I see that my indirect message to you four years back was not enough. Let me ask you once again—do you think you can match the opulence of this house, the class, and strata that Abir is used to seeing in women, like how he has seen me, his mother?"

"With due regard, you did not earn all this opulence. You just got it for free," said Shyamoli quietly.

Abir marveled at her level tone, surprised and somewhat shocked at her statement, and almost smiled as his mother let out an audible gasp.

"You dare to even utter this?" said Mother sharply.

"There is no fundamental difference between you and me," said Shyamoli, her voice serene and devoid of any emotions. "You and I are both women who pursue their intellectual passions. You come from a family that has strong Indian values. So do I. You are just lucky because you were married to this family. There is no reason to be proud or arrogant over it, with due respect. You take pride in the opulence of this home, its dignity, but you are merely lucky to be associated with it. You did not earn it. You simply got it for free."

Mother remained silent, as if not believing that Shyamoli dared to even utter these words.

"Too long have some women lost their power by attributing their greatness to the families they get married into," said Shyamoli, her tone serene, but reverberating with a strange power that made Abir awestruck at its force. "Too often have some women basked in the glory of things and material wealth for which they made no contribution, overlooking their own inner strength. I am sorry if I sound rude, but you did nothing to earn them. And that's the truth, whether you like it or not. You are proud of this magnificent bungalow, which you did not build—you got it for free by just being an IAS officer's wife. You are proud of your opulence, of the society that you mix with, but again, you got it for free by being a distinguished IAS officer's wife. You did not have to work for it—you just got it for free. If there is something you *should* be proud of, it should be your personal achievements. As a teacher. As a mentor. As a mother and as a human in this society."

Abir heard Mother stand up abruptly, moving the sofa in the process.

"You are the most impertinent woman I have ever met," Mother said, her voice shaking in anger. "First you reject my Abir, for which he suffered for years. Yes, you were the one responsible. A mother's heart knows exactly what is going on in her son's mind. I could see the pain that you gave to him. And not content with that, you brought this accident on him again!"

"I rejected Abir because you rejected me," said Shyamoli softly. "You had rejected me, and I would have suffered, and my mother would have suffered her daughter's heartbreak. I rejected Abir because I stood up for centuries of abuse that dark-skinned women like me have faced from society."

"What high ideals!" said Mother scornfully. "You think too much of yourself and broke an innocent man's heart for your ideals!"

"Yes, I certainly did," said Shyamoli, her voice suddenly sounding tearful. "I do accept that Ma. Not a single day had gone by in these last years when I had not thought about the expression on his face when I cut him off from my life. I was absolutely horrible to a wonderful man like him. I will never forgive myself for what I did with him. But I had to. I stood up for what is right and what is wrong."

"Whatever you say, because of you, my Abir suffered for years."

"Your Abir suffered because of your rejection of me," said Shyamoli quietly. "Men have often suffered, sandwiched between us women, and we are the last ones to know. Men are less prone to seek emotional help. Especially men like Abir, who are too busy trying to make this world a better place to really care about their own well-being. Men like Abir are always supposed to be strong and don't have a way to just let down their heads, cry, and ask for help. You harmed your son, and you didn't even get to see it. Your Abir suffered because of your rejection of me, the love of his life. You did this with disdain, with utter indifference to his feelings, because he never showed his feelings of being hurt to you, because men don't cry, right? You did all this without thinking of him, of what we stood for, but only thinking about what you would get from our union."

"You dare to blame me for my own son's unhappiness, despite me giving you a chance to stay at this home and look after him, knowing very well that I have every right to kick you away? How can you be so ungrateful, Shyamoli?"

"Ungrateful. How strange this word sounds, Ma. I took your Abir in my heart and cradled him, protected him, nurtured him, when he was with me. Yet you rejected me, the very thought of me, with disdain, with insults, with utter ungratefulness. And you are saying *I* am ungrateful? I am looking after your Abir for days at end now, yet not a single day has gone by without you passing some barb at me, taking efforts every now and then to belittle me. I don't need to do all this. Ungrateful. It's a strong word and certainly does not sum up what I am doing, just because I am in love with him."

"Love? How does it matter if you are in love with him?" said Mother scornfully. "Any woman who knows him well will fall in love with him. I can get twenty girls lined up for Abir, and he will forget you in no time."

"It's not about what you want, or what you can do, Ma," said Shyamoli, "It's your son's life. It's for him to choose. You imposed

Riya on him. What happened to it? Riya treated him like an animal, bullied him at her own convenience, and physically abused him with utter impunity."

"What!" exclaimed Mother.

"Yes Ma—Riya physically abused him and insulted him to the core. You measure people by values that have nothing to do with their character; as a result, you are completely blind to their lack of empathy and kindness. You should really, truly listen to what your son talks about in his TED talks, in his blog posts. Then you will understand what empathy and kindness is all about."

"Stop this lecture and tell me what happened with Riya and Abir. What is this physical abuse that you are talking about?"

"You asked Riya to come over to get back in Abir's life again today," said Shyamoli, her tone polite, but radiating a strange fierceness. "You did not seek to understand why Abir went away from Riya's home in the first place and came to me. I did not ask him to come. He was helpless and alone in the city, and I gave him shelter, after Riya physically abused him, almost injuring him by throwing a vase at him, and literally threw him out of her home. You overlooked all that, just because you had already placed Riya on an altar, despite what she means to him. Yet again, Riya got things for free, without earning them, and that's why she threw it all away with disdain. She bullied him with disdain, and you never got to see that side of her."

There was a silence.

"You probably hate me for saying all this, hate me for my dark skin, for daring to be a love object for your son. I know that, and I have stopped caring now," said Shyamoli, her voice sad. "As I promised, after I get Abir up and running, I will leave this house forever and never show my face to you again. But I wanted to tell you something. All I wanted was acceptance from you. Acceptance and respect. That's all."

Mother remained silent.

"When I looked at you for the first time, back those four years, as you entered our home, I felt Goddess Saraswati had entered our house. At your age, you radiate beauty and intelligence in your demeanor that your Abir has inherited from you. I was in awe with you and expected your behavior to reflect your radiating beauty and aura. But your behavior was not at par with your appearance."

Mother remained quiet, as if at a loss of words.

"The only thing I wanted was a little appreciation for me. Just one glance. Just one smile from you. Just one little appreciation of what I did, or where I stood in your son's life. When you came with Abir to our home, I wore my best saree, just to impress you. I made my best dishes, hoping to impress you. But you saw none of that. You only saw the dark color of my skin."

Mother remained uncharacteristically quiet. A tear trickled down Abir's face, as he laid down quietly inside the room, breathing softly lest he disturbed Shyamoli's flow of thoughts and feelings.

"I walked these stairs every day, for these so many days, every day wishing to get that one smile from you," said Shyamoli softly. There was profound sorrow in her voice, and Abir rolled over, feeling a surge of desperate sadness at her silent battle. "Not a single day had gone by when I had not asked for your permission before entering this room, because I know you, and you alone, have the right to be by his side and not me. Not a single day had passed when I had not gazed upon your pictures with Abir when he was small, your arms around him to protect him. Not a day had gone by when I did not take your textbook on mathematics and gone over it. Not a single day had gone by when I did not look at the rows of awards that you received over your career. Best teacher. Best mentor. Every day in these past weeks, I wished to be included by you, to be induced in this family. I have tried so hard, Ma, but I have failed."

Abir felt both his eyes get wet with tears.

"Why does God love me so less, Ma? Can you tell me why He loves me so less? He took away my most precious possessions. My father. My mother. He took them away and made me utterly lonely. I had to throw away Abir, the most innocent and wonderful man that I have seen walk this Earth, the only person who stood by me like a rock, the love of my life. I was left with nothing in my life. Nothing and nobody. Why, Ma, can you tell me why? Is it because I am dark-skinned, Ma? Is it because I am dark-skinned in a culture which does not want or like dark-skinned women? Is it so? Is that why you would rather have Riya bully your son, break his mind and spirit, abuse him physically, but still accept her, but would not hear of me or even glance at me? Why Ma, is it because I was made to be loved less? Why is there no more love left for me, Ma?"

Abir could feel the grief in her voice, and he cried softly, his tears wetting his pillow. There was a long silence, and he lay down quietly, lest he made his presence known, let it be known that he was listening to a conversation which was not meant for him.

"Are you done with your emotional outpour, Shyamoli?" asked Mother after a long silence, her voice hard. "Then let me tell you something. Nobody cares about your education, or upbringing, or nature, or accomplishments. The first opinion that people in our culture make about women is based on their skin color. Period. Everything else is secondary."

Shyamoli remained silent.

"So now let me tell you one last thing," said Mother, venom spewing in every syllable, as if mustering enough negative energy to finally speak her mind clearly. "Look at yourself in the mirror, and you will realize why you will never fit in this house. Even the maid-servant who does menial jobs in my house is fairer-skinned than you. And that seals *your* place in our society. Got it? Now get lost and never show your dark face in this house ever again."

Abir's heart felt like they had stopped. His mother's harsh words felt like daggers which pierced him through and through. His head spun around, as if the Earth was shaking, and he buried his face in his palms, quivering in distress.

There was an uncanny silence that filled the void—a deafening silence which consumed all sounds around him.

Then he heard Shyamoli burst into tears.

"When Abir was being hit, I wanted God to take me away and save him," said Shyamoli, sobbing, her voice getting shrill with agony, her words choking in her tears. "I wanted those monsters to hit me on the head and get done with, and spare him. I asked them to hit me instead, but God would not listen. Why, Ma, can you tell me? Why did God not take me away, Ma? Take me away to his home in the clouds? Then I could be with my father. Be with my mother. To be with them, to see their faces, their eyes on me, the only people who loved me unconditionally, look at my eyes, and not at the dark color of my skin. Can you tell me why I did not die that day, to leave this world where there is nobody for a person like me? Can you? Why did God not take me away that day? Why? Tell me why. Can you tell me?"

Abir curled up on his bed and wept, tears flowing all over his face, wetting his pillows. He wanted to get up and rush to her, bury her head in his arms and comfort her, and tell her that he was there, even if nobody else in the world was there for her; tell her not to heed his mother's words; to tell her that she was a precious child of God, and that she was beautiful beyond words, and that everybody loved her—everybody except his mother, whom she had tried to make her own, but had failed.

He tried to get up from his bed, his head hurting, his feet trembling, his tears blinding him. But before he could go to the door, he heard Shyamoli run down the stairways, sobbing hysterically.

He heard the main door close downstairs as Shyamoli ran out of his home.

And this time, he knew she was gone for good, and would not come back.

He realized that Mother had successfully banished the dark-skinned woman who dared to try and become the other special woman in her magnificent and glamorous son's life.

Torn

Abir woke up, trying to remember why he felt so depressed and worried. He racked his mind for some time and recalled that it was because Shyamoli was gone from his home. He had overheard Shyamoli and his mother's discourse the previous evening. He closed his eyes, thinking of her story. Would this battle for acceptance always continue? He recalled what she had said four years back and also in the email that she sent. This was an unbalanced equation, never meant to be balanced. Perhaps she had been right.

He got up from his bed slowly and realized that he could walk without much effort. He touched his head—the Band-Aid had gone. True to her words, Shyamoli had seen him through his sickness till he felt better. He was feeling better now. And, she was gone from his home. This was what she had said to his mother too.

He stared at his phone. Should he call Shyamoli? He was sure that she would respond to him, but she had left on her own accord. Would it be right to ask her why she left and make her emotions surface again? Did he have any right to even speak to her, given the terrible way his mother had banished her the previous evening? He realized that Mother had, yet again, broken that trust between Shyamoli and him; a trust that he had painstakingly rebuilt in these last few weeks. He did not have any more right to expect anything from Shyamoli, or tell her anything. The only thing he could do now was to apologize to her for his mother's harsh words.

But then, the conversation had been between his mother and her. It was not meant for him—he had merely overheard them talking. It was a battle of ideologies and views between the two most important women in his life. In this battle, he was to remain invisible and had to exercise his influence through rational thinking, akin to how he had trained his mind to handle adverse situations.

It was early morning. Perhaps Shyamoli was still not awake, but he decided to call her anyway. He video-called Shyamoli on

WhatsApp. After the first ring, she picked it up. Her eyes were puffy and red, and he realized that it was due to hours of crying alone and not sleeping for the entire night. His heart bled for her plight, for her sorrow, and his eyes moistened automatically. They stared at each other into the video call, none of them speaking.

"You look tired, Shyamoli," he said after a while. "You should rest today."

Shyamoli smiled at him, the way she did every time she saw him, and he stared at her solemnly.

"Are you feeling better now?" she asked softly.

"You took care of me for all these days, Shyamoli. How can I not feel better?"

She remained silent, staring into the screen, and he stared back at her.

"When is your flight back to the USA?" she asked, her voice oddly casual.

"I have yet to buy my flight ticket," said Abir. "And before I buy it, I have to do something. I will call you back tonight."

He disconnected his phone and got out of his bed slowly.

* * *

Abir took his first steps confidently after many days. He could climb the stairs to the terrace above his second-floor bedroom without any support. His head did not pain when he walked, and he felt as if he did not have any accidents at all.

It was late morning. A horde of people had accumulated on the terrace to watch Abir take his first real walk after weeks of being sick. Rimjhim and her parents were there. Dadu was sitting on the mat on the terrace floor. Manik and his father stood by as Abir crossed the entrance door to the terrace. His parents stood at the door of the terrace, looking at him with a mix of anxiety and happiness. Manik started clapping when he entered the terrace. The others joined in, in a unified show of delight that Abir was feeling fit and fine.

The terrace was decorated with balloons and confetti. The table was laden with a typical Bengali breakfast—*luchi, aloor dom, begun bhaja,* and *payesh.* Manik had arranged for a small box speaker with a stereo, which played popular Bengali songs. Abir sat down on one of the chairs, as people flocked around to get their breakfast on the terrace. There was general rejoicing in the air. People talked enthusiastically, laughed at each other's jokes. Abir smiled at their rejoice to see him up and running.

His mind, though, was on the selfie he had just taken after coming to the terrace. When he found some time to himself, he quickly opened WhatsApp and sent the selfie to Shyamoli. And almost immediately, he received a big heart sign from her. His heart filled with joy and, at the same time, sadness that she was not there to celebrate this occasion.

He looked around his family, all coming together to celebrate him. And somewhere a little far off in north Kolkata, Shyamoli must have gone to her extended family of uncles and aunts in the morning, as was her ritual on weekends. For the past few weeks, she had visited him every day, even on weekends, just to look after him. This weekend, she had gone back to her extended family—the only family she had.

Abir knew that, deep down, her eyes must be unknowingly seeking out his face in her family, the same as he was seeking out her face in this joyous union of his family.

* * *

Abir sat with his parents on the terrace, quietly surveying the setting sun. It was evening, with dull red skies shying away from a reclining sun and waves of birds flying above in the sky, as if waving him hello, welcoming him back to the natural world as they made their way across to their home after the day was over. The day had been that of celebrations and family. The morning started with picnic-style breakfast on the terrace. Lunch, too, had been on the terrace, consisting of all his favorite food.

He was feeling relaxed, and his head did not ache at all.

"I wanted to talk to you about something," he said, breaking the silence, addressing both of them. Mother glanced at Father, as if she were waiting for him to start a conversation. The glance was not lost on Abir.

"Guys, I want to talk to you about Shyamoli," he said quietly, coming to the topic straight away.

"Perhaps I should leave you and your mother alone to have this conversation," said Father hastily, getting up. Abir waved him down.

"No, dad, stay," he said quietly. "You both need to be in this conversation."

Mother got up from her chair and went and stood near the terrace wall. His father remained quiet, and Abir knew that he would not have an opinion. He remained silent, waiting for Mother to speak.

"OK, if you are reluctant to talk about it, answer me this, mom," he said after a while, addressing his mother directly. "Why are you having such a hard time just to accept Shyamoli and me as a couple?"

Mother did not reply.

"Do you have any complaints about her?" he asked.

"No, Abir, I have no complaints," said Mother after a prolonged silence. Abir kept quiet, allowing her to collect her thoughts. "I think she is fine as a person. She is quite well behaved, has good values, and has brains. I don't dislike her as a person."

"But I get the feeling that you don't want her in my life," persisted Abir. "I am really curious to understand this."

An expression of disdain flitted across Mother's face. Abir chose to ignore it and remained silent, waiting for her to speak.

"Abir, your entire life has been about succeeding in your endeavors," said Mother. "I have always pushed you for excellence. I have always had high expectations of you. And you did not let us down. Look at where you are now. You are a star—a role model engineer, a leader. You have made a mark in the world with your TED talks, with your videos. You are glamorous, Abir! You, us, our family, is all about glamour! What you need is somebody who is at par with you in terms of glamour."

"I find your statement very cryptic, mom," said Abir quietly.

"There is nothing cryptic about it, Abir," said Mother. "We hobnob with the upper echelon of society. Industrialists. Ministers. The who's who of the society. There are certain expectations in our society. Will this Shyamoli ever be able to withhold the posture, the veiled arrogance, the disdain, the subtle aura of power? Do you really, *really* think she has that glamour to stand beside you as your wife, to represent us, our status?"

"What makes you think like that, mom?" asked Abir quietly. "What makes you think that she lacks that aura and glamour? Just because she is dark-skinned in a society which does not favor or appreciate dark-skinned women?"

Mother frowned, and he could discern anger in her face. Abir smiled at her ruefully.

"Let me see," he continued quietly. "Shyamoli exudes all the wonderful qualities of a person that one can possibly have. Like you said, she has brains, is well behaved, and has great values in life. You and I, and all of us saw her dedication in putting me back to shape. She is brilliant, from a great family, and in every aspect, she is a person of utmost refinement. Any association with her is a matter of pride. And to top it all off, she is my best friend, the closest one I have ever had in my life—a friend whom I am proud to associate with at every moment of my life. And yet, you are going to ignore all that, everything, just because of her dark skin color?"

Mother looked away from him coldly.

"You talk about women empowerment," he continued. "Yet, when finally a woman of the highest class and substance comes in front of you, you suddenly lose all your ideologies. Instead of empowering her with appreciation for her, you look down on her using an age-old prejudice! Aren't you being hypocritical, mom?"

Mother stared at him as if she could not believe that he could oppose and belittle her standing with such impunity.

He noted the haughty lines on her face, forming an expression of disdain that centuries of prejudice had etched.

An expression of arrogance that had been passed on, genetically and culturally, for ages.

An expression and attitude that mere words and logical reasoning could not erase.

An expression created by a subtle sense of superiority and entitlement, supported by society at large, that had given some people like her the right to persecute and not accept anybody whom their society did not perceive as equals.

Mother's expression changed from anger to loathing, and Abir felt as if the sky had clouded over suddenly, without warning. He stared at Mother, troubled at her mutinous expression, but at the same time, a quiet determination built inside him that refused to get bogged down by her vibe. He could also see what Shyamoli had said to him so often—that it was an equation that could perhaps never be balanced because of the years of colored, prejudiced numbers in those equations.

Mother got up from her chair abruptly and walked out of the terrace. Abir and Father exchanged a silent look.

* * *

Abir stared at the ceiling fan morosely. It was night time, and he had come over to his room to lay down without joining his family for dinner. His father had come to call him for dinner, but he refused to go down. He was in no mood to sit down with his mother, whose lack of empathy and openness stung him. He felt he had not known her at all. It seems incredible to him that even after Shyamoli looked after him for weeks, Mother remained negative about her presence in his life, without an iota of thankfulness.

He realized that the time had come for him to make a big decision. He had to go back to the States in another week. He wanted to have some sort of a solution with the complex dynamics between him and his mother. To go back to the States without any definitive answer about his relationship with Shyamoli would be heartbreaking for him. He was away from her only for a day now, and already he felt an emptiness in his life—a void that only Shyamoli could fill.

The door opened, and Mother came inside, carrying a tray with food. She put the tray on the table beside his bed and hovered around for a while. As she sat down beside him on a chair and took a plate of food on her lap, he rolled over to face away from her.

"Stop sulking and eat up," she commanded. Abir did not reply and looked away.

"Why are you treating me like this?" she asked, her voice tearful. Abir saw tears in her eyes, and automatically, he reached out his hand and wiped her tears away gently.

"Why are you having such a hard time accepting Shyamoli, mom?" he asked after a silence. Mother did not reply and looked away from him, holding his hands.

"You said you read all my blogs on empathy and mindfulness," he said gently, pressing the palm of her hand with his. "You said you follow all my TED talks. But I believe you have not really understood the content there, mom. Empathy can truly arise when we let go of colors—the color of skin, colors of elitism—truly let go of the *me* in *myself* to really understand the *them* in *others*. You see Shyamoli through the colored eyeglasses that have been imposed on you through generations. Instead of looking at her eyes, which had nothing but yearning for acceptance from you, you looked at her skin color, as you have been conditioned to do through centuries of prejudice. I am not blaming you at all. I just want to tell you that you have to look at the right things, mom. The right things, at the right place, with the right intent. Shyamoli makes me happy. It's as simple as that. Like you make me happy. You and her are the two most important women in my life. It's hard for me to live without one or the other. Her presence brings me peace, the same as your presence brings me comfort, mom. In her presence, I can forget all my worries, the same as I forget all my troubles in your presence. In all these four years, you have seen me become a well-known blogger and TED talker. Do you know who has been inspirational in my talks, my ideas? Shyamoli's father, Biren sir, along with dad. It was Biren sir, who embraced me in his life and ideals, even as I followed dad's footsteps to be of service to others. You see your's and dad's photos in my purse that I carry with me all the time? It was Shyamo-

257

li, five years back, who had asked me to keep them with me always. You just need to take off your shaded glasses mom, to truly see what she is and what she means to me."

Mother shook her head and put her fingers on her lips as if wanting him to keep quiet.

"You are too young to understand all this," she said soothingly, patting his arms. "You are infatuated with the wrong person. I chose Riya for you, but you would not have her! If you don't like Riya, never mind. I will look for another girl like her for you. You need to get over your silly obsession with this dark-skinned Shyamoli. And also, stop sulking and eat up the food. I heated it up just for you."

Abir stared at her in disbelief.

"Your views on Shyamoli amazes me, mom," he said, letting go of her hand and sitting up. "So finally you see a woman who is exemplary in every sense—by her education, class, behavior, beauty, kindness, nobility. A person who has painstakingly made her presence in this prejudiced world by sheer hard work and goodness of heart. So what do you do? You downplay her by that one *single* thing which she cannot control—the skin color that she was born with! Then you use that *one* single aspect to pin her down and belittle her—again—and again—and again—and again—and again! Looking beautiful? No, too dark! Really a nice person? No, too dark! Fit to be a queen? No, no, and no—just too dark! Nothing she does can impress you, nothing she does can make you accept her."

Mother looked away, her expressions frigid, contemptuous.

Abir sat silently, contemplating the extraordinary lack of empathy and kindness in his own mother. His own mother, who had taken supreme pride in her son's fame due to being an empathy engineer, yet ironically failing to follow the fundamental tenets that he had been preaching.

"I finally see your reasons now, mom," Abir said quietly after a long silence. "I think this is because, finally, a dark-skinned woman worked her way to get respect from the most important man in your life—respect that you have been so undeservedly getting all your life for free, no?"

Mother got up abruptly, the food from the tray falling all over the floor. She glared at him, her eyes blazing fire, and he stared back her apprehensively, startled at how similar she looked like Riya all of a sudden. He perceived the same aura of disdain, the same expression of arrogance as that of Riya, something which he had failed to recognize in his thirty years of life.

Abir recalled Mother's sermons a few hours back on the terrace. He finally understood what she meant: an attitude of veiled arrogance, of undeserved and freely acquired sense of superiority, condoned by an ever biased society. A sense of entitlement, which she had gotten all her life, for free, without having to work an iota for it.

Mother raised her hands, and he closed his eyes, getting a strange sense of deja vu.

She slapped him hard across his cheek, her fury manifesting itself fully.

"You wretched brat!" she spatted, her face white with rage. "How dare you even compare me with that dark-skinned woman?"

She turned around to leave, shaking in anger, and stopped near the door.

"Stop calling me mother from now on," she said, her voice trembling with hatred. "You are no son of mine."

Then she went out of his room, banging the door shut in a fury that shook the entire house.

Abir looked at the closed door in a daze. His mother had slapped him for the first time in his thirty years of life.

She had asked him to stop calling her mother, something he, even in his dreams, could not imagine her utter, even in her wildest anger.

He realized that she had finally disowned him.

* * *

Abir stared at the clicking clock. Everybody was asleep. He had to take a heavy dose of painkillers to get over the pain in his head. The wound on his head was hurting again after his mother slapped him. It was midnight. He stared at his phone, his mind in a curious whirl, and decided to video-call Shyamoli on WhatsApp, knowing that she would be awake, waiting for his call. As always, she picked up his call immediately. He smiled at her, feeling happy to see her as ever, and she smiled back at him shyly. Shortly, though, her smile faded away.

"You are looking sickly again," she said, her voice quivering slightly. "What happened, Abir?"

"You go away from me for just one day, Shyamoli, and I feel my protection has gone," he said quietly.

"Oh, Abir, don't say that," said Shyamoli, tears dripping down her face. She stared at him for some time, and he looked back at her silently.

"Did you buy your ticket for San Francisco?" she asked, wiping her eyes, her lips quivering.

Abir did not reply and stared back at her.

"When will I ever see you again in person, Abir?" she said, tears falling from her eyes again. She covered her face with her palms and started sobbing.

Abir held out his hand, as if to wipe her tears from the phone screen, and she stopped crying, wiping her eyes.

"Do you remember that day Shyamoli, four years back, when you asked me not to be spineless?" he said.

"Yes, I do," said Shyamoli, suddenly looking anxious. "Please, Abir, don't remind me of that day."

"Don't look so anxious!" he said, smiling at her gently. "I just think that I still am a pathetic spineless little boy and not a real man—a pathetic coward who can't even defend the women in his life."

"No, you are not!" said Shyamoli fiercely. "You stood up and fought like a man to defend the honor of all the women in that shelter. You single handedly fought with three goons, not caring for your own safety. You are a role model for bravery, for doing the right thing at the right time. Don't ever call yourself a coward again! I can't tell you how proud I am of you, Abir."

"Well, maybe," said Abir. "But there is one thing I was distinctly lacking to make me a real man. But not today. Not anymore, Shyamoli."

"I am happy to hear that," said Shyamoli.

"Shyamoli, did I ever tell you that I love you?" Abir said quietly.

Shyamoli's eyes welled up with tears again.

"I love you, Shyamoli. I have always loved you, but now I cannot hold it in me anymore. I love you, and I cannot stay away from you for one moment of my life."

Shyamoli's tears fell freely, as she looked at him through the phone screen.

"I love you too, Abir," she said, looking down at her hands shyly for a while and then looking up and him. They stared at each other.

"Do you remember what I told you a few weeks back?" asked Abir quietly.

"What, Abir?"

"I told you that I see my yet unborn children in your eyes, Shyamoli," he said.

Shyamoli blushed scarlet red and covered her face with her palms.

"And you said that day that this can never happen until and unless our society accepts it," he said, almost in a whisper.

Shyamoli sat still, her face covered with her palms.

Abir got down from his bed on the floor and placed his phone at a little distance so that Shyamoli could see him in entirety. His head hurt him again, and he felt slightly imbalanced. He could see Shyamoli on the little phone screen, covering her face with her palms, shaking, tears falling freely, wetting her hands.

He knelt down slowly on the floor and stretched his hands toward the phone, his hands trembling slightly.

"Miss Shyamoli, my Goddess," Abir said quietly, "will you marry me tomorrow morning?"

* * *

Abir and Manik got down from their Uber taxi near the marriage registrar's office in Behala in Kolkata. He had come off in the early morning with Manik. The Kolkata roads were already heavy with traffic. All kinds of people strolled around in the vicinity, the monotonous humdrum making up the noise and vibe of the romantic city of joy. Shyamoli had brought Aniruddha along as a witness, as he had brought Manik with him. As usual, her sight made his heart skip a beat, her large beautiful eyes looking dazzling, her graceful demeanor seemed to make everything around dim.

Abir went and stood in front of Shyamoli, his eyes locked on hers. She looked back at him, as if in a trance.

"I still did not get accepted by your family," she said, her big eyes looking anxious.

"We will work on it, Shyamoli," said Abir softly. "And who says my family doesn't accept you? I am sure everybody in my family fell in love with you after they saw you for three weeks! It's just my mother who is not on board, but then, how can two simple people like us eradicate centuries of prejudice over skin-color passed on from generation to generation? It will take time. But I need to stay with you every moment of my life. I am done waiting. We will fight the battle together. You and I."

He held her hands, and she held onto his tightly, her eyes on him. As always, everything dimmed around him, as if an invisible knob had turned off everything around them. He felt he was floating in the air, to be in her presence.

They heard a soft cough, and turning around, they saw Aniruddha and Manik grinning at them.

"You two can stare at each other all you want after you get married," said Aniruddha, his voice sarcastic as always, but his eyes smiling. "But let's get it done now. I am in a hurry."

With their two witnesses, Abir and Shyamoli entered the marriage registrar's office.

* * *

"Dad, do you have a minute? I have something to say."

"Where the heck are you, Abir?" said his father, sounding annoyed. "Where did you disappear to? You told me briefly that you are leaving for the city with Manik in the morning, but it's past lunchtime now, and you are not back yet. You did not even pick up my phone—I have been calling you for ages! The doctor ordered you to continue resting for another few days—you know that, right?"

"I am in the city right now, dad," said Abir. "And I have news for you. I wanted to call you earlier, but your line was busy. Is mom nearby?"

"No, I am on the terrace alone. What's going on, Abir? What's the secret?"

"I have huge news, dad."

"Wait—I have a feeling I know what you are going to say, son."

"Really? What is it that I want to say, dad?"

"Oh, cut the suspense," said Father gruffly. "Did you elope with Shyamoli? Did you marry her?"

Abir almost dropped his phone in surprise.

"How in the world did you know that dad?" he asked in wonder.

"I anticipated it," said Father solemnly. "But you could have told me instead of doing all this drama! Listen, you and I were always pals, son. Why didn't you tell me you were going to do this? Why such filmy drama?"

"I am sorry, dad, but I just could not delay this anymore," Abir said, suddenly feeling supremely happy at the very thought. "I married Shyamoli today, dad. She is my wife now, and it's the happiest day of my life."

"Of course it is, son," said Father. "Your girl is an absolute sweetheart, and I am surprised you took so long to come to such an obvious conclusion to your love story! I am glad you finally got your act together. You acted like a man, and I am proud of you, son."

Abir felt his heart soar in happiness. Relief spread through him like a wildfire that warmed his heart with affection for his ever-supportive father.

"Thank you, dad," said Abir, hardly able to suppress the choking sensation in his voice. "I feel I am not alone with Shyamoli."

"Of course, son," said Father briskly. "I support you whole-heartedly. Listen, just bring Shyamoli over. Right now. We should give your queen a royal reception today. With what little arrangements we can do in a few hours."

"I don't think I can do that, dad," Abir said quietly.

"Why—are you worried about how your mother will react to all this?"

Abir did not speak, his throat suddenly constricting him at the thought that his mother had finally disowned him.

"Listen, Abir," persisted Father. "Do not forget that Shyamoli is now our daughter too. She is a part of this house, our name, our presence in this society. We need a proper celebration and all the traditional formalities. This is a great day, a great occasion, and it should be celebrated like so! I would like to welcome her to her new home, wholeheartedly."

"I don't think I am welcome in that house anymore, dad," said Abir.

"Well, this is *your* home, Abir," said Father.

"Is it *really* my home, dad?" asked Abir quietly.

Father became quiet for some time, and Abir remained silent, waiting for him to speak up.

"Listen, son," said Father after a while. "Whatever may have transpired, you should let your mother know that you got married. I know she will be shell shocked at first. I know it is going to be hard—for you and, more so, for dear Shyamoli. Give your mother some time, Abir. She expects you to come back home with your wife."

"I don't think so, dad," said Abir, his voice choking up, his tears falling freely. He waited for some time, unable to talk, and Father waited gently.

"I am sorry that I am crying, dad," Abir said at length, feeling abashed at the way he let his emotions flow at that moment—ashamed that a grown up man like him could cry like this.

"You are doing what every human being does—cries when they are distressed," said Father gently. "I can't tell you how proud I am of you, Abir. I am so proud that you refute that false male bravado, which condones a false sense of toughness, making them think that crying is a sign of weakness. Cry, Abir, cry. It's OK for men to cry. There is absolutely nothing wrong in men crying and showing their emotions on the surface."

"I can't come home, dad," said Abir after a while, steadying himself. "Mom has really disowned me this time, and I think she would not like to see my face again."

"No mother can ever disown her child, Abir," said Father gently. "You are a grown-up man now, but you will always be that little child to her. This is beyond a difference of opinion between a mother and her son. For once, I think you are not just a son to your mother, but a person who started a revolution—a person who has questioned her ways of thinking—a person who is making the society rethink the fundamental tenets of what empathy and kindness is all about. I think you shook her coveted place as a privileged person in the society, Abir—a society which gives privilege to a certain section of people just due to their external facade and appearance and elevates them to a position that makes them forget the fundamental notions of empathy and kindness."

Abir listened silently to his father, wiping the tears from his eyes.

"I know you are having a difficult time with your mother, Abir, but sometimes, you need to face these things. I know, for you, it's an extraordinary irony that your mother, of all people, failed to follow your algorithms of practicing empathy. But I firmly believe it will become alright over time. Your mother and your Shyamoli are the two most important women in your life, Abir. Be aware that there will always be this subtle fight for your attention and love. Be patient. Be wise. I know I sound pedantic, given that you are the master of removing yourself from a situation and putting yourself in others' shoes, to be empathetic, to be kind. But even a great heart and a great mind like yours needs help sometimes, Abir. I do understand your dilemma and plight. And as your father, I can only wish that God gives you the strength to stick to your beliefs."

"Thank you, dad," said Abir, feeling better.

"And one more last thing, son," said Father. "Try to stick to traditions. Traditions will make you happy and give weight to your actions. So make a decision about today carefully. In fact, before making a decision on your own, make it a habit to ask Shyamoli about your decisions too. Take her opinion. She is a wise person and will guide you in the right direction when you need light. And let me know your plans. I think you and Shyamoli will do the right thing."

* * *

Abir stared at his phone as his father disconnected. He remained silent for a while, looking afar at nothing. Then he turned to Shyamoli.

"We have two choices now, Shyamoli," he said. "Either we go back to my home today, or we don't go back at all, and stay back here in Kolkata till we fly back to San Francisco in a few days."

Shyamoli turned a shade pale. She remained silent, staring at him.

"Don't worry, I am not asking you to come home with me," Abir said gently. "In fact, I was planning for us to stay at the Marriott here in Kolkata for a few days, then go for a trip to Europe, and then, finally, take you back to San Francisco with me. But I wanted your opinion."

He waited for her to make up her mind.

"I would like to visit your home first, Abir," she said softly, after a long pause.

"Shyamoli, my mother will surely insult you," he said, feeling anxious. "She might create a scene, and our moment from today might go down in our history as a moment of agony."

"This is a beautiful day in my life, and nothing can take it away from me," she said softly, holding his hands, her large eyes suddenly brimming with tears. "I want to go to your home today, Abir, because that is where we belong. Maybe we will experience negativity—maybe it will come like an avalanche, like a storm. But I know that it will surely pass by. I want to get your family's blessings today. I want to be acknowledged as your wife by your family. By your father, Rimjhim, and her family. By Manik and his family. By your Dadu. I would like to see them all today, even if your mother does not accept me. For the three weeks that I went to your place to look after you, I felt they were part of my family. And after we go away from here, to San Francisco, I will continue to fight for your mother's approval, for her acceptance, and if God willing, perhaps she will one day truly see me and not the dark color of my skin."

"You are an extraordinarily strong woman, Shyamoli," Abir said quietly.

"I don't want a mother to become distant with her son," she said, her eyes brimming with tears again. "If my parents were alive today, they would have counseled me to do the same. We cannot run away on the first day of our new life, Abir. We will have to face it. Together. Be what it may."

Abir put his arms around her, and she rested her head on his shoulder. They sat silently for a while, savoring the moment of togetherness. Then they got up and went outside from *Shiraz*, where they had brought Manik and Aniruddha for a lunch treat.

Manik and Aniruddha were smoking outside.

"Well, what's the plan now, brother?" asked Manik.

"We will go home, Manik," said Abir quietly.

"That's the spirit, brother," said Manik happily, looking at Shyamoli with reverence, as if realizing that it was her wish to go there. "I know your mother will be—err—a bit upset. But don't worry, brother. I will phone my friends right now, and we will plan a careful decoy to whisk her away before she can create a scene! But I wish you were not so dramatic. Then I would get some time to give a proper surprise and arrange a grand welcome for my new sister-in-law."

Shyamoli smiled at Manik, who made a grand bow to her and touched her feet.

"Oh, what are you doing, Manik?" she asked, looking embarrassed.

"You are officially my *boudi*, and as your younger brother in law, I am paying my respect," said Manik solemnly.

Abir and Shyamoli waited for Manik and Aniruddha to finish smoking. As they threw their finished cigarette stubs down on the ground, which was already littered with cigarette stubs, Abir raised his eyebrows slightly. Manik and Aniruddha, as if reading his mind, hastily picked up their cigarette stubs from the ground and threw them in the trash bin. Abir picked up the remaining discarded cigarette stubs himself and threw them in the trash bin.

"Always following your empathy algorithms, aren't you?" said Aniruddha sarcastically, his demeanor, paradoxically, exalted in reverence for Abir. "Empathy for people, empathy for nature. At every step, at every instance."

Abir smiled, and Aniruddha suddenly went over and hugged him. Then he turned to Shyamoli and hugged her too.

"I will leave from here, Abir and Shyamoli," said Aniruddha. "Wishing you a very happy married life. I wish I had a gift with me today, but you guys did this all so suddenly. Anyways, give me your address in San Francisco, and I will post a personal gift for you."

"Thank you for everything, Aniruddha," said Abir. "You are a true friend to us."

"Stay in touch," said Aniruddha, waving to them as he walked away. "You are truly an empathy engineer, Abir. Let the world learn and follow your empathy algorithms, as you have always dreamed of!"

As the Uber taxi came to pick them up to take them home, Abir, Shyamoli, and Manik hopped on to it. Manik sat on the front seat, talking on his phone excitedly, giving instructions to the boys in the local neighborhood club, apparently preparing for an impromptu grand reception of sorts for Abir and Shyamoli.

"Dad, I am coming home with your daughter in law," texted Abir to his father.

"Hurrah! Let me consult with Rimjhim immediately, so that we can create a plan to make it a grand reception in such a short time," his father texted back immediately.

He smiled at the exuberance and warmth in the message and showed the texts to Shyamoli. She looked at it and smiled, her eyes apprehensive. He saw the apprehension in her eyes, and he put his hands around her shoulders reassuringly, and she put her head on his shoulder.

Abir stared thoughtfully at the road ahead, as buildings and trees ambled past. These roads would take him back to his home. And there, perhaps, he and Shyamoli, the newly wedded couple, would not be received by his mother. Maybe Mother would create a scene, be rude with Shyamoli. Maybe she would not see his face at all. Maybe she would not probably even come to see them off at the airport when he took Shyamoli back with him to her new home in San Francisco.

Despite a sense of foreboding, he felt oddly relaxed, knowing that whatever was to happen, he had Shyamoli by his side. His Shyamoli, who was there to protect him, as he was there to protect her. Perhaps it was going to be a long battle for acceptance for Shyamoli, but he was going to be by her side at every moment. Be what it may, they would face it together.

After all, he called himself an Empathy Engineer. He would engineer and create empathy in his mother's heart for Shyamoli eventually. And not only for Shyamoli, but perhaps for many others in the society who faced prejudice due to the color of their skin. He was confident about it. It would take time, but it would happen.

After a while, Shyamoli turned and gazed at him into his eyes. As always, he forgot everything, as he stared at her big, beautiful, and intoxicating eyes. Eyes that quietly comforted him, eyes that were on his, for now and for eternity.

CPSIA information can be obtained
at www.ICGtesting.com
Printed in the USA
BVHW030250240320
575824BV00001B/65